Adventures on Brad

Books 1 - 3

by

Tao Wong

Copyright

This is a work of fiction. Names, characters, businesses, places, events and incidents are either the products of the author's imagination or used in a fictitious manner. Any resemblance to actual persons, living or dead, or actual events is purely coincidental.

This eBook is licensed for your personal enjoyment only. This eBook may not be re-sold or given away to other people. If you would like to share this book with another person, please purchase an additional copy for each recipient. If you're reading this book and did not purchase it, or it was not purchased for your use only, then please return to your favorite eBook retailer and purchase your own copy. Thank you for respecting the hard work of this author.

Contents

Book 1

A Healer's Gift

Chapter 1

"Daniel Chai. Miner. I'm here to join the Adventurer's Guild." Answering the guard's questions, Daniel looks across the 10-foot wooden wall that separates the dungeon town of Karlak from the wilderness behind him before letting his placid brown gaze rest upon the guard and his pike once more.

The fair-haired guard, clad in a simple leather tunic and wool pants, stares at Daniel, waving his hand to summon Daniel's status screen to confirm the truth of his words. The guard reads over the information before he gestures for Daniel and his employer to enter. With a flick of the wagon's reins, Atrieus, who has sat beside Daniel during and undergone the process just moments ago himself, sets the wagon rolling.

"I turn off to the right here, boy. You okay with being paid now?" Atrieus grunts at Daniel, a hand absently coming up to scratch at his matted beard.

For a moment, Daniel is irritated but he quickly dismisses the emotion. At twenty-one, Daniel is well past the age when the term boy is appropriate, but as Atrieus has watched him grow up working the mines since he was an actual child, another thousand protests at the term are unlikely to change the old man's mind. Instead, Daniel just answers politely, "That's fine. Thank you."

"Damn waste, boy. You sure you want to do this?" Atrieus growls out, digging through the bag at his feet to pull out a small coin-laden cloth purse to hand over to Daniel.

In answering, Daniel just shakes his head, accepting his wages and waving goodbye to his temporary employer as he hops down from the ore-laden wagon. Daniel has no desire to retread that conversation either, one that has happened in many forms these past few weeks of travel. Reaching behind before the wagon leaves, he grabs his backpack and his only weapon, a 20-pound sledgehammer.

Heavy as it is, Daniel carries it with little effort, muscles from years spent working the mines flexing.

After parting with Atrieus, Daniel starts off to the town center and the Adventurer's Guild, enjoying the feel of the brisk late autumn air. Home to barely more than a few thousand people, Karlak is a small town with only a single Beginner's Dungeon of ten floors. Like most dungeon towns, Karlak has grown out of the need to serve the Adventurers who bring in the majority of the town's income, and so, the entire town splays outwards from the Guild and the Dungeon entrance.

As Daniel walks deeper into town, buildings shift from simple wood to stone, prosperity showcased in architecture and materials. Around him, townsfolk weave through traffic with casual ease, most dressed in plain woolen tunics and dresses. For a town, Karlak is quite uniform in its race profile, only on occasion does Daniel spot a figure that is not human, with Beastkin the most common minority. The growth of the town has stabilized in the last few years, its presence near the contested border between Brad and the Orc nations a significant dampening factor in immigration. On the other hand, the Dungeon that provides the main source of income for the town has been around for over twenty years, and is well-mapped with a well-known and well-balanced mix of monsters, ensuring a constant stream of new hopeful Adventurers.

The latest of these hopefuls walks down the street, drawing more than a few glances his way. All new Adventurers are a potential source of income for the town, and many of the townsfolk are making quick assessments of the likelihood of his survival. His impressive musculature is a point in his favor but most quickly downgrade his chances of being a true earner. Hair so brown that it is almost black, the broad-shouldered newcomer is only 5'8" tall and human, his stature and race creating a significant disadvantage that the youngster will need to overcome.

That smells good… Daniel twists his head, searching for the aroma's origin as his stomach wakes to remind him that his last meal was early that morning. Spotting the roadside stall that has awakened his hunger, he picks up his pace before a sickening crunch followed by a chorus of screams draws his attention.

Just behind him, a child lies on the ground, his body damaged after being hit by a speeding cart. An errant wind, a loosely held flower and a hurried attempt to catch his gift are all that was required for this tragedy to happen. Unable to stop, the cart's wheels have first pushed and then rolled over the child. The child's caretaker finishes her dash out from the alleyway, a moment of distraction now twisting her face with shock and regret.

Daniel is moving without conscious thought; his worldly goods dropped behind him as he dashes to the small, crushed body. His eyes narrow as he draws upon a portion of his Gift and assesses the damage as he touches the slightly twitching body.

Shattered collarbone, crushed ribcage and heart, severe bleeding in chest cavity and stomach. Hairline cracks in the spine, a minor concussion, and a broken arm. The damage jumps out to him as he touches the child, information pouring through his mind as he catalogs and instinctively understands both the natural state of the child's body and the damage done. Information continues to flow, though he dismisses most of it from his mind. A slightly lower quantity of blood than normal, previous damage to the tendon in his ankle still a week away from healing, improper placement of the hip socket….

Even as the information comes to him, Daniel speaks familiar words, "I'm a healer. Please let me do what I can."

From the viewpoint of the child's caretaker, what Daniel does next is nothing short of miraculous. The child's caretaker is an experienced Adventurer and is well-versed in the forms of healing magic available in the world. Nothing short of a Greater Blessing by a senior priest could have saved her nephew, and yet the stranger, without uttering a single word or calling on a God, is healing her nephew before her eyes. Bones knit, lungs inflate, and the bleeding stops within minutes. All there is to indicate that anything is even happening is the gentlest of glows coming from Daniel's hands which surround his small patient. As the glow fades, the boy's eyes open and he draws his first conscious breath before proceeding to scream and cry into his aunt's arms.

Clutching her nephew and rocking the child, the blonde-haired Adventurer looks over to Daniel who's slumped over, breathing heavily, and mouths her gratitude. Daniel just nods weakly, slowly regaining a sense of himself after the use of his Gift. As always, there is a price to pay. This time, only a half-a-day of his past - memories and lessons learnt during a fight with an overgrown badger that blocked the ore-wagons way and conversations with Atrieus - are sacrificed to his Gift.

Around Daniel, the watching crowd and the cart driver gawk at the miraculous healing; the gossip mill among the townsfolk will have new grist tonight. A good Samaritan carries over Daniel's dropped items, patting him on his back in congratulations before he leaves to finish his own errands for the day. The Samaritan's actions break the spell, with others crowding around and thanking Daniel and murmuring congratulations and consolations to the blonde-haired Adventurer, who still clutches her nephew to her chest.

Eventually, the child calms, and the crowd disperses as Daniel's attempts to make them leave finally make a dent. Work done, he stands with a groan and bends to pick up his pack and hammer but is stopped from leaving by a hand on his arm.

"Thank you." Her voice is soft, cultured and feminine, a sharp contrast to her bearing and appearance. Short-cut yellow hair, an aquiline nose, and piercing blue eyes rest upon a face that many would call striking. The adventurer holds herself with a martial air, a hand unconsciously resting on her sword hilt, the shape of her toned and firm body easily seen under the loose cut blouse she wears. "My name is Mary Lavie, and this is Charles."

"Daniel Chai." He smiles at the boy, impulsively reaching out to ruffle the child's hair, "You'll watch yourself running out into the road next time, right?"

The boy nods slightly, his face hidden in Mary's pants. He peeks out with his own pair of blue eyes around her pant leg before burying his face once more. In the child's mind, he will still feel the breaking and the healing, a stark contrast of experiences that will, thankfully, fade in the coming hours.

As Daniel sways slightly, the Gift always taking a little of his own strength to fuel, Mary queries, "Are you okay?"

"Yes. Just a little tired and hungry. I'll be fine after a meal."

A smile brightens Mary's face, and she gestures down the road, "My sister runs the Spinning Top, just down this way. She'll want to thank you too."

For a moment, Daniel considers refusing, but he reconsiders quickly, remembering the weight of his purse. Even the payment from Atrieus is insufficient to truly fatten it out, especially with his expected expenses in the next few days. He nods gratefully in acceptance and Mary smiles, her blue eyes sparkling at his acceptance.

"This way."

Chapter 2

The Spinning Top is a typical smaller inn – at least in Daniel's limited experience. The Top is positioned close to the center of town and is made up of a mixture of wood and stone, though the inn does come with expensive blown-glass windows. The entrance of the inn leads through to a small dining room filled with rustic wooden tables and chairs flanked by a simple, worn wooden bar and a doorway to the kitchen, while a staircase opposite the entrance leads to the top floor and the rooms that the inn rents out. Like most inns in a dungeon town, it's likely the rooms can be rented on both a short and long-term basis. Daniel's musing is cut short as the smells from the kitchen set his stomach growling.

Inside, the sole worker is another tall, striking blonde woman, clad in a simple brown frock, whose matronly curves put her sister's to shame. The moment they cross the threshold of the inn, Charles squirms out from the shelter of his aunt's arms and into his shocked mother's.

"Mary…" the aghast mother and innkeeper says, bending a knee to hug her child and to survey the blood and damage. She holds Charles away from her, parsing his words while she checks him over for injury before coming to the surprising conclusion that there are none.

"We had an incident, Elise." Mary steps forward abashedly, explaining the accident in quick, concise sentences. Charles gets angry as the adults talk over him and he glares at the two, before deciding it is time to sulk. Mary flicks her hand back to Daniel, who has taken to leaning against the bar and staring into the kitchen in longing while the two sisters talk, "… and so I thought we could feed Daniel and maybe house him for a bit?"

"Jar, one plate with extra bread!" Elise calls out to the kitchen before marching over to Daniel and giving him a tight hug. "Thank you! Thank you so much!"

In a few minutes, the bustling Elise has Daniel settled and eating before she drags her bloodied child upstairs to get cleaned up. Mary takes over the counter, watching Daniel eat with a pensive look on her face, glancing between him and his hammer. It doesn't take long before Daniel is done, leaning back against the chair after mopping up the last of the stew with his bread.

That was very good. Looking around, he doesn't spot Elise to thank. He frowns slightly, impatient to complete his task but unwilling to leave without thanking her for the meal. As he debates what to do, his thoughts are interrupted by Mary.

"Are you going to join the Guild?" she asks, nodding to his hammer. The guess was not hard since the vast majority of fit young men coming into town had only one goal. She purses her lips as he acknowledges her question with a nod. "And that's your weapon?"

"Why? Is it a problem?" Defensive, Daniel places his hand on the hilt of the hammer.

"It is. It's too big and unwieldy for a dungeon." As he opens his mouth to reply, Mary raises her hand and forestalls him, continuing, "I'm sure you used it while traveling here. Probably killed a few monsters too. There's no arguing that it's a fearsome weapon.

"But you have to land your blow. You need space to swing it and time to recover after you've swung. In a dungeon where you might face two or three different monsters at the same time, often faster and smaller than you, it won't work."

Daniel grunts, hunching slightly at each of her words. He knows it is not perfect; it's not as if he hadn't experienced much of what she said himself. "It's what I have."

His words are not unexpected, and as soon as they leave his mouth, Mary turns to the staircase, calling upwards, "Elise, we're going out. I'll bring him back later! Jar, put his bags in room 3!"

The blonde stands swiftly, pushing her chair back into place before walking to the exit. When she notices Daniel is not moving, she barks out a single word. "Come."

"Umm… what's going on?" Hurrying to catch up with her, Daniel stumbles along, trying to gauge their destination in this strange city. Even as they hurry, human townsfolk offer Mary a quick smile and greeting, each acknowledged by Mary with a short nod.

"We're going to the Guild to get you registered. You do have the twenty silver, correct?" She doesn't acknowledge his hasty nod, continuing to speak even as she strides along. "After that, we'll get you the training you need to wield a proper weapon."

"Training! I can't afford that!" Daniel exclaims, catching up with her and trying to slow her down to speak.

"Who asked you to pay?" Arriving at the doors of the Adventurer's Guild, she strides in and heads to the nearest empty counter. An attendant walks over unhurriedly, tall and thin with a full mop of curly black hair. He smiles slightly as he spots the harried Daniel behind Mary before focusing on her entirely.

"What can I do for you, Mary?" The attendant smiles, his face wrinkling and adding to its lines as he runs a hand through his hair to bring some order to it.

"Got a newbie who needs to be registered, Liev." She gestures behind, indicating Daniel who's staring around in confusion. Liev smiles placatingly at the young man, pulling some papers and a small crystal ball out from beneath the counter.

"Not a problem. Just put your hand here; don't be shy." Smiling encouragingly, Liev has Daniel place his hand on the crystal ball while he coaches out the information that he needs to finish the registration. "Good, good. A Level 7 Miner. Ooh, very good, a Minor Healing spell. Yes, we can definitely register you as an Adventurer."

At the end of his words, a low azure light glows on the crystal bringing another contented smile to Liev's face. "And done. That'll be twenty silver."

As Daniel finishes paying, he can't help but wonder if all his dreams have come true already. Another barked command to follow pulls him out of his contemplation as he hurries to catch up with the impatient Mary as she strides out of the Guild house. While he rushes after her, he calls up his Status Screen to marvel at his new position.

Name: Daniel Chai

Class: Level 1 Adventurer (0%)

Sub-classes: Level 7 (Miner) (14%)

Human (Male)

Statistics

Life: 164

Stamina: 164

Mana: 129

Critical Hit Chance: 4%

Attributes

Strength: 17

Agility: 12

Constitution: 23

Intelligence: 14

Willpower: 16

Luck: 13

Skills

Unarmed Combat: Level 2 (47/100)

Clubs: Level 3 (21/100)

Perception: Level 3 (21/100)

Mining: Level 7 (78/100)

Healing: Level 5 (84/100)

Herb Lore: Level 3 (31/100)

Cooking: Level 2 (37/100)

Singing: Level 2 (14/100)

Skill Proficiencies

Mapping (II)

Spells

Minor Healing (I)

Gifts

Martyr's Touch - The caster may heal oneself or others by touch and concentration, sacrificing a portion of his life to do so. Cost varies depending on the extent of the injuries healed.

It's a surprise for Daniel when Mary finally comes to a stop and thrusts a shield and mace at him. He reaches out and grabs the items automatically and then frowns, dismissing the Status Screen to pay proper attention to what he has been given. The mace is a simple construct, though instead of metal, its top is padded with wood and wrapped in cloth. A training weapon, though of better quality than he's ever wielded before. The shield is a simple wooden shield banded with iron around the corners and weighted with extra lead at the back.

He pauses, looking at the weapons in his hand before looking up and around himself for the first time. Although the training hall they are stood in is made of stone, its high ceiling is vaulted with wooden beams. Windows are thrown open to bring in fresh air, but where wall space is available, weapon racks full of training gear hang. The ground beneath his feet is hard-packed soil, though in the corner he notices a rougher training ground. All around him, adventurers, and those who wish to be adventurers, train.

"Mary…"

"Litzburn!" Mary ignores Daniel again, waving to a towering, bald, ebony-skinned man who seems to be in command of the training floor. The man strides up to them, smiling widely at Mary and then nodding in acknowledgment as she speaks. "This is Daniel. He's joining today."

Litzburn chuckles as Daniel opens his mouth to protest to Mary's already departing back. He drops a surprisingly delicate hand onto the new Adventurer's shoulder and gently but firmly guides Daniel onto the training floor, "Don't bother, kid; she isn't listening. Now, follow along, you'll want to know this."

Chapter 3

Hours later, Daniel lies on his back groaning in pain, unwilling to move another inch and feeling thankful that he's not training in the heat of summer. He hasn't felt this tired in years, not since his first year as a miner. For hours, he has been put through various exercises. Firstly, basic fitness tests and weight carrying before moving on to more intricate martial forms with both mace and shield. Once he had spent fifteen minutes working with his new training equipment, Litzburn had walked over and ordered the young man to return the set that he had been working with to the walls, before providing him with even heavier equipment.

Hours of drills then came, at first beginning with simple actions such as stepping and striking before evolving into more and more complicated sequences as Litzburn realises Daniel isn't a complete novice. Every time Daniel flags, Litzburn is at his side, barking at him to pick it up and move faster, driving the young man on. Still, he can't complain as he stares at the blue notification window floating in front of his eyes.

Skill Increase

Clubs: Level 3 (27/100) +3

He's interrupted in his thoughts by a shadow falling over his still form and a booted foot prodding him. He turns his head to meet the gaze of his smiling tormentor. "You did well today. Litzburn tells me you have good stamina and some adequate training for a beginner."

"Thanks..." Daniel mutters before pulling himself up from the ground shakily. Normally he'd heal himself slightly with his gift, just enough to take away the fatigue to let him work more but after this morning's events, he decides against it. Enough has already been lost for one day.

"Come on. We're heading back to the Top. Tomorrow, Litzburn will have you work with some of the other students, and I'll train with you in the evening." Mary is already walking off, and the bemused Daniel follows along, accepting that the young lady doesn't seem to have any desire to waste time.

"Mary, thank you for the training. But, don't we have to pay or something?" Catching up, Daniel gestures back to the training grounds that they have just left.

Mary snorts, before she stops, realising that, of course, Daniel wouldn't know, "I own these training grounds. Well, my sister and I do," she corrects herself, before continuing, "Litzburn is the Master-at-Arms my father hired before he died and while Litzburn might run it, we do own it."

"Oh." Pondering the news for a moment, Daniel continues, "Is that where you learnt to fight too?"

A nod confirms his guess which makes Daniel fall silent, a part of him considering how strong Mary might actually be. She moves with a fluid grace, every action like a part of a dance. Perhaps he too could learn some of that?

It takes them only a few minutes to reach the Top, where Elise seems to have been joined by a pair of waitresses. Spotting her sister, Elise waves them over before directing Daniel to a seat and placing a tankard of beer and an evening meal in front of the weary youngster. The heavenly smell of roast lamb with vegetables and mashed potatoes is all the enticement Daniel needs to throw himself at the meal with gusto. Leaving the young man to eat, Elise drags her sister off and begins a furious conversation with her.

Daniel digs into the meal, casting an occasional curious glance at the arguing pair, but after a moment, he dismisses it. Best not to get involved in a family fight. Instead, he spends his time eating and surveying the various other customers, many of whom look to be guards and adventurers. Each group sits with others of their kind, clustered in tables and partaking of the food with relish.

Daniel is so caught up in people watching that it's a surprise when Elise speaks to him, "I know it's been a hectic day, Daniel, but you really should have stayed for me to say thank you properly."

"I'm sorry," Daniel tries to explain. "Mary dragged me off and then…"

"I know." She gestures with the dirty washcloth in her hand. "She told me. She says she'll be teaching you for the rest of the week before you go into the Dungeon. Good."

"About that…." Daniel opens his mouth, wanting to protest about being given free room and board.

"Daniel, you saved my son's life. The least we can do is increase your chances of surviving in the Dungeon." She suddenly snorts, shaking her head, the long-time resident of a dungeon town adding her two cents, "I don't believe you intended to use that hammer in there. You won't make it past the second floor with that thing."

"Come on, it's not that bad!" protests Daniel.

"Yes, it is. I've lived here all my life and let me tell you, Daniel, one in four Adventurers die on their first foray into a Beginner Dungeon. Of those that make it past the first zone, only one in ten ever completes the Dungeon. Being an Adventurer is dangerous." As she speaks, Elise holds Daniel's gaze. Though she is telling the truth, what Elise leaves out is that many Adventurers do not complete the Dungeon by choice. There are significant riches to be made continuously 'farming' the dungeon monsters for their mana crystals and other dropped items. Riches that an experienced Adventurer could gain with minimal risk.

"That bad?' Daniel's eyes widen, completely taken in by Elise. For a moment, doubt creeps in, and he second guesses his new future and his decision to travel, to adventure, to be his own man. It is a brief moment of hesitation that is soon pushed aside as Daniel refuses to give up before he has even begun. "Thank you. For the advice and the room. And thank Mary for the training."

Satisfied that she has won, Elise bestows a kindly smile on Daniel before she hurries off to care for her patrons. Left alone, Daniel makes his way to his assigned room to wipe himself down and rest. It has been a long day, and tomorrow Litzburn has promised that the real training will begin.

Chapter 4

In the morning, a hurried breakfast is all that Daniel has time for before he rushes over to the training hall. Litzburn is already waiting and directs Daniel to join the other trainees in a slow warmup jog around the hall. The remainder of the day falls into the pattern of the previous day –calisthenics and weight training for a few hours before they dive into the meat of the program, focusing on the use of his mace and shield. Outside of a short lunch break, Daniel is given very little time to rest, which makes him truly grateful for the packed lunch that was pressed on him by Elise as he left that morning.

By the time late afternoon has come, Daniel is beaten and ragged. Numerous other trainees have come and gone throughout the day, most only spending only a few hours in the hall before leaving to run other tasks. Only a few trainees stay throughout the day, each of these is given extra special attention by Litzburn for their dedication. Daniel is focused on a paired movement and striking exercise, attempting to keep his feet, shield and mace moving together and so he never notices Mary's entrance and silent consideration.

"Hold!"

Caught in the middle of a swing, his opponent freezes and steps back, putting distance between himself and Daniel. Daniel freezes too, his shield half-raised to block the blow, his mace swinging from below in return and paused too. Daniel stands there, frozen for a moment before he remembers to step away from his opponent as well, ensuring a safe distance is created. Only then does he look over to Litzburn who is gesturing him over to where he and Mary stand.

"Take a ten-minute break. Then you'll be sparring with Mary," Litzburn calls out to Daniel as he nears before turning away from the tired young man and walking over to address the rest of his students.

Stifling a groan, Daniel flops down in the corner of the training floor before reminding himself to grab a drink of water. As he rests, he stares at his newly updated skill screen, the second one to appear after his rests.

Skill Increase

Clubs (Basic): 37/100 (+3)

Skill Increase

Shields (Basic): 11/100 (+5)

I'm learning very fast, muses Daniel as he dismisses the skill screen. *I guess that's what a real trainer and training ground will do.*

Even to his untrained senses, Daniel can sense the Skill stones that dot the building, helping him to learn faster, even while Litzburn corrects his mistakes with a critical, experienced eye. Still, he can feel a wave of apprehension rising in him at the thought of actually sparring with Mary. He could tell that she was going to be significantly more experienced.

Damn it. Stop worrying. She isn't going to hurt you. Drink some more water and let's get going. Chiding himself, Daniel pushes himself up and walks over the water barrel again before approaching the waiting senior Adventurer.

Mary's dressed in a near replica of her clothing from yesterday - a simple white blouse with a black lace vest and tight, brown pants that show off her trim body. Her sword is strapped to her right side, still sheathed, and in her left hand, she holds a training sword. She looks Daniel over critically, her bright blue eyes clinical in their assessment before she waves him onto the training floor, before following along behind.

A brief salute is exchanged, and immediately, Daniel hunkers down beneath his shield, his mace at his side near his waist as he circles her probing for an opening. Mary turns, only shifting her blade slightly to cover the exposed angles until Daniel lunges forward, committing to an attack. With the barest of motions, the attack is deflected, and Mary returns a riposte aimed at Daniel's shoulder which he barely dodges by jumping back. Regaining his footing, Daniel hunkers back down and works to calm his nerves, the barely moving form of Mary an intimidating presence. Again, he begins to move forward, this time attempting a blow from over his shield. Mary catches his mace in a casual block, and as he recovers, she casually strikes him on his upper arm.

He growls, trying another attack which is just as quickly and neatly defended before her words ring out, "Stop leaning in before each attack."

The sparring continues for an hour with short breaks as she corrects his form and attacks. Not once does he even come close to landing a blow on her, each attack nonchalantly deflected with a flick of a wrist or twist of the elbow. After each committed attack, Mary launches a single return blow of her own, forcing Daniel to scramble to block or dodge in turn.

"Hold!" she says. Daniel pauses and steps back, ensuring he is safe from a return attack before lowering his tired arms.

"Good. We're done. We'll work on what we talked about tomorrow. I'll see you for dinner at the Top." With that and a final salute, Mary turns and strides out of the training ground. Daniel sighs, watching her go and feels somewhat inadequate at his failure to land a single blow. Before he can begin to get too morose, a hand lands on his shoulder.

"Don't worry about it. Even experienced Adventurers had a hard time landing a hit on her – and that was before she first entered the Dungeon and leveled up. That girl, her ability, it isn't normal. You did well for your first time." Chuckling, Litzburn pushes Daniel towards the racks. "Best get dressed and moving; she hates to be kept waiting."

At the Spinning Top, Mary waves Daniel over to her table where a meal is already set, awaiting him. Taking a seat gratefully, Daniel speaks, "Ummm… so, thank you for today."

"It's fine. Now, eat. You need it." She waves him towards the food before she continues. "What do you know about the Dungeon in Karlak?"

Caught between two conflicting orders, Daniel chews quickly and swallows before answering. "It's a Beginner Dungeon, so it's suitable for those just starting out Adventuring. There are ten levels, with the monsters growing stronger at each level. The Dungeon is considered extremely suitable for melee fighters starting out and… umm…. that's about it."

"So, nothing really. Do you know what kind of Dungeon this is? What monsters spawn in the first sector? Do you even know about sectors? How about how many mobs you can expect to see per level? Who is the Dungeon boss? What kind of weaponry is most suitable? Why are melee fighters most suited for this dungeon?" Mary fires question after question at Daniel, waving her own fork as she speaks.

Daniel stops chewing at her words, hunching a bit into his chair as he realises exactly how unprepared he is. Seeing his reaction, Mary relents a little.

"It's fine. It's just a typical beginner's mistake. Just, do your research next time, alright?" Mary waits for Daniel's sheepish nod before leaning forwards and meeting his eyes, "Melee fighters have a bad enough reputation for never using our heads. There's no reason to foster that reputation further. Prior research about a Dungeon is what separates the professionals from the dead."

Pausing to emphasise her point, and making sure it sinks home, she continues to answer her own questions, "It's common knowledge that Dungeons are a way for Erlis to cleanse herself of the corruption that Ba'al releases into the mana flows. The monsters created in a Dungeon are patterned upon the various minions of Ba'al, though they do not truly 'live'. It's why they do not often exit the Dungeons and when they do, most break down in short order. Of course, a

Dungeon that isn't regularly cleared of monsters will have no choice but to strengthen those monsters, eventually giving them sufficient strength to leave the Dungeon itself. In time, an unchecked Dungeon can become the source of Ba'al's infestation, leading to tragedies like the Abandoned Lands. Of course, as Adventurers, we're mostly concerned about the mana crystals – the seed that Erlis uses to create the monsters and our main source of income.

"There are two kinds of Dungeons - the permanent Dungeons like the ones in Karlak and the capital Warbis, and then the temporary Dungeons which randomly appear. Permanent Dungeons rarely change their overall structure, often fixing their floors and the monsters for years at a time. While minor changes in designs and traps do occur, the overall structure of a permanent Dungeon stays the same and, as such, they are often considered 'safer' than temporary Dungeons.

"Temporary Dungeons, or instances, are rare. They appear in places where mana and Ba'al's corruption have built up and by their very nature, are extremely chaotic. Monsters and layouts may change significantly from one trip to the next which make them extremely dangerous to clear. However, because they are built from corrupt mana sources that have temporarily congregated, these Dungeons often do not last longer than a few completions."

Having finished his meal, Daniel places his utensils down and stays silent, listening to the lecture. It is pleasant to not move, and the information she provides is important, even if some of it is well known. Seated, Daniel can feel his body recovering already, regaining the strength it lost through the day.

"Now, for ease of understanding, the Adventurer's Guild has split each Dungeon into sectors - a sector ranging from a single floor to ten. Sectors are grouped due to the nature of the monsters, the traps and the layouts of the floors. At the end of each sector, it's possible that there are sector bosses - monsters whose strength is significantly greater than the average mob already encountered.

They aren't even necessarily a similar monster to those that you have met on that floor, though most Dungeons keep to a theme of some form. Though this isn't always true, it is in the case of Karlak.

"In Karlak, there are three sectors which consist of three floors. The tenth floor isn't a true 'floor', but a single room with the Final Boss monster of the Dungeon. The first sector in the Karlak Dungeon is inhabited by Kobolds. They move in groups with a maximum of three Kobolds at the third level, but for the first level you'll at most run into two of them, and even then, that's highly unlikely."

She pauses for a moment, taking a drink from her tankard and Daniel takes the moment to ask a question, "What are they like?"

"Kobolds?" For a moment Mary racks her brains, trying to recall the looks of the creature. It has been many years since she has fought one of those herself. "Small – about three to four feet tall at most. Extremely thin, very fast with elongated ears and pale grey skin from living underground for so long. They rarely wear much in terms of armour and in the first level wield a dagger-like item, though some carry slings for ranged attacks. Overall, they are the perfect mob for beginner melee fighters."

Daniel nods in thanks, and seeing he has no further questions Mary continues, "Due to the prevalence of the Kobolds in the first few levels, corridors are small and cramped in many areas. There are numerous side-tunnels in the first few levels with no safe zones for healing. Large weapons like a spear or hammer," she flashes him a quick smile at that one before continuing, "are not advisable due to the lack of room. All adventurers should carry a backup dagger for close combat fighting due to the layout, and they should expect potential sneak attacks at all times."

Opening her mouth to continue her lecture, she's interrupted by her sister, Elise, who is accompanied by a young boy clad in a ragged tunic who could at best be eight years old. "Sorry about this, Mary, but young Pierson needs to speak with Daniel."

The young boy impatiently pushes forward, placing a hand on Daniel's arm, "Sir, Charles mentioned you healed him. Healed him good when he was hurt." At Daniel's nod, he rushes on, "Please, will you come and heal my mum?"

Chapter 5

Following Pierson through the lightly illuminated streets of Karlak, Daniel is struck by the thought that this is his first foray into the town at night. Old tales about the dangers of the city make Daniel's hand open and close in want of his hammer. Unknown to him, Karlak is actually a very safe town as guards routinely patrol the streets looking for trouble. Regular troublemakers were sentenced to work in the Dungeon, collecting a set number of mana stones before they were released. Troublemakers and thieves would either die in the Dungeon or just became Adventurers after their term was done since the work was easier and more regular than anything they could do on the outside.

Unfortunately, Daniel knows none of this, and he continually twists his head around, peering into the shadows of alleyways and doorways as they pass expecting to be robbed. It is only Pierson's words that distract him from his obsession. "You can heal my mum, right, Sir? Please?"

"I'll do my best," Daniel hesitantly promises, knowing that even his Gift has limits. Not many for sure, but the cost did increase. Still, the conversation does take his mind away from the supposed dangers of the night as they leave the center of town.

"Charles said you brought him back alive. My mum's not dead. So you can heal her," the child continues, pulling on Daniel's hand to hurry him along.

"He wasn't dead…" realising he forgot the child's name, Daniel trails off. Instead, he changes the subject before Pierson can continue. "Are we heading to your home?"

"No. We're going to the Clinic!"

Even Daniel can hear the capitalization in the child's voice, forcing him to enquire, "The Clinic?"

"Yeah, that's where we all go. The poor. Kyra treats us all." Pierson happily imparts his knowledge to the adult. "She's real pretty, but she never lets me eat any sweets. And she said she couldn't help my mum… but you can! So you're better."

"Kid…" Daniel trails off, shaking his head. No use trying to dissuade him and destroying the child's hope just yet. Instead, he asks another question. "Who's Kyra? Is she a healer?"

"Yeah, the best. Well, other than you. Mum says she opened a clinic years ago and since then, she treats everyone, even if you're poor. She never says no, but it's boring going because there's always people there," Pierson explains.

Much of the information imparted by Pierson isn't particularly surprising to Daniel. Healing potions and spells were expensive as materials, and experienced users were rare. Healers rarely ventured into Dungeons to gain experience faster which meant they could only increase levels by practising their craft. Unfortunately, most skills had diminishing returns in their experience gain if the same action was taken over and over again – which of course was what healers mostly did. There really wasn't anything new to be learnt, dealing with the common cold for the hundredth time. Powerful healing spells drained mana at a significant rate, and with individual mana pools taking up to eight hours to refill, common folk rarely had access to powerful healing magics.

The rarity of healers is one reason Miles, the mine overseer, and many of his miner colleagues had tried to convince him to stay at the mining camp, or at the very least, to not waste his Gift and train to become a healer. Daniel's healing Gift was rare and powerful, especially since it drew upon his experience and energy and thus was a source of energy separate from his mana. Daniel could have become a truly miraculous healer, able to heal using two forms of energy - along with more mundane skills. Even the Royal Healer was known to do very little actual magic-assisted healing since he would need to husband his mana in case of a sudden need for his abilities.

Still, the fact that there is a location in Karlak where the poor can find some form of healing, overworked and crowded as it might be, is a surprise. Daniel can't help but wonder what kind of person this Kyra was. All idle thoughts come to an end as they finally arrive at the Clinic. A weather-worn sign hangs outside with the universal symbol of healing, a crossed pair of hands with jagged lines coming from the hands to indicate an aura. The two-story building itself sprawls across two lots and is by far the best-kept building in the neighborhood with fully working windows and doorways, even if obvious signs of wear and patching are visible.

Pierson doesn't even pause before pushing open the door and is closely followed by Daniel. Inside, what looks to be a waiting room is filled with the poorer denizens of Karlak awaiting treatment. Few even bother looking up from their seats as the child and Daniel enter, lost in their thoughts as they are. Ailments range from simple open wounds that need stitching and broken bones to the disease ridden. Pierson doesn't spare a glance to those inside, instead rushing to the corridor behind and leading Daniel up the stairs to a second-floor room.

In the room, a surprisingly young woman lies, wasting away. Pierson's mother's face is drawn, any excess fat removed, and what would have been once a beautiful face is drawn in pain. Through the room, an obnoxious stench of puss and other unmentionables permeates, making Daniel gag at the stench.

"Mum, I brought him. You'll be fine. He'll heal you." Pierson's voice comes to Daniel as he walks over, a hand landing on the young woman's shoulder so that he may activate his Gift.

Oh, so that's what it looks like when it's advanced. None of the men I treated at camp ever let it get that far before they saw me. His eyes locked on her groin area as he followed the lines of infection spreading outwards and invading her body. He senses the raised temperature, body struggling to fight off the infection and failing. *She will be dead in a few days if I do nothing.*

"Why are you waiting? Come on. Heal her." Almost stamping his feet in impatience, Pierson pushes at Daniel's leg. Then, a trace of fear crosses his voice as he realises where the young Adventurer is looking, the young child's voice beginning to tremble, "You aren't not going to heal her are you? Because she's a... a... whore?"

Shaken by the child's voice, Daniel pulls himself away from the mother to look at Pierson. "It's not that, kid. I just needed to know what I was healing first. My magic isn't like the others... I need to understand what I'm going to fix before I can do it."

She's too weak to use her own energy. We have to drop her temperature first then we can cleanse the infection from her body. After that, we'll have to seal the wounds, so she's not re-infected. Exhaling forcefully, Daniel reaches out to place his hand on the delirious woman's head as he kneels down. "Pierson, this is going to take a while. So don't worry if nothing seems to be happening, I'm going to have to go slow with your mum."

As he finishes speaking, Daniel calls forth his Gift and sends it into her, easing his energy just a little bit into her body at a time. He pushes it slowly, letting it fill her body without attempting to guide it at all at first, the energy lighting up along the meridian pathways of her body starting from her head downwards. As his energy fills her, her breathing eases, and her heartbeat steadies under the passive influence of his Gift. When he is ready, finally, he begins to actively manipulate the energy, working to lower her over-heated body before beginning the long, slow process of flushing her body of the toxins that permeate her blood and the infection that causes it.

The healing isn't easy; each moment a sacrifice. He doesn't speak of the cost of using his Gift to others, though his grandfather and a few others have guessed long ago. In Brad, the Gifted were believed to be blessed by Erlis herself, in others they were considered curses laid by Ba'al for the toll each Gift took upon their users. In truth, none knew where the Gift came from. Like all Gifts, Daniel's had a cost and his tore away knowledge and experience with each moment of use. Knowledge of past actions, past conversations, training and experience drawn from his body.

Hours later, Daniel opens his eyes and tries to stand, pushing against the bedframe. Legs locked in a single position for hours are unable to hold the weight placed on them, and Daniel stumbles forward, caught from crashing into his patient by a steadying hand.

"Thank you," Daniel croaks out as he sways slightly. He is quickly guided to a seat by his unexpected helper, a matronly older lady.

"No, thank you. Peony would be dead without you." The old lady guides him to a waiting seat before turning back to her task of wiping down the patient. It's only then that he realises how much worse the room smells now. All the toxins and infection from Peony's body have leaked into the room, creating a truly horrendous stench that not even an open window can aid.

"I do hope all your work isn't as smelly as this," the old lady continues as she bathes the newly-healed young woman.

Daniel grins weakly before quenching his thirst with a glass of water. It's been ages since he used so much power on a single individual, even Charles's healing was simpler than eradicating the disease that had ravaged Peony's body. Still, he cannot help but smile as he watches the young woman rest easier, Pierson curled up at the base of her bed asleep.   As he contemplates his work, another figure strides in, one that causes his jaw to drop. An elf!

Never having seen an elf before in real life, Daniel stares at the elf with undisguised awe. The elf is tall, clad in a simple green frock that hugs her slim upper body on top of a buxom chest, waist-length blonde hair spilling out behind long pointed ears. The elf moves with a lithe grace over to Pierson's mum, a delicate hand moving in arcane gestures as she checks on the condition of the patient. Satisfied, the blonde elf turns to Daniel who has managed to close his mouth at last and stand up.

"I'm Daniel. Would you be Kyra?" He offers his hand to shake which is promptly taken. Her skin is surprisingly soft and smooth, a sharp contrast to his own rough and calloused hands.

"Khy'ra," she corrects his pronunciation off-handedly, not expecting him to get it right as she turns to point at Pierson's mum. "Your Gift, it's incredible. It's at least the equivalent of a Tier 4 Healing Spell, maybe 5. Are you able to use it again today?"

"Kind of. That took a lot out of me…" as he speaks, he meets the enthusiastically nodding Khy'ra's gaze. Sparkling green eyes meet his own, and Daniel's excuses catch in his suddenly dry mouth. "Maybe a bit."

"Good. I'm not much of a healer; I only know a single Tier 3 spell so there's much that I cannot do for these people. There are a few others I'd love you to see if you are willing?" She casts an entreating look at Daniel who sighs, consoling himself that he will get to spend more time with the beautiful creature before him.

"I'll do what I can."

"Excellent!" Gripping his arm to her full chest, Khy'ra drags Daniel out of the room to visit her patients, already beginning to list the many issues that they face. Behind them, the matronly old woman is left alone, smiling slightly at the departing smitten young man.

Chapter 6

The following days for Daniel each fall into the same pattern as the day before. An early breakfast in the Top followed by training with Litzburn at the hall. In the late afternoon, Daniel spars with Mary before retiring for dinner with her and a lecture about the basics of Adventuring. The moment dinner is over, he is escorted by a grateful Pierson to the Clinic where he works alongside the minimal staff, using his healing skills, spells and on occasion, his Gift to reduce the waiting line. The line at the Clinic never seems to reduce, no matter how much he does, but the work itself is rewarding.

Each day is packed, every morning a struggle as Litzburn berates him for forgetting part of what he learnt the day before, driving the willing Adventurer ever harder. On the fourth day of training, he finally manages to make Mary move from her spot, the casual blocks insufficient. On the sixth, after chaining together a series of strikes, he makes her move regularly and pick up speed. On the seventh day, he finally breaks through.

Level Up!

Adventurer Level 2

You have gained 5 attribute points and 1 skill proficiencies.

The Level Up notification is dismissed, leaving Daniel on the floor rubbing his jaw. The level up had caught him unawares, distracting him for a crucial moment leading to the blow that he forgets to block properly. Still, he can't help smiling. Sure, the first level was always easier to gain after any class change, but in a week!

Mary stands over Daniel, offering him a hand up and a murmur of, "Congratulations."

"Thank you. You and Litzburn. This, this will help a lot," Daniel says as he lets himself get pulled up.

"It's your hard work." Mary smiles, clapping him on the back. "We're done for today. You might be rather useless in the mornings from what Litzburn says, but you work hard. You should spend the evening deciding where to put your points. I have dinner with Elise and Charles tonight as I leave tomorrow."

Daniel nods, a bit impatient to review his Status Screen. It's been such a busy week, he hasn't had time to review it, but he can certainly see the wisdom of her words. After all, he's going into the Dungeon tomorrow for the first time. "Thank you again."

"Daniel, your Gift – don't take it for granted. Most others have to start out slow, buying potions from the apothecary for healing and if they run out or are too gravely injured, leave the Dungeon until they are healed. You don't have to. It's also a double-edged sword as you may come to rely on it too much. Just, don't push yourself too hard. That includes the Clinic," Mary adds. She hasn't asked what his Gift costs him as yet, but it was common knowledge that there must be a cost of some form. Still, his performance in the morning has given her an inkling, but it was his secret to keep. As they talk, Mary leads him to the corner where she hands over her training sword to be put away once again. The clerk returns after setting her training sword in its special spot in the armory with a real mace which she takes from him with a nod. Mary then turns to Daniel, offering him the mace. "This is the last thing I can do for you for now Daniel. The rest will be up to you."

Daniel takes it and murmurs his gratitude, hefting the mace and looking it over.

Steel Mace

Damage: 3 - 7 + .5 Strength + 2 Quality Bonus

Durability: 50/50

Item Class: Common

Quality: Good (+2 bonus to damage)

Daniel can't help but marvel at the weapon, the nicest he has ever owned before eventually slipping the mace through a loop in his belt, "I talked to Khy'ra last night. I'll visit once in a while, but I won't be there every day anymore. As much as I like helping, I can't. She understands. Mary, all this - the training, the mace, the advice, how can I ever thank you?"

"You don't need to. I'm leaving tomorrow for Starhaven. My team's waiting for me, and I need to get back. If you are ever in Starhaven, buy me a drink as thanks if you must. Just don't come too fast." Mary smiles slightly at that, clapping him on the shoulder once more before turning to leave. Daniel understands her message - Starhaven only has Expert level Dungeons and was no place for a novice Adventurer like him. Not yet, at least.

That evening, after a rushed dinner by himself, Daniel lies in bed and debates what to do with his new attribute points and skill proficiencies.

5 attribute points and 1 skill proficiency to allocate. Unlike his previous class as a Miner, the Adventurer class was much more open-ended on its attribute point allocation. Strength, Agility and Constitution were all key to his needs as a melee fighter, but it was his Intelligence and Willpower that dictated his ability to heal. He frowns for a moment, deciding to put a couple of extra points into Agility and a point each into Constitution, Intelligence and Wisdom. He was more than strong enough for now.

That done, he calls up his skill proficiency tree and stares at the new options available for him. All that training has increased his skills in both Shield, Dodge, Combat Sense and Club offering him more options than he knew what to do with. As he gains ability in each skill, new skill proficiencies would become available that allowed him to enhance the basic abilities of each skill. This even translated to his healing skill, with both mundane options like First Aid or at higher levels, powerful healing spells. Unsure of what to do, Daniel decides to peruse his proficiencies again, musing over his options.

An upgrade to his Minor Healing Spell would reduce the mana cost and increase the amount healed slightly. It was a good option for both the Clinic and the Dungeon. However, he had the backup of his own Gift which should be enough for now, so he dismisses that option.

In terms of defense, he could learn Hard Block, offering him a chance to beat aside an opponent's weapon and potentially riposte on the line of attack. A truly successful hard block could even damage or disarm an opponent. On the other hand, Tumbling under Dodge would provide a more efficient means of getting out of the way of large attacks or groups, though Sway was a passive skill proficiency that would offer him the chance to dodge blows by inches without giving ground. Daniel knew Mary favored that option, allowing her to hold her ground even against the strongest opponents. Sway was a skill particularly useful for the smaller, lighter Adventurer but after consideration, Daniel discards it. It just doesn't suit his fighting style, especially as he intends to specialise in the use of a shield when he could afford one.

Dueling from Combat Sense would give him a bonus to hit and his critical hit skill while fighting a single opponent but as he was a solo Adventurer, multiple mobs were a guarantee at some point. While Daniel has no shield or armour to his name at this time, he has more hit points than most beginning Adventurers since he started out his career later than most of them. Trusting in his ability to take damage, Daniel dismisses all but his combat skill proficiencies to review.

Shield Bash

An attack with your shield, turning it into an offensive weapon as well as a defensive tool.

Skill: Active

Cost: 12 Stamina

Effect: User's Bash does 1-2 points of damage + 0.5 per level of the Shield Skill. Has a 1% chance per level of Shield Skill chance to Stun for 5 seconds.

Power Strike

Powerful single strike that causes additional damage to an opponent.

Skill: Active

Cost: 15 Stamina

Effect: User's Power strike does 50% more damage + 2% per level of Club skill.

Double Strike

Cross strike allows the wielder to launch a chained attack, striking twice in the time it would take an inexperienced attacker to attack once. Each strike (if it lands) is at 70% of the damage.

Skill: Active

Cost: 25 Stamina

Effect: User strikes twice in quick succession. Each strike does 70% of normal damage. Damage increases +0.5% per Club skill level of user.

Power Strike was a very common attack for most melee fighters. It provided a high level of damage and could crush many lower level enemies if he could increase his skill level with clubs sufficiently. Shield Bash was probably the next most common attack form, a safe skill that made both hands dangerous and one that was favored by shield users like himself. The stun effect could be very useful in a fight, but unfortunately, he didn't own a shield at this time. Still, as Daniel thinks about the various sparring sessions he's had with Mary, Daniel can only choose Double Strike. It was only with a flurry of blows did he ever make her move, make her take him semi-seriously. Satisfied, he selects the Skill Proficiency and stares at his newly updated Status Screen.

Name: Daniel Chai

Class: Level 2 Adventurer (0%)

Sub-classes: Level 7 (Miner) (19%)

Human (Male)

Statistics

Life: 176

Stamina: 176

Mana: 136

Critical Hit Chance: 4%

Attributes

Strength: 17

Agility: 14

Constitution: 24

Intelligence: 15

Willpower: 17

Luck: 13

Skills

Unarmed Combat: Level 2 (47/100)

Clubs: Level 7 (21/100)

Shield: Level 5 (18/100)

Dodge: Level 3 (16/100)

Combat Sense: Level 2 (12/100)

Perception: Level 3 (21/100)

Mining: Level 7 (78/100)

Healing: Level 7 (07/100)

Herb Lore: Level 3 (31/100)

Cooking: Level 2 (37/100)

Singing: Level 2 (14/100)

Skill Proficiencies

Double Strike

Mapping (II)

Spells

Minor Healing (I)

Gifts

Martyr's Touch - The caster may heal oneself or others by touch and concentration, sacrificing a portion of his life to do so. Cost varies depending on the extent of the injuries healed.

Chapter 7

"Listen up, children." The guard in front of the dungeon entrance stares at the group of Adventurers before him. The beginner Adventurers grouped around him vary in size and clothing though most are in their mid-to-early teens and sport a single weapon, most often a short sword. The Adventurers are mostly human, though on occasion Daniel spots a Beastkin and even one dwarf in the group.

"This is your first time in, so I strongly recommend you stick to the first floor. If you do manage to find the stairway to the second floor, you may go down but only to access the transportation gem. That'll allow you to travel to the second floor directly when you are ready to take it on.

"The number one cause of Adventurer deaths is overconfidence so don't think about going down to the second floor until you cleared the entire first floor. Never start a new floor injured - it's the fastest way to get yourself killed. Remember, the Guild buys mana stones of all sizes so make sure to collect every single drop that you get. The blacksmiths have asked me to remind all of you not to bring Kobold shanks back. They don't want them or need them. Any questions?"

Barely waiting for the Adventurers' answers, the guard steps aside and waves them into the Dungeon. Gripping his mace in hand, Daniel nods his thanks one last time before stepping in, his hand slightly clammy on the grip of his mace. On entering, Daniel is immediately greeted by a simple stone room lit by the sunlight behind and the soft white glow characteristic of the Dungeon's mana-imbued walls.

Grinning slightly, Daniel shifts his bag once more to ensure it is properly seated before following the sole corridor that leads into the dungeon proper. The exit immediately splits into three earthen passageways, and Daniel pauses, listening for the movements of the other Adventurers before choosing the middle pathway.

As he moves deeper, a mental mini-map of the dungeon begins to form in his mind from the Mapping proficiency. Daniel gained that option as a Miner, like most others, and chose to level it up a couple of times rather than other more traditional mining proficiencies as he knew it'd be more useful for him in the future. You never wanted to be lost in the dark. *I wonder what other Adventurers do…*

Spending time thinking about inconsequential things like that is never a good idea in a Dungeon, a fact that Daniel finds out to his chagrin when he turns a corner and walks into a Kobold. A runt even among its kind, the three-foot-tall creature looks like a gray, gangly, slightly malnourished child clad in peasant garb, other than its rather elongated ears and too-wide eyes. Somehow, even after Mary's description, the Kobold looks nothing like he had pictured it. The Kobold reacts first, thrusting its only weapon, a shank made of metal and bone, into Daniel's chest. It hits hard, plunging through cloth and skin and grating against a rib. Daniel jumps backwards, groaning in pain as he feels blood begin to dribble from the wound, waving his mace to ward off the Kobold.

Taking to the offense, Daniel lashes out once and then again, the Kobold scurrying backwards and staying out of range of his attacks. As Daniel is recovering from his swings, the Kobold darts in again and attempts another stab, and only a last-minute hasty parry by Daniel forces the Kobold to stop its own attack or have its arm crushed.

Daniel again steps forwards, attempting to strike the Kobold who dances back and swings at Daniel's arm, nicking him. This fight is completely different from his earlier sparring matches with Mary. The Kobold is smaller, more prone to feints and is focused on short quick strikes to Daniel rather than a single painful attack.

As blood continues to run from his open wound, Daniel pushes forward to finish the fight. He throws another overhand right and then as the Kobold ducks, he charges forwards and activates Double Strike, his mace swinging faster as the proficiency activates. The first attack from the left is blocked, but using the force of the block, Daniel swings the mace around to strike on the Kobold's unprotected right side. The mace crunches into the Kobold's shoulder, cracking bone and mashing muscle.

Panicking, the Kobold pulls itself away from Daniel and attempts to stab its attacker again with its shank. This time, Daniel is ready though, and he smashes his mace onto the Kobold's outstretched attacking hand, crushing its fingers and forcing the monster to drop its weapon. As the Kobold flails, Daniel swings again, landing a Critical Strike on the top of the Kobold's head to deliver a fatal blow. A moment later, the body dissolves into acrid smoke leaving behind a small mana crystal.

Daniel barely pays attention, slumping into the corner and holding a hand over his wound as he chain casts Minor Healing on himself. It's only when the bleeding stops that he pays attention to the notifications he received during the battle.

Critical Hit! 29 Damage Dealt. Kobold killed.
Minor Healing cast on Daniel. 14 Hit Points Restored.
Minor Healing cast on Daniel. 10 Hit Points Restored.
Bleeding has stopped.

Seeing nothing important in the information, Daniel dismisses it and resolves to stop looking at such information. Daniel bends to pick up the dropped mana crystal, looking around warily before heading deeper into the dungeon. He'd used over nearly a third of his mana already, and he had just started. For the first time, he begins to truly understand Mary's point.

A half-dozen Kobolds later, and a chance meeting with one other Adventurer, and Daniel has found the staircase down. The other battles since the first one have gone quite well, with little additional damage dealt to him they have bolstered his flagging confidence. As long as he pays attention, with his skill and level, he should be able to deal with a single Kobold. Unlike most newbie Adventurers, this wasn't his first class, and as such, his Health was significantly higher than theirs. Of course, he had paid a price in time – most Adventurers who survived to his age were at a much higher level than him and would not even consider stepping into a Beginner Dungeon. Confident and impatient, Daniel

makes a decision and takes the steps down, ignoring the guard's advice.

Chapter 8

The staircase down to the second floor leads to a small ten-foot-wide oval cavern that is currently empty. Unlike the first floor, the soft drip of water can be heard through the Dungeon; stalagmites and stalactites dot the floor and ceiling. Lighting on the second floor is worse too with the mana-imbued walls occasionally pitch black.

Daniel feels the hair on his arms stand out a little more; the second floor actually felt dangerous compared to the first. The exits from this cavern are smaller too, more cramped and Daniel soon realises he'll have to shorten some of his strikes. For a moment, he considers going back upstairs before he spots the portal stone and recalls the directions given. He walks over swiftly and places his hand on the stone where it gently lights up, 'remembering' his mana. The temporary distraction is enough to push the creeping doubts away.

"Let's see what I can find down here…" whispers Daniel to himself, filling the oppressive silence. It only takes a few minutes of walking for Daniel to run into his first Kobold, a far cry from the relatively quiet first floor. The fight does not take much more time than his fights on the first floor, though the Kobold is more skilled and is able to leave a long cut across his left arm. Daniel ignores the damage, only spending enough time to wrap a simple cloth bandage around his arm to stem the blood flow.

Emboldened by the successful fight, he journeys deeper into the dungeon, stopping only occasionally to check his surroundings and his mini-map to ascertain his location. Another fight with a Kobold brings him a third of the way to his next level up as an Adventurer. Obviously, actual Adventuring and fighting were a faster form of levelling than training.

It has been hours since the day began and the intense concentration required is wearing on him. The mental fatigue he is experiencing is something different from mining, and once again, his wandering mind betrays him as he doesn't notice the Kobold that creeps up behind him. His first impression of it is a sharp one, the shiv plunging into his back and nicking a kidney.

A hasty back kick glances off the Kobold's body, Daniel's larger size managing to push the monster away long enough for him to spin around. Daniel snarls, stepping forward and swinging his mace to injure the Kobold who ducks into the smaller passageway that it came from to dodge the strike. The side passage is much smaller, barely five feet in height with almost no lighting.

Daniel crouches to follow the shorter Kobold in, hoping to extract his revenge. Forced to shorten his swings and to jab the mace forwards in strikes, he doesn't have much room to attack properly, but the Kobold is still forced to back away from the stronger human or risk getting injured. Both parties trade insignificant blows for a few seconds, before another sharp pain in his buttocks makes Daniel realise that he's surrounded.

Trapped! For a moment, Daniel panics as the tight quarters, monsters in front and behind him and open wounds make his chest tighten and his vision narrow. He freezes, body locked in fear as he realises he might truly die here, his momentary pause allowing the Kobold he faces to lunge forward and stab his arm.

Instinctively, Daniel grabs the smaller Kobold's arm and holds the monster to him, picking the creature up and rushing forward to escape the confines of the passageway. Almost trampling the monster as he shoves the creature ahead of him, his panicked body attempts to create space away from his pursuing attacker and fails, the shiv from his attacker behind him plunging again into his back and eliciting another grunt of pain.

The Kobold he holds tight scratches and bites at the arm holding it but is unable to do significant damage without the use of its weapon. Daniel continues rushing ahead, crouched over and finally, the pathway breaks open into a larger room. Still gripping the Kobold, Daniel spins around and flings the smaller monster into its brethren's path before he falls back away from the two monsters, blood from his back continuing to pour out with every exertion.

In the larger room, Daniel's moment of panic begins to subside. The two monsters pull themselves apart and beginning to flank the novice Adventurer. Realising he cannot let them set themselves for an attack, Daniel rushes forward and activates his Double Strike proficiency, attacking the closest Kobold of the two. A pair of strikes lash out, one dodged but the second landing properly. It forces his attackers to grow warier as Daniel begins to swing his weapon with abandon, able to properly wind up in the larger space. Every time he is able to, he activates his skill proficiency, the mace suddenly moving faster.

It takes only a few more passes before the fight finishes, a lucky blow to the top of one attacker's skull stunning it long enough for a second attack to finish it. Faced one-on-one by Daniel, the second attacker falls with relative ease, and the injured Daniel slumps to the ground in pain. Out of battle, he feels the additional wounds on his arm and torso he received during the last few moments of desperate fighting.

Grunting in pain, Daniel focuses on calling forth his Gift and begins to stitch the wounds in his body together, cutting off the bleeding immediately. Once that important task is done, he proceeds to heal up the last of the damage with his mana, casting Minor Heal on himself and watching the last of the wounds stitch close.

"Well, that didn't go well…" Daniel whispers to himself before finally pulling himself to his feet. He looks around before sliding one of the Kobold shanks into his belt, finally recalling Mary's initial advice on having a shorter reach weapon on-hand.   It definitely would have been helpful in the smaller passageway he had been trapped in. Thank Erlis he had more vitality and experience than a typical novice Adventurer. With a last stretch and quick looting of the mana stones,

Daniel stares at his mini-map and ponders if he should head back upstairs or continue searching the second floor.

Chapter 9

"Damn. That's six." Sighing, the guard hands his friend a silver piece and shoots Daniel's tired form an unfriendly glare at his loss. Who would have thought that another beginner would show up this late at night? Most of the beginners from this morning's batch had called it a day hours ago, those that survived that is.

Daniel barely notices the look or the words, dragging his feet towards the awaiting Adventurer's Guild. He had long ago eaten all the food and drunk most of the water he had carried down, and he just wanted this to be over. Adventuring seemed to take more energy out of him than even the mines, and he was thoroughly ravenous. Vowing to carry more provisions the next time, all Daniel wants to do is to sell the mana stones he has collected and sleep.

In the Guild, Liev is finally coming to the end of his long shift when he spots Daniel. A flicker of relief breaks his professional facade as Mary would have been thoroughly upset if Daniel had died. His demeanor restored, he calls out, "Working hard I see!"

"Hi, Liev. Got a few stones for you…" Daniel empties the pouch on the counter, the shower of mana stones making Liev raise an eyebrow.

"That's quite a haul you have there…" Practised hands dance across the stones, pushing and sorting the stones by quality as he continues. "You went to the second floor didn't you?"

"Umm…"

"There are no rules barring that, Daniel. The Guild does not monitor, condone or judge such decisions. No matter how foolhardy," Liev states as he works on a piece of paper, totaling up Daniel's earnings.

"How did you know?"

"These here are all D Grade 12 stones and 11 stones, what I'd expect to see from the first floor. These three though are D Grade 10's which you'd only get if you were really lucky or were hunting on the second floor." As Liev speaks, he points to each pile before he twists his pad around and shows Daniel his total. Knowing that some of their clientele are unable to read, he states as well. "4 Silver and 3 Coppers. Third best haul among your group."

Daniel nods jerkily at the announcement automatically, picking up the coins as Liev deposits them on the counter. A decent amount, though an experienced miner could earn five silver a day for much less risk. After a moment, Daniel recalls what the attendant said, "Third?"

"Yes. Two of the Novices managed to find the chest on the first floor."

"Chest?" Feeling like a parrot, Daniel leans forward. Truth be told, after his nasty encounter on the second floor, he had grown a lot more careful and worked the second floor with caution, checking each side passageway carefully before moving on. Unfortunately, that meant he encountered Kobolds at a slower rate.

"You didn't even look for it did you?" Liev smiles, slightly bemused, reaching under his desk to pull out a mana stone. Almost the same size as the shards that Daniel has been bringing in, this one is noticeably clearer than his. "On each floor, there is a chest which contains a mana stone which is a number of grades higher than what you'd find defeating the mobs on that level. It moves around after it is found, respawning every two to four hours but it's always guarded by an Elite of that floor. This one here is a D Grade 8."

"Oh…" Daniel falls silent, tapping his fingers on the counter before looking up at Liev. "It's a matter of quantity over quality then isn't it? If I stay on the first floor, I'll be trying to find the chest to get a good, high-quality stone. If I go push down to the second floor again, I'll be able to fight more often, but it's more dangerous, and I wouldn't be able to get a chest yet."

Liev nods, internally surprised that Daniel has come to that conclusion that quickly. Most Adventurers take a while longer to work out those options by themselves.

"Thank you, Liev. I'll keep it in mind. Goodnight!" Daniel waves goodbye, moving away from the counter. It's been a long day, and it's time to get to bed.

"Morning, Daniel. Sleep in, did you?" A laughing Elise waves him over to the bar where she is busy cleaning up from the breakfast rush. "Breakfast will be out soon."

Daniel nods, plopping down onto the stool. He has his gear with him already, but a good meal to start the day seems like a great idea. That and coffee.

"So, Daniel. I know you saved my son and all…" Elise smiles as she drops a plate before him along with a steaming cup of coffee. "But you know, I run an Inn…"

Daniel blinks and then understands where Elise is leading with this and hangs his head slightly in shame, "Yeah, uhh… about that. How much for room and board for the week?"

"Since you're almost like family, a silver a day for all the food you can eat and we'll even wash your clothes," Elise pronounces unashamedly.

"Ummm… here you go." Daniel empties out the silver from his pouch, feeling how empty it is now. He shovels the last of the gruel in, already thinking of the Dungeon and refilling his purse and his many expenses. He will need a new shirt soon if he continues being stabbed so often, a shield to protect himself, soap to wash his clothing, another purse so that he can separate his mana stones from his coins. The list goes on.

As he finishes, Elise waves him towards a wrapped box that she has placed on the bar. "Here you go. Lunch and a snack."

"Thank, Elise. I'll be back late, I think." Scooping up the box, he stuffs it into his bag and hurries towards the Dungeon. He definitely needs to do better than yesterday, his current and future expenses piling up behind his eyes.

Watching his departing back, Elise smirks to herself. They were all like that, getting lazy after their first run. A little kick in their ass was what they needed. Whistling to herself, Elise walks back to the kitchen to begin washing up. That boy would do well.

Chapter 10

Waving to the guards as he passes them by, Daniel trots into the Dungeon's first floor without slowing down. A single Kobold didn't really pose too much danger to him after his experiences yesterday, certainly not those that lived on the first floor. However, unlike most other Adventurers, he had not bought a map, trusting his own proficiency to glean the layout. Recalling his talk with Liev yesterday, Daniel decides to work out the full layout of the first floor by himself and hopefully find the chest at the same time.

Moving at a slower pace once he is inside the actual dungeon, Daniel still paces through the passageways at a faster rate than the previous day, able to marvel at the strangeness of the dungeon. To his experienced eyes, the layout of the first floor made no logical sense as a cave network, even if it would to the ignorant. Small incongruities jumped out at Daniel; the floor was too smooth, the changes in the size of both the tunnels and chambers they joined making no natural sense and each cavern is too symmetrical. After encountering and killing a few more Kobolds, Daniel even begins to realise that the layout seems to repeat itself.

It takes Daniel almost three hours to make his way through three-quarters of the floor. He passes by a number of other novices, many moving more slowly and cautiously than he does. More than one pair have teamed up, an action that makes Daniel wonder before dismissing the option for now. At some point, he would need help, but a part of him revels at working alone after years of working in teams in the mine. In addition, he fears that any Adventurer he joined with would slow him down and he had a lot of ground to catch up on.

Not that I really want to deal with teenager angst either… Daniel chuckles to himself quietly, oblivious to the irony of his thoughts.

As he nears the next corner, Daniel hunches forward to peer into the chamber. His eyes widen, and he pulls his head back, hiding again. *Well, I found it. And him.*

Most Kobolds were four feet tall at most, but the Elite was obviously a paragon of its kind - standing four and a half feet tall and having actual, visible musculature. At least, what wasn't covered by what looked like badly-stitched-together soft leather armor. Thankfully, it was still armed with just a shiv.

For a moment, Daniel hesitates. Then, recalling that it was just a Kobold that at least two other beginners had beaten before him, he firms his resolve and steps out to meet the monster. The Kobold spots him almost immediately, growling a low challenge as it crouches down in front of the small chest.

Surprised that the Elite doesn't attack him straight away, Daniel hesitates before taking a step forward and throwing a cautious strike. The Kobold barely moves, seeing the feint for what it is.

Daniel's eyes widen further in surprise at this unexpected reaction, and he stops, hovering outside of the Kobold's reach. The Kobold moves first this time, throwing a rock it had concealed at Daniel. Instinctively, Daniel bats the rock aside and pays for it when his opponent lunges forward, plunging his weapon into Daniel's extended arm, twisting the blade as it exits to widen the wound. Before he can retaliate, the Kobold dances out of range again and flashes Daniel a predatory smile.

The next few passes have Daniel and the Kobold cautiously trading blows, neither fully committing to the attack. Daniel receives another light wound on his thigh, the Kobold suffering a bruised arm as it manages to foil a blow by pushing its arm forward into the mace's handle.

Frustrated, Daniel engages his double strike to watch the Kobold back away from the attacks, forcing Daniel to pursue him. A few more passes clarify Daniel's initial impressions. *Little bugger's fast. Hold still will you!*

Eyes narrow at a sudden thought and then Daniel shifts to slightly wider swings, focusing on herding the Kobold to a corner. It is his time to smile as the Kobold realises what is happening, but the human's greater reach foils the Elite's ability to get away even as Daniel receives a few more light injuries. Finally, backed into a corner, the Elite is unable to escape its end beneath the mace, though a last-minute surge by the monster leaves its shiv planted in Daniel's thigh as it dies.

Swearing to himself, Daniel collapses and tugs the shiv out of his thigh, slumping against the nearby wall as he takes his weight off his injured limb. A flash of red catches his eye at the passageway he entered, but he ignores it, focusing on healing himself first before turning to his notifications.

Level Up!

Adventurer Level 3

You have gained 5 attribute points to distribute.

Immediately, Daniel puts a few points into Agility before he shuts the window. He will figure out the rest tonight, but it is obvious to him that he needs to be faster against these monsters. Smiling in glee at the thought of the mana crystal that awaits him in the chest, he pushes himself up.

Was it open before? I was sure it wasn't… With dread filling him, Daniel walks over to the chest to find it empty with no sign of the thief.

"Bad day?" Liev asks the young Adventurer as he sorts and counts Daniel's mana stones. A slightly raised eyebrow at the lack of a more powerful mana stone, especially since the number that Daniel brought back was actually less than before. In fact, the way the stones told the story, Daniel must have spent most of his day on the first floor.

"I fought and defeated the Elite, but someone stole the stone while I was recovering," Daniel explains, looking morosely at the smaller number of coins Liev pushes forward as payment. Sighing, Daniel picks up the coins and puts them away.

"Ah, yes. That does happen occasionally." Liev shrugs, thievery in the Dungeon while uncommon was not unknown. Since there was no way to tell who owned a mana stone, thieves could steal stones with impunity in the Dungeon so long as they were not caught. Occasionally, bandits would even try their attempts at extortion or robbery, but those did not last long. Theft, while annoying, was an accepted part of Adventuring life. Since the only place to sell mana stones was at the Adventuring Guild, any bandit who came back with too great a haul regularly was bound to be caught.

Daniel nods glumly, having already decided not to make too much of a fuss over his loss. After all, he had no proof of who could have stolen his stone.

"Might I make a suggestion?" Liev smiles slightly at the young Adventurer, catching him just as he is about to leave.

"Of course." Daniel perks up, hoping for some earth-shattering advice from the experienced attendant. Surely he knew things that a young Adventurer could learn.

"There's a bathhouse a few blocks from the Top to the East. You'll find most Adventurers find it prudent to visit the bathhouses every few days." Liev smiles gently, eyeing the dirty, smelly Adventurer. Washcloth baths could only do so much, especially after a number of days fighting, killing and bleeding in the Dungeon.

"Oh!" Daniel blushes, realising Liev's unspoken implication. "Right. Thank you!" With that said, Daniel rushes off to the Top with what remains of his dignity.

Chapter 11

"15, 16, 17, 18!" Daniel sighs, staring forlornly at his small collection of coins as dawn light streams through the window. 1 Gold, 18 Silver. Still not enough to buy the shield he so desperately wanted. Armour, decent armour, was still a distant pipe dream, but a shield he could buy. Even with his increased skills and abilities, getting regularly wounded was becoming a pain.

A knock on his door brings Daniel out from his morose musings. "Yes?"

"Daniel, you're up?" Smiling Elise looks him over. "I need a little favour."

"What favour?" Daniel looks at innkeeper warily.

"Oh, nothing much. I just have a friend who needs some company today. You know, someone who needs to get out of work, stop doing the same things they've been doing non-stop," she smiles slightly while looking at him knowingly.

"Umm… well, I was going to go to the Dungeon…," Daniel mutters. He ignores the implication Elise makes, even though he has yet to take a break in the three weeks since he has first entered the Dungeon.

"It's fine; you'll love it. Anyway, you haven't really seen much of the town yet, have you? This would be a great opportunity, and it'd let you get in some shopping." She points to his rather threadbare, often-patched set of clothing.

A short twenty minutes later, Daniel is standing outside the Spinning Top, muttering about a wasted day and wondering who this friend was. When Khy'ra walks up, he can't help but smile at the blonde elf. He has barely had time to visit the Clinic with his activities, and when he has done so, it has often been late at night after returning from the Dungeon when Khy'ra was not around. "Khy'ra! It's good to see you."

"And you. Did you see Elise…?" Khy'ra is looking around, frowning. "She asked me to come over."

"Umm…."

"Good, you're both here." Stepping out of the inn as she wipes her hands on her apron, Elise nods firmly. "Kyra, Daniel needs a guide around town. He's yet to actually see anything, and he could do with some new clothes too."

"What…?"

"Oh and don't bother going to the Clinic or the Dungeon. I told them not to let you guys in." Smirking, Elise walks back briskly into the Top and shuts the door behind her.

"Couldn't she be a bit more subtle…" mutters Khy'ra as she stares at the door, blushing slightly.

"Yeah…" Daniel agrees with her before he tilts his head, struck by a thought. "Do you mean…?"

"Shopping!" Smiling brightly, Khy'ra grabs his hand and drags him down the street. "I know just the place for some new clothing."

"Actually… I was saving up for something."

"Something?" An arched eyebrow has Daniel quickly explaining.

"A shield. I'm getting stabbed a lot, especially when I'm fighting two Kobolds. It'd be nice to be able to guard one side properly. Nothing too big of course, it's a bit cramped you know, but yeah…" Daniel trails off, realising explaining the intricacies of using a shield to Khy'ra might be a bit much.

"Then let's go!" She tugs Daniel down the street, half-dragging the man down to the river with her. "So, you're a mace and shield fighter, eh? I'd have thought Mary would have converted you to the sword."

Daniel laughs, shaking his head. "She's amazing, but the sword requires real skill to use, you know? And the mace just feels right."

"Oh, I get that. I hated the sword myself. Especially in those tunnels! I could barely swing without hitting the walls at times." Khy'ra reminisces, miming a swinging action as she speaks.

"You were an Adventurer?" Daniel tilts his head to Khy'ra, bemused at the thought of the bubbly creature beside him in the depths of the dungeon, searching for Kobolds and killing them with a smile.

"Yes. I was one of the first to enter this Dungeon actually. Came here with my brothers." Khy'ra smiles, shaking her head reminiscing. "We couldn't get the reward for completing it first though, and they left soon after. I decided to stay for a bit. Here we are."

Daniel nods comfortably as she talks, both of them weaving through the busy morning traffic. It takes him a moment to realise that the last sentence wasn't part of the initial conversation and he looks up to spot the sign of an armourer swinging above him. Even as he gets pulled inside, Daniel realises where they are.

"Maxwell, I have a customer for you - we need your best shields," Khy'ra announces as they enter the armoury, the forge at the back increasing the temperature a few degrees even out at the front of the shop.

Stepping away from his forge and beckoning to an apprentice to take over, Maxwell grins as he spots Khy'ra, "Definitely not for you. Oh, it's you!" He nods firmly to Daniel while he gestures behind him to where the shields hang. "Stock hasn't changed."

Daniel smiles politely, stepping further into the shop to survey the pair of styles available. A simple buckler and a larger round wooden shield, both banded by metal are his choices. His fingers trace the round wooden shield with lust, the larger shield perfect for his fighting style and what he has been saving up for before he looks to Maxwell and asks, "A gold and fifty still?"

Maxwell nods before Khy'ra clears her throat loudly. "You know, Max, Daniel here has been helping out a lot at the Clinic lately. Why, he helped me deal with that rather nasty situation with Peony. And her friends."

"Peony?" Maxwell's face goes blank. "I don't, well, if he's been the one helping you, Khy'ra… A gold and…" A slight smile from Khy'ra makes him stop. "A gold."

Daniel watches the byplay, a small part of him feeling slightly guilty about the deal. It is only a small part though as he snatches up the shield and pushes the gold into Max's hand. "Thank you! A gold it is."

The pair spends the rest of the day shopping, stopping by to pick up some basic household supplies for both themselves and some additional supplies for the Clinic. Khy'ra occasionally name drops Daniel and his connection to the Clinic, though Daniel finds it hard to understand when and why she does so. After a time, he gives up on it and just enjoys her company, the two chatting amicably about Khy'ra's past exploits and the city.

While they shop, Khy'ra takes her role as guide seriously, pointing out reputable shops and food establishments as well as laying down town gossip with undisguised glee. Having lived in the city for over twenty years and being one of the original inhabitants, Khy'ra is a fount of information about local history, and more than once, Daniel is amazed by the knowledge that she exhibits. It is clear to Daniel that Khy'ra holds a deep affection for the town and its inhabitants, one that she is happy to impart to him.

Evening finds them on a hill overlooking the town at Khy'ra's bequest, a small indulgence that takes her away from the city. The first snows of the winter have yet to arrive so while the evening has a brisk air to it, they were still dry, and the chill kept the hill empty except for themselves. As the sun sets, Daniel takes a moment to truly look at the town he has spent so many weeks in.

Karlak is bisected a third of the way in its circumference by a river, surrounded by a lightly patrolled wooden wall. Built between the rolling forested hills that make up the vast majority of the lands around here, Karlak draws its stone and ore from the distant mountains that Daniel came from. Lying on the outer frontier of Brad's borders, the town is surrounded by unexplored forests, connected by a network of dusty roads. The vast majority of the buildings in the town are made up of the easily secured wood, clay tiles or dirty rushes marking differences in prosperity from the hilltop.

"You puzzle me, Daniel." Khy'ra, propped up on her elbow stares at the young man next to her, interrupting his thoughts. "Are you really that naive or just that nice?"

"Huh?" Daniel, caught off guard, blinks at the non-sequitur.

"You don't exploit your Gift. You don't even mention your connection to the Clinic to the merchants we visit. Yet you use it without hesitation…"

"Ah…" Daniel sighs, flopping over to stare up into the darkening sky. That question. Why always that question? He raises his hand up, shading himself from the non-existent sunlight for a moment before he speaks. "My grandfather, he used to say, do good, just don't ever expect gratitude. What I do, when I heal, it isn't for them."

"Then who is it for?"

"Me." Daniel shuts his eyes. He falls silent, letting the word stand between them. Unwilling and unable to explain the extent of guilt that he harbors, that comes from having a gift like his and not exploiting it to the fullest. The constant pressure by others the moment his Gift manifested, the constant demands to use it, to be someone important. The pressure and the fear of even more were why he didn't speak of the extent of his Gift, both its cost and its full ability. The less people knew, the less they could use against him. This way, they could ask, they could suspect, but they couldn't know.

Pursing her lips, Khy'ra watches the play of emotions on his face before making up her mind. She swings her leg over his prone body, straddling him to lay a kiss on his lips. As his eyes pop open, she smiles. "Well, Elise did set this up. So, are we?"

Laughing, Daniel rolls her over and returns the kiss, banishing deeper considerations for the moment.

Chapter 12

A shiv comes speeding towards his left eye, but Daniel doesn't flinch, raising the shield just enough to catch the light blade. Once his arm begins moving, he trusts instinct to get it in the way correctly and focuses instead on lashing out at his other attacker and triggering Double Strike. The first blow is hastily dodged by the Kobold, the second crushing its knee.

Rather than pushing his luck, Daniel jumps back to separate himself from his assailants. He catches the second Kobold's attack on his shield again and deflects it to the side this time, creating an opening for his mace to crash down onto the monster's head. The Kobold staggers under the blow, a choked scream emanating from it as it struggles to stand up but is quickly dispatched before Daniel focuses on the remaining maimed Kobold to finish the fight.

Exhaling in relief and concentrating to slow his breathing down, Daniel checks his surroundings quickly before pocketing the mana stones. Still no sign of that damn red cloak… Pushing the thought away, Daniel grins over the progress he has made. Another level and a shield have made the second floor and the Kobolds warriors he fights significantly easier to handle. A higher level of Agility means that he can now keep up with the Kobolds and their fast, short attacks, while his greater strength allows him to occasionally smash aside their defenses with impunity.

Looking at his mini-map and the two passageways that split before him, he picks the one on the right where a larger cavern awaits. He knows that the larger cavern will normally hold a few more Kobolds if it had not been cleared already by another Adventurer. Hunting Kobolds was almost fun now that he wasn't getting stabbed nearly every other fight.

Two hours of further fighting, and he finally gets the notification he's looking for.

Level Up!

Adventurer Level 4

You have gained 5 attribute points and 1 Skill Proficiency to distribute

He doesn't even have to think about it, having spent more than a few idle nights plotting what attributes and proficiencies he requires to progress further. A quick selection and he pulls up his Status page to review the results.

Name: Daniel Chai

Class: Level 4 Adventurer (1%)

Sub-classes: Level 7 (Miner) (19%)

Human (Male)

Statistics

Life: 201

Stamina: 201

Mana: 152

Attributes

Strength: 18

Agility: 19

Constitution: 26

Intelligence: 16

Willpower: 18

Luck: 13

Skills

Unarmed Combat: Level 3 (01/100)

Clubs: Level 9 (11/100)

Shield: Level 5 (78/100)

Dodge: Level 4 (36/100)

Combat Sense: Level 6 (72/100)

Perception: Level 5 (16/100)

Mining: Level 7 (78/100)

Healing: Level 7 (47/100)

Herb Lore: Level 3 (31/100)

Cooking: Level 2 (37/100)

Singing: Level 2 (14/100)

Skill Proficiencies

Double Strike

Shield Bash

Mapping (II)

Spells

Minor Healing (I)

Gifts

Martyr's Touch - The caster may heal oneself or others by touch and concentration, sacrificing a portion of his life to do so. Cost varies depending on the extent of the injuries healed.

Satisfied, Daniel continues his search for the chest. It is another hour before he locates it, the second floor significantly larger than the first and consequently requiring much more time to map and search. He's not even surprised to see two Elite Kobolds guarding the chest. The second floor's guardians seemed to vary depending on the luck of the Adventurer, either presenting a single Elite and a regular Kobold or two Elites.

Checking behind himself once more to ensure he is not followed by an opportunistic Kobold, or a red cloak, Daniel peeks about the corner till both of the Kobolds are no longer facing his entrance. He sprints forward immediately, keeping as silent as a 5' 8" man carrying a shield and mace can be in the cave. It gets him about halfway there before the first Kobold notices him, screaming a warning that is cut short soon after as Daniel gets close enough, at last, to swing with his mace down overhand to crush the creature. Only a last-minute jerk of its head saves the Elite Kobold's life, but the mace still smashes into its shoulder to crack the collarbone and drive it to its knees.

The moment his feet are set, Daniel spins and utilizes Shield Bash on the other Elite who is already winding up its own strike. Daniel's attack is hastily thrown, but it smashes into the out-thrust shiv with force, sending the shiv and arm spinning aside. The Elite is not stunned, but Daniel now has more than enough time and space to face his first opponent and engage Double Strike. A fast series of strikes, both hitting for once, manages to end the injured Elite's life.

Daniel doesn't pause, already turning to deal with his last opponent. His quick turn keeps the Elite's strike from doing more than superficial damage to his arm, and Daniel hunches down beneath his shield, ready to finish the fight. The remainder of the fight is relatively one-sided, though much less spectacular as Daniel hounds the Elite with quick, fast strikes that force the Kobold to defend itself till a failed attempt at a dodge ends it.

As is his tradition now, the moment the monster falls Daniel spins around to check his surroundings. Still no red cloak. He strides quickly to the chest to take his rightful prize before collecting the remaining mana stones, a wide smile on his face. Today was definitely a good day.

Chapter 13

"Har!" Daniel grins, feeling the shiv skid off his newly bought chausse. No more getting stabbed in the thigh by these too-short monsters. It was a pain trying to block attacks that came so low with his shield - he either had to stay crouched really low for hours on end or keep his shield at a comfortable height and risk missing a block. A few weeks later, Daniel finally has some armor after more skimping and saving. It cost him more than he cared to think about, nearly three times what he would have needed to live on as a miner, but it was worth every penny.

Of course, Daniel isn't wasting time just gloating. His mace whistles down in a diagonal strike onto the Kobold he has been targeting, smashing it into the ground. As the Kobold attempts to stand, he winds up and kicks it in the side, keeping his shield close to him to foul probing attacks from the other two Kobolds he faces. The kick picks up the smaller monster, smashing it into his friends and throwing the group off-balance.

A chained attack that keeps the group of Kobolds staggering and injured ending with a Double Strike ends the fight soon after. New armor, new tactics, and another level have boosted Daniel's fighting abilities significantly. He confidently fights two or three Kobolds these days without fail, only receiving the most minor of injuries in most cases. Daniel no longer even bothers with trips to the first or second floor, only working the third floor and the more numerous Kobolds there. Until today though he has avoided the location where the Sector boss and main floor boss lived, preferring to work his skills safely. Today though was the day he would challenge the monster.

The trip to the Kobold Chief's lair takes Daniel another hour, the Adventurer pausing after each battle to rest and recuperate. As he nears the chamber, he hears a scream, and he picks up his pace. His sudden, noisy entrance surprises the combatants for a second, giving Daniel time to assess the situation.

An Adventurer is curled up on the floor missing his arm, bleeding out while his companion stands facing the Kobold Chief. She is the screamer, her sword and dagger combo wavering as fear grips her. The Kobold Chief sports a single large gash on its arm but is otherwise unharmed. To Daniel's surprise, the Chief is no taller than a normal Kobold at a short four feet though the monster wields an actual short sword, chipped as it is and wears rusted chainmail for protection on its torso. The other major change in appearance is that the Kobold Chief is significantly more muscular than a regular Kobold with defined musculature in its arms and chest.

Pushing aside other thoughts, and concerns for the other Adventurers, Daniel rushes the Kobold Chief who jumps away with ease and speed. The movement is quicker than any of his previous opponents by a significant margin. Narrowing his eyes over the shield, Daniel hunkers down for a long fight, realising that he cannot take chances here. Recalling his first fight with an Elite, Daniel begins to feint and attack with wider swings, intent on cornering the Chief.

The Chief growls at Daniel, deflecting a swing with the mace with its own short sword, but Daniel's surprising strength throws it aside slightly, forcing the Kobold to compensate for its balance by taking a step backwards. As it recovers, Daniel's backhand catches the Chief on its forehead, sending the creature stumbling again. Daniel steps forward again to push his advantage but is distracted by the sound of metal on stone behind him. The female Adventurer, exhausted and panicked, has dropped to her knees, her weapons clattering against the ground.

Daniel turns back to his fight, having taken his eyes away from the Kobold but for a second, and is greeted by black smoke rising from where the Kobold Chief was. A tentative swing through the smoke shows that it is just smoke, so Daniel spins around searching for his opponent.

The Chief reappears behind the shocked female Adventurer. Shouting a warning, Daniel is too late as the Chief stabs downwards, targeting not the female Adventurer but her injured friend, cutting his throat with relish. Screaming in anger, Daniel crosses the floor and Shield Bashes the bloodthirsty smile from the Kobold, watching the creature stumble back stunned. Not giving the creature any further chances, Daniel smashes it with quick strikes, his technique falling by the wayside as rage consumes him.

Daniel is panting and leaning over after the Chief finally falls, having never let the monster a respite after the original stun. Somewhere along the way, the Kobold Chief had managed to slip a thrust under his breastplate, right above his hips and only now does Daniel truly feel it. He has no time though to worry about his own wounds as he hurries over to the pair of Adventurers.

"Miss. Are you okay?" Provided no answer, he places a hand on her shoulder and sends his Gift into her body, finding nothing major to heal. He bends down to touch the armless corpse, again sending the energy of his Gift out in forlorn hope. It finds no purchase in the soulless corpse, coming back to him and Daniel bows his head in silent grief for the two for a moment.

Unable to do anything for either, he turns his attention back to his own injuries and the loot. A series of quick Heals puts him right again before he loots the room. Coming back to the body, he rolls the Adventurer over and does a quick search, pulling out the money pouch from the Adventurer's body. He presses the pouch into the lady's hand and helps her sheath her weapons. The Adventurer responds to direct instructions and guiding hands but otherwise does little else, her body already beginning to shiver from shock.

Hours later, Daniel finally manages to guide the lady out of the Dungeon. The moment the setting sun hits her face, she screams and rips off her belt and weapon, throwing them onto the ground before running away from the Dungeon. Daniel steps toward her fleeing form but is stopped by a hand on his shoulder.

"Don't." Daniel turns to see the guard, the one who lost the bet on his first night out. Brown concerned eyes stare out from a bearded face as he holds the young Adventurer still. "We'll keep an eye on her, make sure she doesn't do any harm. To herself or others. Then when it's time, we'll get her to a Priest. You did your part; you got her out."

Daniel slowly nods. A part of him wants to help, but mostly, he's glad. His Gift was powerful, but it had limits, and the mind was one thing he could not heal. This was outside his purview, "Okay."

On the other side, the guard's larger, balding companion bends down to pick up the weapon sheath, belt and its attached coin purse for safekeeping. The bearded guard considers Daniel, tilting his head in thought, "You don't look too shaken. Most newbies find their first death hard to deal with."

Daniel grunts, looking back into the Dungeon before he answers, "It's not my first. The mines weren't safe either."

The guard grins, clapping Daniel on the shoulder. "Good man. Keep that in mind and you might just make it to the bottom. The name's Ken, and that silent lunk is Curtzman."

"Daniel." Daniel looks back to the entrance before he mutters about what is bothering him, "I left his body back there. Couldn't carry it and watch her…"

"Don't bother; it's gone. The Dungeon will have taken it already. That's the Adventurer's Grave for you." Ken shrugs before he shoves Daniel on the shoulder. "Best hand in your stones; you're buying tonight at the Top."

Daniel opens his mouth to protest the guard's insistence, but after a moment, shuts it. He did need a drink, and rough and selfish as it was, the invitation was meant in a friendly manner. "Tonight then."

Chapter 14

A finger traces down his chest as Khy'ra smiles at Daniel in her bed. Outside, the town was blanketed in white from another snowfall, broken up by the criss-crossing tracks of carts getting ready for the day's work. The last few weeks had deepened the budding relationship between the elf and human, though due to their nature and profession, an agreed upon mutual emotional distance was still kept. Life had fallen into a comfortable routine, seeing each other when their schedules allowed, but neither insisting on more than the other would give.

For Khy'ra, the relationship with Daniel would always be a temporary one, as any relationship with one not as long-lived. It was a curse of their kind and why so few Elves deigned to live and work amongst the shorter-lived races. Few desired to deal with the emotional toll of watching one after another of their friends grow close and die, again and again. Khy'ra herself was considered highly unusual, not only on her insistence in interacting with the shorter-lived races but by becoming a healer amongst them. It would not be entirely fair to say that other elves saw her work among the destitute humans and Beastkin as futile, a delaying of the inevitable, but it was not far off.

"How are things going?" Khy'ra asks, just enjoying touching Daniel's hairless chest. Certainly, she might be slightly unusual, but she felt no carnal desire for those hairy rugs that many other humans and dwarves sported.

"Mmm… good. Very good. I went down to the fourth floor yesterday, registered myself, and then finished the third again. I think, I think I'm ready to try tomorrow." He rolls over, kissing her and grins as he waggles his eyebrows. "Today's another… shopping… day though."

She snorts, pushing at Daniel's chest. "No…. some of us actually have to work."

Grinning, Daniel plays his trump card, leaning down and gently nibbling on her pointed ears. She moans slightly, whispering softly, "Maybe I can be late…"

Whistling as he leaves Khy'ra's house, Daniel reflects on his luck these past few months. The initial free training gave him a leg-up, honing his fighting skills sufficiently to let him utilise more advanced attacks and tactics than see-smash. In the last few weeks, at first reluctantly but now routinely, he has joined Ken, Curtzman and the other guards and even some senior Adventurers drinking at the Top in the evening when he comes back. Elise kept an eye on the young Adventurer when he did so, often cutting him off and sending him to rest when he stayed too long, her mothering done with the deft hand of an experienced innkeeper.

It was the advice from the Adventurers and guards that drove his agenda for this shopping trip. The fourth floor saw a major change in the dungeon layout with the introduction of the Draxillan Crawler and Dungeon-built traps. The Draxillian Crawler was a strange beast that was tougher individually than any Kobold, skittering around in its grey shell and twelve legs up walls and down passageways with ease. The monsters routinely avoided traps that caught unwary Adventurers. However, their greatest threat was not in their fighting prowess but what they defecated. Joined together, the Crawlers feces and a chemical it extruded were mixed together to create a fast hardening substance that had the strength of stone. It was highly prized among the construction companies, but in the Dungeon, the Crawlers would often cover chamber entrances and exits, constantly changing the layout of the floor and driving Adventurers into traps and cul-de-sacs.

The city hired Adventurers to constantly break down the newly-created blockages, but it was a constant battle that made the Guild-sold map of the floor both a necessity and a waste.

"4 vials of glow moth serum, 40 feet of rope, attachment for the ropes and a hammer." In the general store, Daniel lists his requirements to the proprietor. "Also, 2 dozen trap balls, a dozen bushels of sage and the cotton balls."

The proprietor of the store, a short older man, hurries off before coming back with the goods neatly packed. "Fourth floor?"

Daniel nods as he pays before he is stopped by the proprietor whose hand comes back from under the counter with a smaller glass canister with glow crystals shedding a soft, warm light. "For you. It can get dark down there. Good luck, Daniel."

Daniel automatically takes the light, at the same time querying, "Have we met?"

"Not me. My cousin works at the Clinic and pointed you out a while ago."

"Oh…" Daniel nods his thanks, taking the bundle and heading to the armourer. Like most Adventurers, Daniel's interactions with the regular townsfolk was limited to a select few shops that directly catered to their needs. Armourers, blacksmiths, the apothecary, a few inns where the Adventurers congregated. Yet a town could not survive just on those things, and outside of the Adventurers' direct sphere of interactions lay farmers, tailors, shopkeepers, masons and more who thrived off the funds that flowed from the Dungeon. It was only Daniel's continued presence at the Clinic, and his relationship with Khy'ra, that highlighted his presence to the townsfolk.

At the armoury, Max pokes at Daniel's pauldrons before making him jump in place while holding his hands up to ensure it fitted properly. Grunting in acceptance, Max makes Daniel spin around again and bend over, checking the links and closures before Max finally grunts acceptance at the work, "It'll do."

"Thanks, Max. It feels great, just great. I barely even feel the weight anymore," Daniel gushes, grateful for the free fitting that Max offered to do last night. He even cleaned some of the blood off the used armor, bringing it back at least partly to its glory days before Daniel's abuse.

"The fourth floor is bad enough without adding ill-fitting armour. You just come back for some proper steel armour before you reach the seventh, yes? Those Ogres will smash right through this," Max says.

Nodding enthusiastically, Daniel makes his final payment and heads out, not even bothering to get undressed. The newly refitted armor was so comfortable, and Daniel secretly thought he looked rather dashing in it. He couldn't wait to try the fourth floor tomorrow.

"I hate the fourth floor," grouses Daniel as he slumps in his seat next to his usual drinking partners the next evening. Draining his mug, he waves to Elise for a refill.

"Har!" A huge hand claps his back, sending Daniel sprawling forward in his seat as Ken and his friends laugh at the new Adventurer. "Now, you're a real Adventurer."

"Real Adventurer?" Daniel says.

"Oh yeah, you ain't one till you've done the fourth floor." Laughing, Ken raises his glass and voice, "To the Crawlers!"

The cheers and resounding toasts make Daniel look around suspiciously. Ken smiles and explains, "There are two groups of adventurers who go to the fourth floor. We call them the farmers and the Adventurers. Farmers love it - it's good, consistent money killing the Crawlers for their stones and sacs. Combine it with being paid by the Guild to open up the passageways, and you can earn a decent living. That's them..." Ken nods to those who joined his toast.

"Then there's the real Adventurers. You guys hate the middle floors because all you want to do is get strong and get down. Not easy to do when you spend half the day checking for traps, backtracking from dead-ends that weren't there the day or even hour before and only occasionally fighting.

"You, kid, you're an Adventurer. Knew it the first time we talked."

Daniel sighs and nods his head in acceptance. The fourth floor, with proper preparation, wasn't hard. It was just slow and frustrating.

"Just remember, kid, it's all good training. Don't rush it - the Ogres in the next sector would squash you flat," says Ken.

Ken's cautious advice still ringing in his mind, Daniel is up and early again the next morning. If it were not for the fact that Crawlers had significantly better mana crystals than the Kobolds, he would have seen an even more drastic drop in his income, even with the addition of the sale of the chemical sacs which were an additional part of the loot. As it stood, he still had lost a third of his regular income yesterday.

Journeying to the fourth floor via portal stone, Daniel readies himself before touching the stone. He gasps as the mana from the stone flows out and enters his body, the cold so intense that he is unable to breathe for a moment before pins and needles shoot through his body. The pain is exquisite and lasts for a moment before he finds himself on the fourth floor next to the portal stone. Daniel raises his shield automatically, crouching down and finds no enemy waiting for him, only then relaxing and stopping his shivers.

Mentally surveying the map he created yesterday, Daniel picks the path to the right, climbing over fallen rocks to peer into the cramped passageway. He moves forward cautiously, pushing against the stone with his mace at each step, ensuring that it is solid and able to take his weight before he moves forward.

The passageway is short, breaking out into a small cavern. He pulls a trap ball from his pocket, dropping it beneath him to test the ground before eyeing the corners of the cavern. Seeing no additional problems, he clambers down from the passageway slowly and picks up the ball to send it rolling across the floor ahead of him.

In this way, Daniel journeys through another two passageways before he encounters his first Crawler of the day. The Crawler is squatted at the end of the passageway that Daniel is walking through, patting newly laid waste into shape as it secretes the chemical from its mouth. Daniel spots the creature first and takes off at a run, hoping to catch it unaware. That hope is dashed as the Crawler looks up at the last second, swinging its carapace clad body to the side and shedding part of Daniel's blow. Skittering legs on one side start moving as it backs away, intent on giving itself space to attack Daniel, but it is hampered by the Adventurer smashing some of those legs into paste.

In pain, the Crawler swings its body back to Daniel and attempts to use its greater weight to crush the smaller Adventurer. Daniel jumps back, barely able to dodge the monster in the cramped confines of the cavern they fight in. He swings again, crushing a mandible as the monster rears back to bite him and then as it reacts to the pain, he smashes his mace upwards before triggering a Shield Bash. The Crawler staggers backwards, injured, and Daniel pushes his advantage. Too fast, for he forgets that the creature can swing its back too. The blow catches Daniel high up on his body and smashes him into a nearby wall.

Daniel struggles back to his feet, shoulder and chest in pain, but the Crawler is hurt too. Shouting in anger, Daniel stands and jumps forward, bringing his hammer down onto the creature's head, braining it and ending the fight. Panting, Daniel waits for the smoke to dissipate before collecting both sac and mana.

A good start, though painful. *Now to find more monsters,* he thinks as he walks off into the passageway. Slow and patient, that was the way to go.

Chapter 15

"No."

Daniel jerks to a stop, pulling his foot back from the step he was about to take. He turns to survey the area, only then spotting the figure seated on an outcropping a few feet to his right. He frowns, the figure, covered in an extremely dirty cloak, is tiny but looks utterly relaxed.

It is his first day on the fifth floor, and so far, it has been every bit as frustrating as the fourth floor, if not more so. Traps, delays, surprise attacks and more. He hunches down, trying to spot the problem while he speaks, "Why?"

"Trap."

"I figured." Daniel huffs and then takes hold of his irritation. "Thank you. But what kind of trap is it?"

"Deadfall." Seeing Daniel's puzzled face, she points up.

He looks up and eyes the stalactite before slowly taking a deep step back. A single ball has already rolled over the ground, part of the precautions he uses, so he pulls two now and rolls both at the same time down the corridor. This time, the pressure is sufficient to cause the trap to trigger and one other trap further down the corridor.

"Noisy." Its hands raised to its head, the other Adventurer hops down lightly next to Daniel. The figure before him surprises Daniel for a brief moment; Beastkin were an uncommon sight, though he knew that they made up a higher proportion of the Adventuring population than their minority numbers would lead one to believe. Standing just slightly shorter than his own 5' 8", he notes it is a feline Beastkin with black fur and wide, jade eyes. She leans forwards, her whiskers tickling his face from her slightly elongated muzzle as she sniffs him before dropping down from her tiptoes, her proximity giving him a quick whiff of her fragrant musk. A part of him notes that she looks more animalistic than many others, more like a grown Jaguar forced to walk upright than a human with Cat features. From his time in the city, he knew that the Beastkin varied greatly in their appearance, though many leant towards more human in appearance. The female Adventurer points down the way, indicating the leftmost branch as she continues to speak. "Hive. Help?"

He puzzles over her words for a few moments before he realises she's asking him to join up to deal with the hive. Daniel has only run across a small hive once before, and the fight had left him drained and injured. A half-dozen Crawlers, even with his new armor had nearly been his undoing. "Maybe. How many?"

"One. Two. Many?" She pauses, watching him wince before grinning at her own joke. "Nine."

He snorts, brown eyes tightening in thought as he runs the odds in his head. "Yeah, okay."

She grins widely at him, stepping forward and leading the way. When he gets to the balls, Daniel picks them both up, noting one is badly chipped. He sighs, realising he might need to go shopping again soon as his stock is nearly depleted.

It only takes ten minutes for them to make their way to the hive. Peering in, Daniel grimaces and looks at his new companion to speak about strategies. Daniel is too late though, and he just catches the quick movements of the Catkin as she ducks past him, already throwing knives at the Crawlers.

Daniel groans, rushing forward to attack the nearest monster, noting it's been blinded already by the Beastkin's accurate throws. He smashes his club down, crushing the carapace before booting the monster up and then smashing it aside with his shield onto another incoming monster.

The first monster slain, Daniel steps back, resetting his stance as he readies himself to fight the swarm of crawlers that have targeted him. At the corner of his eye, he notes the Catkin has swarmed up the side of the cavern and is throwing her knives to distract and injure the foes that rush him now, ignoring the pair that have begun crawling up the wall to her. The blades are well aimed, most finding gaps in the carapace, but after even a few moments of fighting, Daniel judges that the throwing knives are no more than painful annoyances for these creatures. It will be up to him to finish their opponents off.

Sliding to the right, he dodges a lunge by a Crawler and activates Double Strike, smashing its legs on one side before he boots the creature away again. Another attack is caught on his shield, and he takes the time to Shield Bash this assailant, using its temporary disorientation to land a few more blows. Even as he finishes dealing with that monster, another one takes his first opponents place, mandibles skittering off his armour as it fails to gain purchase.

The battle is hard pressed, the Crawlers swarming Daniel at every turn. Forced to focus on damaging and hampering them, Daniel is unable to finish a kill as he continually moves and attacks. A bad step though has him lose balance for a precious moment, one that a Crawler uses to attach itself to his leg and yank him off his feet. Its mandibles close on his shin attempting to shatter the bone, delayed only for a brief period by his greaves.

The Catkin's jump onto the creature from her perch smashes it down, and she reaches forward, daggers plunging into the Crawler's eyes. It releases Daniel who scrambles back and onto his feet as the Catkin jumps away, neatly avoiding an attack from behind.

The remainder of the fight passes without further life-threatening incidents and, in the end, Daniel slumps amongst the bodies, sweat covering him and sticking his brown hair to his face. He pulls his helmet off to let it cool, noting that the Catkin does not seem to be sweating at all. Then again, did cats sweat? After a brief rest, they work to collect the mana stones and the additional sac drops. Thankfully, they didn't need to haul the faeces upstairs - the hired Adventurers who worked for the Guild did that with the broken-down exits where alchemists dissolved them again into their component parts to await the chemical sacs.

Housekeeping done, Daniel turns to the Catkin who is busy cleaning her daggers with a cloth and water. "Thank you."

"More?" She points down the way while putting away her cloth amongst an impressive array of knives.

"Why not?"

"Why haven't I partied up before?" Daniel muses to himself as they exit the Dungeon after a very successful day into a brisk winter weather. The Catkin's ability to sense traps and sniff out the Crawlers meant that he travelled faster and backtracked less today. On the other hand, more than once, he was able to help guide her around a faster entrance or exit due to his own mapping skill. And it was obvious, at least to Daniel, that the Catkin had been having trouble fighting the Crawlers. She could kill one or two on her own without issue, but on the fifth floor, the Crawlers often came in larger numbers. Without the raw strength to shatter their carapace, the Catkin must have been forced to fight a battle of slow attrition in great danger to herself.

There was one thing that bothered Daniel about their partnership though, and as the Catkin heads off, he rushes forward to touch her on the shoulder. She snarls, hunching down and popping a pair of claws before realising it's him and relaxing slightly, though she still backs away from the Adventurer.

"Sorry! I just don't know your name." Daniel apologises, pulling his hand back.

"Asin," she purrs resting a hand on her chest. She points to him and mutters, "Daniel."

"Yeah." He wonders how she knows his name, but dismisses it. "You know, we did pretty well. Do you want to do this again tomorrow?"

Asin pauses, looking the young man up and down. Daniel was not unknown to her, the Clinic was one of the few locations that took in Beastkin for treatment, and as such, all the workers in the Clinic had a level of notoriety among the Beastkin minority in Karlak. In addition, she has secretly watched the young man's progress for the last few days as he worked through the level. In truth, Daniel's judgements about her progress were spot on, and she had been considering travelling back up a floor to gain strength before attempting the fifth floor. All these thoughts pass through her head quickly before she nods affirmatively, waving goodbye to the young man as she heads into the Guild to sell their collected loot.

"I tell you, my cousin says there's been a lot of activity in the Borderlands this winter. Last time that happened, we saw raids all through the winter," Ken expounds from his usual table. The guards around him nod in understanding, recalling that his cousin's a Griffin Scout for the Kingdom. While the guard was a loudmouth, he did not lie about the important things, and orc raiders were definitely important.

Daniel waves to the group, catching the tail of the end of the conversation as he joins them at their table, a mug of beer in his hand. He plops down in his seat with a contented sigh, drawing deep of the beer.

"Good day?" Unusually, it's Curtzman who speaks first after the initial round of greetings as he spots the more relaxed mood the young man is in.

"Yeah, it was. Did very well today. I met a Catkin today, and we worked on clearing the fifth floor together. Finished off quite a few nests," Daniel answers quite proudly. Working with Asin, Daniel had made more today by a significant margin than any previous day, and they hadn't even spent the whole day working together. He couldn't wait for tomorrow. As such, Daniel isn't ready for their reactions.

"Beastkin," one guard spits to the side, the rest grimacing at his choice of companions. More than a few shake their head, their estimation of the young adventurer falling a little.

"What! Why?" Daniel frowns, wondering what is up with his friends.

"Look, we're not prejudiced or anything, Daniel, but, we're guards you know." At Daniel's nod, Ken continues, "Beastkin, well, they make up half our work for being such a small number. Seems like every time we turn around, we're catching another one of their kind and locking them up. They just, well, they're just criminals, most of them. Petty thieves, swindlers, con artists and more. They're either thieves or Adventurers, and the Adventurers aren't much better."

"Just trouble. We should just kick them out," grumbles another red-headed guard.

Daniel frowns, staring at his friends and considers their words. He wasn't a guard, so he couldn't talk about their experiences, but… "She was real helpful to me. Knew where all the traps were and backed me up when I needed it. We made really good time."

Ken holds his hands up placatingly, "I'm sure she's good. There's always a few good ones. Just, you know, the rest of them."

Somewhat mollified, Daniel turns his attention back to his meal despite a part of him being disturbed by the conversation, though the young adventurer is unsure what it is exactly that concerns him.

Chapter 16

The next morning, Asin is surprised to see Daniel waiting for her at the Dungeon entrance, chewing on a loaf of bread and cheese. Since neither of them had thought to arrange a meeting time, Daniel had decided to just get up early and wait for the Catkin. The Catkin slows down for a moment, pulling her cloak tight around her body as she struggles with her feelings. Daniel has been the first human Adventurer who has agreed to and kept his promise of partying up with her again, a fact that stung Asin's pride. Now faced with a human that keeps his word, the Catkin finds herself confused at her own reactions.

The storm of emotion is pushed aside as Daniel finally catches sight of Asin and waves to her, gulping down the mouthful of bread. Asin will test him today, see how he reacts. Even if Daniel worked with Khy'ra, humans were still not to be trusted.

"Morning, Asin." Daniel smiles and stretches. "Are you ready?"

Asin nods in confirmation, hands doing a quick pat down to check that all her weapons and supplies are on-hand. Next to them, the pair of guards who are on night duty watch the Catkin with ill-disguised suspicion. Daniel's eyes narrow slightly, for the first time noticing the guards' reactions. Yet it is not the time to say anything about it as the Catkin strides right past them all, walking into the entrance and heading for the portal stone.

At the stone, she waits for Daniel to catch up before she raises her hand with all her fingers spread to confirm the floor they will work. Daniel nods agreeably and after she has been transported down, places his own hand on the portal stone.

"Cold!" Daniel mutters after checking his surroundings for dangers. Asin can't help but agree with his comment. It always took her a while to get the bone-chilling cold out from her bones. Bent slightly forward, her ears swivel as she listens to the noises coming from the passageways that surround them. There is slight noise coming from two, the third there is none, and in the fourth passageway, she can hear the regular ring of pickaxes on set excrement. That rules out the third and fourth passageways. Prowling to the other two where she hears faint sounds, she sniffs at the air, sorting through the scents before making her final decision.

Daniel watches Asin work without comment, having seen this particular routine a few times already. He marvels at the way her whiskers twitch, sensing the shift in air currents - something that he had to purchase the sage brush for and wave around to notice. It was useful knowledge to have since passageways with higher airflows most likely meant more openings that were available for travel. It was no guarantee, but nothing on these floors was.

As Asin sets off ahead of him, Daniel follows a short distance behind. Neither Adventurer moves quickly, Asin scanning the floor and ceilings for traps, Daniel watching for monsters ahead and behind them as best he can. It is only fifteen minutes in before Asin finds her first trap, a simple deadfall that had been covered by the thinnest level of excrement and dirt. She pauses to point it out to Daniel before moving forwards, leaving Daniel to smash the trap open with his mace. It is only a temporary solution, for a Crawler would be by soon enough to fix it or perhaps even the Dungeon itself would do so.

Scholars still debated how Dungeons fixed traps, and even why traps were present in Dungeons. Many felt the traps were like the monsters, formed out of the corruption in mana by Ba'al. However, that explanation fell short of why Ba'al or the corruption would even bother as traps themselves were inanimate, unlike the monster children of Ba'al. Alternative explanations have risen - that there was not one type of corruption but many and that each type related to a different monster or trap or that the traps themselves were created by another, unseen monster. In the end, the truth was, as far as Daniel could ascertain, no one truly knew, and neither Erlis nor Ba'al was telling.

At the first Crawler they encounter, Asin rushes ahead to fight it alone, ducking beneath the first strike of its mandible to slash with her daggers. The space ahead is too tight for Daniel to join in the battle, not effectively, so he stays behind to watch. Asin's techniques are different from his, relying entirely on speed and precision to cause damage, dodging attacks by inches before lashing out. It makes Daniel feel like a lumbering ox, slow-moving and ungraceful. At least, he comforts himself, her techniques against the Crawler are less effective due to its tough carapace. On the other hand, she must have been a nightmare for the Kobolds to face.

The next Crawler they encounter, Asin smugly hops aside and onto a ledge with a chuffed, "Yours."

Daniel snorts and steps in, bashing the creature with his shield before pounding on the carapace. When the Crawler recovers, its return bite is caught and deflected on his shield and mace, Daniel taking the momentary leverage to kick it with his foot before going back to pounding on it with his mace. The fight is brutal, rough and lacking the finesse of the previous one, but it is shorter.

Panting, Daniel stretches after the fight to force more air into his lungs. Thank Erlis Dungeons somehow circulated their air. Otherwise, it would have been much more difficult to survive this far down. Pushing aside the unnaturalness of it all, Daniel nods again to Asin to continue their exploration.

Fight after fight, cavern after cavern, the two explorers move through the passageways with brutal efficiency. Each trap they find they set off, each monster they kill. It is only when they encounter the Elite of this floor that they pause. A single Elite Crawler, larger than any others with legs tipped with serrated claws, guards the treasure chest.

A shared look is all that is needed before the two Adventurers throw themselves at the monster, both of them knowing what lies in the chest. By now, they've worked out a simple system of fighting. Daniel would stand in front of the monster, keeping the mass of its attention while Asin would work its middle where the creature could not as easily reach her. Against tough opponents, she'd work to cripple the monster, cutting at the legs on one side till it could no longer move.

At first, the battle goes much the same way their previous fights did. Then, in a blink, it changes. As Daniel attempts another Shield Bash, the Elite rears back and clamps its mandibles around the shield. Gripping it tightly, it twists its head and flings Daniel into a wall. He smashes into it, grip lost on the shield which is dropped.

Instead of following after the fallen Adventurer though, the creature turns its attention on Asin, surging in the middle to knock her aside. A leg stabs down, attempting to spear her, cutting a long line across her back as the Catkin rolls away.

Woozy and short-of-breath, Daniel staggers to his feet, Asin scrambling to stay away from the attacks. A dagger flashes out, catching a leg as it attempts to spear her, but before Asin can counter-attack, she has to move again.

Forcing his Gift into his own body, he pulls and rips, fixing the crack in his head and righting the swelling that has begun, pain exploding through his body as he works fast without his usual precautions. No longer injured, Daniel rushes back into the fray with a roar, intent on finishing this battle and repaying the pain he has suffered in spades. The Elite spins back to Daniel, instinctively understanding that the larger Adventurer is the greater threat to its life.

Roaring, Daniel triggers his Double Strike, smashing the first blow into the mandible that comes at him, and following up with a second attack to the same spot. It cracks, and Daniel grabs it tight, pulling down and ripping the mandible off. As the Elite rears back in pain, Asin leaps, climbing swiftly up its back and plunging a knife into an eye. The creature shakes its body, throwing Asin aside into a stalagmite and her body smashes into it with a meaty thump before collapsing in a heap.

Distracted by the attacks and in pain, the Elite feels its own mandible stabbed into its lower body. Unable to keep itself upright, the creature plunges down, impaling itself on the point, driving it deeper. Its chittering takes on a frantic air, its movements erratic, as pain and damage accumulate. Daniel moves away to pick up his discarded shield, stalking the monster as its movements slow and grow less erratic. Once that happens, he moves in to finish the fight.

Under narrowed eyes, Asin watches Daniel finish the Elite. Time to see if he leaves her and takes the crystals. It would be a shame, one that Asin would be sure to return, but better to know now than later. It is to her surprise that Daniel does not do so, instead hurrying to her body – leaving both crystals unguarded! – to check on her immediately once the Elite bursts into smoke. Warm healing energy fills her body as soon as Daniel nears, bruises and torn muscles knitting swiftly as Daniel chants his Minor Healing spell.

Asin rolls up to her feet, no longer playing at being unconscious and nods her thanks. This one had some Horst then, perhaps more than a little. Asin licks at the fur on the top of her hand as she waves him to pick up the crystals, cleaning away the accumulated dirt. He would do.

Chapter 17

Daniel sighs, stretching and rubbing his left shoulder absently. A crawler had managed to get around his shield and crushed his shoulder earlier today, and though he had healed it with careful application of his Gift and then a Minor Healing spell, it still felt sore. Nothing a good night's rest wouldn't heal, but the pain still crept up on him occasionally.

The door of the Clinic opens again, the next patient enters, and Daniel flashes the man a smile. Asin had requested a short delve today, and so, without anything better to do with his time, Daniel has made his way to the Clinic to provide Khy'ra with some additional help.

"Healer…" the old man shuffles over and sits down, his bare feet unkempt and swollen.

"No healer," Daniel chides softly. He does not have the Healer class and thus will never have access to their specific class skills. He, certainly, is looking forward to reaching Level 10 as an Adventurer and discarding the need for physical baggage as he would gain access to their mystical Inventory class skill.

Even as he thinks these idle thoughts, he is asking questions to ascertain the problem, though it is relatively clear to him. He does not call upon his Gift, seeing no reason to use it in such a simple case. Most of his work in the Clinic was like this in-truth, simple injuries and illnesses that only required non-magical treatment by a knowledgeable healer. Yet, as always, there were few enough people who cared to apply themselves to gather the knowledge and skill to become healers themselves.

"Soak your foot in crushed Wylie leaves. You should be able to get some at Lianne's shop. Make sure she sells you the fresh ones though. Three times a day for a week. A week mind you! If you stop earlier, this will just come back, and you'll have to start again," Daniel says and then makes the man repeat his instructions to him twice before he sends him on his way.

It only takes a minute before the next patient is darkening his doorway, Daniel again absently rubbing at his shoulder. *No time for that, there's always the next patient.*

Hours later, Daniel realises it has been a few minutes since a patient has walked into his office. He stands, stretches and groans, wondering how long he has been at this. Darkness fills the room and his stomach clenches in hunger. Well past dinner time at the very least then.

Khy'ra smiles as she enters the doorway, seeing Daniel standing up. The blonde elf is clad in a tight green dress, its plunging neckline hidden behind a white shawl with yellow flowers edging it. She steps in, letting the shawl fall apart as the two are alone, and she smiles at the admiring glances Daniel sends her way.

A swift step takes her to Daniel, and she kisses him tight, moulding her body against his. Such a pleasure to find a human who didn't tower over her she thinks.

"Hi," Daniel says breathlessly when they break from the kiss.

"Hi," Khy'ra replies, smiling up at him but not moving from his arms. "I've sent the staff home for the evening. So if we're quiet…"

Daniel grins, not needing another reply and picks her up, walking to the nearby table. Such a pleasure to find a human of her height who was so strong amends Khy'ra. Then she's not thinking much of anything for a while.

Stomach rumbling, Daniel pulls his pants up and looks at Khy'ra who comes back from the restroom, "Care for dinner?"

"Yes, I do believe so," Khy'ra says, leaning forwards and kissing him. "Your technique is improving."

Daniel grunts, pulling her closer and mutters, "You know, that's not what most men want to hear."

"You do though," she giggles and taps his nose. "It's what I like about you, Daniel, you're quite willing to listen to instruction."

Daniel snorts and gives her another kiss before letting her go. "Come on, let's get some food."

Outside, after locking up, the two walk down the lightly illuminated streets. At night, few are out to walk the streets. In this part of town, the mana lantern crystals are interspersed at great distances, making both of their shadows stretch out before them. The two chat quietly, nodding in greeting as a pair of guards walks past them on patrol.

"Khy'ra, Daniel! Good to see you!" Mikey, the owner, calls out and waves them into a pair of free seats. As the closest late night dining establishment to the Clinic, he is not at all surprised to see the two. "Late night again?"

"Two plates for me, Mikey!" Daniel calls out as he sits down.

"The usual," Khy'ra adds.

Seated, Khy'ra takes Daniel's arms in hers while they both turn to watch Mikey work. Mikey first takes a scoop of batter, ladling it into the oval, scooped cooking pans before him, swirling the batter around as he works them in. A quick flick of his hand ensures that the batter covers everything properly on each of the pans that he starts before he turns around. Hands pick up knives and flicker, slicing off thin slices of meat from the roast that rotates behind him. Slices, perfectly sized all are placed on the thinly applied, already cooked bread. Hands dance then as cheese, slices of red pepper, cucumbers and mushrooms are added before the bread is rolled together. Each roll is then quickly slid into a small oven, the cheese and entire dish toasted for just a minute before the rolls are ready.

Khy'ra and Daniel enjoy the show; Mikey is a known master of his craft. Even as he gets their order ready, he begins others, constantly moving to ensure that none of his plates are ever over-cooked. Business, even this late, is always busy at his location.

When dinner arrives with a thump, the two dig-in with gusto, blowing hard at the rolls and huffing around too-hot mouthfuls. Eyes crinkling in amusement at each other's antics, the two lovers only stop when bells begin to ring throughout the town.

Daniel pauses, tilting his head to the side, never having heard these particular bells before. Next to him, Khy'ra has her head hung down, whispering a soft prayer. "QuanEr, for pain, peace. For anger, forgiveness. For hatred, love."

It is only when he hears Khy'ra's prayer that Daniel knows what the bells are for, and he too hangs his head, repeating the prayer. It is no surprise, for all the myriad gods that meddle in mortal life, only one is revered through all the lands. She who rose from humanity like many others, but who refused to ascend. She who walked among mortals still, providing aid and care without price, without cost, without judgement. Once a year, bells are rung and remembrance given to QuanEr throughout the lands.

Silence reigns before Mikey lets out a little yelp, and his carefully orchestrated dance of food preparation is broken. Muttering, he tosses the burnt food aside amongst the others that will go to those less fortunate later on before restarting his work.

Dinner is soon finished by the two famished healers, and they quietly deposit the plates and money on the counter next to Mikey. As they walk, Khy'ra notices Daniel rubbing his shoulder again and places a hand on it, murmuring a soft chant to complete the healing process. Idiot must have used the last of his mana earlier in the day.

"Thanks," Daniel repeats, and Khy'ra just shakes her head, leaning her head on his shoulder as they head back to her apartment by unspoken consent.

Chapter 18

Months later, spring has finally arrived. The snow has melted, the sun arriving earlier and earlier each day. With the setting this evening, Daniel and Asin are back in the Adventurer's Guild, collecting another day's earnings. As usual, Asin is taking care of this, leaving Daniel to wander around the Guild Hall till she is done.

"Liev, what's this?" Daniel points to the appearance of the new board in the Guild Hall. It's obviously been moved, and after a moment's recollection, Daniel remembers seeing it in the far corner previously. The board stands to the side of the attendant booths, positioned such that Adventurers may peruse the board without blocking access to the booths themselves.

"It's the request board. Now that spring's here, we're getting more and more requests for Adventurers to help around the town and surrounding villages. We move it up every spring, since during the winter it's mostly Quests for more advanced Adventurers," Liev explains, looking up from the papers he is working on. The redhead runs a hand through his hair, messing it up even further as he purses his lips, trying to decipher the handwriting before him. Liev would curse the writer, if the writer were not him. Instead, he reminds himself to take notes with more care. As Liev finishes speaking, Asin comes up next to Daniel and hands him his share silently before joining Daniel in staring at the board. It takes her a moment to let out a chuff and turn back to licking at the black fur on top of her hands.

Having received his answer, Daniel turns back to study the board in more detail with renewed interest. The board itself is split into four parts with a carving above each portion indicating the type of request it was, with a simple rating system consisting of the Guild's seal beneath each portion in ascending order of difficulty. A single seal meant the quest was suitable for Beginner Adventurers, with up to four stamps being the highest on the current board. That one consisted of a request to hunt a manticore which had taken residence in the Borderlands near a village. The four categories showcased were for Hunt, Supply, and Guard quests with a final miscellaneous section that currently consists of numerous scouting and exploration requests. Each Quest had a written portion that detailed the quest and a simply drawn image below it for those who couldn't read, allowing most Adventurers a quick idea of what each quest entailed.

Daniel quickly relays his findings to Asin who nods her head at the words before pointing to the Hunt and, with a slight hesitation, the Supply portions of the board. Preference offered, Daniel turns back to the board to search for an appropriate Quest. After spending the entire winter working the Dungeon, a change of pace was called for.

"Liev, what's the circle for?" Daniel points to a notation that he has spotted that appears more regularly on the Supply side than the Hunt sections.

"Repeatable quests. Most unique quests require a deposit by the Adventurer and have a time limit. The repeatable ones don't since multiple Adventurers can work on them at the same time. Most of those quests are from traders looking for new material, though the Guard, of course, have their regular bounties on Orcs, Goblins and Kobolds," Liev clarifies.

"These two are in the North of Karlak and are around the same area, I think. 40 Silver each," Daniel points and Asin looks up for a brief moment, considering the pieces of paper before an eloquent shrug provides her answer.

Daniel sighs, having gotten used to the ever-eloquent nature of his friend and party member after many weeks of working with her. He pulls the papers down and walks over to Liev. A change of pace would be nice after being stuck on the fifth floor for weeks, crawling through passageways and fighting the same monsters again and again. Twice before, the two had attempted the sixth floor out of frustration, and both times they had found fighting on that floor too difficult. The Behemoth Crawlers that inhabited the floor were not only larger than their upper floor brethren, their armour was significantly tougher, and it took both Adventurers working until exhaustion to kill even one.

"That's 40 Silver then." Liev takes the two papers, glad for the momentary distraction from his paperwork and looks at Daniel whose jaw has dropped. Liev just smiles, knowing the two Adventurers between them have enough - they did just pay them out for the day.

Grumbling to himself, Daniel casts a beseeching look to Asin who hands over her portion too before they receive confirmation that they are now assigned to the requests with a three-day completion requirement.

"This is rather nice, isn't it?" Daniel makes conversation the next morning as they head out of the North gate. Asin provides the unspoken agreement by running ahead of him and then squatting down to grab a handful of newly bloomed flowers in her hands, the yellow and pink flowers contrasting with her black fur. She sniffs them and then slides one into her brooch before offering the other to Daniel.

A shake of his head makes her wrinkle her nose, her whiskers bouncing around at the motion before she drops the flower and joins Daniel as he walks.

"So, we've got to find a Shadow Cat and an Owlbear that have come too close to town and are threatening the farmers in the area," Daniel muses before glancing at his companion. "Do you have any tracking skills?"

Asin pauses, tilting her head up she sniffs disdainfully at Daniel and then continues.

"Is that a yes?" Daniel queries, and not getting an answer, hurries up to catch up with her. He's hoping that's a yes. It is a 40 silver deposit they've put down already, and while he has some minor experience in the woods himself, he would not call himself a tracker. When he asks again, all he gets is silence, so he lets the topic drop. The rest of the walk is finished in companionable silence, both parties enjoying the nice change of pace as the Spring sun shines down on them with the just the barest hint of cold in the air from the night before.

The pair has walked for hours, taking them from the outskirts of the city where farmers work towards the edge of the settled lands that border Karlak. Here, gently rolling hills dotted with large farms worked by dedicated farmers have transformed into smaller farms where pioneers work to build their lives. Many of the farms in this part of the world are small, the space between each farm large, and most are threadbare in their fittings with a single building. Many of these farmers stabled their animals in their houses themselves, both as a safety precaution and to add additional heat to their dwellings. Now, with the snow gone, they are hard at work felling new trees for fences, wood and just to extend their plots.

"This is where the quest says the Cat was last seen." Daniel gestures around the forest, which just gets another disdainful sniff from Asin. Using the map provided by Liev at the Guild and his Mapping proficiency, Daniel has been able to guide them to the appropriate spot unerringly.

Asin prowls away from Daniel, walking in a slow circle as she stares at the ground and occasionally sniffs at the air, taking over now that they are close to the monster. Daniel sighs and falls silent, letting her get to work as he pulls his shield off his back.

It's a few minutes later when she gestures for him to follow. The two begin walking into the woods, Daniel following after Asin when she turns and points to his feet and then her ears, hissing at him in disapproval. Daniel grimaces and tries to walk quieter, though the glare he gets from the absolutely silent Catkin tells him how well he is doing.

After a few hours, Daniel realises there is a reason why these quests paid so well - spending hours tramping through the woods not killing anything was significantly less interesting than the Dungeon itself. For Adventurers who craved excitement and adventure, tramping through the undergrowth was less than rewarding. Thankfully, Asin seems to know what she is doing, or at least she seems confident, extremely confident to Daniel, as she follows a trail that only she is able to see.

Unfortunately for them, a certain city dweller's heavy feet have given their prey more than sufficient warning. The Shadow Cat has doubled back, crawling up a large oak tree and crouches on it, waiting for its prey to arrive. Watching the two cross below it, the Cat decides to attack the larger of the two and launches itself from its perch, smashing into Daniel with its claws. One claw catches on Daniel's shield, the other on his armour as the beast knocks him to the ground. Claws rip into him, and a paw rises to finish the foolish Adventurer.

The paw never completes its journey, a thrown knife slamming into the fast-moving limb. Hurt and angered, the Cat shifts to snarl at its new assailant which gives Daniel enough time and leverage to throw it off his body with a heave. Rolling back onto his knees, Daniel throws a clumsy and hasty swipe of his mace to force the Cat to back off. The Cat lands on its injured paw, hissing in pain as the blade drives deeper and Daniel is able to stand fully and bring his shield up on guard, bloodied but alive.

The Cat lets out a low rumbling growl, assessing the two creatures before it, taking careful steps backward into the shadows that surround the trees above it. A second knife tumbles through the air, but the Cat is gone, fading into the shadows before their eyes. Daniel moves to place a nearby tree to his back, shield held up to guard himself, and Asin moves to join him, both Adventurers awaiting the next attack. No attacks come, and after a time, Daniel squats to begin healing the deep cuts in his back and across the back of his head as Asin moves around the clearing carefully to see if she can pick up traces of the creature. When Daniel has finished healing himself, she beckons him over, pointing to the trail of blood that she has found.

Together, the two follow the trail, eyes peeled for danger. After an hour of careful navigation, they come across a slow-moving river where the trail stops. Snarling in anger, Asin moves up and down the river and even crosses it, attempting to pick up the trail again but is unable to do so. The Cat is gone and hours of further searching yields no further result. Disappointed, they make camp for the evening and, realising that they no longer have a lead, decide to switch targets to the Owlbear. Perhaps the Cat will make itself known while they deal with the Owlbear.

Chapter 19

The Owlbear's lair is a simple cave hidden in a depression surrounded by trees, the perfect place for the creature. Outside, there are scattered bones from its recent meals of stolen sheep and the larger bones of a bear - the cave's former occupant. For a time, the pair of Adventurers watch the Owlbear's cave to ensure the monster is alone before ascertaining their plan. Of course, since neither are tactical geniuses, their plan is simplistic in the utmost.

Daniel moves to the depression, shield and mace at the ready. Once he's set, he strikes the mace against his shield boss, drawing the creature out. The strikes are loud in the forest, drawing the ire of the monster. When the Owlbear lumbers out, Daniel pales at the sight of the nine-foot-tall feathered monstrosity whose front limbs end in paws instead of eagle claws. Yet, the humanoid body structure and face itself is that of a bear, with only vestigial wings at its back.

As the Owlbear roars, daggers flash forward one after the other to sink into the creature's flesh. The blades are targeted to the creature's softer underbelly, the Owlbear's tiny inset eyes too difficult a throw for the hidden Asin. Instead, she goes for quantity over quality, injuring the creature and distracting it as Daniel rushes forward.

Ducking beneath the first paw strike, Daniel targets a knife that is stuck in the creature's body and drives it deeper with his blow. He keeps moving, getting out of range of the return attack, forcing the Owlbear to turn to chase him. Another knife flashes out, taking the creature in the back but failing to draw its attention away from Daniel.

Daniel ducks the first lurching strike and blocks the second on his shield, using the opening to smash against the claw. The Owlbear hisses, ducking forwards with its head to bite Daniel. Fetid breath from rotting flesh stuck in its teeth misses Daniel by inches as he ducks to the side, swinging a backhanded strike to the creature's muzzles. The combatants are too close for thrown weapons now, so Asin instead rushes forwards on silent feet and launches herself with daggers extended, landing on the monster's back and allowing her own clawed feet and daggers to dig into the monster.

The creature roars in anger and rears back, the Owlbear's claws unable to reach its new assailant. Daniel matches the roar, raising his mace high to smash down with all his strength on the creature's exposed chest. The Owlbear's bones are surprisingly brittle, and Daniels mace sinks deep into the creature's chest. The unexpected lack of resistance forces Daniel off-balance for a brief moment and a rotating claw catches him high up on his shoulder, ripping muscles and tendons apart as Daniel loses grip of his weapon.

Daniel stumbles away, catching the next strike by reflex on his shield but is sent sprawling to the ground. Behind, Asin uses the dagger to repeatedly stab the monster in its neck, who gurgles as blood rushes into its throat. In a desperate attempt to kill at least one of its assailants, it stomps down at Daniel who rolls away, the attack tearing his back open. Strength finally gone, the Owlbear collapses forwards, forcing Asin to throw herself into a roll to escape harm.

Daniel groans, lying on his back and focusing on healing his wounds with his mana. The monster's claws were sharp and the creature strong, shredding the hardened leather armour on his back as if it was paper. "Why am I the one who always gets hit?"

Asin does her version of a laugh, chuffing as she takes the loot from the monster. She points to herself as she finishes pocketing the mana stone and claws, "Fast. Smart." Her hands come up to point at Daniel, and she finishes, "Strong. Slow."

Daniel snorts, rotating his shoulder as he finishes healing and stands up. "You're just using me as a meat shield."

She chuffs more and then points back into the woods before continuing, "Cat?"

Daniel nods, heading back to their backpacks, "Yeah. Though I think we need a new plan."

She nods in agreement, jade eyes narrowing as she remembers how the Shadow Cat had counter stalked them and managed to run away even with one of her daggers in its paw. She really liked that dagger too.

A couple of days later, the two are standing in the Guild Hall, handing in the Owlbear's claws as proof of their success. They are dejected, however, as their various plans to deal with the Shadow Cat - from using bait to laying crudely built traps - were a failure. It is only on the last day when they are heading back do they hear of a good lead but by then, it is too late. Only once more did they come across a pair of tracks, but Asin had waved them off, fearing that the creature was likely luring them into a trap again.

"Cat got the better of you?" Liev chuckles softly, handing them their pay and half their deposit back. The glum nods make Liev chuckle. "It's okay, those things are tough. Really, Rangers are the only ones who stand a chance finding those Cats."

"You could have told us that earlier," Daniel mentally groans but when he takes the coins, he has to smile at the new pop-up.

Quest Completed
Hunt the Owlbear (1/1)
2,000 XP Received

Level Up!
Adventurer Level 5
You have gained 5 attribute points

As the happy purr from Asin attests, she probably received the same Quest completion. *Well*, Daniel thinks, *there might be at least one other reason to complete Quests.*

With a little bit of time on his hands, Daniel walks into the training grounds for the first time in months, marvelling at how little the grounds had changed in the intervening period. The same old smell of sweating bodies, oil and metal fill the air, and the same grunts and occasional groans of pain or frustration.

He waves to Litzburn, who breaks out into a wide smile before making a last few comments to his current students before walking to Daniel. They share a quick handclasp, Litzburn looking over his old student with a practised eye. Daniel had put on even more muscles than before, though the way he held himself spoke of a better sense of his own body as well. The slight tilt of his body to where the combatants were, told of a new wariness the novice youngster had previously lacked. Overall, Litzburn was satisfied – the young man was coming along well. Of course, he couldn't let the youngster know that. "You need a haircut."

Chuckling, Daniel runs a hand through his brown mop of hair and nods, "Yeah, got to get that done."

"Well, go get ready then," Litzburn pushes him to the walls where the training weapons are. "Floor 3."

Daniel nods happily, hurrying off to get the training gear. When he arrives back on the floor, he's surprised to see Litzburn casually stretching, light glinting off his oiled bald head. For a moment Daniel feels trepidation, before he grins, realising this is a great chance to see how far he has come.

The moment Litzburn nods his readiness, Daniel launches an attack, stepping forwards and using Double Strike. Litzburn blocks the first, dodges the second, and has to skip backwards slightly to avoid the Shield Bash that comes his way next. Daniel does not let up, pushing the tempo of the fight to keep the more experienced fighter off-balance. Litzburn continues to block each strike with minimal motion, batting Daniel's mace aside and forcing wider and wider strikes before he lunges, having created the opening he was looking for. Struck full in the chest, Daniel stumbles back, his breath forced from his body.

"Hold!"

Daniel nods in thanks, getting his breath back as Litzburn walks forward. "Good. You're faster and stronger, and you kept up the training yourself, didn't you? Your basics are solid."

Daniel grumbles, "Didn't hit you though."

"No. You're too direct, no real feints. That's fine against dumb monsters, but against smarter opponents, you need to create the openings you need." Watching Daniel he continues, "There are two major kinds of feints – movement and attack feints. You can feint by committing to a movement and then shifting." Litzburn showcases it, shifting his weight to the front foot, his entire body angling to the right before bouncing to the left.

"Or you can feint an attack, forcing the opponent to create an opening. Feints are all about making the opponent move, but they don't work if you aren't seen to commit. A feinted attack should look, should feel, like a real attack." Litzburn lips twist in wry amusement. "Or you can just attack and change it mid-way like Mary."

Daniel absorbs the information in silence, before raising his mace once more. Litzburn steps back, and they begin. Almost bored, Litzburn adds as they fight, "Don't fall into a pattern either, especially of using your special attacks. A smart opponent will see it and do something like THIS!"

Litzburn blocks the Shield Bash, and then wraps Daniel's shield and arm with his own before Daniel can pull back. A quick step puts Litzburn inside Daniel's defence as he begins to pull Daniel downwards, stretching the shorter Adventurer over his knee. Free hand raised, it flashes towards Daniel's neck and stops at the last moment, completing the demonstration.

"Now, let's begin again."

Chapter 20

"This way!" Khy'ra pulls on Daniel's arm, dragging him down the pathway, blonde hair flowing in the wind. He smiles, enjoying the view as the elf in the light summer dress hurries along, wind pushing the dress against her body, hugging her full curves. It is a touch chilly, a last-minute frost the night before slowly thawing in the spring sun.

"Come on, Khy'ra." Daniel laughs, shaking his head, "You told me to take a day off, and now you're dragging me around. It's not like I don't mind taking a day off, but couldn't we spend some time actually resting?"

She snorts, turning around and waiting for him to catch up before kissing him on his nose. "Sex later."

Daniel blushes slightly, still uncomfortable by the frank way Khy'ra deals with certain topics. "I didn't mean that!"

"Of course you didn't." She grins, pulling him on. "Anyway, the only reason you agreed to come was that Asin refused to work again today. I believe she eloquently put it as you being work stupid."

Looking ahead, all that Daniel can see as a potential destination is a small hut at the end of the curved pathway, the only apparent structure among the rolling green hills that they traverse. He ignores hers and Asin's pointed comments, knowing they were correct and that he could get a touch focused at times. However, they just needed to level up and then maybe they'd be able to deal with the next floor. Just a little bit more. "Are you really not going to tell me what this is about?"

"Patience!"

As they near the hut, Daniel notes that the clothing line outside seems to be built on a small pulley to raise and lower it. The hut itself looks to be relatively well kept, no obvious holes and the thatched roof recently redone. Khy'ra does not wait to knock on the door, instead stepping in directly. The inside of the hut is a contrast to the neat external and is a complete mess with tables filling up every inch of space and laden down with a wide array of items - shields, swords, maces, jewellery and more. In a rare clear space on the table in the centre of the room, a series of etching tools and a small beaker sit, containers filled with copper, silver and gold dust next to it.

"Khy'ra, lass, you made it!" A low voice rumbles from the kitchen, soon followed by its owner. The dwarf whose residence this is comes out from the kitchen holding a frying pan and wearing an apron, his full brown beard braided to remove itself from danger. Brown eyes twinkle as he hefts the pan, slabs of heavenly smelling bacon roasting on it, setting Daniel's starving stomach clenching.

"Tharuk, boy, I told you I'd be here today," Khy'ra says, stepping into the hut and pointing behind to Daniel. "This is Daniel; he's a friend."

"Tharuk. That smells amazing." Daniel greets the dwarf and then angles for an invitation.

Tharuk laughs, leading the way into the kitchen, "Come. There's more than enough for everybody!"

A short thirty minutes later, Daniel is patting his stomach having stuffed himself. *Tharuk was definitely a very good cook, better he would say than even Elise, though he knew better than to ever say that!* "That was wonderful, Tharuk. Thank you. I'm now glad Khy'ra dragged me out here."

"Any friend of the lass is a friend of mine." Tharuk grins, standing up to begin putting away the dishes. "Even if he's stolen her away from me."

Daniel blanches and shoots a look at Khy'ra who just smiles blandly at him. Tharuk seems to be missing the awkwardness his words have created, coming back and offering further nourishment. "Cake?"

"Uhh...," Daniel stares at the cake and then shrugs, taking the plate. "Thank you."

"The lass says you've been having trouble with the sixth floor?" Tharuk mentions around his mouthful of cake. Khy'ra stays silent, savouring her own piece as she lets the two talk.

"Yes. The Behemoth Crawlers are just too strong. We can kill one, but it takes forever, and if there are two, we just have to run away," Daniel grumbles, waving his fork around. "There's always a few of them in a nest at a time, and I don't even want to think what the boss is like."

"The Crawlers are horrible. Tough carapace makes it nearly impossible to smash through or stab. Most Adventurers have to level up a few times or party up enough to beat the floor. Khy'ra says you're too impatient for that though, got places to be and all that."

"Well, I'm… you know…" Daniel grimaces, shrugging his shoulders.

"Young." Tharuk laughs heartily and points to the front of his hut and his workshop as he finishes up his cake. "Alright, I got something that can help. You and your Catkin."

Walking past Daniel, he pushes the Adventurer down as he tries to stand up to follow. A few minutes later, Tharuk returns with two pairs of bracers with etchings inlaid in copper on them. "Normally, I don't work with such low materials these days, but I couldn't say no to Khy'ra."

"What are they?" Daniel picks one up, frowning at the etchings. There's something about the bracers, a feeling of power that he can sense at the edges of his perception. He extends his senses a bit further, feeling the bracers through his mana and realising that the bracers seem to contain and hold mana themselves. "These are enchanted!"

Lesser Braces of Lightning

Effect: When worn, Braces add 3 – 5 Points of Lightning Damage per successful attack. 5% chance to stun (resisted by Magic Resistance).

Durability: 30/30

Item Class: Enchanted

Quality: Excellent (+2 to Enchantment Damage)

"Well, I am an enchanter." Tharuk gestures to the bracers before him, smiling slightly in pride. "These are enchanted with lightning magic. If you wear them, your aura will be imbued with lightning magic itself, and each of your attacks will do a small portion of lightning damage. The Crawlers themselves are susceptible, so you'll be able to kill them a lot easier."

Daniel's grin widens even further as he caresses the bracers. "Thank you!"

"You are very welcome. I'll also need 12 Gold for the bracer sets," Tharuk states. Daniel's jaw drops open, the sheer amount staggering. A thrifty man could survive on a single gold for a year; twelve was a fortune. "Each."

Suddenly, the heavenly brunch he ate feels like lead in his stomach. He had been earning a decent amount for a while now, but still. "I uhh… don't have that much."

"Of course not. Just give the money to Khy'ra when you can. I trust you!" Khy'ra just smiles, raising her cup as Daniel reels from the news. This was his first enchanted item, but for so much. He pushes down the feelings of trepidation. He always knew that being an Adventurer was an expensive proposition; it seemed it was time for him to truly decide. Would he strive for the top or become just another low-tier Adventurer, working small-time dungeons and earning enough to have a comfortable, but unexciting life.

Put that way, there really was little choice. If Daniel had wanted comfort, he had simpler, easier options, "Thank you. I'll repay you as soon as I can. We will."

Unable to stop himself, Daniel quickly straps the bracers on. The moment both are equipped, a surge of energy ripples through him, invading his aura. Concentrating, he can feel the flickers of lightning mana that are now imbued into his aura, stretching forth to cover him. As he picks up a fork, he can feel how it flows down even to the fork, charging it with a slight measure of the lightning mana and his own aura. The two old friends just watch as he plays with his new toy, sharing knowing smiles.

"Mrs. Hearth, what did we say about overdoing it?" Daniel grumbles later that evening, raising the elderly woman's arm to inspect it again and then letting it drop.

The octogenarian cackles for a moment before wincing in pain, "Young man, at my age, you take what time you get and make full use of it."

Snorting, Daniel sighs and reaches out with his Gift, slowly reknitting the torn tendons and muscles in the shoulder. Healing in this way was old hat to Daniel by now, though with Khy'ra's guidance, he had learnt to use less power, making smaller adjustments to allow the body's natural healing abilities to take over. However, his biggest gains in skill were when he helped the diseased and the elderly, their various ailments and illnesses outside of his previous experience in the mining camps. The hard life of the camp was no place for the weak or elderly, so what he mostly treated were injuries, not the common ailments he dealt with now.

Finished with the old woman, he sends her out before turning to Khy'ra who has wandered in. After exchanging a quick kiss, she announces, "That's it for the day. Thank you for coming in with me, Daniel, I felt bad about taking the morning off."

Daniel just nods, accepting the thanks gracefully. It wasn't exactly what he would consider a rest day but who was he to complain, "Khy'ra, one question."

"Mmm…?"

"I've noticed some of the patients, well, they seem to refuse to go to you." He gestures to the now empty waiting room.

"Oh, mmm… not refuse. They're just more comfortable with you," Khy'ra explains, looking over to the youngster.

"Right…" Daniel's eyes narrow before he flinches as Khy'ra punches him in the arm.

"Don't," she warns him, and he sighs, nodding. No point making a fuss about it, even if their actions just made no sense. As his grandfather pointed out, fools would be fools. Still, he might make those wait a little longer next time and use more traditional methods with them. No point in wasting his gift for those… "Ow!"

"I said, don't." Khy'ra holds her fist up, glaring at Daniel before he nods quickly.

"No fuss, no fuss."

"Good. I much prefer being hit…" Khy'ra grins lasciviously at the suddenly blushing Daniel. He still rejoins, however.

"You do, do you…"

Chapter 21

"This."

Smash.

"Is."

Smash.

"Awesome!"

Smash.

Lightning dances again as Daniel's mace crushes the Behemoth Crawler. The creature shudders again, the lightning piercing through its shattered carapace. It doesn't go down easy though, swinging its head around to strike at Daniel with its mandibles. The jerky attack is caught easily on Daniel's shield though, and its body is levered up long enough for Daniel to swing an underhand blow to its thinner under-armour. The Crawler shudders once more and falls dead, allowing Daniel to survey the rest of the nest on the sixth floor.

To his right, Asin is throwing knife after knife into the squirming mass of junior Crawlers. They struggle to get to her, but as they close she lightly leaps away and continues her attack. As each strike hits, the tell-tale flicker of lightning arrives, shocking the crawlers. Asin switches targets as one Crawler gets too close, twisting the knife in her hand and sending it into a spiralling movement as she activates her skill proficiency, Piercing Throw. The newly imbued knife shatters the carapace as it lands, lightning mana doing further damage inside the unprotected flesh. Through experimentation, the novice Adventurers have learnt that Asin's knives hold the enchantment for a short distance before fading away, though imbuing the knives with her Skill Proficiencies aided in extending the range.

As the injured Crawler finally manages to close the distance, Asin backflips out of the way, her trailing foot kicking the Crawler in the face as one last spiteful farewell, lightning dancing as the blow lands to kill the creature. Daniel enters the fray then, his mace making quick work of the last few wounded junior Crawlers. As they loot the bodies, neither Adventurer can hide their glee at the speed they completed this nest.

"So…." Daniel tilts his head to Asin, hefting his mace and trying to sound professional. "Boss?"

The Catkin in her usual crouch looks up at Daniel, wrinkling her muzzle though her eyes sparkle as well. She takes a moment to act like she's thinking about it but her mind is already made up as she nods firmly.

Unfortunately, actually finding the Boss in the sixth level was a chore in itself. Nearly half as large again as the fifth floor, the two Adventurers have to call it a day before they are able to locate its lair. Even with Daniel occasionally wiping their fatigue away with his Gift, he could do nothing about the mental exhaustion of crawling through the dark in constant danger.

They have no luck either for the next three days, and on the fourth, they arrive too late as another party finishes the monstrous Crawler off just minutes before they arrive. Glumly, the pair leaves the celebrating party to their spoils, knowing the Boss would likely respawn in a new location. The only major gain during the last few days was that they had found the stairs down to the seventh floor where they registered themselves but did not explore.

"I'm feeling lucky today!" Daniel states as they transfer down to the sixth floor once again. Asin just chuffs, having heard this pronouncement four times already, though she is as excited as to get this done as he is. However, this time, he speaks the truth as they come across the sixth floor's boss after only a few hours of searching and just a single fight with a nest.

As Mary had initially mentioned, the boss in the Dungeon was of the same form as the other monsters before it, just more powerful. Having seen the corpse of the boss before, neither Adventurer is surprised at the Titanic Crawler's size, but a part of them still wonders how it managed to make its way around the tight tunnels of the sixth floor.

The Titanic Crawler was twice the size of a Behemoth Crawler, its head alone four and a half feet wide. Its body stretched behind it, curled up in what looked to be sleep and stumping their guesses, though it was at least twenty feet long. Its carapace gleamed darkly in the faint light, the creature resting while its prey searched for it.

The two do not need to speak, having worked out sure-fire tactics when dealing with a single enemy. Asin enters first, silent as only a Catkin could be and quickly clambers up a wall, putting herself out of danger. Hidden in the shadows, she readies her attacks and begins the battle with a Piercing Throw. She follows up immediately with another, targeting the same spot in the middle of the back, looking to shatter the carapace. Too far away for the bracers enchantments to work, the shots still shatter the carapace in small chunks, sufficient to allow the knives following to land in unprotected flesh.

The Crawler roars, shaking the cavern as it comes under attack and rears towards Asin's newly revealed presence. Daniel takes advantage of this, charging the creature to Shield Bash it. The creature stumbles back, lightning dancing as Daniel proceeds to target the legs on one side to cripple the Boss's movements.

It is only two blows in, a single leg among multitudes shattered before the Crawler spins, using its bulk to smash against Daniel. He brings his hands up together in time to block, using both his Shield and mace to support his block. Safe the from the immediate retaliation, Daniel begins to hammer at the creature, keeping it focused on him as Asin drops from the ceiling and runs the creature's length to reach her embedded knives. Once there, she begins tearing at the shattered carapace to get at the unprotected flesh inside.

The Boss thrashes, attempting to throw Asin off while simultaneously trying to crush Daniel with his mandibles. Daniel fights defensively, foiling attacks against him and only lashing out when he can to send sparks of lightning damage against the monster. The repeated bashings, it seems, have hardly slowed it; as Asin finally creates an opening wide enough for her own liking, she plunges her knife into its back.

The Titanic Crawler then does something unexpected, rolling over entirely. The Catkin throws herself off, but the momentary surprise means that she is unable to leap clear of the body entirely. The Titanic Crawler's bulk lands on her legs, forcing a choked scream from her.

Daniel leaps, using both arms to swing his mace at the softer carapace that the Crawler has exposed. The blows force the creature to roll again to protect its body, a foot spearing Asin in the stomach as it does so. She lets out a choked groan, pain radiating from her broken feet but the Catkin pushes past it, chopping at the leg with her knife to free herself. Once she is able to do so, she begins to pull herself away from the monster, letting out choked off whimpers of pain with each movement.

Luckily, Daniel has the creature's attention now, allowing Asin to crawl away as he triggers his proficiencies, again and again, battering at the creature to keep its attention. He can feel the strength of his blows slowing, fatigue catching up as he attacks and dodges in a desperate attempt to save his friend. Finally, a lucky Shield Bash stuns the creature for a few seconds, allowing Daniel to run and grab his teammate to escape into a nearby tunnel shaft.

Inside the smaller tunnel, safe for the moment, Daniel spins around to focus on healing his teammate. He doesn't need his Gift to tell she is gravely injured, both her legs shattered by the weight of the behemoth and the Crawler's leg still sticking from her stomach.

Focused, he pushes his Gift out even as he extracts the leg and begins to rearrange her leg bones manually. Asin chokes back a quick scream before falling unconscious from the pain as Daniel sets her bones with quick, efficient movements. His Gift begins to take from him almost immediately, pulling memories of previous battles, stretching muscles and nerves as it strips it of their gained experience to fuel the healing. What feels like days later as memories and experience both good and bad disappear, Daniel comes to from his trance and slumps next to his friend.

He shudders, his body slowly accustoming itself to its new state. Asin is awake by the time he is fully aware, staring at her healed body with awe. She points to him, and Daniel just nods, and she chuffs out, a low rumble coming from her. Still not having learnt to speak Catkin, Daniel just shrugs and forces himself to stand up.

"You know, I bet that Boss hasn't healed yet..." Daniel muses, his mace slapping into his hand.

The agreeable yowl from Asin indicates her agreement and Daniel's face tightens into a grim smile. Time to get some experience back.

"Ugh..." Daniel shakes the remnant of his shield loose, tossing it to the side in disgust. The Crawler had attempted its smashing move again, this time dropping its weight on Daniel. Unfortunately for the Crawler, it hadn't expected the Adventurer to just block it, the strong ex-miner catching the full force on his extended shield arm and just about able to hold it off the ground. The mistake was fatal for the already wounded creature, Asin sliding underneath to savage the creature from beneath and pierce its three hearts.

The creature dead, its body dissolving, the two Adventurers rest for a few moments before they move to pick up the Boss's chemical sac and mana stone before walking to the chest. Inside, they grin at the largest mana stone either has seen, glowing with clear light.

Now, this is a real stone, Daniel thinks, picking it up to admire it. Asin purrs for a moment, and then her face closes down, looking between the stone and Daniel. She then points to him and states, "Yours."

"Huh?" Pulled from his greedy contemplation, Daniel shakes his head at her implication. "Ours."

"Yours." Insists Asin, now pushing at his arm to make the stone get closer to Daniel.

"No. Ours." Daniel pauses, realising he's falling into the rhythm of her speech again. "This is ours. We're partners. You save me, I save you. That's the way this works."

Asin chuffs, letting out a low growl and pushes again at the stone. "Yours."

"No." The two then exchange glares, eyes locked in a contest of wills that neither wants to give up. The tense silence hovers around them for long minutes, neither willing to look away or give in. It is only the sound of approaching Crawlers that make the two break their gazes. Daniel glares at her one last time then shrugs, tossing the stone back into the chest.

"Fine. No one's then," Daniel grumbles, turning to walk towards the incoming monsters. If they weren't taking the stone, at least he could start making some money back from the other Crawlers.

Asin just stands there shocked at this frustrating human, a low rumbling growl in Catkin arising from her throat. That was money he was throwing away, a lot of it! *Why would he not let her show her gratitude for saving her life?* Frustrated and unhappy that she lost, she grabs the stone out from the chest again and scrambles after him. *At least she wasn't willing to leave good money behind to make a point.*

Chapter 22

"You two should talk," Liev says to Daniel as he waits around for Asin to finish up with their day's take.

"I don't know what you're talking about," Daniel replies, looking back to Liev and the older attendant sniffs, running a hand through the curly mess of his hair again.

"You two are having problems. It's affecting your work. I've seen the tally for the last few days, and you two are down. And it's not just the shorter hours you are working either," Liev says and raises a finger. "Though that's part of it. I've never seen you or her out of the Dungeon before eight bells two days in a row before, and this is the fourth day you are both here."

Daniel crosses his arms, replying, "You all keep saying I should take a break, maybe that's what we're doing."

"Is it?" Liev reiterates, and Daniel shifts uncomfortably, looking away from the attendant. "I thought so. Talk."

Standing up, Liev walks away, and Daniel sighs. Liev was right, the past few days, the uncomfortable silence between the two Adventurers after their first real fight had affected their teamwork, and the unspoken topic between them hangs in the air, suffocating them in the crawl spaces of the sixth floor. It was so heavy, it drove the two up, early.

Asin comes over, handing a pouch over to Daniel. He hefts the pouch, a part of him wondering if she's giving him more than his share before he shakes his head, clearing it. Liev is right; this was beginning to be a distraction.

While Daniel battles with his doubts, Asin has turned away and started off.

"Asin!" Daniel calls out.

Shoulders hunching slightly, the Catkin turns to look at Daniel, golden eyes glinting with expectation.

"We need to talk," Daniel says as he approaches her.

She chuffs, then nods finally, waving him ahead. Daniel rolls his eyes, wondering why he's always leading. For a time, Daniel debates where to go before defaulting to where he feels most comfortable – the Spinning Top.

The Top is surprisingly quiet, and Daniel blinks, surprised at the lack of patrons. Elise smiles as they come in, waving them over to a table and coming over to serve them herself. "Daniel, and this must be Asin?"

Asin nods and Elise smiles, "I know what he wants, but we have Burdock root if you wish? And the roast is just about ready."

Asin lets out a little yowl of delight, nodding to Elise's suggestions who smiles, moving off to get their order sorted. Daniel shifts uncomfortably in his chair as Asin turns to regard him, silent. They just sit there, waiting for the food to come, the silence growing increasingly uncomfortable before Daniel finally gives in.

"We're having problems," Daniel begins and waits for a reaction from Asin. Getting none, he forges on anyway, "We aren't working as well together, we're getting in each other's way, and well, it's just not going well."

Asin finally relents and offers him a short nod before Daniel continues, "It started with the fight with the Boss. And the healing. I guess, I guess you want to know why I didn't tell you about it before."

Asin tilts her head for a moment before letting out a little chuff and shakes it. "Stone."

"You are upset with me about the stone?" Daniel blinks, not exactly what he was thinking.

"Yes. I give. You refuse," Asin continues, shaking her head. "Throw away."

"Of course I refused it," Daniel states. "I can't take everything for myself. That would be wrong. You don't take from your team."

"Throw away!" Asin snarls and points. "No respect Asin."

"I do respect you. That's why I refused the stone!" Daniel protests and Asin huffs, nostrils flaring out as her tail swishes out behind her, straight as a sword.

"No respect. Throw away!" Asin snarls again and thumps her paw down, claws coming out slightly.

Daniel leans back away from the Catkin, the snarl sending involuntary shivers deep down his back, "Asin, I do respect you. You're my team."

Asin snarls again, but before she can speak, Elise appears carrying their drinks. "You two, calm down. Or do it outside of my inn."

Daniel blinks and notes how everyone is watching the two of them. He hangs his head slightly while Asin looks around, realises she's actually jumped up onto her chair as she speaks with Daniel and hops back down, looking slightly abashed as well. Elise, seeing the two have begun to behave themselves points her fingers at the two of them. "You two should actually try talking."

"We are!" Daniel exclaim and Elise reaches over, smacking him on the top of his head.

"I said talk, not shout the same things over and over again. Explain your side of things!" Shaking her head Elise walks out, muttering, "Youngsters," under her breath.

As Elise leaves the two of them, it is Asin who breaks the silence first, "Asin give gift. Gift! Daniel throw away. Throw away gift. Throw away respect." Finishing, Asin chuffs and reaches for her drink, guzzling it down.

Daniel frowns, shaking his head. "But I couldn't take it from you. You earned it!" At Asin's glare, he holds up a hand, trying to figure out how to explain. "You know I grew up in the mines, right?" Asin nods and Daniel continues, "The mines, you work in a team. Always. The stupid ones, the prospectors, the fools, they work alone and die alone. Real miners, we work together because the mine is always looking to end you. Cave-ins, monsters, bad pockets of air. Without your team, you are nothing. *Without Asin, I would be nothing in the Dungeon.*

And you never take all the ore, all the mana from another. If you do, they might not be able to come back the next day."

Asin snorts at the last bit, but chuffs a little, shaking her head. She's slightly mollified by what Daniel has said, but is still upset. As the two Adventurers ponder the matter, Elise arrives with their dinner, shooting them one last quelling look as business is finally picking up. Hurrying away, Elise leaves the two to sit in silence, enjoying the roast.

When dinner is finished, Asin fishes in her pocket and lays out a pair of silver. She looks Daniel straight in the eye and says, "Dinner. Gift."

Daniel nods at her words, murmuring a soft, "Thank you!" This was one battle he would not fight. Satisfied, Asin slinks off, the crowd of Adventurers and guards eyeing the Catkin and smiling as she leaves.

Chapter 23

"This is the Adventurer you mentioned?" The speaker is broad-shouldered with an erect bearing and a small, faded scar on his left cheek, wearing the green and gold uniform of the Army. The man speaks to Liev as he points a finger at Daniel who is enjoying his breakfast in the early morning.

Liev nods, hands folded behind his back, and surprisingly his unruly red hair combed flat, "Yes, Champion, he is. This is Daniel Chai, Healer and Adventurer."

Striding over, the Champion barks to Daniel in an authoritative voice that brooks no argument, "I have need of another Healer. Pay's a gold and a half a day for a Healer; we'll be gone for a week at most. We leave tomorrow."

His mouth full, Daniel chews and swallows quickly, casting a pitiful glance at Liev for a further explanation as he does so.

"This is Champion Eronin from the Duke's Guard. It seems that an Orc raiding party has been spotted two days' ride from here and the Champion has volunteered to fight it. You'll be joined by a dozen other Adventurers and a platoon of the Duke's Guard."

Quest Offered

Accompany Champion Eronin in battling the Orc Raiding Party.

Reward: 1 and a half gold a day as a Healer.

"Umm…" Daniel scratches at his chin as he finishes swallowing, "I'd be happy to do so, but I do work with another Adventurer, Asin. She uses knives, but she's a much better tracker than me."

"A gold a day," Eronin states and begins to turn around. He stops as Liev clears his throat, waiting for the Champion to turn to him. "Champion, I am afraid I must inform you, as per your request, that she is a Catkin."

"What?" Eronin turns and looks at his potential healer and then the Guild attendant. "Forget it. We don't need those thieving creatures in the group. Just you, Healer."

"Then no," Daniel states calmly, though the words make the entire room fall silent. Elise, having come out from the kitchen winces, matronly brown eyes narrowing in concern.

"Do you know who I am?" Eronin growls, leaning forwards to stare straight into Daniel's eyes. "You will come with me."

"No." Daniel meets the gaze for a brief moment and then is forced to look away, unable to meet the pressure exerted by the man's presence. Yet, stubborn nature refuses to give in to the man's demands. He would not abandon his team.

A hand slams into the table again, Eronin snarling, "I could destroy you for this insolence."

"Champion…" Liev intervenes, coughing into his hand. "As per Guild charter, an Adventurer may turn down any request, for any reason, so long as he has not previously accepted it. Daniel is within his rights, if not his mind."

Eronin snarls, a hand trembling on the table before he regains control of his temper and stalks out of the room, shoving the door open with a crash, Liev following silently behind. As they leave, Daniel feels a hard smack on the top of his head, Elise holding the offending spoon.

"You idiot! That was the Duke's Champion!" Elise complains, pointing towards the recently departed figure. "If you had played nice you could have gotten personal quests and more!"

Daniel rubs his head, trying to figure out how to explain this to Elise. She needed an explanation, probably one that was complicated, but it was simple really. Asin was his friend and his partner, and you always worked with your team because that's what you did in the mines. Once you had a partner, you worked together, no matter what. Eventually, he tries with, "I work with Asin."

Elise's groan is what he expected, though having overheard their previous conversation, she understands his thinking, to a point. Still, the damnable stubborn child! While she is standing there, frustrated, Daniel switches topics to something that puzzles him. "I didn't think Liev disliked her too."

Elise rubs her temples as she stares at Daniel, a headache forming while she explains to him, "Liev is just doing his job. The Champion doesn't work with Beastkin, and probably made that clear in his quest."

"Oh," Daniel frowns and looks at his hands, trying to understand the reasoning behind such a decision. In the end, he shrugs and dismisses it. It was not his concern why others chose to do what they did, just what he chose to do himself. Gulping down the last of his meal, Daniel stands and gives Elise a peck on the cheek. He and Asin were going to try fighting a single Ogre today on the seventh floor. Working the seventh floor was tough, and they had avoided the Titanic Crawler for the last few days as their close defeat was still fresh in their minds. Perhaps trying the new floor would provide much-needed variety, even if Daniel still didn't have the money for proper chain mail.

"This was not what I was expecting," Daniel mutters, staring around the seventh floor. The ceiling stretches for a good forty feet; glow stones are interspersed throughout the ceiling so that it looks like daylight itself in the cavern. The ground is covered in lush grass and occasional small trees, and more often bushes range across their view.

Asin nods firmly, gliding soundlessly across the grass in her light leather armour and boots before tentatively poking at a bush. When nothing happens, she squats down and eyes it closer, before shrugging and moving to the next type to repeat her actions.

Daniel keeps watch of the cavern while she does her thing, a part of him glad that he's no longer forced to crouch. If not for good massages, and a constant barrage of healing spells, he felt he would be stuck in a permanent half-crouch after the last several months.

A low rhythmic thudding brings both Adventurers' attention back to point, Asin pulling her cloak tighter before working her way into the shadows. Daniel steps forward to face the new threat and then gulps as he spots an Ogre for the first time, his hands growing clammy. Nine feet tall, wearing a ragged loincloth and wielding a club, the creature sports a potbelly and a pig-snout that is just the tip of a truly ugly but humanoid visage. It roars at seeing an intruder in its domain, rushing forwards to punish Daniel.

Daniel tenses, watching for the club to begin its strike as he forces himself to breathe slowly. The first battle was always the most dangerous as no knowledge of the monster's proclivities were available to draw upon. Rather than rushing in, Daniel intends to focus on defence instead. The club begins its downward swing, but Daniel does not move, instinct telling him to hold still until the Ogre is fully committed to the attack. The Ogre does not feint though, continuing the motion with ever-increasing speed so that Daniel has to throw himself aside, forced to give up an opportunity to counter to just dodge the blow. This is not like fighting the Crawlers or Kobolds; the fight reminds him more of training against Litzburn, a situation where his opponent had cunning and guile.

As the Ogre winds up to swing again, it is shocked by Asin's knife thrown from her hiding place. The knife pierces the Ogre's back, digging into its spine and stunning it for a moment. More knives land in quick succession and Daniel takes advantage of the momentary opening to slam his mace into the Ogre's knee twice before he springs back from the retaliatory attack. As the Ogre swings again, Daniel sheds the swing with his shield but is over-powered by the Ogre's strength and is driven to his knees. The Ogre continues to swing, each blow smashing aside Daniel's attempts at parrying, staggering the Adventurer beneath his shield. Each parried blow sends shudders of pain through his body, his shoulder and arms taking the abuse as his shield begins to crack.

As the Ogre steps forward again, Asin throws another Piercing Shot, this time aimed at its already injured knee. The knee gives way, and Daniel throws himself into a roll to avoid the falling monster. Asin continues to pelt the Ogre with her throwing knives, each knife sinking into its body with little resistance and shocking the creature with lightning, even as Daniel returns to beat on the Ogre with his mace. Crippled, the Ogre does not last much longer before succumbing to the attacks of the merciless Adventurers.

As the body fades, they find only a few coins left behind and a mana stone. The now experienced Adventurers immediately eye the stone, satisfied at the increase in quality once again before Asin tucks the stone away.

"You know, I felt kind of bad there…" Daniel says as he rubs his shoulder. The repeated attacks have numbed his arm and injured his left shoulder, the shield slightly cracked under the onslaught. His knee throbs as well from where he was forced to the ground. Nothing that a simple Minor Heal would not fix, which is what he does immediately, sighing in pleasure at the lack of pain.

Asin shrugs, not understanding Daniel's feelings on this. It was a monster. The Ogre needed to die, no matter how much it looked like a human or how helpless it was at the end. A Dungeon-created monster wasn't even real, not in the sense that sentient races were real. Just constructs.

Daniel looks out over the landscape before them before turning to Asin, "Up or stay?"

Asin ponders the question, thinking about the hallways above. The mana stone they had just received was definitely a level higher, which meant more copper. She hated being in debt, especially with her other obligations. More money faster was good, but it was dangerous too. Daniel had struggled to fight a single Ogre – what if two came? On the other hand, her daggers were much more effective against the Ogres with their current lack of armour.

Daniel is doing the maths in his own head as well, weighing the risk and reward of staying on the seventh floor. It seemed they could handle a single Ogre without injury. Two might be problematic, especially as Asin's knives were damaging but not deadly. He would have to focus almost exclusively on defence if he had to fight two.   Still, he probably could do it…

"Stay." The two speak at almost the same time and then Asin chuffs in amusement. Decision made, she lopes ahead to check out potential problems, though a part of her resolves to avoid having to fight more than one at a time if it can be helped. Best to be careful.

"Elsa." Daniel smiles slightly, spotting the attendant in the Guild hall as the pair limp in, looking the worse for wear. The seventh floor had been tough, and thrice they had decided to stay hidden or bypass corridors rather than fight a pair of Ogres. However, the floor had been highly profitable in both experience and mana stones.   He passes her the collected stones, watching her tally the stones. "Where's Liev?"

"Mmm…? Oh, he took the day off." Elsa smiles at him, her dirty blonde hair momentarily covering her eyes. She sweeps her hair aside, smiling up at the young Adventurer. He and his Catkin associate were the talk of the Guild, their progress the best the Guild had seen in the last few years. Why, they were down on the seventh floor already! Most Adventurers who chose to complete the Dungeon found themselves stuck on the sixth floor for at least a year, grinding levels till they could gain enough strength or a Skill Proficiency to destroy the Titanic Crawler.

"Really?" Daniel frowns, concern flashing across his face. Was the old bureaucrat sick?

"Mmm… most people don't work every day," Elsa says.

"Yeah, but…" Daniel doesn't know what to say to that, after all, Liev has been here every time he's been here.

Asin is chuffing beside him, obviously amused. Elsa just points a finger at her and says, "You're his partner. You're in here just as much as he is."

"Makes. Me."

Elsa just looks at the money crazy Catgirl, after all, Elsa was Asin's unofficial attendant. She was the one who Asin came to when she needed to find a partner who would work as hard as she did and who wouldn't hold her race against her. Asin pretends to miss the look, scratching at her own ear.

A gentle cough reminds Elsa that they still haven't been paid out yet, at which point she returns to her work, point having been made. Sometimes, these youngsters really didn't know when to stop.

Chapter 24

Days after the not so subtle hinting by Elsa, Daniel finds himself standing outside the Top, dressed comfortably in his only other pair of clean, non-adventuring clothing, waiting for Asin. He sighs, wishing for once she'd turn up on time for something other than a dungeon delve.

Just as he thinks that, he spots her and Khy'ra walking together, chatting amiably. As he gets over his surprise at Asin's apparent talkativeness, he gets another one as they close enough for him to hear the meows and growls that the two speak in. He didn't know Khy'ra spoke Catkin!

"Khy'ra!" He gives a quick peck to the offered cheek, sliding a hand around her waist and copping a quick feel. She rolls her eyes, but hugs him nonetheless, melding her body comfortably to his. "You didn't tell me you were coming."

"Asin came by the Clinic a few days ago to invite me." Khy'ra smiles and Asin nods in confirmation. Pointing down the street, the Catkin heads down, the mixed-race trio garnering more than a few quick stares. Daniel ignores it, focusing on his companions.

"Where are we going?" Daniel asks once again. Perhaps this time he'll get an actual answer.

"Celebration. Anika," Asin replies in her usual terse matter. Daniel rolls his eyes and is suddenly glad of Khy'ra's presence. He shoots an imploring look at Khy'ra who runs a hand through her hair, green eyes sparkling.

"It's the Beastkin celebration for Anika, their First Hero," Khy'ra says. "I believe today would mark the 497th anniversary of the founding of the city of Marloo by Anika, the first major step to the creation of Garhwa and thus the first Beastkin nation."

Daniel scratches his head and sighs, somewhat abashed at his lack of knowledge. Spending most of his time in the mines, dominated by humans and the occasional dwarf, he had little knowledge of the other races. It just had never been part of his world view till now.

Asin does not lead them straight to the Beastkin district though, instead stopping by a butcher's first. Unlike many, the butcher seems more than happy to see Asin, as Asin is one of her most regular and best customers. Today's order was noteworthy, even for the small carnivore, and Asin quickly drags Daniel over to help with the large sack.

"This thing must weigh a good eighty pounds! What did you do? Buy a whole pig?" Daniel grumbles as he lifts the sack. Asin's cheerful nod makes him groan again, but he stays silent as they continue the walk, Khy'ra regretfully detached from Daniel's arm now.

They continue to journey through the streets of Karlak, Khy'ra, as always, smiling and nodding to those she recognises. The elf, as usual, garners more than one admiring glance, though most either dismiss Asin's presence or watch her extra carefully. After a time, the trio leave the normal thoroughfares that Daniel knows, the roads becoming narrower, buildings growing older and more rundown, though still well washed and well kept. The transition is gradual at first, but as they step out from another alleyway, it's like walking into another city.

The streets are filled with Beastkin of all kinds, from arrogant Wolfkin to the statelier Catkin, grumbly Jackals, lazy Ursines and more. As great a surprise for Daniel, however, are the riot of colours and smells that make up the streets. A wild divergence from humanity's boring pastels are the vibrant colours that the Beastkin coat their dwellings in, yellows and greens and reds cover walls and wood trim and are even layered on roofs. For the celebration, strings of red and white flow from one side of the alley to the other, with trailing hand-painted scrolls depicting memorable scenes beneath. Food and other scents cling to the air, mixing with wild abandon and assaulting Daniel's senses and he reels, wondering how the Beastkin are able to handle all this. Even his human senses are over-whelmed, how do they cope?

By his side, both Asin and Khy'ra watch with amusement, treasuring the view as Daniel struggles to deal with the overload. When he finally recovers, Asin tugs on his hand and points, leading him to a cooking pit that has been set up in front of a shop where he is directed to set the pig.

A rumbly, growly conversation ensues between Asin and the presiding cook, both getting more and more agitated. Daniel frowns, hairs prickling on the back of his neck and he unconsciously reaches for his non-existent mace. Khy'ra reaches for and grabs his hand, pulling him close to whisper, "It's okay, they're just arguing about how to cook the meat. Beastkin are loud amongst themselves."

Daniel grimaces and sighs, watching his normally quiet companion get into a shouting match. Unsure what to do, the two lovers stand and watch the scenes around them, ignoring the arguing pair; Beastkin children stream through the streets in a never-ending game of tag, miraculously dodging busy adults without fail. A large, black Catkin dressed in a garishly coloured yellow tunic and blousy white pants strides up to the pair, hands splayed with paws facing the sky in greeting. He is a mixture of human and Catkin traits, a feline-angled face but lacking the over-abundance of fur that marks Asin's own visage. "Khy'ra and Daniel, it must be. May you find safety at our fires."

Khy'ra copies the hand greeting, and after a brief moment so does Daniel. She intones the ritual response as well, "Elder Chetan, may your fire burn forever safely."

Unsure if he should repeat the message, Daniel just falls back on being silent. Elder Chetan turns to the young Adventurer, black fur wrinkling in amusement before he speaks, only the slightest of growls marring his voice, "Thank you for coming. And thank you for taking care of my daughter."

"Daughter…" Daniel catches on quickly enough and shakes his head. "We take care of each other. We're partners."

The Elder chuffs and continues, "Yes. It is good that she has found one who is willing to accept her. Asin has not had it easy, being closer to the progenitor than many other Kin."

Daniel's puzzled look encourages the Elder to explain further, first stepping closer to allow himself to lower his voice, "It is strange. In Garhwa, she would be exalted. Here, in Brad, we strive to be closer to you humans, and she is despised." Ears drooping, the Elder shrugs. "I love my daughter, but she could have made it easier on herself too. She is stubborn and prideful, much like her mother."

Daniel smiles slightly, having noticed both aspects of his companion on more than one occasion. She could be frustrating at times to deal with, but so could he, he had been told.

"Still, this is not the time for this! Come, you must drink some saboo and dance!" The Elder claps his paws together and drags the two off, growling out his intentions to his daughter who just waves him away. The argument with that obstinate cook who wishes to use wyxli spice on her pig had to be completed. *Wyxli spice! Everyone knew you used jylin leaves and cracked esper spice to get the best taste from roast pig.*

The ensuing hours pass in laughter and amusement, the Elder happy to play host to the two guests. As the day progresses, Daniel notes that his and Khy'ra's presence is a notable exception, the Beastkin having the run of this neighbourhood to themselves. That is other than a loud and boisterous Tharuk, partaking in a drinking competition with a bear which neither seems ready to concede. Through the day, Daniel has food and drink stuffed into his hands continuously, meats of various types such that even his own carnivorous nature is more than fulfilled.

Only once is there silence, when the sun reaches its zenith. The Beastkin pause, staring at the sky, the silence lingering for minutes. At first, the growls are too low for Daniel to hear, though he can feel it in his bones as the voices of the assembled Beastkin surround him. Slowly, it goes higher and higher, the growls resolving into an animalistic song that tugs at a deeply hidden part of him. When the song is over, Daniel finds himself breathing heavily as if from a long run, his face flushed and his eyes sparkling. A glance at Khy'ra shows that even the Elven beauty is affected, the smouldering look she gives him makes him wonder briefly if he can find an empty room somewhere.

Asin joins them soon after the ceremony and drags Daniel to a nearby warehouse where a small arena has been created. There, Beastkin challenge each other in various feats of athleticism. Once, even Daniel is dragged into the centre to join in the feat of strength, though he is quickly outclassed by the massive Ursine and Buffalo Beastkin who make up the majority of the contestants.   It is Khy'ra who proves the surprise, laughingly dancing and stealing ribbons in the game of tag and agility that the Catkin and Snakes dominate otherwise. Eventually, even she is caught but many of the Beastkin eye the Elf with new respect.

During a lull in the evening, Daniel finally manages to ask the question that has disturbed him all day, "Asin's very talkative, isn't she."

"Yes, yes she is," Khy'ra answers.

"So, why doesn't she talk to me?" Daniel grumbles.

"Do you talk to her in Beastkin?"

"No…" Daniel frowns. "She seems to understand me well…"

"Yes, dear," Khy'ra sighs and touches his throat and then hers. "Now look at hers."

Daniel does as she says, finally looking and then slowly blinks, feeling ashamed, "She has trouble speaking doesn't she?"

"In Brad? Yes."

Daniel falls silent then, absently chewing on the rib he is given. He stops, grimacing and puts the food down again as his stomach catches up to his hands. Way too much food. Khy'ra pushes his shoulder with her own, and he meets her eyes, where she just shakes her head slightly. Getting the message, he focuses on having fun. This is not the time for such thoughts. Smiling, he holds a hand out and Khy'ra takes it, letting herself be pulled onto the dance floor again with a laugh.

Chapter 25

"There you are!" Liev's sudden appearance makes the two Adventurers jump, Asin making it half-way up the nearest wall while Daniel drops into a crouch, shield up. They then both blink, after all, they're both on the seventh floor working their way through a couple of Ogres and Liev had never been spotted anywhere close to the Dungeon before. "Take my hand."

Daniel frowns and Liev sighs, no longer asking and reaching out to grab his hand and Asin's arm in short order. A surge of power takes them both out of the Dungeon directly into a room that neither has seen before. The two Adventurers stare around themselves dumb-founded, a window to the outside room indicating that they are in town and in the Guild itself.

"How…?" Daniel says.

"Group Teleport. It's a level 50 Adventurer's Skill Proficiency," Liev explains as he gestures to Daniel. 'Come, you're needed."

Daniel automatically follows but then stops short, Liev is pointing to Asin who has started to come too. "Your presence will be unhelpful, my dear. We go to see the Champion. And don't give me that look, Daniel, we need your Gift."

Daniel wipes the mulish look off his face, grimacing and following after the fast disappearing attendant. He frowns in thought though, surprised to find that Liev was, or perhaps still is, a high-level Adventurer. Liev certainly didn't have the bearing of a fighter. In fact, the thought of Liev holding a sword makes Daniel chuckle to himself internally, the bookish and fastidious red-haired older gentleman ignorant of Daniel's amusement.

"The Champion and his party were ambushed. Most died in the attack, and the Champion himself is gravely injured. We need you to heal him, Daniel," Liev says.

"Uhh…" Daniel's initial amusement is wiped away at Liev's words as he struggles to catch up mentally.

Liev turns, getting into Daniel's face and speaking emphatically, "Young man, I understand your position. I almost admire it. However, this is not the time or place. The Orcs haven't sent a raiding party; they sent a War Party. There are over three hundred Orcs rampaging through the province at this moment and that man, for all of his distasteful views, is the most powerful weapon we have. If. He. Survives."

Daniel gulps, the thought of three hundred Orcs laying waste to the countryside enough to force him to cast aside any personal feelings he had. While he was no Healer, he understood their oath – to treat all that needed it, no matter their personal feelings. Daniel nods firmly, and in silence the pair hurry to the barracks where the Champion lies injured.

The sight that greets Daniel when he enters makes him pale. The Champion, once a larger than life presence is gravely hurt, multiple open wounds on his chest and limbs. Most dangerous of all was the distorted skull - pressure and shattered bones causing it to bulge out. For a moment, Daniel can only stare before he takes a deep shuddering breath.

A hand touches Daniel's, gripping tight and he notices for the first time the presence of others in the room. The Guard Captain he knows by sight, Khy'ra obviously, but the other three are unknown to him. The first seems to be another healer from the way he works on the Champion's wounds but who the other two are he is unable to guess. One is a portly human with a beard, the other a female with a thick gold chain around her neck. The chain clues him in on her at last – that was the Merchant Guild's seal on it. Khy'ra squeezes his hand again, bringing his attention back to her.

"Can you heal him?"

Daniel nods mutely, a part of him already assessing the damage and what he would need to do. The greater part of his mind though stalls at the cost of the healing, a cost that would dwarf anything he had done in years. Only once before had he attempted something this powerful, and in that case, he had eventually failed. No Gift could win against the ravages of time, not in the end.

"Daniel," Khy'ra turns her lover's gaze to meet hers, concern etching her voice. "What's wrong?"

"My Gift…" he struggles against his irrational fear of telling them, the fear that they will exploit him, what they will ask of him, force on him. His hand, entwined with hers begins shaking violently.

"What is the holdup?" the portly human speaks imperiously, pointing. "Heal him, Adventurer. I won't have the Baron's Champion die in my city!"

Khy'ra turns to the man, shooting a glare that would have killed if it could. Liev steps in, holding a hand up, "My Lord Mayor, this space is no longer suitable for non-Healers. I believe we should retire."

"I'm the Mayor!" Snapping, the portly man begins to set himself when the woman leans over, whispering in his ear.   He grunts and finally stomps out, followed closely by the woman and Liev. Just before she leaves, she casts an assessing glance at the pale Daniel before turning away. The Healer, after a glance at Khy'ra, moves to a corner, giving the two space.

"Daniel, talk to me. Please…" Khy'ra implores him, holding both their hands up and placing a kiss on the top of his.

Daniel draws a deep shuddering breath and then whispers, softly, "When I use my Gift, I lose a bit of myself. A part of what I've learnt, a part of my memories, a part of my skills and some of my energy. The Gift, it strips me of these things when I use it. It's normally not much, just a few minutes here or there, an hour or two sometimes. This though…" He shivers again, clutching her hand, "I could lose a lot more."

Khy'ra's eyes widen, remembering all the times she blithely asked him to help her in the Clinic, all the times he seemed a bit forgetful or slow afterwards. All the times he acceded without protest when he should have said no, "You… you… idiot!"

"Yeah." His secret out, he seems to relax a bit. "This has to happen, doesn't it?"

Lips pursed, Khy'ra nods, "It does. The Champion's another Gifted. If he is able to use his Gift, only a Master Mage or another Gifted can challenge him on the field of battle."

Daniel lets her hands go, and walks past her to put his hands on the struggling Champion. Almost plaintively, as he thrusts his Gift into the man, he says, "Couldn't he at least be a little nicer?"

Khy'ra watches for a moment as Daniel begins, then turns, gesturing for the other Healer to keep an eye on them. She has another place to be; there are words to be spoken. If what Daniel fears is true, he will lose much in this, and she intends to ensure he is well compensated for it.

Focused, Daniel misses the byplay. His Gift tells him all the details he needs, the punctured lung, the shredded intestines, the broken skull and the ever-growing pressure in the head, barely relieved by other methods. A normal human being would have been dead a score over, only the Champion's stupendous health and the magic used on him are managing to keep him alive. Yet his health falls with each breath; he will not last long without further healing.

Damage assessed, Daniel begins the process of fixing things. Plugging the most dangerous wounds first, he heals and lowers the pressure in the Champion's skull while bones shift back under the skin to their appropriate locations. Each pulse of power pulls another memory, another shudder through his body as his Gift strips him of recently learnt skills, of muscle and real memory. It is an uncaring taskmaster, removing both pleasant and unpleasant memories, caring not of their origin. The Champion's health works against Daniel now, muscles and organs that would be pliant and easy to heal in another being requiring more energy, more time, more experience than any previous patient.

What feels like hours, but is barely half of one, passes by before Daniel pulls his senses back into himself. He stumbles, collapsing into a thoughtfully positioned chair as the Champion's breath eases. The Champion's wounds are mostly healed, the majority fixed and he no longer does injury to himself with every breath. Bruises and some cuts still lie across the Champion's body, but Daniel knows he is no longer in danger. Regular magical healing or plain time will do the rest.

Level Lost!

You are now a Level 4 Adventurer

Attribute Points Lost

That could have been worse… Daniel stares at the little sliver of Experience he has left keeping him from falling another level and groans. So much experience; so much time lost. Months of hard work, stripped from him, his memory of recent Dungeon delves and fights gone. His body aches from the use of the Gift, his nerves and muscles feel stripped raw. However, the job is not done, and so he forces himself upright, placing his hand on the Champion's chest and invoking his healing spell. He was so close to getting the option to learn a Moderate Heal the next time he received proficiency, so close to becoming more than he was before. Once more, he has been dragged down by his Gift, and he can't help but feel a flare of resentment. He forces it down, focusing on burning through his Mana to finish the job. Later. Later he'll deal with this.

With the last of his mana drained from him, Daniel turns away to leave. They can deal with the rest of this. All he wants is rest. As he steps aside, an iron grip grasps his arm.

"You healed me," the Champion rumbles, awake.

"Yes," Daniel says, tugging at his arm. The Champion releases him and stares at the youngster who dared defy him days ago.

"Why?"

"It was needed," Daniel begins and falls silent.

"And the Cost?" Daniel hears the capitalization; he understands what the Champion asks. Another one cursed/blessed with a Gift at birth understands all too well the Cost incurred. It was no simple matter, no matter what the others thought. The Champion's own Gift allowed him to ignore any attack he chose to when invoked, but the price was paid in pain days later. The longer the Gift was activated, the worst and longer the pain it inflicted. The payment could be put-off, but not indefinitely.

Daniel shakes his head, refusing to answer. He owes this man no answer. He owes him nothing more. Duty done, all Daniel wants is to be left alone now, and so he tugs again at the arm, the Champion finally releasing him. Daniel walks away, leaving the Champion to the care of the Guards' Healer. Behind him, the Champion growls, displeased at being so casually dismissed once again. *Damn the child!*

In another room, while Daniel works, a larger and more intense argument is happening. In that room, the Mayor and the Merchant Guild Master and Khy'ra face-off over what Daniel's fee for the healing will be. Liev watches, taking no side in the argument directly, though he subtly helps by pointing out the rarity and exclusivity of Daniel's Gift.

It is only when the Guards' Healer arrives to announce the successful restoration of the Champion that the argument finishes. Like all good negotiations, no single party leaves happy, but Khy'ra is grimly content at least. If the child would not value himself, then she would ensure that.

Back in the Top, in his room, alone, Daniel calls up his Status Screen to see how much he has lost in detail.

Name: Daniel Chai

Class: Level 4 Adventurer (2%)

Sub-classes: Level 7 (Miner) (14%)

Human (Male)

Statistics

Life: 201

Stamina: 201

Mana: 152

Attributes

Strength: 18

Agility: 19

Constitution: 26

Intelligence: 16

Willpower: 18

Luck: 13

Skills

Unarmed Combat: Level 3 (01/100)

Clubs: Level 8 (14/100)

Shield: Level 6 (28/100)

Dodge: Level 4 (36/100)

Combat Sense: Level 5 (48/100)

Perception: Level 5 (36/100)

Mining: Level 7 (78/100)

Healing: Level 8 (17/100)

Herb Lore: Level 3 (31/100)

Stealth: Level 2 (14/100)

Cooking: Level 2 (37/100)

Singing: Level 2 (14/100)

Skill Proficiencies

Double Strike

Shield Bash

Mapping (II)

Spells

Minor Healing (I)

Gifts

Martyr's Touch - The caster may heal oneself or others by touch and concentration, sacrificing a portion of his life to do so. Cost varies depending on the extent of the injuries healed.

Chapter 26

"Asin, we have to do the fifth floor today," Daniel announces to his friend the next day. She stops from touching the gem that would bring them lower, tilting her head as she considers Daniel. He did seem weaker today – perhaps his healing had drained him more than she thought. She chuffs out, slightly annoyed but touches the fifth-floor gemstone.

Relieved that she will not enquire further, Daniel follows his friend down. It's time to see how much he has lost. Three nests later, Daniel takes out his frustration on a single Crawler that they have come across, slamming down again and again with his mace. So much lost. He's a step slower, a beat off and while he feels he should be faster, he's not, and he knows why.

Behind him, Asin watches with deep concern. Daniel's normal calm, slightly amused but entirely engaged mode of adventuring is gone, replaced with a short, sullen ball of fury and resentment. On the other hand, as Daniel kicks the Crawler away and moves on to the next cavern, he certainly is making up for the quality with quantity today. Grabbing the mana stone, Asin moves to keep up with her friend and to ensure he doesn't walk into any traps. Well, if Daniel keeps this up too long, she'll find a barrel of water and dump him in it. Till then, she is content to let him work his feelings out on the Crawlers.

In a room far above the Dungeon, the titular leaders of the city of Karlak work out plans to deal with the rampaging War Party.

"Daniel, a word?" Liev is waiting for them when they finally surface from the Dungeon. Daniel nods, moving to the side to allow to Asin handle the sale of their mana stones and other loot.

"Firstly, thank you." Liev does not stop though, knowing the young Adventurer was uncomfortable with thanks, "Secondly, there has been a general request for Adventurers to join the army as ancillary troops due to the War Party.

I have taken the liberty of assigning you and Asin to Maximillian's team as melee fighters. I believe that is where your particular skills will be most useful."

Daniel frowns and Liev sighs, explaining, "Doing so ensures you are not conscripted as a Healer if the number of volunteers is deemed insufficient. In addition, it will be good experience for you, young man. Brad does not have to keep a large standing army because it relies on its Adventurers to provide additional troops when necessary. If you intend to progress as an Adventurer, you will find that such requests become more and more common. This particular event is as safe as any general Army sponsored-quest will be."

"Yes, sir," Daniel finally agrees. He is still not certain joining the army was a great option for him, but if Liev felt it was the right thing to do, he would accede to the man's request. The attendant had yet to steer him wrong.

""Lastly, you are going to be very popular among your peers in short order. Word of your Gift has finally reached their ears after yesterday's incident." Liev hesitates and falls silent, leaving any additional advice unspoken. Truthfully, Liev had done as much as he could. Getting the young man out of town under the watchful eye of a friend ensured that those who would use him just for his Gift had no target, at least for the short term. In the meantime, he and Khy'ra would work on making his return as uncomplicated as possible.

Seeing no other conversational threads cropping up, Daniel wishes Liev goodbye and returns to Asin. He quickly informs her of their new quest to which she replies, "Pay?"

Daniel pauses, realising he never did ask that. Asin lets out an annoyed chuff, slinking back to talk with Liev directly, grumbling all the while about how lucky Daniel was that he was such a good distraction for her. Finding a comfortable corner, Daniel settles down to wait, knowing Asin will more than handle matters for both of them. He had spent the day fighting, going from one nest to the next and now he was drained, all his anger and regret smashed apart like the Crawlers he had met. When Asin is done, and has provided him with the details of their pay, he thanks her, and they part ways, Asin to spend an evening with family and Daniel to the Top.

At the Top, Daniel is startled to see Khy'ra waiting for him, chatting amiably with Elise. Khy'ra sends a smile his way, walking over to kiss him before wrinkling her nose at his smell.

"I was thinking dinner, but I think a bath would be better," Khy'ra says and points upwards. "Hurry up; I'll be waiting."

Daniel nods dumbly, deciding that it is best to go with the flow here. He did need a bath after all, or at least a wash. A quick trip upstairs to get a boar of soap and a change of clothing is all that is needed before he returns, Khy'ra taking his arm as they bid farewell.

The walk to the bathing room is short and pleasant, the two quickly catching each other up on their day's activities.

"…now Leon comes in with this barb in his foot, about two inches sticking right out of it. And he's sitting there, dripping blood in the waiting room and every time we go to get him in, he sends another patient in!" Khy'ra continues, shaking her head. "I eventually had to do the damn operation right there in the room and push it out in front of everyone. That big baby was so scared of it coming out that he nearly died of blood loss!"

Daniel laughs at her words, holding the door open for Khy'ra as they enter the bathtub. Both experienced hands, they deposit a silver coin each for their personal use and then Khy'ra deposits another three silver to get them a private room. When Daniel moves to protest, he is quelled by the smouldering look Khy'ra offers him.

A silly grin crosses his face as they head in, first to their respective sexes changing rooms before they make their way to the marked private room. Daniel is surprised to find Khy'ra in first, lounging in the circular wooden bath that is large enough to fit four in it. Steam comes from the hot water, a pair of small ladles and even soap set aside for their use. As he nears the tub, he realises that she is naked under the water.

"Mmm… I hadn't brought a change of clothing," she says in answer to his look.

Daniel grins, sliding in with her. Before he can move to get a kiss, she points to the soap, and he sighs, getting to scrubbing. As he moves to clean his back, she moves over and takes it up, scrubbing at his back.

"Liev tells me that you'll be joining the Army tomorrow," Khy'ra says.

"Yeah, he said it's good for me. I never really considered it, you know," Daniel says.

"Liev is somewhat traditional in his thinking. Not all Adventurers take as much part in the Army quests as he did, or thinks most should do. I rarely did," Khy'ra says, smiling and splashing his back before pushing back.

Daniel turns around, ducking under the water to get the last of the soap out of his eyes before he lies back, enjoying the heat as it releases his muscles, "Oh! That's nice…"

Smiling as she watches him, Khy'ra sighs and swims over, sliding between his legs and straddling him. When his eyes open, she puts a finger to his lips and murmurs, "Daniel, focus. I wanted to tell you something. You need to be careful about the quests you take. Most are, well, normal, but some might not sit well with you. Army quests aren't like your normal quests – you can't take one and then leave it just because you don't like how it works out or the information wasn't complete. You have to finish Army quests or face their censure."

Daniel pauses, staring into her eyes and then nods slowly, "Okay. I'll be careful."

Khy'ra smiles and then kisses him before murmuring. "Good, now we've got this room for another hour. Let's make the most of it."

The next morning, Asin and Daniel exit to meet up with the Army in the clear fields north of Karlak. Already, the first few divisions have gathered, their supply train pulling in behind them. In contrast to the orderly line-up of the army divisions, the Adventurers mill around in loose groups, individuals occasionally breaking off to chat with other groups.

The two friends glance around, feeling somewhat out of place. There are few Beastkin in the group, clustered together in small clumps. For the first time, Daniel realises how little interaction he has had with the general Adventuring population of the town of Karlak. Even the regulars he sees at the Top often receive little more than a nod. His own free time was mostly taken up by Khy'ra, the Clinic or training with the occasional night drinking with the Guards thrown-in. Unlike most Adventurers, his social circle was the town residents.

As the two stand around awkwardly, a tall, blond swordsman walks up to them clad in plate mail. He smiles as he nears, showing off perfect teeth on top of a chiselled jaw and Daniel feels a sudden twinge of jealousy. "Daniel? Asin?"

Receiving confirmation from both, the swordsman offers his hand, "Maximillian. You'll be in my party for this."

Daniel shakes it, impressed by the casual strength he feels through the handshake. Obviously, all those muscles were not just for show. Asin chuffs a greeting as well, eyeing the surroundings with casual interest.

"Come on; I'll introduce you to the rest of the group." Maximillian leads them through the crowd, offering quick nods and greetings as he walks through, the man's presence obviously well known. It takes them a short while to wind their way to their own party as there are nearly a hundred Adventurers gathered already. Daniel feels somewhat impressed, never realising there were this many in the town. Most are out-fitted like he is with varying degrees of protection for armour and weaponry, the vast majority being melee fighters. Only a small portion seem to be carrying a visible ranged weapon, and of those, crossbows seem to be the most popular option.

"Daniel, Asin, this is Kilroy and Mia. Mia's a Ranger and is our main ranged weapon dealer. Kilroy's, well, Kilroy's Kilroy," Maxmillian says. "Have you shot a crossbow before Daniel?"

Daniel shakes his head, glancing at the weapon that Max holds out to him.

"No problem. We'll head down the way and get you familiar with it. It's simple compared to the bow, so you should pick it up easily. We'll all be using a ranged weapon, other than Asin for obvious reasons, and the crossbows and Mia's bow will be our first line of offence."

Daniel nods, hefting the crossbow and following along. He voices one hesitation first though, "Don't we have to join up the army?"

"There's no need right now. It'll take them forever to get moving, and we'll catch up once we're done training," Maximillian says, gesturing for them to catch up.

Daniel repeats quietly in his head the instructions he's been given - exhale, remember to adjust for the wind and drop, pull gently on the trigger – and feels the jerk as the crossbow bolt releases, flying to the target. Breath held, he watches the arrow arc through the air and miss once again, this time by 5 meters.

"I think you're getting worse," Maximillian says with awe.

"Worse," chuffs Asin before going back to cleaning her paw.

"I'm sorry," Daniel sighs, dejected. He reaches for another bolt and realises he's shot them all. A glance to the side shows that the others are done, for now, so he calls out his intention of retrieving the bolts, hurrying to do so. Four hours of training and he hasn't managed to hit the stump a bare 20 meters away even once.

When he returns, Maximillian shakes his head as Daniel begins to load the crossbow. "No time, we need to get going. We'll have you carry the crossbow and reload for Killroy instead."

Daniel looks away, shame filling him. A hand claps on his shoulder, Maximillian waiting for Daniel to look up before speaking, "It's okay. Not everyone can be good at everything. Now come on, we've got a bit of a hike before we're caught up."

Chapter 27

"Is this all they do?" grumbles Daniel, slogging along behind the army. He'd enjoy the countryside, but since the Adventurers were stuck behind both the army and the supply train, most of what he got to see was dust clouds and the turds he had to walk around.

"Pretty much," Maximillian chuckles, seemingly completely at ease even after a day and night of this. "Joining up with the army is mostly a lot of boredom, punctuated by a few hours or minutes of excitement."

"At least they get experience out of this," Daniel grumbles, waving his hand forward. Unlike Adventurers who mostly gained experience from exploring, killing and questing; the army gained theirs from training and marching for the most part. It was, in the opinion of many learned scholars, certainly better for professional armies to gain experience by training for war rather than actually waging war. Musing on this, Daniel is struck by a thought, "Max, how do Orcs gain experience?"

"Ah, you don't know?" Maximillian asks rhetorically. As more than one rookie Adventurer moves in, Max raises his voice, "Orcs are kind of like us – they gain experience mostly from killing and questing. However, unlike us and like the army, those in positions of power also gain a steady boost of experience. It's why your average Orc grunt is easy enough to fight, but their bosses are much more difficult."

"How much more?" Daniel asks.

"An Orc Boss is about twice as dangerous as you'd expect based on its level. Stronger, faster and smarter. Don't fight them if you can, that's what the Army Sergeants and the Advanced Adventurers are for," Maximillian responds, making sure to look at the rookies. There are more than a few nods including from

Daniel and Asin. Daniel especially agrees, feeling particularly vulnerable after his recent loss of level.

At night, the campfires spread out over the plain. Each Adventuring group has created their own little camp, each scattered haphazardly, unlike the army. On cooking duty today, Daniel stirs the pot, ignoring the occasional proffered recommendation from Asin.   Rumours swirl around them, that the Orcs were sighted earlier today, that they have left, that they destroyed one, two, no eleven villages already. After an exhausting first night listening to Rumours, Daniel resolves to ignore them all, focusing on what he can control - the stew.

It was strange, being out in the city, travelling to do battle with sentient creatures he had never seen before. He knew of the Orcs from rumours and late night tales, after all, their lands bordered Brad in the West, and they conducted regular raids into nearby villages on a regular basis. Yet, his upbringing in the mountains meant he had had no direct interaction with them. Unlike humans, it seemed most of their levelling options required constant battle, forcing them into constant raids and attacks against each other and Brad itself. More than once, Brad had launched campaigns into Orc lands to destroy settlements and reduce the population, but the sprawling, untouched lands that the Orcs claimed meant that eventually the army campaign was called back and the Orcs would return. Rumours had it that Orcs gave birth in litters, their constant attacks and seemingly unending numbers resulting from their animalistic breeding patterns, unlike the more civilized and sentient races.

Daniel stirs the pot once more, tasting the stew before waving over his party members. It felt strange, to be grouped with so many others when it was just Asin and him for the longest time. Strange, but nice, even if this was temporary. His new party members were all good people, Kilroy, a joker; Maximillian, stern but kind; and Mia, quiet and competent. The quiet (and not so quiet when Kilroy was around) camaraderie was soothing, even as they all felt the tension of the upcoming battle.

Perhaps it was because they all risked their lives on a daily basis in the Dungeon that the Adventurers seemed to take it in their stride. Certainly, they were louder and more exuberant than their Army counterparts. More than once, he had caught the glowers from passing army personnel, almost as if they were angry that the Adventurers were willing to laugh. Yet, Daniel mused, what else could they do? Risking life for money was their way of life, and whether it was a Crawler which had dropped from the ceiling or an Orc who smashed their skulls in, it didn't matter how their lives ended. If you could not learn to laugh at upcoming death, you had no place being an Adventurer.

As Daniel sips on the stew and accepts praise for his cooking from all his party members but Asin, his thoughts turn to motivations. It was strange, how those in the Army, the Guard and Adventurers were so similar but so different. Each led a life of violence when a more peaceful life was an option, yet the individual motivations for each group were different - patriotism, service or adventure. Each gained strength in different ways too, training, peace or conflict and would eventually gain skills from their classes that marked them differently too. The Adventurers' inventory ability, the Guards' Truth Tell or the Brad Infantry's Shield Wall were all individual skill proficiencies that were available only to those who dedicated themselves to the lifestyle. Perhaps it was the class skills, the distinction those created that motivated an individual to go one way or the other – or perhaps it was the way experience was garnered. Certainly, the Guards in his experience were steadier, more prone to finding peaceful solutions than your average Adventurer.

It was a life that was far different from his time as a miner. Sometimes, he wondered if the others who chose a more peaceful, less dangerous life were correct – but like many of his peers, none of the other choices had felt right. No resource gathering, farming or crafting job would ever give him the chance to test himself like an Adventurer did. No guardsmen or soldier would ever have the freedom his vocation had.

Perhaps that's why he felt so much more at home among these Adventurers now than he ever had while mining, as the choices each of them had made separated them all from common society. Though, did perhaps the thrill fade away? Certainly, it seemed that old Adventurers stopped being Adventurers if Khy'ra, Liev and Tharuk were anything to go by. Perhaps Adventuring was a young man's job.

Daniel smiles slightly, accepting the bottle of spirit from Kilroy and pushes aside those thoughts as he joins them for a game of cards. Musings like this were interesting, but in the end, it made no real difference. He was an Adventurer now and soon they would fight.

"Well, I guess the easy money is over," Maximillian chuckles, eyeing the increased activity among the army personnel ahead of them. The army has been moving ahead on the road, heading closer and closer to the border with each mile across the rolling grassy plains. Perfect land for farming, with fertile soil and plentiful rainfall, if you discounted the constant slopes.

"Hmm…?" Daniel turns away from the exaggerated story told by Kilroy – there was no way three goats and a wolf did that with a farmer – when Maximillian speaks. He brushes a hand through his brown hair in absent thought, peering at the movement in the distance.

"Trouble looks like. If I'm correct, we'll get a message soon, and the wagons will be pulling to the side," Maximillian says, gesturing for them to hurry up a bit to stand next to their assigned wagon. Events fall true to his word, as word is soon sent back for the supply wagons to pull over and set-up for a potential attack in a small glen. The moment the wagons do so, the Adventuring groups spread out to stand guard while the wagon drivers and their attendants hurry to pull out any equipment needed. Ahead, the army pulls away from the road to the top of the hill, spreading out with the infantry in front and archers behind. At the top of the hill, the commanders and the Champion take their place, watching.

Daniel shifts from foot-to-foot, wanting a better view. Wanting to actually see the Orcs, but their job was simple – guard the supply train. Other Adventuring groups pull away, forming a smaller but more mobile force awaiting instructions, situated just behind the hill and to the right of the army. *Those lucky Adventurers would see actual battle,* thinks Daniel. That force would be used to help flank or reinforce the army as needed, a secondary reserve to the Army's own.

A hand drops on Daniel's shoulder, causing him to stop moving. Maximillian smiles, pointing to Daniel's back and speaking, "Might want to check that over. Don't load it yet though, we'll get a signal when things are about to start, but there's no reason not to check it now."

Daniel nods gratefully, falling to the task of checking the crossbow he carries as requested. Maximillian smiles, noting how the youngster calms down a little with something active to do. Of course, as Maximillian glances up to Daniel's original partner and thinks, some people could afford to be a bit more excited. Asin sees the glance and guesses Max's thoughts but just yawns, sharp teeth flashing in the sun as she stretches on top of the wagon they are guarding before lying back down.

Next to the nervous Daniel, Kilroy sets up with his crossbow, sticking a few bolts in the ground as does Mia. She strings her bow swiftly and with ease, testing the pull before going through a series of eye-catching, slow stretches. All around them, various other Adventurers take part in their preparation rituals, getting ready for the battle.

Time stretches on with no battle though, ticking by an hour after hour. No fight, no battle, and no sound from across the hill. The Adventurers get impatient, annoyed and then finally bored. They relax, sitting around and one group even starts a card game.

When the drums sound, everyone perks up again. Noise that was at first ignored brings everyone's attention back to where they are, the danger they are all in. Adventurers stand, and even the army that had been resting for a time straighten. The drums begin to grow in volume, accompanied by shouts and growls that travel across the hill. The roars grow louder, bugle calls of the Army finally sounding. Archers in the back row pull back and fire, sending arcs of arrows above the heads of their comrades, blows falling unseen by Daniel and the other Adventurers.

When the clash finally comes, the meaty smack of blood and bone against steel and wood, it resounds through the glen, amplified between the two hills. Screams begin soon after, cries of rage and pain intersperse between the all too regular sound of metal against metal and metal against flesh. The battle happens on the other side of the hill, for the most part, only the work of archers shooting over the hill seen, yet Daniel can imagine it.

Soon enough, the Adventurers grouped to the right are sent around the flank at a run as the Champion strides away from the command group, disappearing behind the hill in a straight line. Others from the command tent break away at intervals to meet greater threats in the Orc army directly. All this Maximillian explains to the novice Adventurer standing beside him, his eyes glued to the action that they can see.

The battle rages on for another thirty minutes then peters out as the drums change. Bugle calls bring the Adventurers back to their original position as the Champion strides back to the command post, shaking blood off his sword. A quick shake of his head negates the question asked of him while all around, soldiers and healers work to deal with the toils of combat.

Time drags on, runners moving between the supply wagon and the front to provide drink and replacement equipment. A command is given, and within the circle of wagons a series of cook fires are started. Without warning, the drums begin again, though the cooks in the centre ignore it all, working on their task.

Daniel finds his stomach rumbling, hunger risen from the constant state of excitement he has been in. He can do nothing, see nothing, just guess at what is happening, yet his excitement will not decrease, nervous energy draining and energising him at the same time.

The battle this time seems to go much the same to start with, but after ten short minutes, a human roar begins. The line at the back, at first orderly, suddenly breaks apart in the centre and then spreads outwards quickly, the army disappearing past the hill in pursuit. The Adventurers quickly break up into hunting groups, tasked with dealing with the flanks even as the commanders take leave, following along behind the army themselves.

For a time, silence reigns on the battlefield and Daniel looks to Maximillian, unsure if that was it. So much time for so little gain. Even before he can open his mouth, a low growl from Asin makes him look at her. She points, and he follows her finger, following its path across the road to where a group of Orcs reveals themselves from amidst an untouched copse of trees.

Chapter 28

There is not much time to say anything as the Orcs, realising they are spotted start off at a run to the group. Cries of alarm resound around Daniel, and he does not realise his voice has been added to the throng.

Mia and Kilroy turn themselves to face the oncoming horde, other Adventuring parties streaming up to reinforce the line from behind them. They are on the far right of the too-thin line, and Daniel can feel his mouth go dry as he sees the lumbering enemy. The Orcs are clad in a variety of clothing ranging from filthy rags to battered leather armour, though a pair of massive Orcs behind are clad in full chainmail. Outside of their clothing choices, Daniel is unable to spot differences in the screaming green, tusk-filled, hatred spewing creatures that bear down on him.

Mia begins firing first along with a few of the other competent archers, sending their arrows into the horde. A few falter, arrows catching them in shoulder, chest and leg but most other shots miss. It is only a short moment later, and another twenty meters before the crossbowmen among the group start firing, adding their bolts to the deluge. Kilroy does not even look, handing over his crossbow to Daniel who passes him his own before beginning to load Kilroy's. Daniel forces himself to stay precise, ensuring that he gets the bolt seated properly before he begins cocking it. The moment he is done, he hands the crossbow over and notices how close the Orcs are.

How did they get so close? Daniel thinks, surprised as he drops the crossbow Kilroy passed to him and grabbing his shield and mace to join the battle. The melee fighters like Maximillian have already taken off, charging the larger group to ensure they are not bowled over. However, the line is too thin, and Orcs swirl around the Adventurers, rushing the line behind them.

Having barely had time to set himself, the Orc facing Daniel almost bowls him over entirely from the initial rush. Daniel staggers back and only the sudden push from behind as Kilroy throws his shoulder into the younger man helps him keep his feet. Thankfully for Daniel, the Orc is unready for the burst of electricity that arcs through him from contact and Daniel is able to duck beneath the mistimed strike. He brings his own mace into play, smashing the Orc in the face twice before booting the creature away from him.

Above the fighting, Asin is working her throwing daggers into the rushing horde, catching Orcs in the feet and face and causing them to falter in their headlong rush. The initial rush stalled, she begins to target her throws with care, picking on Orcs that attempt to flank and gang-up on nearby Adventurers.

Mia and Kilroy, having dropped their ranged weapons have drawn a sword and a pair of knives respectively and work next to Daniel as he pushes forward, using his Shield Bash ability to create space for them to attack. In the centre of the fighting, the Adventurers have fallen into a quick circle to back each other up and avoid being surrounded entirely. Maximillian still stands, wielding his sword and dagger combination expertly, catching and turning aside blows with his dagger and striking back with the sword in quick, precise movements.

Daniel continues to push forward, instinct driving him to close to his party member and help him. A blow to his left is caught on his shield, Kilroy taking the opportunity to slip in behind the Orc's attack to drive his daggers into the Orc's chest. Daniel brings his own mace down in a crushing blow on another Orc facing Mia who is forced to abort its own attack to dodge the strike, giving Mia a moment to recover her footing. As the Orc steadies itself after the dodge, a thrown dagger drives through its throat, piercing it completely through. Distracted and choking on its own blood, Mia ends the creature's life.

A loud roar catches Daniel's attention just as he finishes engaging Double Strike, smashing the next Orc in line before him aside. Both of the massive Orc Warriors that Daniel first spotted have joined the fray in the centre, smashing aside the flimsy circle through brute force. Maximillian spins away from an attack against him, blade flicking upwards to slice tendons in the arm as he faces one Orc Warrior. The second Warrior rampages through the remains of the line.

Distracted for a brief moment, Daniel is almost struck by the Orc facing him, only a last-minute jerk of his head stopping the blow from braining him. It lands against his shoulder though, numbing his left arm for a moment. Daniel growls, ducking forwards and closing with the Orc to give himself a moment, punching the creature in the face with his mace in hand. When the Orc backs away, he backhands the creature and then shoves it to the right to allow Mia to finish the creature off.

Maximillian dances away from the large Orc Warrior, the creatures wide, inexperienced swings giving Maximillian brief breathing room as other Orcs are forced to scramble away to ensure they too are not hit. He uses the time to launch his own attacks, striking arms and legs when he can. As the Orc grows angry, it steps forward to end the fight, and that is when Maximillian steps forward in a perfect lunge, his sword glowing briefly and punching through the chainmail. The impaled Orc Warrior finishes its initial attack, though the weakened blow is easily turned aside by Maximillian's dagger.

Unfortunately, before Maximillian can retrieve his sword from the Orc Warrior's body, the other Orc Warrior returns, swinging his sword at Maximillian. It catches the Adventurer under his chest but is unable to pierce the plate breastplate the man wears. Still, the blow is strong enough to lift the Adventurer off the ground and throw him several feet away.

Kilroy roars, pushing away from the group to become a blur of flickering blades as he whirls through the last few remaining Orcs between him and his party leader. The blows leave long, bleeding gashes on all his opponents, drawing their attention to the dagger-wielding fighter in their midst. As they concentrate on him, Daniel and Mia rush them from behind, laying waste to the distracted fighters.

Behind, Asin has jumped down from her wagon and is working her way among the remaining Adventurers, killing their opponents with quick strikes of her daggers from behind before pulling them into a cohesive unit. Unknown to Daniel and his focused friends, they have pushed deep into the main group and created a flanking manoeuvre by themselves, and Asin works to finish rolling up the Orcs with the others.

Daniel finally closes in on Kilroy and Maximillian. A Shield Bash pushes one last remaining Orc off Kilroy, who is bleeding from multiple wounds already but refusing to move away from his downed party leader. Spotting a brief moment of respite, Daniel drops his knee and places a hand on Maximillian's prone body to cast Minor Healing. The casting takes precious seconds but is quicker than his Gift and less dangerous to use in such circumstances. Above him, Mia and Kilroy fight aggressively to keep the Orcs off Daniel to give him time to work.

As Daniel looks up from casting the spell, he is greeted by the sight of Mia's sword being driven aside as she mistimes her block and is overwhelmed by the sheer strength of the remaining Orc Warrior. The blow enters her left shoulder blade, shearing through muscle and bone and leaves her stunned and bleeding. Daniel surges to his feet, triggering a Shield Bash into the Orc Warriors mid-section, though it is Daniel who is sent stumbling backwards. The Orc Warrior is not deterred from his attack, swinging its sword again at Mia. Daniel throws himself in the way, bracing his shield with his other hand and staggering back. He keeps staggering as the Orc Warrior does not relent, swinging blow after blow at Daniel, never letting him set himself properly, each blow widening cracks across the shield.

The relentless attacks of the Orc are suddenly halted as a pair of throwing knives sink into its deltoids as Asin and her collected Adventurers finally arrive. Asin herself moves to flank the creature, throwing her knife with Piercing Shot to distract the creature further as Daniel charges ahead with his Double Strike.

Working together, the two Adventurers fall into the routine they have developed to deal with Ogres on the seventh floor, whittling the more powerful Orc Warrior down with each blow. Beside them, the other Adventurers work to finish mopping up the remaining Orcs, leaving the two to finish the job.

In contrast to the desperate battle only a few moments ago, the battle with the Orc Warrior now is almost too easy. Injured beforehand, and with no other distractions to bother them, the Orc Warrior is no match for the two rookie Adventurers. When the Warrior collapses from Daniel's final blow to its forehead, the two adventurers step aside to look for further danger and find none. The battle for the supplies is done.

Chapter 29

For a brief moment, Daniel relaxes, relief flooding through him that he survived the carnage. A moment later, he sheaths his mace and shield as he rushes over to Mia's body. Her wound is wide open, blood no longer pouring from it, and even as he bends down to check, he knows it is too late. Still, he tries but the soul has fled, and his Gift finds nothing to purchase upon.

Grief threatens to overwhelm him but is pushed aside as Daniel moves to do his job. Kilroy limps over, tears running down his cheeks as he stares at his friend's body. The grieving Adventurer goes to one knee, holding her as sobs rip themselves from his chest.

Only Asin sees this, for Daniel works feverishly, moving from body to body to do what he can. Other Adventurers work to triage the situation, pulling the grievously injured aside while Daniel and the other healers stabilise them. Daniel uses his Gift sparingly, only doing so twice to quickly heal and stabilise Adventurers that would otherwise expire. Those that are injured but who will survive are cared for with more traditional means, mana saved for all but the most critical.

It is only when the critical work of healing is done that Daniel is able to check the notifications that have been piling up, scanning through the various pieces of information he has received during the fight. It is only the last piece that is of particularly noteworthy.

Level Up!

Adventurer Level 5

You have gained 5 attribute points.

When the first army division returns and no other attacks come, the healers turn back to their patients, using their mana to speed up the healing process. All efforts are taken to conserve some mana for potential additional life-threatening injuries, but with the immediate danger over, the healers have wider leeway to use their spells.

Maximillian is among those critically injured but stable, ribs shattered but the internal bleeding halted by Daniel's quick fix. Daniel himself works on his wounds, using his healing skills to patch the unconscious party leader together. Kilroy has been pulled away by now from Mia's body, and he sits next to Maximillian, clutching the departed Adventurer's bow as he watches Daniel work.

Asin works with the quartermasters while Daniel heals, first stripping the Orcs of their valuables and then categorising it all. A part of the Catkin is disappointed that the Army will be taking it all, but she accepts it without complaint. This is neither the time nor place to discuss the terms of their hiring after all. In either case, it is a better task than the distasteful one of burying the Orcs and her peers.

It is in the evening that the Champion finally reappears with the rest of the Army. Tents staked and perimeters secure, the party begins. Losses were more than acceptable; the Army once mobilised had managed to destroy the grunt Orcs with ease. Only once was there true danger when the Orc War Chief himself had joined the battle, but the Champion had met him in combat himself. The tale of the Unbreakable defence of the Champion's Gift and the ensuing fight travelled the tents with speed, growing with each telling.

Those guarding the supplies have their own tale to tell, and while the celebration is at first muted, it soon picks up. The Adventurers understand loss, they understand death, and while this was not the way they expected their friends to go, it was still part of their job. Grieving could happen, would happen, later – for now, it was time to celebrate the fact that they were alive.

In their own camp, Daniel and Asin find themselves in a cook-off much to the delight of surrounding camps. The two cooks have beer pressed into their hands while they work to feed the hungry crowds, laughter and good-natured ribbing passing between them. Or as much ribbing as Asin ever offers.

In the morning, the camp breaks up, and the Army begins its long journey home. A select few of the Adventurer parties do not go back, instead moving to the border to ensure that the Orcs are gone. Daniel and his group are not chosen, their group too few and new to take part in such an endeavour. Daniel is relieved – as instructive as this quest has been, he is happy to return home.

The journey back to the city is quiet and relaxed, even the Army personnel seeming to loosen up after the battle. Daniel spends his time alternating between the healers' wagons and walking alongside Asin to start learning Catkin.

At the city gates, Daniel never makes it all the way to the Adventurer's Guild to file his completed Quest. Instead, he is dragged away firmly by Khy'ra to celebrate his safe return. After the throes of passion, she expertly drags the tale out of him, letting him work through his emotions. Asin completes the Quest for both of them, giving Liev a quick hug before departing to see her family. In their own way, the Beastkin debrief her, making her tell the tale of the battle again and again to different groups. It is only the next morning that Daniel manages to make it to the Adventurer's Guild, lighter of step with a portion of his grief eased.

"Daniel, good. I have something for you," Liev smiles slightly, waving him over.

"Morning, Liev. Asin let me know." He nods to his friend, looking around the relatively quiet Adventuring Guild. It seems most of the others who went with the army are taking a day off.

"Come with me," Liev beckons and brings Daniel to a private room. There, he pulls a small packet out of his jacket pocket, offering it to Daniel. When opened, it contains a simple iron ring with a cut blue-purplish stone. Yet, when Daniel picks it up, he gets a notification:

Moonstone Ring of Experience

On sleeping, wearer re-experiences events occurring within 24 hours, learning new lessons.

Effect: +2% experience and skill gain over previous 24 hours

"This…" Daniel's jaw drops. He has heard of enchanted items like this before of course, stories told by Adventurer to Adventurer, their status raised to almost mythic proportions. Enchanted items like these were passed on as heirlooms in Adventuring families, guarded as some of the most precious items they could acquire. It was said the Crown itself was made of Moonstone, granting the wearer a 10% boost. To hold a ring like this in his hand exceeds his expectation.

"It's yours. I would caution about speaking about it to anyone else. Khy'ra, of course, knows as she negotiated it as your payment for the healing of the Champion," Liev says. He reaches out, closing Daniel's hand over the ring.

Daniel fights his feelings, truly conflicted. His first, instinctive reaction is to refuse the gift. It is too much, way too much. Yet, a more honest part of him realises how powerful and appropriate a gift it is – letting him gain strength and experience even as he loses it while using his own Gift. It could never truly make up the ground lost or the memories forsook, but it would help.

"Thank you." Head bowed, Daniel opens his hand and slides the ring on.

"No need. I'm just the messenger." Liev smiles, patting the young adventurer on the shoulder and guiding him out.

Outside, Asin waits patiently with a slip in her hand. She glances at Daniel and live and sees the new ring but ignores its presence, instead proffering the quest slip to Daniel. Daniel smiles at his friend, taking the slip and reading it over before raising an eyebrow. "Shadow Cat, again?"

Asin nods firmly, caressing her knives. Their one failed quest. For a moment, Daniel hesitates then he smiles, acceding to her request and walking to the counter. "Back to work it is then."

###

Book 2

An Adventurer's Heart

Chapter 1

As the sun begins to set, a pair of Adventurers approach the Northern city gates of Karlak. The small dungeon town is bisected by a river, overlooked by rolling hills, and surrounded by wooden walls. The town radiates outwards from its chief income source, a Beginner Dungeon with buildings closest to the Dungeon and the town center made of stone, and those further away with cheaper materials such as wood and clay. As the pair near the walls, the Guards relax as the pair are well known, and their presence barely missed. After all, these two Adventurers had left only two days ago.

The taller of the pair is only five-foot-eight, a friendly smile gracing his face as he nods to the guards. The friendly Adventurer is broad and stocky, his muscular frame currently burdened by a large bag slung over his shoulder. The second of the two is a shorter Catkin female, black fur and bestial, cat features on a slim build. She is dressed in a jerkin and shirt, with a dirty, once dark-blue coat trailing behind her. A brace of throwing daggers lie across her torso, another larger pair rest on her hips as she glides alongside her partner.

"Matthew, Jason!" the human Adventurer calls out, waving in greeting as he shifts the bag behind him again.

"Daniel, Asin. A successful trip I take it?" The two guards grin, glancing at the bag and the roll of dark fur that lies strapped to the top of it.

"Yes!" Daniel answers them, pride radiating in his voice.

"Well, best get in. We'll be closing the gates soon." The two guards beckon the Adventurers into the town, and Daniel nods in thanks. Asin chuffs a greeting as well, the guards flashing a quick, narrowed eye once-over at the Beastkin before stepping aside.

When the pair is a distance away, Asin moves closer to her friend, grating out in a low purr, "They like you. The guards."

Daniel nods, smiling slightly as he rubs his nose as it attempts to get used to the unwashed, rotting stink of the city, "Yeah. They're a decent lot mostly."

Asin chuffs again, shaking her head at Daniel but failing to contradict him directly. His experience and hers differed greatly as the Beastkin were an unwanted, barely tolerated minority in Brad still. If she had arrived alone, Asin knew she'd have to pay the toll for coming in and would have been hassled for leaving, even though she was a registered Adventurer like him. Daniel, however, had managed to build a good reputation in the town – his work in the Clinic as a free healer and his time spent socializing with the guards stood him in good stead. His presence shielded her and those with him, even if he himself never realized it.

The pair head deeper into the town, bypassing alleys that would take them into the various shopping districts and head directly to the Adventurer's Guild. The Guild is one of the few buildings in town able to afford the mana stones required to light the building all night long and does so, staying open all hours of the day and night. They could afford this as the Guild was the exclusive purchaser of mana stones from the Adventurers who ventured into the Dungeon, their monopoly guaranteed by Kingdom law. It is also at the Guild that the two expect to turn in their successful quest.

It is no surprise to either of the Adventurers to find that Liev, the red-haired senior Guild attendant, is still on duty. He rarely leaves the building and is often seen working the busy shifts late into the night when Adventurers returned from their Dungeon exploration. When the pair step into the building, Liev smiles as he spots them, straightening up for a moment from his usual slouched posture before the usual impassive demeanor returns.

"Asin, Daniel. Back already?" he says to them when the duo finally reach his window.

"Yes!" Daniel unslings his bag and unties the skin, dropping it on the counter as proof of their successful hunt.

A brief check is all that Liev requires to confirm the kill, and then he hands over their reward, a staggering 75 silver, and their deposit. A single silver could let a day laborer who skimped eat for a year, so the sum they have just earned still makes both Asin and Daniel grin. After all, it has only been a bare nine months since they first started Adventuring. The enormous sum for the Quest was due to the continued failures by other Adventurers to complete the quest. As was custom, the city raised the bounty after each failure, using a portion of the failed Adventurers lost deposit to pay for the increase.

A brief moment later and both Adventurers receive a notification, the glowing black lines floating in their sight before disappearing.

Quest Complete!
+5,000 XP

The pair of Adventurers quickly take their piles of coin, thanking Liev before exiting to run their next errand. Asin leads Daniel to a butcher shop, having organized the additional trade to supplement their income. Shadow Cat meat was a rare treat and would be highly sought after by certain clientele, and the butcher had agreed to pay very well. Once again, Asin chuffs in pleasure at the thought of the coin they are about to earn and the fact that her party member had done most of the hard work carrying the meat back to town. In truth, while the work had been hard, Daniel knew the additional funds would help in paying off their accumulated debts.

Absently, Asin strokes the matching enchanted bracers on her arms. While they had greatly aided the pair in their battles, enchanted weaponry was extremely expensive and had driven both of them deeply into debt. Even now, with their recent windfall, they would have been unable to pay for the bracers if Tharuk, the enchanter, had not generously agreed to allow them to pay what they could, when they could. For Asin though, owing anyone, especially a Dwarf, was not something that sat well with her.

Meat deposited and payment received, the two Adventurers part ways. Asin to meet her family and Daniel to head to the Spinning Top, the inn where he resides. At the inn, Daniel greets Elise the innkeeper and owner before asking for food to be brought to his room, taking the time to wash himself down in the provided washbasin. After dinner, exhausted from a hard day's work, Daniel lies back on the clean sheets and falls asleep, completely forgetting about the dinner he had ordered.

As he sleeps, his enchanted ring of experience begins to draw forth the stored memories from its stone, replaying them through his mind and body in flashes. It is a strange experience as the memories and experiences that flow through his mind are always somewhat scattered.

In the morning, Asin is cooking breakfast, spreading herbs on the omelet and working the pan with little flicks of her hand. Mushrooms, field onions and more.

"Ugh, no mushrooms!" Daniel complains and Asin sniffs, ignoring his constant complaints about the delectable fungus. "I'll cook mine!"

Daniel takes over when Asin is done. Borrowing the pan, he cracks the eggs with professional ease. Instead of borrowing from her herbs though, he pulls his own out from his pack, separating each pouch and adding in the herbs with practiced flicks. Asin sniffs as she watches, though an eyebrow arches at his last addition.

"Papricha," Asin grates out.

"Yes, paprika. Love it," Daniel smirks and finishes up, tossing the omelet onto his plate and pulling out some bread to toast as well. "Want some?"

Asin pauses, nose wrinkling and whiskers trembling in the still air before she bobs her head, tail lazily waving behind her.

The Shadow Cat is crouched above Daniel, snarling at the downed Adventurer. He groans, pushing against the monster but it's already jumping away as Daniel tries to lever the monster off him, blood pooling on the ground from the cat's attack. A knife catches the Shadow Cat as it jumps away, Asin's Piercing Shot drilling into the creature's body, the knife twisting as it rotates in. Attached to the knife is a long iron chain, the end of which is wrapped around Asin's torso.

The creature's jump pulls the chain taut, jerking it to a stop and forcing the monster to fall with an ungainly crash. Asin, who is lighter, is pulled off her feet and falls on her behind. The snarls of pain and dismay from the pair of cats sound eerily similar to Daniel as he struggles to his feet.

Standing, Daniel jumps at the monster, slamming the mace down with his full strength onto the cat's prone form. He clips the creature's back leg, bruising and tearing muscle as the cat attempts to stand again. Asin rolls over, gripping the chain and yanking hard to throw the cat off balance and keeping it out of the shadows.

Daniel swings again, the blow catching the cat on its forehead, dazing the creature and then he kicks it away from the nearest shadows to the middle of the path they walk on. As he does, the knife finally dislodges, and Asin stumbles from the sudden release. She catches herself quickly enough to pull another knife to throw at the cat, even as the monster gets back onto its feet in another attempt to flee.

Walking back to the city, back bowed as he carries the quartered meat. Daniel asks, "Where did you learn to skin and butcher like that?"

"Father. Traditional," Asin chuffs, waving a hand around and then goes back to cleaning her claws, working to remove the accumulated blood and filth.

"Ah," Daniel nods slightly, a wry twist of the lips crossing his face. He never knew his father, a casualty of the mines a few years after he was born. His mother had died in childbirth, leaving him to grow up with his grandfather. Strange how that still stung, even after all these years.

Morning. The bells wake Daniel up and he pulls himself from the covers, drenched in sweat once again. He sighs, shaking his head at the memories and unpleasant experiences he has gone through. Sometimes, it seemed that the minor gains in experience he received from the stones were not worth the hassle.

Chapter 2

"Ogres, ogres, ogres. Come out!" Daniel calls mockingly, swinging his mace around as he walks around the massive cavern that makes up the entrance to the seventh floor of the Dungeon in Karlak. Glow stones in the ceiling were so bright that lush grass and small trees grew in the cavern, a massive change from the cramped, cave-like floors above.

Asin's tail waves lazily in amusement, loping alongside Daniel as they search. His noisy entrance brings not one but two Ogres to them, and she shoots an annoyed glare at her companion. The creatures are on the smaller side, barely twelve feet tall, clad in their traditional loincloth and rags and each carries a crude wooden club in hand. Small or not, Asin would have preferred to start the day a little lighter. On spotting the intruders, the Ogres roar, charging the pair.

Bounding ahead, Asin slides a pair of throwing knives from her bandolier, targeting the lead Ogre's right eye with one knife. It roars, raising a hand to block the knife, and is now unable to see the follow-up throw charged with Piercing Shot slice through the air into its chest and lung. Angered at being tricked, and in pain, the Ogre dashes forward to smite the smaller Adventurer, but Asin skips back with ease. As she does, she throws another pair of knives underhanded, the Ogre is so close this time that lightning from Asin's charged aura also strikes the monster.

By her side, Daniel rushes Asin's opponent, using his shield to ram the monster and forcing it back further still with a Shield Bash. The Ogre stumbles, catching its balance and Daniel lashes out once quickly at its knee, cracking his mace against it before stepping back so as not to be surrounded as the second Ogre finally arrives.

As the uninjured Ogre attacks Daniel, he backpedals to the side and puts the other Ogre in the way, forcing his second opponent to pull back on its attack. Staying close behind Daniel, Asin does the same, pelting the first Ogre with a knife each time it tries to move its hand away from its face. Asin moves smoothly, pulling extra knives from her satchel and passing it to her primary hand when she can. Unable to properly see what it is doing, it swings its club wildly, allowing Daniel to duck beneath and attack its knee, smashing again and again into the bruised limb until it cracks and gives way.

Once the first Ogre is immobilized, the two Adventurers turn their attention to the second Ogre. Their time with the Army has given them new ideas, new concepts to play with, and they put these ideas to work immediately. Instead of holding back and providing fire support, Asin rushes forward to join the fight with the Ogre directly. The second Ogre is forced to deal with two opponents, one on on either side, Daniel taking the side with the club and shedding any attacks the creature swings while Asin slices into its body with her long knives, dodging and cutting at the monster's flailing fist whenever it comes close.

As the Ogre swings an overhand blow, Daniel steps to the side swiftly and lashes out twice at the exposed arm, cracking the thumb bone that holds the club and forcing the Ogre to release it. Even as it deals with that pain, Asin ducks in and plunges her knives into its liver, dropping the monster to its knees before it collapses for the final time. Without pause, the Adventurers move towards the second Ogre whose attempt at crawling to them has been too slow. Dispatching it is done swiftly, Daniel shattering an elbow to allow Asin to plunge her knife into the back of its head. As the creature finally dies, it breaks apart in motes of blue light, leaving behind the mana crystal it was made from.

Asin lets out a little meow of happiness, dancing forwards to collect and verify the crystals. The monsters were created from mana by the goddess Erlis in Dungeons to remove the taint her nemesis Ba'al continually introduces into the mana flows of the world. It is the job of Adventurers to travel into Dungeons, defeating the monsters to help purge the taint and, of course, earn a living selling the mana crystals to the Guild. These mana crystals are then used for a wide variety of purposes, such as providing lighting sources, magical ingredients for powerful spells and even fertilizer for farms.

"Just three more floors to go, Asin," Daniel grins, rotating the mace around his hand in idle thought as they make their way to the next cavern. "Then we'll be done here."

Asin nods, nimbly skipping along in front of her companion and scanning the ground for potential traps. As they near the exit, she throws a hand up, and Daniel stops, waiting as she stares at the ground further. After a moment, she digs out her knife, moving to lightly score the earth which gives way with ease, revealing a crude pit trap covered with sod and grass. Standing and eyeing the trap, she leads Daniel around it, neither bothering to set the trap off. The dungeon would recreate it soon enough if they did.

"Dungeon Boss, hard," Asin points out, and Daniel grimaces, nodding in agreement. "New skills."

"True. We'll need more skills for sure. Still, we're learning to fight together quite well," Daniel points out as he waits for her to clear the passageway.

Asin just chuffs in agreement, nimbly moving along the smaller passageway that connects to the next cavern. They certainly seem to have learned to handle two Ogres quite well. Perhaps their time with the Army, listening to conversations and observing the fighting, had not been a total waste.

"Evening, Asin, Daniel. Seventh floor?" Liev asks, sorting through the mana stones with practiced ease and drawing his conclusion from their quality and quantity. Asin nods, chuffing in agreement, eyes tracking the motion of his hands with deep intensity. "You really should get better armor if you are working that floor you know, both of you."

"I wish!" Daniel mutters shaking his head. "I still owe Tharuk another gold for the bracers, and then I've had to save up for the armor itself!"

"Mmm… and you buy from Maxwell, right?" Liev asks, and Daniel nods. "And you, Asin?"

Asin shrugs, waggling her hands sideways a bit, black fur licked clean from their romp.

"Ah, no loyalty. Not surprising I guess, most armorers don't really build for Catkin." Liev finishes his calculations and pushes the document forward to show them how much they earned today. Daniel reads the document over, announcing the total for Asin who nods in agreement. They quickly split the earnings, sliding the coins into their pouches as Liev smiles slightly. "Well, I'd check the Quest Board then. I believe Maxwell posted a job there recently."

"Thanks, Liev!" Hurrying over, Daniel and Asin scan the board before finally finding the one Liev spoke of.

Quest: An Armorer's Masterpiece

This is a multi-stage quest that will require a flexible and dedicated team to finish. Interested parties should speak with Maxwell the Armorer directly.

Rewards: 1 full set of iron armor upon completion of the Quest chain.

"Ooooh…" Daniel stares, salivating at the thought of a full set of iron armor. The cost of his Leather Armor was staggering, especially for one who until recently was just a Miner. The idea of a quest chain that would gain him a full set made him crack a wide smile. Then he stops, realizing it is only a single set. He looks over to Asin, who looks at it and makes a face too.

"Only one," Asin growls, scratching at her ear.

"Yeah, I guess this won't work," Daniel sighs, shaking his head. No wonder other groups hadn't jumped on it yet. Working out who got the set would be troublesome especially since most groups were larger than their pair.

"Split. Me three-quarters," Asin points to herself and then points to the quest.

"What? No, that won't work. We aren't even the same size!" Daniel protests and her tail whips around in annoyance.

"No. Dungeon earnings. Three-quarters." Asin points to herself again, hoping he gets it.

"Oh…" Daniel nods slowly, then realizes something. "For how long?"

"Paid off. Then half." Asin shrugs and Daniel nods, doing the math in his head. At their current earnings, that would be at least another half-year, if not year. Dungeon delving on the seventh floor was good money, but not that good. Though perhaps if they went deeper, they might earn more too.

Having finished his calculations, Daniel nods and pulls down the quest marker, flashing Asin a grateful smile. He walks over to Liev quickly, paying the refundable deposit that is required for the quest. Since it is a chain quest, the Guild have made it a refundable deposit so that Adventurers can back out of the quest once they receive full details from Maxwell. Thanking Liev, the two Adventurers make plans to visit Maxwell's shop the next morning when it opens. That done, Asin heads into the Beastkin's quarter, loping off at a steady pace while Daniel moves to visit the Clinic.

The Clinic, as it is known in Karlak, is in a poorer quarter of the city near the walls. Made of wood and clay, the Clinic spans two whole buildings with only a few rooms for outpatient treatment, with most of the other rooms filled with patients who require on-going care. A free institution run by Khy'ra and other volunteers, the building is always crowded with individuals who needed healing. After all, good medical care is both difficult to find and expensive, especially healing spells.

As Daniel enters, the townsfolk within wave, call out and nod in greeting to the young Adventurer. He smiles at them all, mentally checking his own Mana pool before he heads deeper, stopping only long enough to announce his presence to Khy'ra with a kiss and hug before he enters his room. It only takes a brief moment before he is joined by his first patient in the room who proceeds to ramble on even around his nasty cough.

Hours later, the Clinic doors are finally closed, and outpatients are forced to leave until the next day. Daniel groans, shaking his head as his Mana is entirely drained leaving him with a slight headache and tired muscles. Arms wrap around him, the comforting smell of his girlfriend tickling his nostrils. For a moment, Daniel wonders how even in the midst of a city, the buxom, blonde elf could smell of trees and wet earth, before he just revels in the hug. She squeezes him again, and then he turns around, seeking her lips.

"Hello there." Khy'ra laughs as she breaks away from the kiss, still holding on to him.

"Hello." He kisses her again hungrily, picking her up and depositing her on the wooden slab they use for an inspection bed.

"Ah, we're doing that, now are we?" she teases, not stopping him as his hands wander to the back of her dress.

"Yes!" he growls, and the older elf laughs again, helping him take it off. Young human males were always so energetic!

"Maxwell." Daniel greets the burly smith as he comes out from the back of his forge, wiping sweat from his forehead.

"Daniel. Asin." Maxwell nods in greeting, eyes automatically dropping to their weapons as he assesses them. "More repairs?"

"Actually, no. We're here about the quest." Daniel steps forward, proffering the sheet to show that they have been officially assigned the quest.

"Oh!" Maxwell deflates a little, eyeing the two of them. "Well, I guess…"

Asin's eyes narrow at the less than enthusiastic response and even Daniel seems a bit taken back. Seeing their reaction, Maxwell hastens to add, "It's nothing against you two. It's just, well, most people have turned me down after hearing the details."

"Well, you might as well tell us," Daniel points out, and Maxwell nods, though he pauses first to get some more water to wet his throat. It is only after he comes back with his own glass that he remembers to offer some to his guests who both hastily decline, impatient to hear about the quest.

"Right then. There are multiple parts to this quest, and once you start, I expect you to finish. I'll build your armor as we finish each portion though I won't make final adjustments until the end. That way, if you decide to quit, I can always sell it later on. And I'm not splitting the making of it – it gets made for only one person!" warns Maxwell and both Adventurers nod in agreement. When they decline to speak further, Maxwell huffs and continues. "Right, there are three parts to this, and you'll be traveling for at least two parts. It'll take you away from the Dungeon for at least three months."

Maxwell then stops, just waiting for the Adventurers to decline. Instead, the pair frown in unison before Daniel speaks up, "Ummm… Maybe you can explain what it is we'll be doing a bit more?"

"I am ready to work on my Masterpiece to get my Master's designation." Maxwell unconsciously reaches out and touches the silver chain behind his tunic. "However, I need specific materials for what I have in mind and most of it isn't available in this town. The things that I need are expensive, and none of the sellers are willing to guarantee my delivery. That's where you come in.

"The first part is getting the materials here. I've already made the purchases, but they're all waiting in Silverstone for pickup. Your job is to travel there and then safeguard my purchases on the next merchant caravan that comes back to Karlak," Maxwell continues.

"After that, I need you to bring a half-dozen grade B Type III mana stones. I need to power the forge for three days straight, and anything weaker than a grade

B will not give us enough heat. If you can't get Type III, smaller Grade B stones will do, but you'll need to get more of them," Maxwell points out, eyeing the two. The last he'd heard, these two were only on the seventh floor which didn't give out grade III stones, even from the chest.

"Lastly, I need you to bring me three intact sacs of venom from the Querk Spiders that live in the Pearly Forests. Those need to be done last because the venom only lasts for a week and it'll take you at least two days to get back here. So, you still interested?"

Daniel and Asin look at one another and then Daniel asks hesitatingly, "So, Silverstone is the biggest trip, right? It's nearly three weeks journey from here. Can we work as guards or something on the way there? There's no time sensitivity to that portion, right?"

Maxwell harrumphs for a moment then shrugs, "No. I figured you Adventurers would time your journey there with one of the caravans. I don't care how you get there, but when you come back, your first and most important role is to keep my goods safe."

Daniel looks to Asin who meets his gaze, inclining her head slightly. Daniel smiles and turns to Max, saying, "We accept then."

Maxwell grins and offers his hand, "Really? You sure?"

Daniel nods and shakes the smith's hand, smiling. "We're sure. We'll head back to the Guild to let them know immediately and then work out the schedule of when we can get there and come back. The stones might take a while, but we can do it."

Asin lets out a low purr in agreement as the two leave the smiling Armorer behind. This will be interesting – Asin has never traveled to another city before, so the journey in itself will be a new experience. Traveling as guards will be boring if it is similar to their time in the Army, but she can accept that.

At the Adventurer's Guild, Daniel and Asin move over to the closest free attendant, quickly confirming their acceptance of the quest and the timetable for upcoming caravans traveling to Silverstone.

"Look, Asin; there's a caravan heading out in three days. They are even hiring, so we should be able to get hired and paid for the trip. Unfortunately, we might have to wait a little bit for the next trip back – looks like there's one that leaves a week before we're scheduled to arrive and not another one for at least another three weeks after that. We'll probably be gone then for…" Daniel frowns, trying to do the arithmetic in his head.

"Two months," chuffs Asin smirking.

"Right, two months. Well, not as bad as the three he mentioned, but it'll be a while. I wonder if we can get added as supplementary guards or something on the trip back…" Daniel frowns, scratching his chin. Three weeks of not being paid were viable for sure, but it would not be pleasant. Asin just shrugs, tapping the first schedule and pointing to the attendant. "Right, right. Let's get signed on first."

Once that is done, Daniel looks to Asin who points to the Dungeon. "Best we get working then. I've got a lot of debt to pay off!"

Asin lets out a low purr of humor, nodding aggressively and waving him on. Perhaps they could even locate the chest today – though they weren't entirely certain it made sense to try for it. Still, they could at least check out the danger.

☐

Chapter 3

"Ready?" Daniel enquires, smiling slightly at Asin who nods back. Daniel turns back to Khy'ra who has stayed the night, pulling her close to give her one last kiss before she laughs, pushing him away. He would miss her.

"Daniel!" Elise calls out as the pair begin to walk out of the inn, and he turns, accepting the basket of food from the innkeeper gratefully. "You come back, okay? Both of you."

"It's just an escort quest, Elise!" Daniel says exasperatedly, shaking his head.

Khy'ra nods as well adding, "It's only two months. It'll be over in moments, just you wait."

As the two Adventurers head away, Elise mutters to her friend, "Not all of us live for hundreds of years, you know."

The caravan is pulled up in the merchant's quarter, a baker's dozen of wagons and a pair of well-appointed carriages arrayed before them. Waggoneers move back and forth, checking the load and their wagons, making last minute adjustments as they get ready for the long road ahead under the watchful eye of the permanent caravan guards. A smaller group of poorer travelers gather at the tail-end of the caravan on mules and horses and in a few cases, on foot. Those travelers have paid a small sum to come along with the caravan, sheltering in the additional protection offered by traveling in groups. However, the protection is minimal as the caravan guards are tasked with protecting the goods, not the people in the train. Still, it ensures that most wild animals will not bother them, and for those poor and desperate enough, the willing paid for the privilege of joining the caravan.

Walking together, Asin and Daniel weave forwards pass grumpy waggoneers and foot passengers in thread-bare clothing. As they arrive at the front of the caravan, they spot a small group of other Adventurers who await the pleasure of the caravan master.

The other four Adventurers are all humans dressed in a mixture of plate and leather armor except for the Priest in his blue cassock. Daniel makes a note of him, always happy to see another potential healer in a group. Asin in turn surveys the melee fighters, nose wrinkling as they near. Obviously, this group had spent insufficient time at the bath houses lately.

Finally, the caravan master stumps up to them. A florid-faced, blond-haired and overweight middle-aged man, he huffs and breathes deeply when he sees the group, "Karlak. I hate Karlak Adventurers. Not a single damn archer amongst you lot."

Daniel opens his mouth to protest then shuts it with a snap. The man had a point, and considering how truly awful a shot Daniel was with the crossbow, he felt it was better to stay silent.

"Right then. You lot get to ride with my waggoneers. Keep an eye out for monsters and bandits, fight them off as necessary. You get paid a daily wage for the time you spend with us, but only if you finish the journey. You get paid nothing if you leave before your appointed location.

"Food is included, but you should have your own bedroll and tent. Your task is to guard the wagons, my goods and my people in that order. The passengers in those carriages," the caravan master waves his hand to the two carriages, "are considered goods, so you guard them with your lives. You keep your hands to yourselves otherwise.

"Any questions? Then ask my lead waggoneer, Chip." A last gesture points to a grayed out, wizened man who sits on the front wagon, his face shaded by a wide-brimmed gray hat that looks as old and beaten as he is. "Don't speak with me again unless there's an attack."

His speech done, the caravan master stomps off, leaving the group somewhat surprised. After a moment, Daniel and Asin shrug and head over to Chip followed closely by the other group. Before they can even get to the old wagon leader, another waggoneer waves them over.

"Right, you two can ride with me. I'm third-in-line, and you can just add your bags to my wagon." A hand is stuck out with a wide smile, first offered to Asin and then Daniel. "I'm Gabriel, and I must say, I like the looks of you two."

"Uhh… Thanks. I'm Daniel, that's Asin," Daniel shakes the hand, glancing at the wagon and then to Chip who just offers a slight nod. Gabriel's vehicle was a covered wagon, and after a moment's more consideration, Daniel shrugs and tosses his bag inside and helps Asin get hers in. Asin then proceeds to crawl into the wagon itself, propping her foot up on a nearby chest and nodding to Daniel who gets on the front seat.

"So, what did you like?" Daniel enquires once Gabriel finishes fussing and gets on next to him.

"You're a small group. That's always good. Big groups, they get by because there's a lot of them. A small group like you, you're either very new or good," Gabriel explains and then nods to Daniel's arms. "And I ain't seen many newbie Adventurers with enchanted bracers."

"I guess you meet a lot of Adventurers in this job," Daniel says, mildly impressed at how quickly Gabriel has assessed the pair. As they inch through the streets of Karlak, Daniel lets his gaze wander over the familiar streets.

"Sure, lots. All the same though, you guys. No offense meant, but we do the circuit - the capital to the Gray Mountains to Silverstone and back to Warmount," Gabriel says, smiling. "After a while, you guys blend together. I can even tell you where that other group is going."

"Oh?" Daniel raises an eyebrow.

"Peel. It's about a week and a half and our first major stop. They've got a dungeon of their own, Beginner one like Karlak but smaller. It's actually got tougher monsters though, so most Adventurers from Karlak go there after they're done here. Good training grounds if you aren't entirely sure you want to try out a Journeyman's Dungeon yet."

Nodding in understanding, Daniel files the information away, watching as they slowly trundle along.

"Not that I mind your friend lounging back there, but once we're out of town the caravan master will want her out," Gabriel adds, and Daniel nods, turning to look back to Asin. She just gives him a nod, her sensitive hearing having picked up the words of caution.

"You know, that group reminds me of this other group we once picked up in Karlak. Well, they didn't have a Priest that group, just another fighter. The thing I remember about that fighter was his green leather armor - green! Why…" Gabriel begins, obviously relishing the chance to tell a story to a new audience.

Daniel nods along, curious to hear what Gabriel had to say. Certainly, the waggoneer had to have a different perspective than the Adventurers themselves.

It takes the caravan nearly half the day to get out of town, winding their way through crowded streets and then having each wagon inspected and sent on its way by the guards. During this time, Gabriel never stops expounding on story after story, only pausing long enough to swig water from his waterskin. Next to him, Daniel listens politely, pulling gently at his leather armor as the midday heat begins to get to him.

"Never understood why you Adventurers insist on wearing those things. Why I had this one Adventurer who would put on a full set of plate mail every morning…" Gabriel begins, and Daniel finally tunes him out, swigging at his waterskin as he stares at the rolling hills that surround the town of Karlak.

Strange to think that only nine months ago he had come to town down these roads himself on another wagon to start his journey as an Adventurer.

He eyes the rolling hills, his stomach rumbling and looks up, noting how the sun has passed the zenith. "Are we not stopping for lunch?"

"Not a chance. Quidley hates wasting time, and we're behind schedule already getting out of town. We'll be traveling all through the day now to get to his favorite spot to camp at. As it stands, we'll probably arrive late in the day. Though, it does remind me of the time when we left Pilak…" Gabriel says, launching into another story.

"You know something, Gabriel? I think Asin should take the seat for a bit. I'm going to walk if you don't mind," Daniel interrupts the man, standing up. "Not used to these seats."

"No, it's good. I'll finish this one later." Gabriel smiles, watching Daniel hop down and dragging Asin forward reluctantly. On his feet, he walks alongside the wagon, letting his eyes roam over the countryside. This was going to be a long trip.

Talkative as Gabriel was, he was correct, and it was late in the evening when they finally reach their evening resting spot. Daniel eyes the campground and silently approves. It had very little to distinguish it from any other spot to those unused to travel, but it had a few good points. There was a small stream within a short distance that would provide the camp with easy access to water, the area around the campsite was relatively flat which meant setting up tents would be easy and watching for threats even easier. With only a small stand of trees blocking the view a short distance away, it would be hard to lay a trap here or sneak up on the caravan.

Even though this is the case, it does not stop Chip from directing the various wagons into a loose encirclement around the camp. As soon as the wagons are situated to the old waggoneer's satisfaction, the other waggoneers start unhitching horses and leading them gently to the stream. Daniel watches for a moment with Asin, unsure of what they should do. The pair are not the only lost souls, and they and the other guests are quickly chivvied into action by Chip who directs them on where to sleep and the cook fire that is to be theirs.

"Hi there, I'm Daniel, and this is Asin." Daniel offers his hand to the other four Adventurers when they all convene at the fire which Asin is working on getting started with practiced ease. "We were wondering how we'd be handling the camp chores? Both Asin and I are decent cooks, so we were thinking we could handle that?"

"I'm Marco, that's Delia, Dale, and Palmer," the tallest of the group who has added a dagger to his sword and shield style says, taking and shaking Daniel's hand. "And we'll take you up on that offer. Can you guys deal with lunch too?"

Asin nods firmly, the fire is started so she saunters away to talk to Chip about where to get their portion of the evening meal. Daniel chuckles, watching his friend move and notes the interested look Dale sends to Asin. "Asin doesn't talk much. Though I think that's my cue to get the water."

"Right, we'll get on the latrine then," Marco says and waves his friends away. Split off, the camp chores that they have to take care of are completed quickly with Chip coming by to assign watches for the group.

As Asin warms the water and pulls out a pan to cook the slices of meat they have drawn from stores and warm up their bread, Daniel spots Palmer standing to the side surrounded by various waggoneers and working his healing magic on their assorted ailments. As Daniel watches, coin passes hands, and he turns away, his lips twisting wryly. For a moment Daniel considers helping out, but he dismisses the thought as being too petty. Just because the Priest was willing to take money did not mean that his actions were not justified. Instead he stood up to wander the perimeter.

To the south where they came from, he finds the grouping of poorer travelers getting ready to rest. He watches them for a short time, noticing how some struggle with the simplest of camp duties like setting up tents or starting a fire and he mentally sighs at the city folk. As one particularly burly and well-dressed man attempts to add a densely leafed, newly cut branch to a fire, he hurries over to help.

It is only when Delia comes over, mentioning that dinner is ready, that Daniel realizes how long he has been helping out. A few last words of advice quickly become another fifteen minutes, and by the time he gets back, his food is cold. As Daniel sits with his cold food, he makes a mental note though to make a quick trip back when he is done - there were a few injuries and illnesses among that group that could benefit from a quick healing spell. After all, Daniel justifies to himself, he had no use for his mana tonight. It had nothing to do with a particularly pretty young lady smiling at him.

☐

Chapter 4

For a week and a half, the duo travel with the caravan, visiting a couple of villages along the way. They rarely stop longer than an hour or two at these villages, long enough for various waggoneers to buy and sell their goods before moving on, draining the villagers dry of coin. These villages are the lucky ones - located on main thoroughfares they receive relatively regular visits from caravans of wagons which can provide much needed raw materials and goods. Other villages further out or on less well-traveled paths have to make do with the occasional trader. For those villagers who cannot wait, a trip to the lucky thoroughfare villages will be required to meet the caravans on their scheduled runs. It is why Quidley has pushed the caravan each day, doing his best to keep to his posted timetable. After all, a prompt caravan sees the most customers.

Peel is a small town, smaller even than Karlak, though it has stone walls - or parts of one at least. The wall was built such that the bottom half was made of stone, wooden posts sandwiched between the stone exterior. As funds and materials became available, the next level of stone was added to the walls, strengthening the entire construction. Instead of entering the small town with the entire caravan, Quidley directs many to park outside while only a few wagons that have business in the town enter it. In this way, the waggoneers avoids the entry fee, parking the wagons in a nearby clearing outside the walls. As they pull in for the night, Chip waves the Adventurers over, four small pouches held in hand.

"Right, you four, this is your pay. Quidley will let the Guild know you've completed your Quest as agreed upon," Chip says as he hands the pouches over to the other Adventuring group before turning to speak with Asin and Daniel. "You two are free to visit the town if you wish, we'll be here for the rest of the day and tomorrow. If you intend to leave, you'll need to be back first thing in the morning two days from now."

"Okay," Daniel says and then looks over to Asin who jerks her head to town immediately. Yes, definitely time to check out a new town. Chip just snorts, their answer being entirely within his expectations. Together the pair trudge down to town after saying some hasty goodbyes. At the gate, they pay their entrance fee and head immediately for the town center without discussion. The town center would be where the Adventurer's Guild, the Dungeon, and inns that catered to Adventurers were located. Inns nearer the city entrance were mostly for the merchants, those who had no real desire to explore the town itself. Not that either of them intended to explore the city per se, their hearts and minds set on the new Dungeon.

"Adventurer's Guild first?" Daniel enquires and Asin nods. Inside, the Guild gives a great sense of deja vu, so similar is it to the layout of the one in Karlak that Daniel almost expects there to be a red-haired, bookish attendant working behind the counter. Instead, a matronly older woman sits flipping through a book looking bored.

"Afternoon," Daniel says as he walks up with Asin in tow. "We just arrived and were hoping you could tell us a little about the Dungeon."

"You're from Karlak, right? Five levels, only one kind of monster. All our levels are full levels, no chests on each floor but each floor has its own champion. In Peel, the monsters you'll face are lizardmen - you'll meet workers, scouts, hunters, warriors, champions, chieftains and warlocks. That's in order of difficulty. What levels are you?" the woman intones, never even looking up from her book.

"Uhh… six," Daniel answers quickly, and Asin adds, "Eight" to which Daniel starts, looking at his companion. He knew he had lost a level, but had she always been a level higher than him?

"Right then, you shouldn't go past level three, and the third level is pushing it. We've got wider corridors so expect ranged weaponry," the woman says. "Also, we close at eight."

Daniel and Asin share a bemused smile before asking together, "Traps?"

"Pitfall, deadfalls, darts and poison gas in the lowest levels. The first level has pitfalls, each level after that adds one more type in order," the attendant says.

"Ummm... How about mana crystals? Size and type?" Daniel asks.

"Grade D Level 8 to start," she declares and sighs, finally looking up. "That's all that I can tell you. The rest you will have to learn yourself."

Daniel and Asin share another look, a bit put-off by the rude and brusque attendant. However, she is correct - there isn't much more that either can think of to ask. Wishing her well, the two Adventurers leave for the Dungeon entrance, nodding to the guards and registering themselves before walking into the Dungeon. Both of them feel a slight chill of anticipation and find themselves grinning in excitement. This is, after all, their second ever dungeon.

"Down," Asin chuffs and Daniel crouches, a pair of throwing knives flashing past his head to bury in the lizardman's chest. Daniel straightens his knees immediately, catching the spear thrust on his shield and stepping forward to deal with the monster. Unfortunately, the lizardman steps back again, thrusting with its rusty spear and forcing Daniel to protect himself. He exhales hastily, drawing a deep breath to fill his lungs as he steps forward again in an attempt to force the monster back, frustration leaking through his control.

This was the third lizardman that they had met. In both other cases, the much wider and taller gray stone corridors of the Peel dungeon had allowed the two Adventurers to flank the creatures, rendering the monsters spears less effective. Unfortunately, they had the bad luck to encounter this particular creature in a smaller, narrower service corridor and were forced to fight him single file. Unable to flank the monster, the pair has to work at whittling it down gradually.

Daniel has pushed the creature three-quarters of the way back, receiving only a light gash on his arm for his trouble but the creature's longer spear has ensured that he cannot close in and finish the monster. Every time he attempts to do so the monster step backs. Stuck behind him, Asin is unable to attack effectively and is forced to take occasional pot-shots.

However, that was about to change as the Lizardman Worker realized it had now been backed up nearly towards the exit. It hisses, the stabbing of the spear getting more agitated as it attempts to keep Daniel back. This is a mistake as Daniel takes a particularly wide strike on the edge of his shield, pushing against the shaft of the spear to pin it against the wall. This allows him time to step in and lash out with his mace, sweat flying from his brow as he twists. The mace swings upwards, biting into the lizardman's body and sending it sprawling backward. Asin hops forward and passes Daniel in the small gap that is created, jumping directly onto the monster's body and jabbing her knives into its prone form, twisting them to add to the damage. Asin snarls slightly, the slightly too smooth skin of the creature disturbing under her furred knees. As it dies, a brief flare of light surrounds the body, and it dissolves, leaving its mana crystal behind.

Daniel breathes deeply, eyeing the crude wooden spear with distaste and letting it fall to the ground. Once again, he wishes he has access to the Adventurers Level 10 Class Skill - Inventory. Without it, neither of them can safely store the spear for resale, and so they have to leave it aside, content with their earnings of mana stones.

Once Daniel catches his breath, the pair continue deeper into the dungeon to find the Level Champion. If the fight goes well, they hope to attempt the second level today as well, though it truly depends on how quickly they can finish this level. Both Adventurers move along the broad stone corridors quickly, Asin's quick eyes having spotted and alerted Daniel of the way the pitfall traps were made of slightly discolored stones early on. Now, even Daniel can pick them out with relative regularity, allowing the pair to move faster.

The differences in the Peel Dungeon did not end at the stone corridors and lizardmen monsters, as even the first floor was much larger and more expansive than their own. Traversing through the corridors, the pair have to fight numerous times before they finally manage to stumble across the Champion's location, after hours of exploration. Together, both Adventurers pull their heads back from the doorway leading into the room after quickly scoping out the Lizardman Champion and another worker. The two Adventurers look at each other before Daniel is the first to speak, "Champion's mine, Miss Level 8."

He smirks at her and Asin rolls her eyes but nods, hefting a throwing knife in her left hand and one of her longer knives in her right. She waits for Daniel to ready himself and then, together, they dash around the corner. Asin activates her Piercing Shot, throwing it at the Lizardman Worker before sprinting over as she draws her other long knife, engaging the creature in close combat. Her first throw drills into the Worker's shoulder, making it hiss in anger.

Daniel charges at the Champion alone, taking the few moments he needs to cross the distance to further observe the monster. The Lizardman Champion wields a better-crafted spear and stands nearly six feet tall, looming over the shorter Adventurer. Covered in dark green scales and wearing a torn, red tunic over its torso and legs, the Champion jabs the spear towards Daniel to keep him away. Hours of fighting spear wielders has taught Daniel some new tricks however, and, instead of catching the spear with his shield, he bats the spear head aside to the left with his mace and continues to close the distance. The spear now out of alignment, he shoves his shield outwards at an angle, riding the spear shaft down even as the Champion retracts his blow. Once he has firm contact, Daniel grins and engages Shield Bash, slamming the spear even further off-course and making the Champion fight to keep hold of its weapon. Unfortunately, the spear does not conduct the lightning that dances on his shield to the monster, but he still succeeds in his main objective - to close the rest of the distance unharmed.

Daniel is now in range, and he immediately triggers his Double Strike skill, sending his mace smashing once then again onto the Champion's head and shoulders. The blows are only partially blocked by a raised claw that has released its grip on the spear. The claw is crushed, and the monster drops its now useless spear to the side, the greater length of the weapon difficult to wield single-handed and in close combat. Instead, the Champion attempts to use its claws to swipe at Daniel. Daniel ducks to the side, then kicks the creature in the legs, upsetting its balance further before laying into it again with his mace. Keeping the pressure up, he smashes his mace into the Champion again and again before the creature falls over, dead.

Slightly out of breath, Daniel grins and looks over to Asin who has finished her monster. The staircase down is just in front of them but it is late, and after a brief discussion, they agree to test the next floor out tomorrow. They will head downstairs, activate the Dungeon glyph and then return to the inn. Better to hand in their money now and get a good night's sleep.

Up early in the morning, Daniel and Asin meet up for a quick breakfast that they barely taste as they cram the food into their mouths. Without a word, they grab the pre-packed lunches they requested from the Inn and head out with a bounce in their steps. Day two of a new dungeon and a new level to boot. What could be better?

The second floor is very similar to the first, its wide gray stone corridors lit by the soft glow of mana imbued stone all around them. A slight breeze could be felt if they paid attention, bringing a dry, slightly sour smell through the level. Corridors turn into rooms where Lizardmen wait, in groups of two or three, playing a game of sticks, training, eating and on one occasion napping.

After the sixth such room, Daniel turns to Asin, murmuring, "This is so strange. It feels less like a Dungeon and more like, well, more like it's their home."

Asin nods at that, scratching at her cheek. It really did feel like they'd invaded the Lizardmen's home and were uncouth, ill-mannered and violent guests, killing their way through their unsuspecting hosts. It felt wrong, even though they both knew that this was a Dungeon. The Lizardmen weren't real; they left no bodies when killed and yet they could not shake the feeling.

For a time, the two stare at each other, battling the strangeness of it all. In the end, they shrug and focus, knowing that as strange as this is, the Lizardmen needed to be killed. Left alone too long, they would spill out of the Dungeon into the town, the corruption induced by Ba'al given a chance to spread. Eventually, such a Dungeon might be the start of a new Blight if left unchecked for too long. It was their job, however strange it seemed, to kill these Lizardmen before it happened.

They move on, pushing through the Dungeon and its monsters, their faces set and the bounce in their steps gone. Experienced Adventurers had a saying - that each new level taught a different lesson, each Dungeon a different experience. In Peel, it seemed the lesson was that whatever they felt, whatever they believed, they still had a job to do.

Focused now, the two work their way through the Dungeon, Asin testing for traps, and Daniel watching for Lizardmen Scouts. The Scouts were annoying as half of them were armed with crossbows, able to attack at range. It forced both Adventurers to move slowly, especially after the first deadfall that Daniel had landed in trying to chase a Scout down. It was only luck and the application of healing magic that allowed him to continue delving today, though the experience forced them to slow down significantly.

The only truly difficult fight comes three-quarters of the day in as they rest in a room for a quick break. As they rest, the Lizardman Scout Champion leans into the room from the doorway, lines up a shot, and fires at Asin. Only their wariness and Asin's quick reflexes allow her to roll out of the way with a long scratch as her only injury. Daniel struggles to his feet quickly, putting his shield in front of him and the two follow the Champion's quickly retreating figure carefully. Annoyed and angry, the two still remember the lessons of the day, making sure to check every passageway for traps and ambushes even as they slowly chase down the Champion. It takes them hours, working their way to the Champion as Daniel blocks the bolts it fires and Asin throws her knives, whittling down the Champion whenever it stops to attack them.

In the end, the Champion can only limp away, out of tricks entirely. It has dragged them into other rooms where Lizardmen wait, through trap-filled corridors and on a long chase through a series of twisting passages in an attempt to escape but now it is finally brought to heel. Out of bolts, out of tricks, it falls to Daniel's mace in short order.

By this time, it is late, and the two Adventurers are exhausted. They journey up to town to sell their mana stones; another lesson learned this long day in blood and frustration. Before they leave, Daniel puts his money down for a new light crossbow with bolts. It is time to learn how to shoot. As for Asin, she comes back with a trio of bolos, chuffing to herself as she spins them around.

Dinner is a quiet affair; the two Adventurers exhausted from their days working the new dungeon. They had pushed hard to do as much as they could, but their lack of equipment and preparedness had stymied their ability to truly progress. Still, they were relatively uninjured, alive and though slightly poorer at least had new weapons.

Daniel smiles at his friend, raising a glass of wine to her and she purrs, sipping on hers. If nothing else, this inn had a good wine selection. They sit alone, the other patrons avoiding their table in the corner and eyeing Asin with trepidation. It seems Peel has an even smaller population of Beastkin than Karlak and while the patrons were mostly Adventurers, none desire to mix with the Beastkin.

As they are finishing up their dinner, a pair of familiar faces wander into the tavern looking the worst for wear. Black-haired Delia, her sword in its sheath but lacking her shield and Palmer, limping and holding his side around his green robes stumble in and find a seat at a free table. Adventurers turn, eye the pair and then dismiss them from their mind, their injuries and hangdog expressions telling the tale.

Asin turns to look at Daniel who sighs and nods, both of them approaching the table cradling the last of their mugs. Daniel takes the lead, murmuring, "Evening."

It takes a few silent moments before Delia looks up, staring at Daniel with blank eyes before a spark of interest kindles, "Daniel. And the Cat. You look well. I guess you didn't do the dungeons…"

"Umm…" Daniel pauses, watching as Palmer winces and tugs at the bandage ineffectually. "Here, let me do that." Quick work is made of fixing the bandage, Palmer gritting his teeth as the bandage is pulled tight around his body and then secured. Briefly, Daniel considers using his Gift, having exhausted all his Mana the moment they had left the Dungeon to heal his and Asin's minor wounds. Briefly, but none of their wounds were life-threatening, just painful.

"How far did you get?" Daniel asks.

"We managed to make it to the fourth today. First few floors weren't hard, so we rushed through them. The third floor was tough, but the Lizardmen, they would stand and fight. But the fourth-floor Champion, he had these Scouts with him. They kept shooting us and shooting us, we couldn't get away, couldn't run…" Delia says, shaking her head. "I told him to wait, told him we should take our time. Marco said we could do it though, said we'd be fine. He cried when they cut off his arm…"

"I'm sorry." Daniel sits down next to her, offering the comfort of his presence. Asin leaves, coming back a few minutes later with beers for the group which are greedily taken and emptied by the two beaten Adventurers. A short while later a waitress comes by, depositing the evening's special.

"I told him," Delia says, poking at the food. Palmer avoids all their gazes, working industriously at his meal, his hands occasionally beginning to tremble before he brings them under control. After a time, Daniel and Asin stand, murmuring a goodbye. As they leave, Daniel wonders if the pair will team up with others now, perhaps someone with ranged weaponry. Death as an Adventurer was a part of life, no matter how experienced you were. Losing a friend, though, was never easy, no matter how inured you were to the realities of the world they had chosen.

Chapter 5

The next morning sees both Asin and Daniel standing beside the caravan at the crack of dawn. Neither having been given an exact time the wagons would leave, they decided to arrive early instead. The moment he spots them, Gabriel waves to the pair and beckons them over to his wagon.

In a corner of the campground, the caravan master is offering his usual, cordial welcome to a new group of Adventurers from Peel. Asin watches the group intently. They are made up of a large yellow-furred Catkin and a pair of human Adventurers. The first human Adventurer wields a sword and shield but the second seems to favor a short sword and bow combination and wears a mottled brown-green cloak. All three adventurers are dressed in a mix of plate and chainmail armor that is worn but still serviceable. Even to the novice Adventurers, they can tell that the weapons and armor are a couple of quality levels higher than theirs. Asin nudges Daniel, nodding to the group to get his attention before purring, "Ranger."

Daniel looks over and spots the Ranger and nods slightly in turn. The Ranger was a rare sight as the famously taciturn and independent Adventurers kept to the borders of Brad. On the other hand, they were known as well for their ability with the bow, and Daniel rubs at his jaw, thinking of how to approach him for help.

"Well, it's good that you returned. Wasn't sure if you would - we lose about half our guards who are supposed to return to us in Peel," Gabriel grouses as he hops on the wagon after hitching the horses to it. "Why, this one time, we had this fair-haired buxom young lass of an Adventurer, all clad in plate who was supposed to be with us to Silverstone. She arrived in Peel and what do you know, she meets up with this sorcerer and priest and they go Adventuring in the Dungeon! Never joins up with us again. Real pity on that too, she sure was pretty. Still, I figure if I had a chance to work with a sorcerer and a priest, I'd join them myself. Especially since I hear they were all women."

The moment Gabriel begins to speak, Asin flashes a grin at Daniel and scrambles to her customary perch at the top of the wagon, her tail lazily waving alongside the canvas top as she sits on the wagon and works on her claws. Daniel glares at the traitor before turning back to Gabriel and his never-ending stories, trying to set his face to an attentive position.

That evening as they come to a stop, Daniel makes his way past the outlying wagons to the nearby river to wash.   Stripped to his undergarments, Daniel completes the ritual quickly, shivering in the cold emerald glacial runoff of the river and laying the thick mat of soap leaves aside. He scrambles out of the water, shaking his blocky frame to free it of excess water before squatting to begin washing his clothing.

At the snap of a twig, Daniel spins, grabbing for his nearby mace. The young lady who surprised him yelps, dropping her washing basket and laundry before blushing furiously at his half-naked state. Realizing it is just one of the hanger-on's, Daniel smiles at her and lowers the mace to his side. "It's okay."

The young brunette with the cute, pert nose shakes her head, hastily picking up the washing. "No, no. I'm sorry."

"Yvette, isn't it?" Daniel says, smiling to the woman as he reaches for and pulls on the extra pair of pants he brought along. She nods jerkily, still not meeting his gaze. "I'm just washing my clothes; you're welcome to join me."

She blushes again and nods, coming over and squatting a short distance from him. She takes out the clothing she brought, focusing on it. Daniel returns to what he was doing, catching the sideway glances the young lady shoots him occasionally. A part of him preens at the attention, a small smile lighting on his face unknowingly. Noticing the rather large amount of clothing she is washing, Daniel says, "Are you washing that for others, Yvette?"

Yvette nods jerkily, blushing again before she looks at Daniel's manhandling of his clothes. She speaks up, hesitantly and shyly, "I could wash yours too. For free."

"Oh, I couldn't ask you to do that," Daniel replies immediately, shaking his clothes and grimacing at the hole he spots.

"No, it's fine. I could mend that too," she raises her voice, nodding. "I have skills in Housekeeping and Sewing, and you've been so kind, healing us. Please?"

Daniel blinks, considering her offer. He really was very bad at sewing - his last attempt had already torn and while he earned more as an Adventurer, paying for new clothing was a constant headache due to the amount of damage they received. In addition, his work in the Clinic had made him realize that allowing others to help or pay him actually made them feel better as well. It was one reason why Khy'ra had a flexible payment policy in the Clinic. "If you're sure. Thank you."

Yvette smiles, stands up quickly and walks over to take his clothing from him. As she does so, her hand brushes against his and she blushes, backing away quickly and ducking her head, embarrassed about her calloused and rough fingers. "I'll… I'll get it right back to you tomorrow when it's done. If that's okay?"

Daniel nods to her, standing around for a moment unsure. "So, uhhh…. Where are you traveling to?"

"Silverstone," she replies promptly. "My father, he's a Master mason. He was offered a job at the new temple they're building."

"A Master mason? That's impressive." Daniel echoes her voice, his gaze resting on the small, pert frame before him, eyes tracking over the way the clothing presses against her body. "And you?"

"I'm… well, I'm just with him for now. My mother, she died a while ago, and I help my Da keep the house while he works." Again Yvette blushes. "He says, well, I'll be a good housewife one day. And you? You're an Adventurer?" Realizing how stupid that sounds, Yvette hides her face in her washing again, not daring to look at Daniel.

"Yes. Just under a year actually," Daniel replies, slowly stretching an arm as he talks to her. Yvette looks over her shoulder at a grunt and notices Daniel with his arm over his head, stretching, and her eyes track over his muscular, hairless chest. Eyes lock on a pocked puncture wound just under a floating rib, and Daniel answers the unasked question. "Crawler in Karlak. They have these big pincers and this one bit right through my armor. Hurt like hell and healing, well, it left that."

Of course, he could have healed it fully and removed the scar, but Daniel had decided long ago to avoid such healings. It created a significant strain on his Gift to do so and wasn't worth the effort. So long as he could move and fight without pain, anything more was unnecessary. It also headed off any requests for cosmetic healings which he really did not want to deal with.

"Oh, you're so brave," Yvette says, looking down at her hands. "I could never do that."

"Well, it's not for everyone," Daniel answers, shaking his head. "But I don't think it's brave, not really. It's not as if farmers or miners aren't in danger outside of Dungeons, and at least we carry weapons."

Yvette nods dumbly along to Daniel's words, putting aside the latest shirt and moving to the next one. Unsure of what else to say, Daniel ends up saying, "I should get back. I've got to get dinner going."

"I'll see you," Yvette whispers and when Daniel has left, quickly hugs the shirt, amazed at how bold she was.

When Daniel arrives back at the camp, he is surprised to find Asin cooking and speaking with the Catkin, the two sharing quiet purrs and growls. He blinks for a moment before shaking his head, moving to put away his cleaning supplies. At his bag, he stares down at his newly acquired weapon, picking up the crossbow and bolts before surveying the area for a good spot.

Setting up a small distance from others, where a small hillock and a fallen tree provide him with a target, Daniel grunts, and strains as he works the crossbow back. Adjusting his stance, Daniel draws a deep breath and exhales, focusing on the half-remembered lessons he received when they joined the Army. As he exhales, Daniel releases the bolt and watches it wing away to dig into the ground four feet short of the target. Pushing aside the rising irritation, Daniel works to cock the crossbow again. Practice. He just needed practice.

Thirty minutes later after having shot through all his bolts twice, Daniel is sweating and swearing. The target was only fourty yards away, and he still had not managed to hit it even once.

"You. This. It's embarrassing." The Ranger walks up, shaking his head at Daniel and unable to watch the young man practice any further. The Ranger is dressed clad in his mottled green and brown cloak, though with the hood thrown back Daniel can see the young, unlined face beneath it and friendly brown eyes. "Let me help you, or else the guards will never let us Adventurers live this down."

At the mention of the guards, Daniel looks back to the camp, having forgotten about everyone else as he practiced. He realizes that more than a few guards have been watching him, a few openly laughing at his lack of progress. Embarrassed, Daniel turns away quickly and looks at the Ranger imploringly. "Please!"

"Right then, let's start with your stance," the Ranger states, moving up to Daniel and correcting his stance. Daniel nods, focusing on what the Ranger says. He certainly needed to improve.

"Well, that's… better?" Iyas, the Ranger says with a resigned tone. The evening had progressed such that even in the long summer days, their practice had to be called to an end. "Gather the bolts, and I'll show you how to care for them and the crossbow."

Daniel nods, staring at his target. Well, he had winged the tree at last. The added pressure had made his first few tries after Iyas arrived even worse than before, but now, now he was beginning to get it. Hurrying forward, Daniel moves to collect his bolts, lips twisting in disgust as he notes one shattered shaft. As he hurries back from his task, he sees Asin still deep in her conversation with her Catkin friend, a hand on the other Adventurer's lap. As he hurries over to the camp, his stomach rumbles and he realizes that he has not eaten. Looking over to Iyas, he points to the cooking pot and the other Adventurer nods.

Having slurped his slightly burnt dinner down, Daniel returns to the Ranger who shows him how to care for the bolts, replacing fletching and ensuring that the bolts were still straight. He even pulls out a stick to show Daniel how he can even make his own if he cares to, though he points out that Daniel will need a carving knife for that. Daniel watches with intensity, soon taking a direct hand and checking over his bolts as Iyas carves.

"You and your Catkin friend, you're both a bit junior to be leaving Karlak aren't you?" Iyas says as carves.

"I guess? We're on a fetch quest actually, to Silverstone and back," Daniel explains, tongue stuck between his teeth as he works on a new feather.

"Ah! I remember those. I used to run a number of them before I joined Niko and Tevfik," Iyas says smiling. "I can't say I miss them at all. Paid good, especially on the Borderlands, but quite boring."

Daniel shrugs, holding up the bolt to inspect. Iyas looks up, shakes his head and Daniel sighs and tries again. "It's our first. We did a few Hunt and Gather quests while in Karlak, but this is our first."

"Well, Rangers are more suited for them," Iyas offers, and then adds, "It's good to get out though, see the world a bit. Too many new Adventurers just fall into the routine of only working Dungeons."

Daniel smiles, basking slightly at the more experienced Adventurers praise. "Why were you in Peel? You three don't seem, you know, of the right level."

Iyas laughs. "Yes. We're not Beginners anymore, but are you aware that you get a minor experience boost for each Dungeon you clear?" Daniel shakes his head, and Iyas continues, "You do. It's why even experienced Adventurers will clear beginner dungeons. Of course, it also helps to keep Ba'al's influence down."

Daniel nods, thinking over what Iyas said and then holds up the next bolt. Getting confirmation from Iyas, he smiles and turns to the next one.

"Morning, Asin, you're up with me today, are you?" Gabriel chatters away to Asin as he climbs on the wagon, clicking his tongue right after to start the horses moving. "Always nice to have you up, though you aren't much of a conversationalist. That's okay though, my Ma always said I could talk enough for two, and with you, I'll need to!

"Well now, we're on the way to the village of Stolin. I bet you haven't heard about Stolin, have you? Small little village, we wouldn't even stop there normally, but it is the only village this side of the border for a good four days. Right in the middle of the plains with all the wheat fields, so that's what we'll be driving through for a bit. Not much to see but the sky and the wheat really, not for a few days. Why you'll get so bored about seeing wheat, you'll want to cry. Reminds of that time when Pini started nodding off on his wagon and drove it right into the ditch. Well, you know Pini, he carries…"

Thoroughly pleased with himself, Daniel slows down to let the wagon pass him by as he walks along the road. He grinned slightly, just happy to be on his feet and away from the chatterbox. He would walk exclusively, but being paid to guard the caravan meant that Daniel needed to be rested enough to deal with problems if they arose. Not that anything major had happened as yet. The worst had been a horse that had tripped and broken its foot when it saw a snake.

True to Gabriel's word, they walk through plains of light green grass and fields of newly sprouted wheat for the next few hours. The land around them slowly shifts from the rolling plains interspersed with stands of trees to flat land divided into occasional managed farm lots. Unimpeded, a strong wind constantly blows, tugging at canvas straps and clothing alike and ruffling the stalks of grass and wheat. The wind carries a hint of morning chill along with the scent of freshly turned earth, newly grown grass and last evening's quick rain shower. Above, the sky almost goes on forever, seeming to stretch on and on before being finally bracketed by the distant mountains in the North.

Walking beneath the sky, Daniel hunches slightly, unused to such a sky. Born in the foothills of the mountains to the North, he was always more comfortable in the forest or underground. Still, at least the plains have the advantage of making travel safe - it would be impossible for bandits and monsters to hide. Tired of walking, Daniel hurries up to jump onto the wagon bed, swinging his feet up and letting the creak of the wagon wheels and the drone of Gabriel's incessant talk wash over him.

A scream breaks Daniel from his reverie, the sound originating from behind the caravan. He hops down from his seat, grabbing his mace and moving to the side of the road as he scans for danger. Two wagons behind, Iyas has climbed onto a wagon top and is scanning the horizon before he releases the tension in his bow, shaking his head. Waggoneers relax as the experienced Adventurer gives an all clear as do the guards. Watching everyone relax, Daniel decides to hurry to the back where the foot passengers walk, and the scream originated.

Pushing past the crowd, Daniel finds a young man crying and holding his broken leg. Another helpful citizen has attempted to straighten it, badly, and

Daniel hisses in frustration. Pushing the man aside, he grunts a quick warning before reaching forward and realigning the bones. He follows this by channeling a Minor Healing. The swelling begins to reduce, torn flesh and bone knitting before their eyes.

"What happened?" Daniel asks, testing along the edges of the initial break. Luckily the bone had not fragmented so healing it was a simple matter that required only a single casting of his spell. "Can someone find some straight sticks? We'll need to provide the leg some support."

"Basher rabbit," the reply comes from behind Daniel, the voice surprisingly high-pitched. Daniel looks over and blinks, seeing the third Adventurer of the group, the swordsman standing there. The swordsman is tall, maybe as much as a foot taller than Daniel with a slight scar near the corner of one hazel eye. "Probably got startled and attacked."

Daniel nods, casting one last minor healing before quickly strapping the leg to the supporting sticks. "The leg will be tender for the next few weeks. You shouldn't put too much weight on it, but…" Daniel nods to the caravan that is already a distance away. "Well, just come and see me tonight and I'll see what I can do."

The peasant grabs Daniel's hand in his, murmuring thanks before standing with the help of his friends. Daniel sighs, flashing a smile at Yvette who he spots standing with her father before turning to the Adventurer who is still watching him.

"So, you're a Healer, eh?" the swordsman says, his hand resting casually on the pommel of his hand-and-a-half sword.

"In a way." Daniel glances at the group who are moving and begins to walk as well, hurrying to get back to the wagons with the swordsman alongside him.

"Interesting. I'm Niko," the swordsman introduces himself as he joins Daniel.

"Daniel."

"Most Adventurers don't take the time to learn enough healing to pick up the Minor Healing spell," Niko adds, looking at Daniel from the corner of his eyes as he walks. "You're pretty unusual actually."

"I don't really understand why though," admits Daniel after a moment. "It's so useful."

"Ah, it's a matter of time and opportunity. Few Healers are willing to spend time teaching those who aren't going to be Healers since it's so time-intensive and for those who can find a teacher, it still takes a long time to reach the required skill level. The way I understand it, to even get started you need about five levels in healing," Niko explains. "Most Adventurers just find it easier to train in their primary skillsets and become better at that, though of course, we all pick up a level or two in healing, eventually."

Daniel nods rubbing his chin. His Gift had allowed him to bypass much of the initial learning stages, teaching him aspects of the body and how it worked on an almost intuitive level. He recalled how surprised the visiting Healer at the mine was at the young boy's knowledge. During his short visits, the Healer had always done his best to teach and convince Daniel to become a Healer himself, becoming ultimately unsuccessful. Now, for a moment, Daniel feels guilty for the time the old man spent with him, guilty about his life choice. He could have been, should have been a Healer. Yet...

"You two!" Chip shouts at them, breaking Daniel from his thoughts. "Who told you to leave the caravan? You aren't being paid to guard them!"

Daniel winces, pulling himself to attention as Chip continues to harangue them for slacking off on their duties. Niko just nods his head, occasionally offering a verbal acknowledgment. When the grumpy, wrinkled old man is not looking he rolls his eyes at Daniel to express his own frustration. Daniel has to cough to cover a chuckle, working hard to keep a straight face as Chip continues to scold them.

Released at last, the two Adventurers bid goodbye to each other and take up their spaces in the wagon train, though Daniel finds himself seated in the front. Asin gives him a wink as he passes her by, chewing on the slice of dried sausage.

As promised, Stolin is a small village with a single-room tavern, a blacksmith and a sundry goods shop dominating the town center. Next to the tavern stands a large bare field where the wagons are directed to park, the caravan master and a select few being allowed to sleep in the tavern. The rest are assigned to the ground around the caravan itself while a few wagons turn off, heading in the direction of the lone mill and the grain barns.

Asin waves Daniel aside as she grabs the cookpot and their empty water skins; Tevfik prowls up to join her at the river with his team's supplies. Daniel smiles slightly, noting how close the two are to each other already, heading towards the woodpile.

"Hi…" the hesitant, sweet voice behind him makes Daniel turn away from the fire he is slowly coaching to light. He smiles as he spots Yvette who holds his washed and darned clothing in her arms. She blushes slightly at the smile, thrusting the pile towards him. The moment he takes it, she blushes again and scurries off, leaving Daniel to watch her swaying behind. He quickly turns away though when he catches her father's glare and has to remind himself that there is nothing wrong with looking.

Smiling slightly, Daniel returns to watching the fire as he waits for Asin to return. And waits. And waits. Growling in impatience after a long hour, he stands and looks around, wondering where his friend is. It should not take this long to get water! Just as he is about to head to the river himself, he spots her hurrying back, fur and clothing disheveled with the full cookpot.

"Where are the water skins?" Daniel asks as he places the pot on the fire. Asin lets out a yowl of surprise and then ducks her head, spinning back and hurrying to the river. As Daniel watches her hurry off, he notes Tevfik is sauntering back like a cat that has eaten all the cream. Just like a cat…

Daniel chuckles to himself, wondering how Kh'yra would react to this news. At the thought of the beautiful blonde elf, he recalls another, much closer young female and ducks his head in embarrassment. Right, he had a girlfriend of sorts.

"We don't serve their kind," the older matron snaps at Daniel. Situated behind the kegs of beer that her husband had rolled out for the thirsty waggoneers, she points to Asin and Tevfik. "No better than animals they are. Why, young Ingrid says she saw the two of them rolling around near the river, yowling and doing what animals do. Disgusting!"

Daniel glares at her, tapping the table with his coin, "Well, is my money bad then?"

"No," the tavern keeper's wife says as she shakes her head to move some of her graying blonde hair from her eyes.

"Then I'll take three," says Daniel.

Eyes narrowing, she waves him away. "I changed my mind. You're not welcome either."

"You just said my money is good," Daniel says, tapping the coin on the table again.

"Well, it's not now, Beast lover." She sniffs and looks past him to the person behind. "You want a drink?"

Daniel shifts, placing himself in front of her gaze again. "Three mugs."

"Go away, or else I'll call my husband," the woman snaps at him.

"Go on then," Daniel challenges and then feels a hand drop on his shoulder. He turns and finds Tevfik shaking his head, pulling him along. Daniel resists for a moment but finds the other Adventurer stronger than him and is forced to move. The tavern keeper's wife snickers even as she pours the next drink.

"Why did you do that?"

"Not worth it, young one. They will not serve you or us and insisting they do will only cause trouble. We wouldn't want to be left behind by the caravan master," Tevfik says, finally letting go of Daniel now that they are away from the tavern. "Come, we've got drink."

"The wagon master wouldn't…" Daniel begins then closes his mouth as Asin just shoots him a disbelieving look. His lips twist, and he growls, knowing that they are right. They were just Adventurers - the village, on the other hand, was the caravan master's livelihood. It would not really be a choice.

"I am glad you care for us, but we are used to such things," Tevfik says as they join the fire where the other Adventurers sit. He disappears into the wagon, pulling a wineskin from his bag and handing it over.

"It's still not right," Daniel grumbles and the others laugh at the naiveté of the young man. Daniel just glares at them back before drinking from the wineskin, coughing at the harsh burn of the unexpectedly sweet but potent drink inside. This was no wine. It was Sabu, the Beastkin's alcoholic beverage of choice.

"Right or not, it is what it is. It will be many years before they accept us." Tevfik shrugs and takes back the wineskin from Daniel, handing it over to Asin whose nose is twitching already at the pungent smell. "Now, come! Tell us about yourself. Asin says you were part of the army's recent Orc Raid subjugation. We were too late to join that."

Somewhat mollified by the better alcohol, Daniel hesitantly tells the tale to his audience who in turn offer some tales of their own adventures. Eventually, a small crowd joins them, listening to the tales of derring-do that are passed back and forth between the Adventurers, the wineskin slowly being emptied.

Chapter 6

Wincing in the harsh morning light, Daniel lets out a little groan and attempts to roll out from underneath the wagon he crawled under for sleep. He blinks, staring at the young lady who is trapping his arm, Daniel slowly recalls the evening before and groans. He had a little too much to drink, and Yvette was there, talking to him and then… Daniel groans again.

At the second groan, Yvette wakes and sees Daniel. She lets out a little squeak of embarrassment, covering her face with her hands and then, noting she is still mostly dressed, scrambles away. Daniel laughs slightly, pulling his arm back as he remembers how the shy young lady had become much less shy last night after a few drinks. The laugh makes him wince again as the headache he has acquired makes itself known once more. Rather than suffer through the hangover, Daniel focuses for a moment, casting a Minor Healing on himself.

Crawling out from underneath the wagon, the caravan is slowly waking up. He moves over to the fire, stabbing it to find some coals and adding some of the prepared kindling as he coaches the fire back to life. Asin comes crawling up to him, poking him with one clawed finger till Daniel relents, casting a short Minor Heal on her too.

After breakfast, the wagon rolls out from the town. Asin pokes him again with a claw and jerks her head to the side of the road, and Daniel sighs, joining her as they walk alongside the caravan.

"Yvette." She points to him and Daniel grimaces and nods. She then points to herself and says, "Tevfik."

"Yes, I gathered." Daniel's eyes sparkle slightly, and Asin pokes him again.

"No tell." Asin glares at Daniel and Daniel nods.

"Of course. I won't. Though…" Daniel shifts uncomfortably, looking at the swaying grass and the bright, clear morning. "Well, I might tell Kh'yra myself." He hears Asin sniff at that, shaking her head and Daniel shrugs. "We're not promised to each other, but, well, I'd feel bad. I think."

"Always bad," Asin pronounces before she shrugs, loping back to catch up fully with the wagon. Surprisingly, she takes the front seat with Gabriel without prompting.

The remainder of the day falls into a familiar, mind-numbing routine as the pair sit and watch the ground roll by, occasionally chatting with each other, Gabriel and the passing guards. That evening, Daniel is pulled aside by Iyas to continue his training with the crossbow, making marginal improvements in accuracy and load time.

In the morning, as Daniel wakes up, he is greeted by a notification.

Skill Gained!

Archery: Level 1 (03/100) +3

He cannot help but smile, the troubled sleep from the evening before worth it to finally, finally gain the skill notification. It had taken hours of practice, but at least he finally had the skill. As the noise from around the camp grows, he dismisses the notification. Time to get to work.

"What's that?" Daniel frowns, pointing to a growing cloud of dust in the distance hours after they started on the road.

Gabriel frowns, standing up for a brief moment before sitting down unconcernedly. "Plains Nomads. They range in the unsettled areas between the villages in Brad and the border. They are normally peaceful."

Daniel nods, watching as other guards take note of the growing dust cloud and after a moments consideration he picks up and cocks his crossbow, sliding a bolt in. At Gabriel's raised eyebrow Daniel shrugs as he sets the loaded crossbow down next to him in easy reach. Better to be careful and ready than careless and dead.

Daniel's jaw drops slightly as nomads arrive. Clad in a mix of wool and linen with the occasional pieces of unboiled leather thrown in, the nomads sit on small, tough steppe horses with a train of at least two additional horses behind each of them. The nomads each carry a short, recurved bow and a pair of filled quivers. However, it is the fact that the nomads are halflings that truly surprises Daniel, the three-foot tall humanoids chattering excitedly with the wagon masters as their horses easily keep pace with the caravan. The halfling nomad's leader is a woman who animatedly talks with the caravan master before coins are exchanged. The caravan master shouts back to his wagons, calling out the purchased goods while the other nomads spread out to the other wagons, their leader having completed her interactions. They stop by each wagon, speaking briefly with the owner before moving on, only pausing when they find something they'd like to buy.

As one of the halflings rides by him, Daniel's nose wrinkles at the pungent smell that hits him. Gabriel chuckles at Daniel's reaction while Asin gags above them. "Horse fat. They rub it over their body to clean themselves and keep them warm. I hear the nomads think it's bad luck to bathe in rivers and lakes. Something about washing away the good luck."

Daniel coughs, rubbing his nose and is glad as the halflings ride right past their wagon to others further behind. Still, he can't help but watch and admire the experienced horsemen guide their animals with just their feet. Soon enough, the encounter is over, and the nomads break off, riding back into the plains, and the caravan is able to breathe easily.

"Gabriel, is it always this quiet?" Daniel asks as he uncocks his crossbow, returning the bolt to its quiver.

"Of course." The waggoneer laughs.

"Then..." Daniel looks around at the many guards and Adventurers who make up the caravan, and Gabriel laughs again.

"The guards and you Adventurers are a show of force. Bandits and monsters stay away from such a large, well-armed group. If we didn't have you, we'd be attacked more, but with so many guards, it'd take a big or particularly desperate bandit group to attack us," Gabriel explains. "It's why Ios dislikes you Adventurers. He has to pay you to keep the bandits away, but because he pays you, he never gets his money's worth or so he sees it."

Nodding in thanks for the explanation, Daniel sighs and leans back, shading his eyes. It was decent money, but it sure was boring.

Days pass, villages blending into one another. It takes them another week to arrive at Silverstone, and there were only three exciting events from Daniel's perspective during that week. The first came a few days after they had left Stolin.

"You, Adventurer! Stay away from my daughter!" shouted the enraged father who waved a finger in front of Daniel's face, drawing the attention of the entire caravan. Behind, an embarrassed Yvettte clutched at her skirts and blushed while Daniel opened his mouth and then shuts it. "You damn Adventurers, sleeping with every young thing. My daughter is too good for your kind!"

"My kind?" Daniel answered stupidly and received another withering stare.

"Adventurers," the father spat to the side, growling. "You think just because you go traveling around, fighting monsters in Dungeons and Leveling up, you're better than the rest of us. Well, you ain't. You keep your hands off my daughter or else I'll deal with you!"

"I'm… I will," Daniel said, changing his mind about apologizing. That evening had been extremely pleasant, and they were both willing adults, even if the young lady was a bit young.

Giving Daniel one last glare, the father stomped away and grabbed his daughter's arm, dragging her off and muttering, "Damn Adventurers! And you, you stupid girl. What will you do if you are pregnant? It's not as if he's going to marry you."

Daniel opened his mouth and closed it, deciding not to explain that he had ensured that no such pregnancy was possible through his Gift. It had required just the barest of touches with his Gift on himself after all. Eyes twinkling, Niko walked up to Daniel, clapped him on the shoulder and guided the youngster away, murmuring, "Right then, let's talk about discretion shall we."

The second incident came two days before they were due to arrive at Silverstone. They had left the plains behind and returned to the forested, rolling hills and cooler temperatures that Brad mostly consisted of. However, it was in one of the forest paths that their first aggressive encounter occurred. A stone bear cub had wandered onto the trail by itself and had been startled by the wagons. Crying out for his mother, the cub had backed off to a corner while the waggoneer had jerked his wagon to a halt. The cub's mother, lingering nearby had rushed out in anger to protect her cub, striking out at the wagon and its guard. Dead after a single swipe, neck snapped and chest torn open, the guard collapsed to the ground as the stone bear mother roared defiance at the unfortunate group.

Standing on his wagon seat, Daniel had swiftly worked to load his crossbow though he was unsure how effective that weapon would be. Iyas jumped down from his perch on top of his wagon, moving quickly to the mother bear without fear. The Ranger spoke to the mother bear, his voice low and calming as he attempted to calm her down. Pulling a bag of berries from his pouch, he offered some to the mother bear before guiding the stone bear and its cub away from the road, a hand on the rough, coarse gray fur. Gabriel breathed a sigh of relief when the animal left and so did Daniel. Knowing one could win did not equal the need to fight, especially against such a powerful monster.

The last event happened the night before they arrived at Silverstone. The three senior Adventurers found the two novices at their cooking fire late in the evening with Niko leading the conversation. "We'll be arriving at Silverstone soon."

"Yes," Daniel said.

"We were thinking, what with you being Adventurers and all. Would you like to see what an Advanced Dungeon is like?" Niko said.

Daniel blinked and looked to Asin, part excited, part scared. As he hesitated, Niko added, "We won't go past the first level. And we'd share out the earnings in four parts, with both of you taking the fourth. It would be good experience for you two, and it'd be good to have a Healer in the party again, even if it is brief."

Tevfik added his own growling points directly to Asin, working to convince her. She yowled a little, pushing against the other Catkin playfully with her arm before she looked to Daniel and offered a slight nod.

"Well, okay. Only the first level right!" Daniel added and the trio nodded, and Iyas clapped Daniel on the shoulder. Once they had received the two novice adventurer's agreement, the talk turned to what they could expect in the Dungeon they intended to enter, speaking of monsters and dangers as well as the required gear. Most of the gear was common, things that they already owned but some were much more extensive.

No other major incidents occurred before they finally arrived at Silverstone, the arches of the tall buildings that make up the city coming into view.

Daniel smiles as they finally arrive, the city spreading out beneath them in the distance as they crest the hill. Three times the size of Karlak, Silverstone is a major trading hub and the second largest city this side of the country, situated as it is on a meeting point for three major roads and the Arq river that flows from the mountains in the North. Most importantly for Daniel and Asin, it also contains two Advanced Dungeons which contribute a significant portion of wealth to the city.

Like its namesake, Silverstone gleams in the evening sun, as the white walls of the houses and the roofs reflect sunlight and even twinkle ever so slightly to their gaze. The white of the city is not in fact stone but from a unique local clay that when applied helps insulate the houses and gives the city its distinctive look.

As they begin the descent into the city, Daniel smiles and pulls up his character sheet for a moment. They are nearly there!

Name: Daniel Chai

Class: Level 5 Adventurer (6%)

Sub-classes: Level 7 (Miner) (14%)

Human (Male)

Statistics

Life: 215

Stamina: 215

Mana: 160

Attributes

Strength: 20

Agility: 20

Constitution: 28

Intelligence: 16

Willpower: 18

Luck: 13

Skills

Unarmed Combat: Level 3 (17/100)

Clubs: Level 8 (84/100)

Archery: Level 1 (18/100_

Shield: Level 7 (04/100)

Dodge: Level 4 (98/100)

Combat Sense: Level 5 (78/100)

Perception: Level 5 (66/100)

Mining: Level 7 (78/100)

Healing: Level 8 (87/100)

Herb Lore: Level 3 (31/100)

Stealth: Level 2 (14/100)

Cooking: Level 3 (21/100)

Singing: Level 2 (14/100)

Skill Proficiencies

Double Strike

Shield Bash

Mapping (II)

Spells

Minor Healing (I)

Gifts

Martyr's Touch - The caster may heal oneself or others by touch and concentration, sacrificing a portion of his life to do so. Cost varies depending on the extent of the injuries healed.

Chapter 7

"Right then, you lot," the wizened old man barks at the Adventurers, waiting for them to gather before Chip passes around small pouches filled with their pay. The wagons having finally arrived at the city, the caravan master had passed the coin pouches to Chip earlier who now did the distribution. Three smaller pouches for the experienced Adventurers, and two larger pouches for Asin and Daniel for their longer journey. Hefting their pay, the Adventurers slide them into their respective belt pouches and take their dismissal with good grace outside the walls of Silverstone.

"Remember, the Wandering Rooster in two days!" Niko waggles his finger at the two novices who nod quickly. The Rooster was located near the center of town, next to the Adventurer's Guild and nearly directly between the two Dungeons. It was perfectly located and well known to provide high-quality food, comfortable and clean beds and thus cost significantly more than the two novice adventurers could afford. As such, they would be taking rooms closer to the outside walls where cheaper accommodation could be found. While many other inns and buildings lay outside the city's walls, those were often more run down and significantly less comfortable.

The group had already agreed that they would meet in two days to run the Advanced Dungeon. Asin and Daniel first needed to make arrangements for their fetch quest as well as locate and purchase some of the recommended items. It also would allow the two time to tour the city itself, uninjured.

Entrance to the city was a simple affair. The pair had to only showcase their Adventurers seals to be allowed in without paying the entrance fee to the city. Daniel and Asin sighed, wishing that this courtesy was extended to them everywhere else. Of course, this tactic was one that the City of Silverstone had adopted to attract and encourage Adventurers to visit their city over others. After depositing their bags at an inn recommended by Gabriel, the two Adventurers get directions from the innkeeper to the merchant they needed to meet for Max.

As they walk through the city, the two Adventurers unconsciously move closer to one another, unused to the press of humanity. Asin constantly wrinkles her nose, the never-ending stench of civilization pressing on her expanded senses while the constant shouts, rumbling of passing wagons and just the patter of feet assault her ears. Daniel, in turn, finds the sight of so many inhabitants slightly unnerving, and he unconsciously keeps a hand next to his mace, glad to have taken Gabriel's earlier advice to keep the majority of his coins in a pouch hidden inside his shirt.

Most of the inhabitants of Silverstone were dressed like those in Karlak, wearing simple tunics and pants. However, even Daniel noted that many of these tunics were made of higher quality material than those in Karlak. Asin prods Daniel who follows her gaze, and they step into a nearby clothing store to make some quick purchases. They leave in short order, Daniel stalking out with Asin following after, the pair of them growling softly as the proprietor refuses to serve the Catkin. Still, Daniel makes a mental note to go shopping for both himself and Kh'yra before he leaves, preferably in a store that encouraged purchases from a variety of customers.

As he stalks forwards in anger, Asin has to tug on Daniel's arm to get him to go in the right direction as he misses a turn, the little Catkin's tail lashing out behind her. Fortunately, an irate Adventurer who was as broad as Daniel generated a significant amount of space around his body, ensuring that neither Adventurer had to deal with any further casual bumps.

It takes them nearly an hour and a half to find the correct building. Asking for directions often resulted in confusing and sometimes contradictory instructions - the sprawling, winding streets and numerous alleyways meant that the 'fastest' way to a location would differ depending on the particular pedestrian. Finally, at their destination, the pair stare up at the larger warehouse. They tug on the rope situated outside the door, listening to the bell ringing inside as they wait to be let in. They are greeted by a large, tattooed bald man whose skin is nearly as dark as Asin's fur when the door opens. "What?"

Daniel fishes out the letter of introduction, offering it to the man, "We're Adventurers completing a Quest."

The tattooed man grunts, closing the door on the two Adventurers, leaving them on the street. Daniel and Asin look at each other before shrugging their shoulders, setting themselves to wait in the busy street. Ten minutes later the door opens, and the door warden waves them in, looking past them to ensure no others follow. Once he bars the door again, he leads the two Adventurers through the warehouse which surprisingly is sparsely filled with wooden crates shelved with great care. Neither of the Adventurers remarks at the state of the warehouse as neither has ever been in one before, unable to realize that the meticulous and spotless nature of the warehouse was unusual.

At an office in the back, their guide knocks and then opens the door before waving them in. The dark giant steps in soon after the two, taking station behind the pair. Asin automatically shifts, putting herself to the side so that she can watch the larger enforcer, her actions eliciting a narrowing of eyes. Daniel, however, steps forward, his gaze fixed on the merchant before them. At first, he assumes it is a woman due to the delicate features and the makeup, but after a moment he realizes he is mistaken. The gentleman before him has rouged his cheeks, mascaraed his eyes and painted his long, delicate fingers but is still very much a man. Fingers gently glide along the edges of their letter, delicately tracing the words before their owner finally deigns to acknowledge their presence.

"Adventurer's Chai and Asin I presume?" Receiving nods from both he smiles, gesturing for them to take a seat, reaching out to pour glasses of tea for them both. "Come, come. Join me in a drink. Please."

Daniel nods and sits down while Asin shakes her head, preferring to stand and watch the tattooed man. The giant flashes her a grin and is given one in return while the merchant looks at the byplay with a resigned expression.

"I am Leonard Regus. Please, relax and drink. You are guests, honored guests here," Leonard says.

Daniel picks up the glass, sipping at the tea, and is pleasantly surprised at the light and fruity flavor.

"It's good, isn't it? It's a blend we import. If I do say so myself, it is very good. If you want, at the end of this, I'll sell you a bagful. Now, did you just arrive from Karlak?"

"Yes, we did," Daniel answers. Leonard proceeds to ask questions about their journey, disguising his search for information on the condition of the roads in idle chatter. Daniel replies, enjoying the tea and after a while, even Asin relaxes and joins him on sipping the beverage and snacking on the expensive and rare treats that Leonard offers. It is only after fifteen minutes that the conversation turns back to their initial reason for coming, Leonard having pulled sufficient information from the pair to satisfy himself.

"Well, you two have been a delight, a true delight. Your employer's purchases, they are all here. Would you care to inspect them?" Leonard asks, and at their nods of confirmation, he stands and struts to the door to lead them to the appropriate crate. His guard proceeds to pick up the crate from its shelf, placing it on the ground for the two Adventurers to review the items within, checking against the list they were provided. Satisfied, the two nod at Leonard and the guard who proceeds to set the items back on the shelf.

"Now, I understand you need to transport these to Karlak?" Daniel and Asin both nod again and Leonard offers them a regretful smile, "How unfortunate, how unfortunate. There is no caravan leaving for a few weeks, and I must say, it's really sad, but I must say, that one will be traveling to Kyris first. As you know, I'm sure you do, that'll lengthen your trip."

Seeing the crestfallen faces of the duo, Leonard continues, "However, there is a smaller merchant who will be leaving in four days who will be headed to Karlak directly. He usually does not take passengers but if I were to make the introduction…"

"What would you want for this?" Daniel asks bluntly, eyes narrowing. This seemed just a little too convenient.

"Nothing much, nothing at all. Just a little favor that a pair of young, strong Adventurers would find simple to complete," Leonard replies immediately, smiling. "I have a small matter, a small problem, with a competitor and it'd be quite, quite useful if you could perhaps have a word with him. Just a small thing, so very small."

"Guild," Asin speaks up, pointing at him.

"Mmmm… How quaint. How very quaint. Unfortunately, I cannot. I truly cannot speak with the Guild about this. It'd make a private matter public. I really wouldn't want that, and it's such a small favor." Daniel frowns and looks at Asin who shakes her head. Daniel nods back to her and then turns to turn down Leonard again but is cut-off. "Oh, that's so sad. Well, if you do change your mind, do tell me. I could always use your help. Really I could."

The moment he falls silent, the guard has moved up to the pair, indicating for them to leave. Leonard is already heading away, bidding them goodbye and the pair are whisked out in a moment, the goods left in Leonard's hands for now. Standing on the doorstep of the warehouse, the pair frown at each other.

"That was… different," Daniel says and Asin nods, rubbing her nose.

"No trust. Bad," Asin replies and Daniel nods, tapping his mace in thought. Still, the merchant was not going to steal their goods. It would ruin his reputation. After a moment, he shrugs at his partner.

"Well, let's check in with the Guild shall we?" Daniel says, and after getting their directions, the two begin the long hike into the center of town.

When they finally arrive at the Guild hours later, after getting lost a few times, the sun has begun to set. The Guild Hall in Silverstone makes both Adventurers stand in shock as they gaze on the large, three story building that makes up the Hall. It takes up two lots with two separate entrances and a gated yard for training. Late as it is, Adventurers stream out from the entrances at a rapid pace, barely even looking at the two who stand there in shock. Many of the Adventurers split almost immediately to the East and West, headed for the respective Dungeons that lie in those directions.

Asin is the first to get over her shock, prodding her partner to get him moving. Daniel grimaces, hanging his head slightly as he realizes how much of a rube he is looking like and starts walking to the nearest entrance. A few minutes later, both Adventurers hurry back out and enter the other entrance, Daniel flushed with shame. How were they to know that there was a separate entrance for the more senior Adventurers? It wasn't as if there was a sign like the wooden, painted one hanging right outside the door…

In the quest hall, the two Adventurers stare around the large room which is both familiar with its desks and attendants and also so much larger than any other hall they have been to before. The sheer hum of business, of Adventurers and attendants moving in an orderly fashion makes them pause at the doorway again as they attempt to get their bearings. At the loud clearing of a voice behind them, the two scurry to the side and out of the way. Movement to their right catches their attention as they spot an entire room that is set aside for quest notifications through the doorway.

"Wow…" Daniel murmurs and Asin wordlessly agrees with him. Such a difference from Karlak. After a moment more, Daniel shakes his head to clear it and walks to the quest room. They needed to see if there were caravan guard jobs available back to Karlak, preferably earlier. Perhaps the merchant had been wrong?

"Asin Chetan and Daniel Chai? Yes, I've got confirmation of your caravan quest here. Well done. As for your other question, the board is correct. The earliest guard job to Karlak is in two weeks. In fact, we have four jobs from caravans available - though I understand you are looking for the fastest to return to Karlak? That would be Elijah's group in two and a half weeks then," the attendant replies, rubbing at the ink stain on his finger as he scans down the list he has in front of him. Daniel and Asin both sigh, their faint hopes dashed.

"Problem?" the attendant asks and the pair shrug.

"We'd like to sign up for the caravan then. And there's no problem, it's just a little expensive living here," Daniel adds, already thinking of how expensive their inn was. They probably would have to move outside the city gates.

"Don't worry. We've got a lot of work for those of your level. Most of our Adventurers refuse to do the low-level quests we receive, so there's always a backlog." The attendant leans forward, his eyes gleaming. "In fact, if you are willing to get started now, I've got a few quests…"

"Uhh…" Daniel opens his mouth to say no as picking up quests today was not part of the plan. It was getting pretty late, but Asin elbows him aside, nodding firmly to the attendant whose grin widens.

"Perfect! Well, being from Karlak, I have the perfect job for you." The attendant grins, pushing forward a small stack of quest markers. Asin's nose wrinkles as she quickly flicks through them, letting out a low distressed growl.

"I know, I know. Sewers, but these have been piling up so much," the attendant replies and then leans forward conspiringly. "I'll tell you what, if you're willing to take them all, I'll even waive the deposit for all but the top one."

Daniel pushes himself up, and Asin hands him the quest notes which Daniel frowns at, reading them over. Rat extermination. Rat extermination. Pest extermination. Rat extermination. On and on, the sheets continue. "So many…"

"Tell me about it! The guards sweep the sewers every few weeks, but they only ever do the main lines regularly and the rest on rotation," the attendant grumbles, shaking his head. "Of course, that doesn't work if you've got an infestation in your neighborhood."

Asin nods absently, her eyes locked on the bottom of each quest notification, mentally toting up their potential earnings. Her grin widens, coins dancing in her eyes as she considers just how much they could earn.

"I don't know; I mean sewers…" Daniel frowns, glancing over at Asin. The Catkin would suffer even more than he would from the smells.

"All sewer quests receive a token for use at the bathhouse too!" the attendant adds, leaning forward and continuing his hard sell. "It's really a good deal."

Asin nods firmly, pushing the quests forward and shoots a look at Daniel. Daniel grimaces, shaking his head and she growls at him. The young Adventurer grimaces again, eyeing the stack before giving in, "Fine. Can you sort them by location and earnings and what we can finish in one day? We'll then take that pile and a map."

The attendant nods, pulling the stack back and working quickly to do as requested, smiling as he does so. Asin nods happily, already counting their earnings in her head as Daniel mentally grumbles. After they receive their quest papers back along with their requested map and have put down their deposit, the two finally exit the Guild Hall to return home.

"You know, we were supposed to take it easy tomorrow," Daniel grumbles at Asin, waving the stack of quest papers in front of her. "Not go on Quests."

"Money. Good money," Asin says, licking at her paw as she walks along, her tail waving out behind her in happiness.

"Uh huh. You're buying dinner," Daniel states and Asin just nods her head, content to have won that fight.

☐

Chapter 8

Deep in the sewers the next day, Daniel grumbles as he holds up the map to ensure they are in the right spot. Satisfied, he tucks the map away in his leather armor, reaching beyond the glowing mana stone he has attached to it and promising himself he will get his armor cleaned for the umpteenth time that day. He rubs at his nose through the cloth covering, glad that they had taken the time to purchase the enchanted cloths which reduce the smells of the sewer. Otherwise, he knew, he would be regretting this day even more.

For all his grumbling, Daniel still had to admire the extent of the sewers around him. Silverstone's city council had spent the money to hire Dwarven architects and Earth Mages to tunnel the necessary sewers beneath the city, an enlightened act compared to many other smaller cities and towns where waste was allowed to collect on streets or at best, was hauled away late at night by waste carts. The creation of the sewers was an act that was greatly praised by the Healers of the city and one that they continually pushed for in other cities but which was often opposed by the City Guard.

By diverting a small amount of the Arq river through the sewers, the city ensured that the accumulated waste was constantly washed away. However, as the Arq changed in height as the Spring thaw and Autumn rains swept through the land, the sewer tunnels had to be built to accommodate the varying flow rates as well. This ensured that most days the tunnels were not filled to the brim, allowing all manner of monsters and ruffians to use them, creating the reason for opposition by the guard and consistent jobs for the Adventurers.

For Daniel and Asin, they have been in the sewers for two hours already, and they have cleared out the first rat infestation. As natives of the plain, the Devil Rats could grow to enormous sizes if they were able to find sufficient food but both Asin and Daniel had yet to fight one larger than three feet long - not including the tails which were currently stored in Asin's backpack as proof.

Even through the enchanted cloth, the smell of the accumulated waste seeped through, making Daniel take short, careful breaths as he led the way through the carved sewer tunnels. The sewer tunnels started off with a single, large corridor that immediately split into a half dozen smaller lines, each of which then split into smaller tunnels which were fed by lead, clay and metal pipes that ran into the various buildings above. While the initial construction of the lines had been extremely orderly, over time the additions and tearing down of buildings had ensured that new sewer pipes now dotted these smaller corridors which Daniel and Asin traversed. As such, they often had to keep a wary eye above them, skirting around these unorganized additions to the gray stone walls.

As they near the next turn off, Asin runs ahead and grabs Daniel's arm, pulling him to a stop. Daniel frowns, glancing over to the Catkin who has a pair of enchanted cloths covering her face as she raises her other arm with a pair of throwing knives in them. Nodding slightly, Daniel crouches down and waits for her to duck around the corner, her knives flashing forward the moment she does so.

Daniel follows soon after and sees what she heard over the ongoing roar of water, a giant black dung beetle. Her knives burrow into the creature's flesh, sinking deep in and Asin skirts close to the wall to let Daniel rush ahead, lashing out with his mace as he does so. The beetle is soon dispatched, the monster barely more dangerous than a Kobold Chieftain and the pair had dealt with a large number of those. The monster slain, Asin walks forward and extracts her knives and removes an antenna before kicking the body into the stream of sewage.

It was pretty clear to both Adventurers by now why the more experienced Advanced Adventurers of the town declined to complete these quests. The monsters in the sewers were little threat to experienced Adventurers and the quest rewards, while decent for a pair of beginners like themselves, held little attraction to the coin one could make in a Dungeon. Not to forget that they would need to wade through the sewers the entire day.

Grimacing, Daniel moves on. It had taken nearly two hours to make their way this far, and they had at least another half dozen locations to sweep. Still, Daniel pushes on without a word. They had taken the quests; they would complete them. That's what professionals did.

Hours later, the two stump into the Guild and to the nearest free attendant's desk. They are immediately rerouted into the Quest room, the main hall devoted to the Dungeon and trading mana stones while Adventurers and attendants hold their breath until they leave. Walking to the Quest room, the pair leave behind looks of disgust and wrinkled noses. Even grumpier than when they started, they finally manage to make their way to the right desk, and Asin drops the bag of rat tails and beetle antennae without prompting. The attendant looks the two over, sniffs and receives the quest notes from Daniel silently, pushing the bag aside without even inspecting the contents.

Minutes later, he has their pay, and their bath tokens, and the pair hurry out, intent on cleaning themselves, their clothing and their armor thoroughly. At the bathhouse, they each hand over their armor and clothing to the attendants to be magically cleansed before they head into their respective sections of the bath houses. Asin, within the female section, is redirected again as she is sent to her own private room due to her fur.

Having washed thoroughly, Daniel relaxes in the hot water pool with his eyes half-closed. Like most other buildings, even the bath house in Silverstone was larger and more grandiose than the one in Karlak. The hot water pool is lined with white marble and situated next to a smaller cold-water pool that is similarly outfitted, sculptures of leaves and vines carved into the lip of the pools. Eyes half-closed, Daniel barely pays attention to the other bathers who move around him till one comes by, letting out a blissful groan as he sinks into the water. Cracking an eye open, he notes the large bruise that covers the man's thigh and hip, and which crawls part-way up his back.

"That looks painful," Daniel says.

"Yes." The man grins, flashing a smile at Daniel as he stretches out in the water and props himself back against the wall. Now that he has more time, Daniel sees that the middle-aged blond man also has numerous other smaller bruises and scratches around his body and a series of older scars. "Life of an Adventurer."

Daniel nods, rubbing his nose before he speaks, "Why don't you get that healed?"

The man laughs, looking at Daniel more closely. "Kid, you don't spend good money on Healers or potions for something this small. Not if you want to save up for any of the good equipment you won't."

Daniel nods slightly, ducking his head down as he realizes that not everyone would have the ability to handle injuries like he did. It had become so routine for himself to fix his or Asin's injuries with minor healing or his Gift that he had forgotten that not everyone had access to that. After a brief pause, Daniel looks up, "I could heal that for you. I know Minor Healing."

The adventurer blinks then laughs, sticking a hand out, "The name's Roy. And I'd be real grateful if you would."

Daniel shakes the man's hand and then while still holding Roy's hand casts his Minor Heal. Roy takes a deep breath when the spell hits him and then relaxes, a wide grin splitting his face as the bruises across his body fade. "Well, isn't that a thing. You actually can Heal. Mighty kind of you."

Daniel shrugs and then blinks as he realizes a number of other Adventurers have come up to him, murmuring about injuries and pointing to them. Daniel twitches, hunkering down a little at the barrage of requests and casts a quick series of spells before claiming to be out of mana. Lips pressed together; Daniel watches the ungrateful Adventurers wade away, the lucky few who were healed laughing at their good fortune and the others quietly grumbling about the Healer who did not have enough mana to heal them all.

"And that's the reason Healer's don't work for free." Laughing, Roy shakes his head at Daniel's pout. "You'll get used to it, kid, you surely will. When you have to fight varmints for everything you get, you start taking whatever you can get for free without thought."

Daniel grunts, unwilling to accept that kind of thinking and regretting opening his mouth at all. At least when he worked at the Clinic in Karlak, he provided a service to those who needed it and who couldn't pay for the services they received. The Adventurers were just cheap and ungrateful.

"So, you're pretty raw for this city. Visiting?" Roy says after watching Daniel mull for a few minutes.

"Yes," Daniel replies, nodding.

"Mmm… and you be having the look of a melee fighter with those muscles," Roy says, eyeballing the broad Adventurer next to him. "What city are you from?"

"Karlak."

"No surprise. Pardon me for asking, but have joined a guild yet?"

"Guild?" Reluctantly drawn in, Daniel leans forward.

"My apologies. I always forget Karlak doesn't have one. No surprise, they rarely bother with Beginner towns, too many flatfoots who will go nowhere there. Adventuring guilds are just a bunch of adventurers who work together in a more formal-like fashion to help each other out," Roy says and his eyes sparkle as he continues. "It just so happens I'm the Vice Guildchair of the Red Roses in this city. Why, we'd be real grateful to have us another Healer."

Daniel blinks, shaking his head slowly. "As I said, I'm just visiting."

"Of course, no rush. As I mentioned, we don't normally recruit Beginners, but you seem like a mighty fine fellow. The guild can provide you some training, some equipment and even have you work with some experienced Adventurers. Nothing like a good old head on their shoulders to keep you safe, you know."

"Okay…" Daniel says, pushing himself up from the pool slightly and smiling back slightly. "Well, I'll think about it."

Roy continues smiling as he nods, "Sure. Sure. Just remember, it's Roy Inverness of the Red Roses. Just drop my handle, they'll know to expect you."

Standing up fully, Daniel wraps the towel around his body once again and nods jerkily, moving away from the rather pushy Adventurer. He sighs when he finally makes it out, relaxing slightly. Well, that was different.

Lip caught between his teeth, Daniel finishes with the letter, setting the quill down with relief. He eyes the sloppy handwriting with distaste, slightly ashamed again about how ugly it looks compared to the flowing script used by scribes. Still, it was what it was. Letting his eyes track over the words again, he wonders if he missed anything.

Dear Khy'ra,

I am writing this letter to you from Silverstone. We have arrived safely and have met with the trader who carries Max's items. Everything looks to be there, but unfortunately, there are no caravans returning to Karlak directly for a few weeks. It seems it will take us even longer to make our way back than we initially planned.

Have you ever been to Silverstone? It is so much larger than Karlak. So much larger than any place I've been to, truth be told. There is so much to see and do! While Asin has been making me do quests with her every day, we still have time to see a little of the city in the evenings. I can't wait to stop owing her money for the armor.

Last night, we went to see a play at a theater. The city is so busy, they even have a dedicated building to host acting troupes all year round! They were doing the Seven Warriors, and it was amazing. They even had a musician playing alongside them. I wish you were here to see it with me.

There is so much to see in this world. I am glad I took this quest even if it took me away ~~from you~~ for a while. Even the quests here are different, and if we ever finish with the sewers, I want us to take a few delivery quests. They are boring and hard work, but it'll give us a chance to see the city more.

We've been invited to test out an Advanced Dungeon with an adventuring party we met on the road. Asin and I are excited to do so, but I must admit, I'm a bit worried. Still, we should be safe with experienced Adventurers around us - they have made it down 6 levels! It's really nice of them to show us around. Don't tell but I think one of the Adventurers is sweet on Asin.

I will see you in a few weeks. By the time you get this letter, it might only be a few days.

Finished reading, Daniel pauses as he wonders how he should sign off. Should he sign off with something other than his name? Perhaps a declaration of love? Yet, neither had said it in person and adding it to the letter seemed wrong. A more formal salutation felt off too. Lips pursed, Daniel stares at the paper, wondering what else to say. Did he even have a right to do so after he slept with another? Did they have that kind of relationship that such things mattered? It didn't seem like it, but then again…

Daniel rubs his temples, making a sudden decision and signing off with only his name and then folding the letter and sealing it. A quick addition of her name and the city and Clinic was enough. Tomorrow, he would hand it to the innkeeper for delivery. Many royal messengers stopped at inns to make some additional coin doing personal deliveries after all, and the innkeeper assured him he had a good relationship with one particular messenger. Lips pursed, Daniel blows the candle out and lays on his bed, troubled thoughts about his relationship keeping him up for a while longer before sleep finally claims him.

Chapter 9

On the second day, the pair finds themselves standing before the Wandering Rooster greeting Iyas and Tevfik. Niko rushes out a few minutes later, still wetting his hair and attempting to get it to stay down as he does so. He grins, waving to the pair as he comes out. Having spent the past few days running the sewers for the Guild, the pair of Adventurers are excited to check out the Advanced Dungeon.

"I see you two brought your bags. Good. And the oil flasks and holy water?" Niko asks, and as the pair nods, he grins. "As we mentioned, we'll take you through the first floor today of Porthos and maybe, depending on how it goes the second floor too. Porthos is better than Aramis for beginners, Aramis being the tougher of the two Dungeons to clear."

The pair nod again at Niko's words, Daniel adjusting his belt to seat his mace better. Niko waits for a moment and looks to his friends before taking the group to the Dungeon entrance. The entrance itself is a simple stone building where a small detachment of guards stand, watching the doors and the Adventurers that enter them.

"Niko, Iyas." The lead guard nods to them, his eyes flicking to Tevfik before moving on to land on Asin and then Daniel. "Additions to your party?"

"Grady. Just showing them the first floor. They're registered Adventurers," Niko replies blithely.

"On your heads. And theirs," Grady says, not even attempting to stop the pair. Why would he after all? Their job was only to stop monsters from coming out and unregistered and foolish children from going in.

Leading the party into the foyer of the dungeon, Daniel blinks as the simple stone room is broken up by a glowing silver portal where a doorway leading to the dungeon itself should be located. Asin beside him lets out a little yowl of surprise and Daniel finds his throat suddenly dry.

"Advanced Dungeons all contain these portals," Iyas replies and claps the pair on the back as he gently guides them forward. "Gave me a real fright too first time I saw one. Don't worry; they work just like the portal stones you're used to in Karlak except that if you're not registered, it sends you directly to the first floor."

"Right then. We're here to give Daniel and Asin a taste of an Advanced dungeon, not kill them. So, Daniel and Asin will be in the center working their long-range weaponry," Niko says. "I'll be in front with Tevfik while Iyas, you'll be scouting. When in the dungeon, my word is law. We'll share the stones and other drops four ways, with Daniel and Asin splitting the fourth share. Any questions?"

Receiving none, Iyas steps forward to the dungeon portal as Daniel hefts his light crossbow and locks a bolt in. As the other party members disappear without a single ripple in the portal, Daniel takes a deep breath and wipes his sweaty palms against his pants before stepping in.

What greets him on the first floor is nothing that Daniel could have imagined. Instead of a small cave, they appear in a single large cavern that seemingly stretches for miles beneath the small ledge that they stand on. Stone walkways are arrayed across the cavern, elevating them thirty to forty feet off the ground immediately, crossing and meeting other walkways that lead higher above to other stone platforms or down to where a rolling white mist forms. Screeches and screams from wheeling birds and other animals echo, along with the slow-grinding of stone as walkways detach from platforms and swing through the air to connect with other platforms or walkways. Light from the mana-saturated stone fills the cave, illuminating the sense-defying scene and giving everything a blue sheen.

Even having had the first floor described to him, Daniel finds himself standing at the entrance in shock as he attempts to grasp the magnitude and absurdity of the dungeon floor. He cannot, even with his elevated vantage point, see the end of the cavern or the ceiling above him, no matter how hard he strains.

Asin next to him lets out a chuff and a low growl of surprise, cursing softly in Catkin as she glares about herself, tail whipping back and forth. At Niko's insistence, she carries a triple batch of throwing knives to make up for the losses that are to be expected through the day. Even now, she clutches a knife in her left hand, the blade sticking out between her fingers.

Having given the pair enough time to view their surroundings, Niko nods to Iyas, signaling him to get a move on. Iyas glides forward, head constantly swiveling to scope out his surroundings, an arrow nocked in his bow. Niko coughs, getting the pair's attention. "Right, come along then. The monsters aren't going to kill themselves."

Walking together, the Adventurers scan their surroundings searching for threats. After a moment, Asin prods Daniel and points to Niko. Daniel frowns and not seeing what she does, raises an eyebrow. She lets out a chuff, her tailing having returned to its usual lazy waving as she points to her eyes and then up. Daniel slowly nods, realization coming as he begins to look upwards for threats. It is not a moment too soon as Niko grunts out, "Trouble."

Daniel spots the Imps a moment later, a dozen scaled, warty figures gliding down with their bat-like wings spread out behind them. The monsters are mostly black with shades of red highlighting claws, pointed ears, and sharp, needle-like teeth. Snapping his crossbow to his shoulder, Daniel waits for the monsters to come near him. At the speed that they are approaching, he will only have one good shot.

Depressing the trigger slowly and gently, Daniel remembers to shoot for where the imp will be and not where it is. The bolt flies true when it leaves, catching an imp in its chest and knocking the monster away. Ahead of him Niko crouches, eyes tracking the pair of Imps that close on him before he draws his sword. Activating a Skill, the swordsman's strike moves so fast, the air in front is compressed into a thin line along the edge of the blade, sending a wave of compressed and super-sharp air tearing into the Imps who dare to attack him. Wings and bodies shredded, the Imps smash into the walkway, what's left of their wings feebly beating against the ground.

"That's how you do it!" Niko calls out as he darts forward to thrust his sword into the Imps bodies. "Otherwise the Mana stones get lost!"

Daniel has no time to answer, working on cranking his crossbow while Asin stands next to him, throwing her knives at the monsters that rush the group. Tevfik keeps close to the two, stepping forwards to strike with his sword when an Imp comes too close, crippling the wing before he stomps on the creature's neck. Ahead of them, Iyas has turned around and sent a pair of arrows into the sky, each arrow bringing a monster down.

Without a word, Asin grabs hold of Daniel and pulls him down, a ball of conjured fire flashing past where his head was. Eyes wide, Daniel drops the bolt and has to scramble for it on the ground even as Tevfik catches another fireball on his shield, enchanted runes flaring to life as they provide additional protection against the heat. Asin is on her knees, charging another blade and sending it straight into a throat, the blade piercing the creature's open mouth. The Imp lets out a little gurgle, falling to the ground and as Daniel finally looks up, bolt seated, he finds the wave wiped.

Niko quickly moves around the dissipated bodies, picking up the mana stones and pocketing them while Iyas keeps a further eye out. "Not bad, eight stones and two imp teeth. Remember, shoot when they are over the walkways."

Asin hops over to grab a pair of her blades that fell on the path while Daniel grimaces, realizing how little he did in that fight. The entire battle had happened so fast!

"Iyas," Niko calls out and Iyas moves on, continuing to lead the party deeper into the dungeon.

The following hours have opened the two young Adventurers' eyes to the level gap between them and the experienced Adventurers they party with. Each attack consists of at least a dozen Imps, often more and yet the party of three cut through the monsters with frightening ease. The fighters never waste any motion, each attack bringing an Imp to the ground to be finished. Skills are used sparingly and with precision, often triggered to take down multiple monsters at a time.

As impressive as their combat skills are, it is their teamwork that makes Daniel and Asin truly jealous. The group rarely speaks, and when they do, it is normally to order Daniel and Asin around. Otherwise, the well-oiled party work together smoothly, never targeting the same monster nor leaving gaps in their defenses as they fight.

"Asin, Daniel, come!" Iyas calls out. Daniel looks up, pushing away his thoughts about the differences in strength and hurries forward. Iyas waves them forward to where a new walkway starts, carefully brushing aside the dirt to reveal a pressure tile.

"See it? Right, watch this." Glancing back to ensure the two are on the platform, Iyas backs off as well and throws a small pouch filled with dirt onto the tile. The weight is enough to depress the tile, and the entire walkway immediately tilts to the side, spinning halfway and tipping dirt and debris into the air before it rotates back.

"Shit!" Daniel shouts, his eyes wide as he imagines what would have happened to any Adventurer unlucky enough to be caught by that.

"Yes. Feather Fall enchantments are quite popular." Iyas chuckles, waiting for the groaning walkway to right itself. When the walkway rights itself, he continues speaking. "See how the dirt, especially on this side, is slightly higher? Comes from the repeated tipping. You got to watch out for that."

Niko waits for the lesson to be over before he clears his throat, waving back to the platform. "Good time to have lunch."

Receiving confirming nods, Iyas elects to be on the first watch while the others eat. Almost immediately, Tevfik and Asin move to a corner of the platform, their tails curling around each other as they growl softly.

"So, what do you think?"

Daniel startles slightly, blinking up at Niko guiltily as he turns away from watching the two lovers. "Ummm…. none of my business."

"Not them, the dungeon!" Eyes twinkling, Niko pokes Daniel who flushes.

"Oh! Of course, that's what you meant." Daniel pushes thoughts of getting berated by Elder Chetan aside as he replies to Niko. "It's amazing. I never thought it'd be so big. And the monsters, they aren't that much tougher than Kobolds, but there's so many of them! And those burns sting!" Daniel rubs at his arm, remembering how Tevfik was unable to catch a fireball completely on his shield, splashing Daniel with just a touch of the explosion.

"It's why we chose Porthos," Niko says. "The Imps aren't that strong, and so long as we keep them focused on us, you two should be pretty safe. Especially with your healing abilities. Aramis on the other hand - well, the Kulark are much harder to fight. They can slither faster than you'd think and their scales are extremely hard. Worst, because they're sentient, they'll target you and Asin first."

Daniel nods at that, looking out at the vista spread before them. In the distance, he thinks he can spot another pair of Adventuring groups, but the level is so large and the pathways so numerous that meeting another team would require significant effort and planning. Running a hand through his black hair, Daniel lets out a sigh.

"Thinking about how far you have to go?" Niko enquires as he spots Tevfik get up with Asin to relieve Iyas.

"A bit."

Niko just nods at that, standing up to have a chat with Iyas. A small smile tugs at the corner of Niko's lips as he stands, a smile that is hidden from Daniel as he crosses over to his friend to plan the rest of the day.

"Right then, you see the big Imp there? That's the Overseer - they are evolved Imps, and while they can't fly, they are a lot bigger and stronger. They can cast Fire Dart too which sends smaller but more numerous fire arrows," Niko explains as he points out the floor champion they have located after hours of trekking through the dungeon. "Iyas and Asin will deal with his minions. I will fight the Overseer directly while Daniel will focus on killing any Imps Iyas and Asin bring down. Tevfik is on guard duty with his shield."

After a series of nods, Daniel pulls his shield off his back for the first time that day, sliding it over his arm. He quickly secures his crossbow to his body with a strap on his leg before hefting it in his other arm, ready to be dropped at a moment's notice. Daniel plans to shoot the single loaded bolt then immediately drop it for his mace. As he finishes his preparations, Tevfik points to Daniel's shield. "Pour the holy water on it."

Preparations complete, the party moves forward quickly at a light jog. There is no way to surprise the Overseer, so it is better to get to the monster quickly before it can call for more reinforcements.

Halfway to the Overseer on the final walkway, Iyas pulls to a stop and begins shooting at the Imps that have begun to converge on them. Asin skids to a stop next to him, throwing knives held out before her while Niko sprints the last few yards. Daniel spots that not all the Imps have left the Overseer's side and brings his crossbow to bear, shooting an Imp that attempts to block Niko's path out of his way.

The next few minutes are a blur for Daniel as he runs from downed Imp to downed Imp, all the time trying to keep an eye out for errant fireballs. Iyas provides cover fire for Daniel without a break, his hands blurring as he fires.

As Imps dart forward to strike at Daniel in ever increasing numbers, Tevfik raises his head to the ceiling and lets out a snarl that raises the hairs on the back of Daniel's neck and arms. He freezes for a brief moment, the primordial part of his mind recalling other beasts before he can push past it. The Imps, the targets of the Skill, are not as lucky and all freeze for a few minutes, struck by fear, and this allows the ranged attackers to attack freely. Iyas does not waste the opportunity, his hands glowing as he constantly pulls on the bow and fires arrows made of green energy at the Imps. Asin spins around and throws her knives as well, each shot targeted at a different Imp.

Daniel is left to run back and forth, swatting at Imps and stomping on them when he can. As the Imps push the fear aside, they screech and divert their attention to attack the greater danger, all of them launching themselves at Tevfik now. Asin scoots to the side, throwing a last dagger before pulling out the enchanted oil flask. She watches, occasionally striking down an Imp that comes too close before snarling out in Catkin as throwing the flask into the air after triggering the enchantment. The flask shatters, sending flaming oil around and catching many of the Imps in the blast radius. Tevfik, warned beforehand is crouched behind his enchanted shield, the explosion giving him a momentary respite.

Behind them, Daniel spots Niko cutting upwards with his sword, the Skill triggering to pick up the Overseer from the ground. Even as the creature begins to fall, Niko cries out and lunges forward, spearing the monster with his blade and then twisting in his hips to tear the wound wide open, ending the monster.

Daniel has no more time to watch as he catches a fireball on his shield from a downed Imp, the backdraft of heat singeing hair and eyebrows. He pushes forward, dropping his shield onto the creature's body and crushing it before it can breathe again, using his lowered body to allow him to swipe at another Imp.

A few minutes of intense battle later, the bodies of the Imps fade away in motes of blue light while the Adventurers catch their breath. Asin rubs ointment into her ear where an Imp caught her as it flew past, and Niko favors his leg while the others check over other minor injuries. Once he is able to, Daniel moves among the group and casts his spells, starting with Niko who proceeds to gather their loot. As he heals them, he receives murmured thanks, Iyas shooting Tevfik a knowing glance after being healed.

Later that evening in the Wandering Rooster, Niko drops a pouch onto the table where the other party members have been waiting, drinking.

"Not too bad a haul for the first floor," Niko says. "Split four ways, that's 1 Gold, 2 Silver and 2 Copper each. As requested, we didn't change the stones that fit your needs, Daniel, and split them into your pile instead as part of your share." He then drops two Copper coins on the table. "Oh, and there's this leftover. Tip?"

He gets nods from his party members of course and at the raised eyebrow from Daniel to whom he explains, "We just add it to the waitress tips when it comes up like this."

"Oh…" Daniel nods in agreement, the mystery of the good service explained. While Daniel is getting the explanation, Asin has pulled the pouch aside and deposited the contents out, quickly shifting the stones to the side before counting the remaining coins. Her ears wilt slightly at how much it has reduced, especially as they were still two stones short!

"So, you leveled up eh?" Iyas says, returning to their prior conversation.

"Yes! Amazing that it happened with just one trip." Daniel nods quickly.

"Mmm… There were a lot of monsters today. It's another reason we chose Porthos," Niko adds.

"What Skill are you going to choose?" Niko asks, curiously. "Are you going to get another Healing Spell?"

Asin tilts her head to Daniel too, nose wrinkling as she considers what her friend will do. More healing would be nice, though Daniel was only a moderately good fighter right now.

"Maybe..." Daniel trails off, not having thought too deeply about his choices yet.

"No! Don't waste your Skill Up on that. You can learn Spells with training," Iyas declares, and Daniel grimaces.

"I wish. The cost alone of renting a Healer's time to train me..." Daniel shakes his head. "It's impossible, at least for me."

"That's why you should join our Guild!" Iyas blurts out and then yelps, rubbing at his foot and glaring at Niko.

"Guild?"

"Yes, we're all part of the Green Robin," Niko replies, tapping at the badge that is situated on each of their cloaks. Daniel blinks, having noticed it before but not recognizing its significance. He had thought it was just a party badge - after all, even Beginner Adventurers in Karlak had done it. "What do you think? Interested? You and Asin could run Advanced dungeons all year long with different parties, increasing levels at a higher rate. And as a Guild member, the Guild would help locate and pay for your lessons just like it does for Mages."

Daniel frowns and then his eyes narrow slightly before he looks between the three experienced Adventurers. His voice laced with suspicion; he says, "You invited us because you wanted us to join your Guild didn't you?"

"Well, partly. We did want to show you around though, we like you guys," Niko hastily adds.

"Why?" Asin says, her tail unwrapped from Tevfik and now sticking out beneath her chair straight down.

"Well, we…"

"Why?" Asin repeats.

"Daniel's a healer. Is that what you want to hear? Healers who aren't priests are really, really rare. And most priests are a pain to work with - their abilities come from their Faith, so the better the Priest, the more Faithful they are to their God. We partied up with a Priest before from Mohin who would never work on the Fifth Day.   So yeah, we want, the Guild wants, any healers they can find," Niko replies exasperatedly.

Daniel looks to Iyas who just offers a short nod while Tevfik growls softly to Asin. She lets out a low snarl in return, moving her hand away from his before she stands, stalking out. Daniel looks between the three before he stands up and rushes out after his friend, Niko calling out quickly, "Think about it!"

As the door shuts, Daniel glimpses Niko berating Iyas for bringing up the Guild so abruptly, disrupting his plans. Daniel has no time to watch though as he hurries after his friend.

"Asin…"

She stalks onwards, not saying a word, tail lashing out side to side behind her as her shoulders hunch. Pedestrians scramble to get out of the short Catkin's way, the glower and array of knives a clear warning to all.

"I didn't know. I mean, there was this other guy who asked me to join his Guild, but I didn't know…" Daniel blathers on, filling the silence. "I mean, they don't even know about my Gift, and they want me this badly. I wonder what they'd be like if they knew. I guess it's good the other Adventurers didn't, but I know Liev mentioned it might be an issue…"

Asin lets out a little growl, and Daniel shuts up, her stalking carrying them through the city streets quickly. After a time, she says softly, "Tevfik no like me. Just you."

"I don't think that's true, Asin," Daniel adds quickly. "I mean, he's always watching you…"

"Idiot," Asin says, and for a moment Daniel wonders who she means. He opens his mouth to ask and then remembering her growl, shuts up, finishing the walk back to their inn in silence.

Chapter 10

"I'm not complaining about being out of the sewers, Asin, but did we have to take quests so far away?" Trudging out of the city, Daniel grumbles as he hefts his backpack. They had only been in Silverstone for a few days, as it stood, and now they had left it again on another quest. This one involved a visit to a nearby village to help the farmers fight off attacking vermin while they completed their harvesting.

It was not a glamorous job, but it certainly paid well as the farmers needed to attract the Adventurers away from the Dungeons. Luckily, with the Skills that most farmers gained, they were able to manage and see to large tracts of land, allowing them to handle the expense. Truthfully, from Asin's point of view, the most important aspect of the quest was for once not the pay but that it got the pair out of Silverstone and away from that traitorous, two-faced Catkin.

Seeing that his partner has decided to ignore him, Daniel glances over to the side and spots a familiar face from the Guild Hall. Not seeing a guild badge on the group, Daniel diverts himself slightly to say hi.

"Morning there!" Daniel calls out, and the group of Adventurers turns to him. The middle-aged, slightly potbellied mace wielder he spotted eyes Daniel for a moment before grinning and waving to Daniel.

"You're the youngsters from Karlak," the older gentlemen replies, smiling.

"Yes. I'm Daniel."

"Lin. This is Ingrid and Jorge," Lin indicates his older companions, a redhead in an old but well-maintained suit of chainmail and a darker skinned, spear-wielding companion in turn. "You heading to Ilquin too?"

"That's right. The quest pays very well," Daniel says.

"Definitely. It's why we do it. I'm impressed you managed three days in the sewers though. Most groups give up after the first."

Ingrid shudders at the mention of the sewers and Daniel finds himself rubbing his nose, the smell coming back to him once again. He is not surprised that the group knows of their exploits, Adventurers had a tendency to gossip worse than housewives. After all, learning as much as you could about the monsters and levels you would face could keep an Adventurer alive.

"Which Dungeon do you run otherwise?" Daniel asks, curiosity filling his voice.

"None," Jorge answers for the group and seeing Daniel's surprised look, he continues. "We're questors."

"Huh?"

"We don't run Dungeons anymore, Daniel. We focus on quests only," Ingrid quickly explains, her voice surprisingly high pitched for such a rough looking woman. "We gave up on all of that dangerous delving a while ago. That's what questors are - Adventurers who only do quests."

"Oh…" Daniel falls silent then frowns. "But we were told there weren't enough quests being taken up."

"Not at your level," Lin chuckles. "Just because we're retired doesn't mean we want to do fetch quests or the sewer."

"Is this dangerous then?" Daniel frowns, recalling that Asin had appeared at his door this morning with the quest already taken.

"No, not really. It's a longer quest since it takes a few days for the harvest to be brought in, but overall, it's a pretty easy quest. The biggest danger is the Spotted Deer which are running, and those are easy enough to scare away. At least for us Adventurers," Lin pronounces, and Daniel nods slowly. "Ever met the deer before?"

"No."

"Har, alright then. Come on; I'll tell you about them and the quest…"

"Smell good," Asin says, walking over to peer at the meal the experienced Adventurers are making. Lin laughs, waving her to take a seat as he flips the pan, sending the thin slices of meat into the air before catching them.

"That's quite a compliment coming from Asin," Daniel says, shaking his head as he sees how fast the group has set up their sleeping area. He and Asin had just finished setting up their own camp and were in the middle of gathering wood, and these three were already cooking.

"Join us then," Jorge says as he brings back a pot of water which he hangs over the fire. The moment it is hung, he moves to the waiting vegetables which he begins to throw in. "Lin always brings more than enough."

"You'd pack more too if you ever got stuck in a snowstorm on Pare Peak like I did. Ended up chewing on our leather vests just to eat something!" Lin replies, a slight smile twisting his face. "Of course, that's when I learned that Derin Lizard brains are quite good."

"Don't corrupt the kids, Lin," Ingrid says, dropping her bundle of wood. "Right, if you add your pile to ours, we'll have more than enough for tonight."

Asin nods with alacrity, leaving Daniel behind as she accedes to the invitation. After a brief questioning, Daniel moves away too to bring along the meat he was to cook and watches as Ingrid slices and spices the meat with deft strokes. Asin prods at the spice, sniffing at the spices with interest as she deposits the wood.

"Why were you on Pare Peak?" Daniel says once he is situated comfortably and out of the way of the smoke from the fire.

"A quest of course. This young nobleman wanted an escort to find the Yeti." Lin rolls his eyes, "Hired two whole parties for three weeks and paid good coin for it. We ended up stuck there for two months when we were snowed in. Luckily, the quest was paid by the day. I bought a pair of enchanted swords from that quest." Lin smiles, dark eyes remembering past glories before he sighs, "Those broke half-a-year later fighting a stone golem."

Putting the cooked meat aside, Lin accepts the newly seasoned slices onto his pan while Ingrid says, "Two swords! I used to have a set of fully enchanted plate. Had to sell it to pay for all the healing potions we needed after a bad delve when we needed to heal Quinn, our Mage. Healers are a damn scam."

"You're telling me. I ended up being a questor because I needed to sell off all my equipment just to cover the bill to regenerate my foot," Jorge adds, shaking his head. "Though I guess I could thank him too."

"Definitely thank him, if that's why you became a questor," Lin follows up before waving them closer to him. "Right, the first batch is ready, get your plates."

The group stops grousing for a time as they work through the bread and meat that is provided, Lin occasionally returning to the pot to stir and taste the vegetable soup. As everyone begins to finish up, Asin turns to regard the experienced Adventurers, "Why questors?"

Lin pauses, spoon halfway to his lips before he lowers it. Jorge sighs, rubbing at his beard when Asin asks her questions.

"You normally don't ask that. It's considered rude," Lin said.

"Why?" Asin prods, scratching at her ear as her tail waves lazily.

"Most other Adventurers consider us failures," Ingrid explains. "In fact, most won't even speak with us."

As Asin opens her mouth to ask why again, Daniel kicks her in the foot. She glares at him but says nothing, turning back to her soup. Lin watches the unsubtle interaction, and his lips twist in amusement before he says, "I was a guild leader once. Just a small one, we only had about forty members. Then we had a few bad months, a few of our parties were lost, and others were poached. We eventually disbanded and then, well, I hadn't done that much delving since I became a guild leader, and I realized I wasn't interested anymore. So, I just started doing quests."

"I couldn't get past the eighth floor no matter what I tried," Jorge speaks up, looking at his bowl of soup as he adds his own story. "I was always the one making the mistakes, always the one holding the team back. They eventually decided to cut me loose after I lost my foot and I couldn't find another team to join permanently. I worked quests when I didn't have a group or in-between delves and eventually, well, I just stopped trying."

Asin and Daniel look to Ingrid whose lips purse before she says, "No." Disappointed, the pair turns back to their meal. Later, when Ingrid has left, Jorge murmurs to the pair as they leave, "She lost her party in a bad delve. Never tried again."

Daniel nods in thanks and invites them over for breakfast the next day in turn. As he walks back, he cannot help but think that being an Adventurer has more paths than the single one that he initially imagined and that for many, those paths ended in heartache.

True to Lin's prediction, the next few days pass without incident. Watching from his assigned spot, Daniel wipes rain away from his eyes before scanning the surroundings again, stopping on the farmers as they finish up the latest field. Barely a dozen in number, the workers had cleared three fields today just by themselves, even while working in the pouring rain. In fact, the greatest delay was in storage as carts struggled along the muddy roads to deliver the produce to the warehouses.

Once again, Daniel smiles as he watches the farmers work. He was always amazed at how so few Farmers can produce such a large harvest - though realistically, it is no different than how experienced Miners can churn out significantly more ore than beginners. If not for the need to continually train the next generation of workers, youngsters like him would never be given a significant role in mining operations.

"Deer," Asin says, her hood pulled tight over her head as rivulets of water drip down around her. As she speaks, she points, and Daniel wrenches his gaze away. In the distance, he sees the Spotted Deer herd run downwind of them, each motion a thing of beauty. They glide across the ground but veer off suddenly as the smell of old and rotten blood carries its way to them. Daniel relaxes and then reaches for his water bottle, feeling the lukewarm water wet his throat.

"So… this is the last day it seems. We'll probably even be able to get back before the evening falls if we hurry," Daniel says.

"Mmmm…" Asin purrs.

"What I'm saying is that we could enjoy a soft bed, warm water, and a hot meal if we decide to." Daniel tries again as he pulls his own cloak tighter, feeling the chill from the rain carry to his bones.

Again, all Asin does is purr.

"Are we going back tonight?" Daniel cries out exasperatedly, and Asin lets out a chuckle, looking up at him from where she crouches, her tail waving lazily in amusement.

"Yes."

"Good." Daniel nods firmly, stretching. "So, you're good then?"

Asin nods and then shrugs after a moment. "Foolish. Over now."

"I still think Tevfik liked you for yourself you know," Daniel adds, but seeing the glare Asin shoots him, he then shuts up. Soon enough, the work is done, and Daniel heads over to wish goodbye to the other Adventuring parties and the Farmers before the pair head back to the city. Asin pauses for a moment, staring back to Daniel before she flashes him a grin and takes off, loping forward at speed through the mud, Daniel growling softly as he hurries to keep up with her. Damn cat.

"Daniel!" Niko waves to the youngster as he walks in, cold and grumpy at having lost the race back. Asin had out-paced him very quickly and never seemed to look back, so all that Daniel could do was follow after her, alternately jogging and running. Having finally made it back to the inn, Daniel only wants to rest in his room and so ignores Niko, heading upstairs.

He is pulled short by Niko's hand on his arm halfway up the stairs, the older swordsman looking serious. "Daniel, I just need a moment. Please."

Daniel frowns and then nods, recalling how the other Adventurers had helped them. He owed Niko at least the courtesy of listening to him. In the dining hall, Daniel quickly orders some mulled wine to warm his body before he turns to Niko, waiting for him to speak.

"I know you're upset we hid our intentions from you. I just wanted to explain it to you," Niko said. "You see, well, finding an unaffiliated healer is incredible. Even someone who only has Minor Healing can make a difference in a party's earnings over the long-term, and if you ever learned more powerful spells, you could make a major difference on a day-to-day basis.

"Few parties ever advance beyond an Advanced Dungeon without a healer in the party. Even including the priests though, there just never are enough of them to go around. Finding a healer that's unaffiliated is a big thing for a small guild like ours."

"I've figured that out," Daniel answers grumpily.

"I still think you should join a guild, even if it's not ours. There's no reason for you to be working a dungeon like Karlak, earning a few silver every run when you could be in a real dungeon. With a guild's help, they could outfit you with proper equipment and ensure you got the right training."

"Out of the goodness of their hearts?"

"Of course not. You're an investment, and they'd expect you to use your skills for the good of the guild. But it's nothing more than what you offered to do in the bath house," Niko points out.

"Oh, you found out about that eh?" Daniel grimaces and Niko nods.

"And I know what you did for the travelers too. You'd just be using your gifts for other Adventurers instead."

"You'd treat me like a Healer though."

"That's what you are. We'll protect you and make sure nothing happens to you. The worst thing you can do is have your Healer killed!" Niko adds, shaking his head.

"Right, right," Daniel sighs and drinks down his wine, standing up. "Thank you for that, Niko. I'll… think about it."

Niko nods, disappointed. As he stands, he offers Daniel a patch from his guild, saying, "If you change your mind, just show this at the reception of our guild hall and state my name. I'll leave word to keep an eye out for you. And Asin."

Daniel nods again, putting the patch away in his pouch as he heads up the stairs. A part of him can see the advantages, the way that joining a guild could make up for his Gift and meet his dreams. However, it meant he would be treated as a precious commodity, a healer that could never be injured. No longer would he be allowed to risk himself in dungeons that might be a little too difficult for him or fighting bosses. Daniel would be a healer, and healers never fought in the front.

Still, this offer would let him make up for lost time. Daniel knew he was old for a beginner Adventurer, old to have just started on this journey. While Levels and experience could help stave off the effects of time, time still always won.

Lying in bed, Daniel stares at the wooden boards that make up the ceiling, his thoughts going in circles.

Chapter 11

"No, it's left," Daniel insists, glaring at Asin. "Who's the one with the Mapping skill?"

Asin glares and points down to the left before adding, "Been there."

"I know we have, but the instructions lead us down there. We must have missed something!" Daniel reiterates, and Asin shakes her head firmly.

"No miss. Nothing there. Right."

"Asin!" Daniel growls again, and Asin sniffs, holding up a finger. When Daniel subsides, the Catkin continues.

"Try once."

"Aaargh! Fine." Huffing in defeat, Daniel shifts the pack he carries once more. When he does so, the scratching coming from within the backpack makes him shiver again. Asin looks over as well, her hearing picking up the noise. "Not doing this again."

Asin nods firmly, shuddering. Delivery quests within the city itself were rare – after all, there were numerous cheaper options. When this quest came up, Daniel had snatched it up quickly as a way to see more of the city. How were they to know that the special delivery was for a box of Umben Beetles.

Umben Beetles were flesh-eating monsters that would swarm the nearest host, burrowing into the flesh and laying eggs where more of their kind would grow, eventually crippling and killing its host. When that happened, the Umben Beetles would exit and find a new host, continuing the cycle. They were also considered a noble delicacy, the creatures carefully cultivated across numerous hosts for the exotic, layered flavors their hosts imparted on the Beetles.

Daniel is brought out of his thoughts by a gloating Asin who points to where the sign of a crossed fork and lamp are painted above the restaurant's name 'The

Fork & Lamp' are painted. Daniel looks once more at the directions and growls, "It says left!"

Before Asin can answer an angry, balding man throws the door open, shouting, "You're late!"

"The directions we were given were wrong!" snaps Daniel and the man snarls.

"I don't care about your damn excuses. Filthy, money grubbing Adventurers. I should complain to your Guild!" snaps the man, reaching out to grab the box from Daniel. Daniel almost holds it back before remembering he wants the box off his back as soon as possible and hands it over. Without another word, the bald man stomps back into his restaurant, already screaming at his employees.

"I hate city people," growls Daniel and Asin wrinkles her nose, eyeing the restaurant. After a moment she shakes her head, gesturing for Daniel to lead the way back. They were unlikely to be served well if they went in to dine right now, which was a shame in Asin's view. After all, the Fork & Lamp was considered one of the premier restaurants in the city. Sighing to herself, Asin follows behind Daniel as they head back to the Guild Hall.

"How about this one?" Daniel asks, holding up a quest note asking for guards. Asin reads over the note, shaking her head and points to the pay rate. Two silver for each Adventurer was very poor. Instead, she taps on another and Daniel reads it aloud, frowning. "Alchemist looking for participants in their experiments. Must have high Constitution."

Asin nods firmly, and Daniel eyes her doubtfully. She lets out a huff and points to Daniel before growling softly, "Heal."

"Oh! Oh...." Daniel frowns, tapping his fingers. Well, it was true that they could probably survive the experiments with his healing and Gift but still... At

Asin's insistent pointing at the bottom of the quest that indicated the rewards which were for each potion they decided to take, he finally relents. "Fine, fine."

Grinning, Asin bounces off with the quest marker to get it assigned to them while Daniel continues to peruse the rather extensive list of quests.

"A Catkin!" The short human grins, pulling on Asin's arm as he leads her to a chair. "This should be…" Daniel and Asin wait, the man turning after a time and spotting the young Adventurer and waving him to a seat too.

"So, let's see…" Muttering to himself, the man tugs at his ear as he walks between rows of potions. Each is marked with tape and a series of numbers and letters. Finally, the human picks and brings across two pinkish red vials. "Take this and drink when I say so."

Pulling a notepad from a nearby seat, the Alchemist jots a series of words down before looking up at the patiently waiting pair. "Well, go on then!"

Asin chuffs out, her tail flicking in irritation before she sniffs at the potion again. It didn't smell wrong at least. Downing it quickly before she can think of a reason not to, she turns to look at Daniel who is more gingerly sipping on the concoction, a part of his mind holding his Gift ready just-in-case. The Alchemist peers at the pair, watching them for adverse reactions.

Nothing happens for a few minutes before the Alchemist nods, smiling. "Good, good… why is that purple?"

Daniel blinks, and Asin holds her nose, skirting away from the Adventurer before suddenly realizing that her stomach needed to release some gas too. Letting out a loud burp, she watches the cloud of purple smoke escape her mouth.

"Well, that's different," mutters the Alchemist, making notes. He grabs a knife, swinging it towards Asin who skirts back. When no one moves to take it, he waggles the knife again. "Well, go on and cut yourself. Do I have to tell you everything?"

"Yes," Daniel says bitingly, taking the knife carefully from the Alchemist. He rolls his sleeve up before gently nicking his arm. Blood wells up as Daniel grunts, waiting to see what might happen.

"Hmmm… No residual regeneration. Okay," the Alchemist mutters and points to Asin. "You."

Asin nods, testing the blade on her own arm as well and finding no change. After a moment, the Alchemist comes back with more of the same potion, nodding for them to drink. "One at a time!" he barks when he notes Daniel about to drink as well.

Again, he watches the young Catkin, keeping an eye on her wound as he tugs on his ear in thought. The wound heals slowly, purple smoke pouring from the wound even as Asin finds herself gassy again.

"1, 2, 3, 4… and that's it. Now, you." The Alchemist points to Daniel before they repeat the procedure. When they are finally done and healed, the Alchemist sniffs, scribbling in his notes. After a time of being ignored, Daniel clears his throat.

"How many more?"

"Hmmm?"

"How many more potions are we testing?"

"Oh, four more with six variations each," the Alchemist answers absently, waving to them to be quiet.

Daniel subsides, looking at Asin who lets out another purple burp. Well, maybe it wouldn't be that bad.

"Yes! That's perfect!" the Alchemist shouts jubilantly while Asin growls, batting at the swarm of flies and other flying bugs that surround her.

"It's supposed to do that?" Daniel says, horrified.

"Of course! It's a potion of insect attraction," the Alchemist says, puzzled at how Daniel could not understand something so simple. "Your turn!"

"That's not supposed to happen…."

"YOU THINK!" Daniel shouts, clutching at the table as he floats up in the air. As suddenly as he lost the ability for gravity to affect him, he finds himself crashing into the ground again. Holding his arm which he landed awkwardly on, Daniel glares at the Alchemist.

"I wonder what a double-dose would do…?"

"Why'd you drink that? That's not supposed to be drunk."

"Uaarggh." Asin would have shouted at the Alchemist, but she was currently hunched over the bucket, throwing up the foul-smelling liquid.

"Application only. Says so right on the… oh, right. Label. My fault!"

"Uaarggh."

"This one works very well," Daniel says, grinning as he lifts the table with one hand.

"No, it doesn't," mutters the Alchemist, shaking his head.

"What do you mean? I'm so strong," Daniel says.

"It's not a strength potion. It's a…."

"A..?

"Skin exfoliator. It's supposed to make your skin shine."

"Why'd you make Asin drink it too?" Daniel asks, puzzled as he lets the table down. It's not as if the Catkin had much skin to exfoliate.

"Science!"

"Now remember, write down any symptoms you experience over the next few days," the Alchemists says, pressing sheets of paper into the Adventurers' hands. Daniel and Asin both nod dumbly, eyes glazed with the sheer variety of things that have happened to them this day. When they finally escape, the pair look at each other and then find themselves hurrying along down the road, their fast walk turning into a run by the end of the street.

Never again!

Another series of complaints had generated a series of quests, and the pair were in the dark again, crawling through the sewers. In truth, after their recent quests, these sewers were quite relaxing. Straightforward and easy kill jobs were so much simpler.

As Daniel finishes kicking away the body of the rat before him, he frowns. Something was wrong. It takes him only a moment more before he realizes what the issue is – light. Light that glowed blue and that shimmered slightly as it reflected off the dark water that ran through the center of the sewer was coming around the corner. Now that he is paying attention, Daniel also realizes that there's a creaking of a cart moving along slowly as well.

Asin hisses slightly and pulls out her daggers, tucking the rat tail away as she steps up next to Daniel. Cat eyes gleam in the dark, reflecting light as she slowly moves forward, followed quickly by Daniel.

The hooded figures turn the corner, a single tall figure leading the way as a cart is pushed along behind him. The figure holds a hand up as he spots Asin and Daniel, lips pulling apart and showing a series of sharp, needle teeth. The Beastkin lets out a low growl, a hand falling to the knife at his side.

Before Daniel can reach for his shield, Asin lets out a low hiss and growl, replying to the Beastkin in the common tongue of their kind. The Beastkin hesitates and then moves forward slowly though Daniel does not fail to notice that his companions have retrieved a pair of crossbows.

A yowly, growly conversation ensues between the stranger and Asin for a few minutes. Finally, out of patience, Daniel elbows his companion gently and asks. "What is going on?"

"Smugglers," Asin replies and gestures to the group.

"Oh…" Daniel tightens his grip on his mace, an act that has the Beastkin tense and Asin shaking her head.

"No, leave. Not our business," Asin insists.

"I…" Daniel frowns, considering. Asin is technically correct – they are not the Guards. However, letting them smuggle some unknown substance or person in did not sit well with Daniel either. "What are they smuggling?"

"Sabu," the answer is a low, rumbly growl that sets the hair on the back of Daniel's neck tingling.

"Oh." The alcoholic drink that was prized by the Beastkin was certainly tasty, but it seemed a bit excessive to smuggle.

"Tax. Very high," Asin answers the unasked question. She frowns, growling back to the Beastkin who answers in Brad.

"Five times the cost of Sabu," the Beastkin growls, spitting to the side at the end.

Daniel's eyes widen, mind going back to the size of the population and how many there are of them. For a moment more, he considers before he slowly slides his mace back into its loop. The Beastkin sees the gestures of peace and gestures for his men to continue pulling the cart, stopping as they pass by to throw over a wineskin that Asin deftly catches.

A quick sniff is all that is needed to confirm the contents before Asin stores the skin. Daniel eyes the skin for a moment, wondering if it is a bribe or a gesture of gratitude. In the end, did it really matter? He had made his decision. "Come on; we've got rats to kill."

Tao Wong

Chapter 12

"Sure?" Asin prods Daniel again as the young Adventurers fights to contain his yawns. Up early in the morning to meet the caravan to Karlak, the pair are walking through the city with their gear on their back. The two and a half weeks in Silverstone had passed in a blur of quests, and now, it was time to head home.

"Yes." Daniel nods firmly. As tempting as the offer to join a guild was, he could not choose it now. Would not, perhaps. He had a quest that needed completing, a Dungeon that he had never seen the end of and a girlfriend he had to confess too. In truth, a part of Daniel knows he is putting the decision off, procrastinating.

Asin continues to chew on the improvised bread wrap she has made, content to let Daniel make the choice without interference. She understood she was not truly wanted by the guild - they would not decline her if she joined with Daniel but she was not their target. If Daniel went, she would follow - the more advanced the dungeon, the more coin there was after all. If he did not, she would get there eventually. In either case, Asin knows her pig-headed partner would not abandon her.

As they come up to the caravan, Asin prods Daniel to take over the conversation, content to let him do the talking. Being in a new city, she had done more talking than she was used to. While she would never tell Daniel, her throat was raw from squeezing out words in Brad. It was so much easier to speak in Catkin and perhaps partly why she had gotten involved with Tevkin so fast. Her tail lashed again as she thought of the Catkin and his luxurious fur, the way he used to nibble on her ear…

Daniel quietly moves slightly further away from his growling friend, having gotten used to the occasional switches in her temperament in the last few weeks.

Tevkin had hurt her, more than she was willing to let on and once again, Daniel wonders how old his friend really was. Was Tevkin perhaps her first real relationship?

Pushing aside those thoughts, Daniel focuses on the job at hand and greets the caravan master, getting their orders. It would be a long few weeks back to Karlak.

Later that day, when things have settled, and the caravan is on its way, Daniel finally pulls up the information on his Status. It was time to allocate his attribute and skill points. He had avoided the topic for days, not feeling the need to rush as the simple low-level Quests that were offered to them were easily dealt with by their existing skills.

Now, with nothing more to do but watch the surroundings and his decision to turn down the guild offers, he could focus on leveling up.

First, it was time to adjust his skills. Of course, he could upgrade his existing skills making each better and more effective, but Daniel was more curious about the new skills he had the option to learn.

Now that he had upgraded his Healing skills and knew the human body better, he had access to two different spells - **Cure Serious Wounds** or **Healer's Mark**. The first was a more powerful version of his current spell, providing almost instantaneous healing but at a higher mana cost. Healer's Mark however just accelerated the healing process of the target over a period of time, allowing the target's body to do the majority of the healing. It was significantly more mana efficient than either of the instantaneous spells and was very popular among Healers who needed to conserve their mana. It did have the potential of failure though - if the host body was not strong enough, the spell would fail to heal the wounds fully and would instead use a significant portion of the target's resources, causing the death of the target.

In terms of his offensive skills, he could now learn **Shield Rush** which was a progression on the **Shield Bash** skill he already knew. Instead of a static attack, Shield Rush would allow him to attack using his shield at a distance by charging the monsters, allowing him to layer a stun and knockback attack. While not as versatile as Shield Bash, Shield Rush was extremely powerful against single opponents, and the Stun effects normally lasted longer too.

His archery skills were still not sufficient to give him any Skill options, but he did have several Club options to review. **Power Strike** continued to be available while two additional options had opened up - **Crushing Blow** and **Perin's Blow**. Crushing Blow was a variation on Power Strike which did less overall damage but which gave additional bonuses against medium to heavily armored opponents. The skill focused on destroying and smashing through armor with pure strength and at higher levels was known for ignoring even physical damage resistances. Perin's Wrath, on the other hand, provided a knockback effect that if used correctly could even throw a monster into the air for follow-on attacks. A similar skill had been what Niko had used to finish off the Overseer in the dungeon.

In addition to all these, Daniel had also gained a few additional passive skill options including **Sprint**, **Greater Endurance** and exclusive to him, **Martyr's Strength**. The last made Daniel pull up the detailed information again to review.

Martyr's Strength

A unique skill brought about by the ongoing usage of Martyr's Touch on the individual's body. Combines an innate understanding of the owner's body with the user's unique Gift to increase regeneration rates.

Skill: Passive

Cost: N/A

Effect: User has a permanent increase of 10% to Health and Stamina regeneration.

In the end, Daniel closes the screen again and rubs at his chin. There were so many options to choose from that Daniel sits quietly, attempting to structure his thoughts. If he focused on his most likely opponents in the near future - the Ogres - both Crushing Blow and Shield Rush would benefit him the most. However, the use of Perin's Blow with his other skills could allow Daniel to inflict significant damage on a single target in a short period of time. In fact, over time, Perin's Blow probably could become the linchpin of his attacks against a tough opponent.

However, that would not benefit him in a fight against smaller opponents. If he upgraded his Double Strike ability, he'd be able to attack four times in quick order, making him a much deadlier opponent against multiple individuals. It would have made him significantly stronger against the Imps for starters.

Healer's Mark would always be useful especially over the course of a day. It would ensure they could stay in tip-top condition while they fought and when they increased their party, it would be even more important as Daniel's mana pool was highly limited.

If he wanted to be selfish, he could even take his unique Skill and increase his health and stamina regeneration. The significant increase in both would make it easier for him in dungeon levels and everyday life though it was probably the least useful group skill.

It was not a simple choice and one that Daniel had agonized over for hours now. Worst, he knew that these kinds of decisions would come even more often as he developed in strength.

Later that evening Asin prods Daniel, taking him out of his contemplation as he prods at the fire. "Skills?"

Daniel pauses, staring at the fire before he finally answers her, "I chose to get Perin's Blow."

Perin's Blow

Named after the God of Storms, Perin, this strike sends concentrates the force of the user's blow to create a knockback effect against its target.

Skill: Active

Cost: 25 Stamina

Effect: User's Strike does 15% more damage and knocks back target. Knockback level dependent on user's strength, Club skill, weight and size of the target and striking area.

"It's a knockback effect, kind of like Niko's," Daniel explains, before continuing, "I think it'd be useful against the Crawlers and Ogres, and if I learn to use it right, it should also allow me to control where the monsters move during a fight."

Asin just nods as Daniel calls up his Status Screen once more, hoping he made the right choice. When he got back, he would ask Khy'ra to teach him Healer's Mark. It was a spell that he had watched her cast before, one of the few Healer spells that the Elf knew. If she was still willing to speak with him after he told her what he had done.

Name: Daniel Chai

Class: Level 6 Adventurer (14%)

Sub-classes: Level 7 (Miner) (14%)

Human (Male)

Statistics

Life: 229

Stamina: 229

Mana: 168

Attributes

Strength: 22

Agility: 20

Constitution: 28

Intelligence: 17

Willpower: 18

Luck: 13

Skills

Unarmed Combat: Level 3 (37/100)

Clubs: Level 9 (04/100)

Archery: Level 2 (18/100_

Shield: Level 7 (84/100)

Dodge: Level 5 (12/100)

Combat Sense: Level 5 (98/100)

Perception: Level 6 (07/100)

Mining: Level 7 (78/100)

Healing: Level 8 (89/100)

Herb Lore: Level 3 (31/100)

Stealth: Level 2 (14/100)

Cooking: Level 3 (21/100)

Singing: Level 2 (14/100)

Skill Proficiencies

Double Strike

Shield Bash

Perin's Blow

Mapping (II)

Spells

Minor Healing (I)

Gifts

Martyr's Touch - The caster may heal oneself or others by touch and concentration, sacrificing a portion of his life to do so. Cost varies depending on the extent of the injuries healed.

Pushing aside those thoughts, Daniel stands and moves to the back of the caravan. He had made his decision. Better to keep busy and that meant helping others. Interestingly enough, the hanger-ons from Silverstone seemed both less numerous and better fed than before, so Daniel expects that he will have less to do.

Days pass in quiet contemplation and evening bouts of training. The other Adventuring group that hired on with this caravan were highly insular, refusing to interact with Daniel and Asin outside of the bare minimum. After overhearing a particular conversation about the Catkin, Daniel was more than happy to keep it that way. As always, Asin just shrugs and moves on with her life, not letting the slight affect her.

Without other Adventurers to train with, Daniel finds himself working with the caravan guards. Once word of his free healing made the rounds, even the caravan manager had taken to speaking with Daniel in more friendly terms - if nothing more than to soothe his ulcerous stomach. The caravan guards were more than happy to train with Daniel for his aid, whether it was for magical or non-magical healing.

A week and a half after they leave Silverstone, the caravan meets its first sign of trouble. The other Adventurers having left to complete another quest, the caravan is sparsely guarded for its size. The lack of guards has resulted in Daniel and Asin having to stand guard every evening, cutting into precious sleeping time. As Daniel rolls over to grab his mace after being woken to take his turn, an arrow strikes his bedroll. For a moment, Daniel just squats there, staring at the arrow as he attempts to understand this strange feathered disturbance.

"Attack!" roars one of the guards and the shout makes Daniel move, automatically reaching for his shield. Crouching low with his shield in front of him, he searches for the attackers and spots a good dozen bearing down on him. Another scream from behind makes Daniel turn, and he spots another dozen human bandits, making Daniel's mouth run dry. They are out outnumbered two to one, and many of the guards are still struggling awake.

Making a snap decision, Daniel rushes the group ahead of him, holding his shield in front of his body. While he might not have the skill, there was no reason he could not use his shield as a battering ram, and so he does, ducking low and scooping his arm as he runs into his opponent. For once, his shorter than normal stature benefits Daniel and the screaming, dirty bandit is flipped over his shoulder to smash into the ground. His first opponent taken care of, Daniel's grin widens, and he stands swiftly, engaging his Double Strike to crush the arm and then knee of his next opponent, flashes of electricity lighting up their fight. As the downed bandit begins to roll over, Asin pounces onto him and shoves a blade into his throat. With the blade caught, she leaves it in his throat as she draws a throwing knife to provide Daniel further support, hissing in anger at the blood that coats her pants.

His second opponent crippled, Daniel spins and steps forward quickly to his next adversary, engaging Perin's Blow for the first time in combat. Daniel strikes low, and to the side, the bandit's clumsy block is smashed aside as the mace catches him on the hip and sends him bowling into the line behind him. Grinning in elation at the successful use of his Skill, Daniel wipes the spray of spittle off his face as Asin works her knives and a bolo into the struggling pile, tangling the group before casting an enchanted oil flask into the mass.

Daniel can feel the heat behind his back, drying his shirt as he steps forward to deal with another bandit, ignoring the screams of pain and the smell of charred meat. He catches the first strike high and raises his mace to strike high but an arrow slams into his unarmored torso, spinning him around. Daniel screams, the coarse wood of the arrow shaft digging into his muscles as he stumbles away from his attacker, a second arrow missing by inches.

Daniel's attacker follows up, swinging his sword once and then again, both blows caught by Daniel's shield as the Adventurer hides behind it. Stepping forward, his attacker hooks his foot behind Daniel's and pulls, dropping the Adventurer onto his back and eliciting an involuntary scream as the arrow in his chest shifts. As Daniel recovers from the fall, the bandit thrusts and Daniel feels the blade sliding into him and grating along his ribs.

Asin meanwhile has spun away from her finished opponent but is forced to dodge to the side as the archer fires, again and again, ensuring that the Catkin is unable to close the distance to her partner. She snarls, her thrown weapons unable to reach the cowardly archer. Not given a choice, Asin jumps back again as the archer fires and throws a knife, activating her newest Skill Fan of Knives. Her single knife transforms into four, each newly created knife mirroring the original's flight path and plunging into Daniel's attacker's back and forcing the bandit away. Even as she lands, Asin rolls and comes up, catching and sliding a short sword that thrusts at her in an attempt to catch the Catkin unaware. She snarls, the blade scoring her shoulder as she fails to entirely divert the attack, jade eyes turning back to her downed partner in worry.

Given a moment's respite, Daniel grabs and pulls the arrow out and then casts a Minor Healing on himself, whimpering in pain as his body forcefully heals the wound closed. The puncture in his chest closes slightly as well, sufficiently enough that Daniel can focus and pull the shield across his body. It is not a moment too soon as an arrow smashes into the shield as the archer attempts to kill the downed Adventurer. Still injured, Daniel is forced to cast another Minor Healing before he is able to stagger to his feet.

Lips pulled tight, Daniel totters to the side, both fighters swaying slightly from their injuries. As his opponent closes on him again, Daniel focuses and triggers a Shield Bash, slamming the shield forward into his opponent's face before he finishes the fight by braining his opponent with his mace.

Realizing that Asin is hard-pressed by two attackers, he rushes over to aid her, barely dodging another arrow. The momentary distraction of the short, stout adventurer is enough for Asin to spin away and draw a throwing knife, sending a Piercing Throw deep into the groin of an attacker and dropping him.

A sudden scream abruptly cuts-off from where the archer shoots at the pair, his demise swiftly ended by a second bolt. Waggoneers, woken from their sleep grab at crossbows and clubs to aid the guards and the Adventurers finally. For a moment the last of the bandits' pause, wavering as they realize so many of their comrades have fallen.

Daniel does not pause, throwing another brutal blow into his opponent's stomach with Perin's Blow, throwing the bandit up into the air. Still, Daniel does not pause even though he struggles to breathe, triggering a Double Strike as the man is in the air, slamming blows into the body and casting blood into the air.

The brutal attack is the last straw for the untrained, ill-equipped group. Screaming, the bandits flee back into the forest, letting Daniel collapse onto the ground in exhaustion. All his strength used up; he begins to feel the injuries that cover his body. When Daniel is finally able to focus, he taps into his Gift to finally finish closing the wounds in his chest. Memories shift, fading away, but for once, Daniel ignores the cost for the pure pleasure of being free of pain. When the wounds are finally closed, Daniel pushes himself up, ignoring the numerous smaller wounds across his body. He has others to heal.

As always, the aftermath of a battle is a sad affair. The smell of iron and voided bowels fills the camp, along with the stifled cries of pain and the slow dragging of bodies as the caravan guards first finish off the seriously wounded and then dispose of the bandits' bodies. No one objected - bandits were the lowest of the low and were killed on sight in Brad, and the caravan had lost many. Three waggoneers had been slain in their sleep, another two guards dead before Daniel can make his way to them. Numerous others carry injuries, too insignificant for Daniel to waste mana or his Gift on.

When the healing he can do is done, the caravan master comes over and offers Daniel a drink. Daniel gratefully takes it, coughing slightly as the spirit burns its way down his throat.

"Bad luck this trip," the caravan master said.

Daniel can only nod, waving Asin over. She sniffs, taking the bottle while Daniel lets a finger linger on her palm, sending his Gift into her body to check for injuries. Finding nothing more than a few treated cuts and a pulled lower back muscle, he leaves her alone.

"Thank you," the caravan master adds, stroking his mustache absently. "It would have been worse without you two."

Asin can only nod again, too tired to suggest a monetary bonus. Perhaps later if the caravan master did not make the offer himself. For now, there were still bodies to put aside and fires to rekindle and a watch to be set.

It is only later that night when others are asleep that Daniel finds a moment of peace. Having offered the excuse that he needed to wait for his mana to regenerate, Daniel hunkers in a corner away from the gathered bodies; his trembling hands clutched beneath his cloak. Daniel forces himself to breathe through his mouth, the smell of blood reminding him of what just transpired.

So close. He had been so close to dying. If his opponent had shifted his aim a few inches, he would have pierced his heart. If the archer had fired an inch lower, the arrow would have pierced his liver, probably incapacitating him for the rest of the fight and ensuring his death.

Daniel at first tries to stop the shaking but eventually gives in, letting his body shudder and tremble as it reacts to his near-death. His mind replays the incident over and over again, and for a bitter moment, Daniel wishes his Gift would have taken those memories. Damn thing – it took memories of evenings with Khy'ra and evening conversations with his Grandfather but left memories like this and being turned by Pearl.

Slowly, his body stops trembling, his mind becoming less of a jumbled mess. Looking up, Daniel sees a streak of blood, and he wonders if it was a bandits' or a friend's. Damn them. Orcs, monsters, Dungeons and more existed, and yet, these bandits felt the need to attack other sentients. There were so many ways to make a living with Skills, but somehow, these scum felt the need attack others for their living. Lips curling up in disgust, Daniel growls softly. Damn them.

Days later, the caravan has pulled to a stop near a river bend, sheltered from the rain by a copse of trees and from attack on two sides by the river. The group is more relaxed now, the caravan master having found replacements for the guards at the next town they had stopped in along with another Adventuring group.

That evening, after dinner, Daniel walks to the water to fill his waterskin and finds Asin sitting by herself.

"Asin?"

At her name being called, the Catkin scrubs at her face before she looks to Daniel. Black fur is plastered down by tears, dark green eyes daring Daniel to mention her weakness. He knows better, instead choosing to sit down next to his partner in silent companionship.

As the silence stretches to the breaking point, Asin finally speaks. "Tevfik liked me. Yes?"

"Yes, I think so," Daniel replies and she nods jerkily.

"Stupid," she mutters, claws coming out to knead her knees. She stares at them for a time, disgusted at her own actions, for reacting so emotionally and blaming him. Yet, she had truly felt betrayed. "I liked him."

"I know."

"No future," Asin says again, rubbing at her knees. "Stupid."

"To fall in love?"

"No love. Like," Asin insists, glaring at Daniel who offers a quick nod. "Stupid anyway."

"Why?" Daniel frowns, on uncertain ground now. After all, they were consenting adults.

"Because over. Always. I leave. He leave. Stupid," Asin insists, shaking her head. "You, Khy'ra, stupid."

"Hey!" Daniel glares at his friend, waving a finger at her. "Just because you don't agree doesn't mean it's stupid. Khy'ra and I are adults. We know what we're doing."

"Stupid. Get hurt," Asin states again.

"Maybe. No, certainly. But in-between, I know a smart, wise, tough, and beautiful Elf," Daniel points out, shaking his head. "We know what's coming, but that doesn't mean we can't enjoy it."

"Still stupid."

"Yes, but it's a good kind of stupid."

Asin lets out a chuff of frustration and then puts her head on her knees again, her tail uncurling from her back slowly. "Hurts."

"Yes," Daniel sighs, unsure of what else to say. So, he says nothing.

After a time, Asin stands up, moving back to the fire. As she passes, she pauses to say, "Thank you."

When she is gone, Daniel stares back into the water, thinking of Khy'ra and the talk he must have. Stupid. Yeah, it probably was.

Chapter 13

"Daniel!" Khy'ra gasps, smiling up at the adventurer as he steps into her Clinic. Weeks of travel with the caravan had finally taken them back to Karlak without further incident of note. This time around, the trip had passed through numerous villages and a few towns but none with Beginner Dungeons. The pair had spent their time at these new settlements sightseeing, for the most part, each stop no longer than a day and often only a few hours. Slightly spooked, the wagons had moved at a quicker pace than normal, and so the pair had arrived in Karlak a day early. Having delivered their goods to an enthused Maxwell, the pair had split up immediately.

Daniel smiles, stepping forwards and wrapping his arms around Khy'ra, kissing her passionately before pulling away as sudden guilt flashes through him. Seeing the change in expression, Khy'ra stops and pushes at him gently, murmuring, "What's wrong?"

"I…" Daniel frowns, searching for a way to say this before just going with the bald truth. "I slept with someone else."

"Oh…" Khy'ra sighs and steps back, blue eyes raking over the man. They glimmer for a moment as she does so before she speaks. "Was she pretty?"

"Umm… a bit," Daniel says.

"A bit," Khy'ra repeats and Daniel nods. "Really? Just a bit?"

"I was drunk!" Daniel adds, grimacing. "I'm sorry, it's not an excuse."

"It's not, but I'm not angry about you sleeping with her," Khy'ra says and smiles slightly at Daniel. "We never made any promises to each other after all. And really, I've been alive and will be alive for many more years. I'll have many more lovers than you, dear boy, so why would I begrudge you yours?"

Daniel blinks, then nods slightly, exhaling. His reasoning had been along those lines too but… his thoughts fall to disarray as Khy'ra raises a finger.

"But, I am disappointed about the betrayal," Khy'ra continues, blue eyes flashing again.

"You just said…" Daniel stutters, confused.

"Not me, yourself." She taps with her finger at his chest, continuing, "You felt it was wrong, did you not? So, it matters not whether I viewed it wrong, you betrayed yourself. And for that, I am disappointed."

Daniel opens his mouth and then shuts it, blinking in understanding. She was right - he had struggled with his actions. He had chosen poorly, and he had felt guilty about it - and even if she did not think it was a betrayal, it was one of himself.

"Oh…"

"For that, dear boy, I must enact suitable punishment," Khy'ra continues, stepping forward and then pushing gently at Daniel, guiding him out of the door. Daniel opens his mouth then shuts it under the firm gaze of the blonde Elf. The door shut on him, Daniel grimaces and stares at the empty Clinic, wondering what to do. After all, he had sent everyone home.

Inside the room, Khy'ra leans against the door, eyes half-closed. She bit her lips, turning to look at the door, a hand raised briefly before dropping it and turning to her desk and the paperwork that awaited her.

"Late!" Asin grumbles at Daniel as he hurries up to her at the Dungeon entrance. He flashes her an apologetic shrug of his shoulders having spent the night drinking alone. His head pounded, and he still wasn't sure - were they broken up permanently? Or just that night? Should he try to see her again tonight? His rambling thoughts are brought to a stop as Asin asks. "Ready?"

"Yes." Daniel shakes his head and winces, finally giving in and casting a Minor Healing on himself to clear the hangover. It was not a good idea to go into a Dungeon, even one as familiar as Karlak, distracted and in pain. He forcibly pushes thoughts of Khy'ra aside and does a final check of his weaponry and armor, adjusting his backpack before they finally enter the Dungeon for the seventh floor.

"Mine?" Daniel asks as they spot their first Ogre. Asin just yawns, hiding her teeth with her furry hand. Not waiting any further, Daniel rushes the Ogre that has started running to him, focusing on the battle.

He staggers his steps, breaking his timing for a brief moment to throw off the Ogre's swing, letting the club pass by him before he steps in and engages Perin's Blow. The blow from under the monster with his mace pushes the mace into the creature's body, throwing the creature upwards long enough for Daniel to slam the rim of his shield into its airborne body. The Ogre falls back, doubled over by repeated strikes to its stomach and diaphragm, and Daniel takes the time to line up an overhand strike on its head. He bends with his knees, putting his weight behind each attack before repeating the strike again and again, never letting up, even as the Ogre attempts to hit him as well.

As Daniel stands over the dispersing body, breathing heavily, Asin calls out a warning and points. In the distance, a trio of Ogres is jogging to the pair to take revenge. Sliding his mace into his belt again, he reaches for his crossbow and loads a bolt quickly, sighting down the weapon before firing. Hours of practice has made loading the crossbow much smoother, Daniel's considerable strength aiding in this endeavor. The bolt flies through the sky, slamming into a thigh and Daniel curses as he works the crossbow. He was aiming for the Ogre to the right of this one. Could he not do anything right?

Asin steps up to buy Daniel time, throwing a pair of blades that blossom into a storm as she activates her Skill. The Ogres duck and twist, attempting to dodge the thrown weapons. Most of the knives miss except for a pair that embed in the unlucky, injured Ogre. The creature groans, blades and arrow embedded in its body and noticeably slows down its movement. Loaded, Daniel aims and fires another bolt, this one targeted to finish off the injured Ogre, and with the close range, he manages to hit.

The remaining pair of Ogres finally reach the two Adventurers, forcing Daniel to drop the crossbow to his side and pull out his mace. A slight smile crossing his face at their ability to injure one of the opponents significantly, Daniel steps forward to the monster on the right while Asin fades to the left, tossing her knives with more care.

Her opponent swings its club at her, forcing the young Catkin to dart forward and to the side, raking the exposed arm with her blade, her enchanted aura sending electricity through the contact and forcing the arm to spasm.

Daniel's Ogre stops just outside of its range, swinging first one then the other arm as it wields two crude, short clubs. Unable to find a good opportunity, Daniel feints to the left and then ducks right, aiming for the last injured opponent that is struggling back to its feet. He feels a club glance off his shield, the blow sending tremors through his body as the Ogre instinctively lashes out and then he's pass and rushing the last Ogre.

He triggers his Double Strike skill the moment he gets into range, taking his new opponent's attack on his shield with a grunt and feeling his arm and shoulder compress, flaring in pain under the heavy strike. Still, he stays focused and lands both blows, sending electricity dancing through the monster at the points of impact, darting to the right immediately as the monster exhales, washing him with its fetid breath. The Ogre finds it difficult to keep up with his smaller and faster opponent, injured as it is and for a moment, Daniel finds himself facing its back. Twisting at his hips, Daniel puts as much strength into the next attack that he can while triggering Perin's Blow, smashing his mace into the Ogre's back, targeting its kidney and sending it flying into its brethren.

The Ogre lets out a breathless scream, bowling over the other monster before expiring and breaking apart. As the other Ogre attempts to stand, pushing upwards with one hand supporting it, Daniel closes in. The stout Adventurer targets its free arm, raining blows on the fragile forearm bones and shattering them to make the monster release its weapon. Devoid of its second club, Daniel alternates strikes with the monster, no longer forced back by the attacks.

Asin, meanwhile, weaves under each attack thrown at her, slashing and stabbing at the exposed arm till the Ogre's arm finally loses all strength and its club drops. She then proceeds to cut and stab the monster, ducking under increasingly desperate attacks, always dodging by the smallest margins, relying on speed and skill. Each attack sends light dancing, making the creature flinch again and again. As her opponent finally collapses, she turns to Daniel to find him beating on his opponent.

Unfortunately, a night spent drinking and thoughts about Khy'ra make him slow and sloppy. An overhand blow that should be easy enough to block comes crashing down onto Daniel's shield. The block is just a touch too slow, the angle wrong and instead of being caught fully, the club smashes past the shield and skips off, glancing off to land a blow on Daniel's temple. He staggers, and before he can recover, a backhanded strike connects with his temple, knocking Daniel out.

Asin yelps, throwing a Piercing Shot before the Ogre can land a third blow. The knife drills into the Ogre's arm, forcing it to drop its weapon even as she charges forward to protect her friend.

When Daniel awakens, he does so with the taste of a dead rat in his mouth. He coughs, pain shooting through his head as his tender temple rings. He whimpers, curling up slightly as pain washes over him, his vision shimmering in and out of focus. Staying silent, he concentrates on his Gift, pulling it from his core to search for the cause of his pain.

Bruising on his face, a cracked skull and minor swelling in his brain from an incipient concussion were the main culprits. Better, much better than he had expected truth be told. Focusing, he lowers the swelling and stitches the skull back together with his Gift to give him relief from the pain before he begins to cast his Minor Healing spell to finish the job.

As Daniel finally opens his eyes fully, he sees Asin squatting a short distance away watching over him. He shudders, remembering the sickening crack of wood on bone, the flash of pain and then, nothing.

"You saved me," Daniel says, working his mouth. "You used a healing potion, too, didn't you?"

Asin nods and then shrugs. Of course she did, they were partners. That was what they did after all.

"Thanks," Daniel says and stands, his body mostly healed. Fighting distracted on this level was a bad idea. Without a full set of heavier armor, any lucky blow could cause problems. Of course, getting a helmet would probably be a good idea, but Daniel was leery of spending the coin for it when he was going to get a full set of better armor soon.

"Ready?" Asin growls and Daniel pauses, rubbing at the dried blood on his temple.

"No… not really," Daniel decides suddenly, shaking his head. "I'm sorry, perhaps we can try this on another day?"

Asin nods. She was not sure what it was, but Daniel was obviously not all here today. Grimacing, she turns to pick her way back to the dungeon entrance. Ah well, she'll head back up to the fifth floor by herself then. No reason to not earn more coin even if her partner was taking the day off.

"Daniel!" Litzburn, the Master-of-Arms at the training grounds calls out in greeting, walking over to the young Adventurer as he enters. The large, ebony-skinned master-at-arms smiles at his former student, shaking Daniel's hand with his own scarred, calloused one. "Are you here to train?"

"Yes, I think so," Daniel says.

"That's not a very sure answer." Litzburn chuckles, running a hand over his bald scalp to clear some sweat. "What's wrong?"

"Nothing. Just, a lot on my mind." Daniel shakes his head, glancing at the training weapons. "Maybe I'll just work the bags for a bit."

"You're always welcome here," Litzburn says, waving goodbye to Daniel as he returns to his other students.

Later, after Daniel has settled in, and Litzburn has watched the young man work the training posts desolately, he walks over and taps Daniel on his shoulder. So lost in thought is the young Adventurer that he completely misses Litzburn's approach. "Enough. You're shaming me and yourself. You won't learn anything but bad habits doing that."

Daniel's lips twist, and he hangs his head, rubbing the back of his neck as he apologizes, "Sorry."

"Come. Let's talk." Waving to his sub-instructors to take over, he walks the young Adventurer to a nearby bench. The older man has quickly figured out the potential cause of the issue. "Problems with Khy'ra?"

"Yes. No. Maybe," Daniel answers immediately and then stops, collecting his thoughts properly. "It's not just that. It's… well, can I ask some advice?"

"Certainly."

Speaking hurriedly, Daniel blurts out the entire story of the guilds, of being asked, again and again, to join, of the potential benefits offered. He speaks fast, trying to get the story out and along the way, he mentions his issues with Khy'ra too, of how he cheated - but it wasn't really cheating, except it was - and what happened. In the end, he runs down while Litzburn just nods. It is a good thing that Daniel speaks with his head down, for at times, Litzburn's lips twitch and amusement dances in the older man's eyes. Ah, the tragedies of youth.

"I would not despair, I do not think that the Elf will cast you aside for such a matter. I believe your current predicament is punishment enough," Litzburn says, lips twitching again before he continues. "I believe you will not make the same mistake again, no?"

"Yes. Ummm… No? I won't make that mistake again." Daniel nods firmly. "It was stupid. And… Not that good."

"Mmm… You bed an Elf, young one. And one who I understand is still quite energetic between the sheets. I fear if you compare your future companions to her, you will be inevitably disappointed," Litzburn replies and then claps him on the back. "At least technically. There is much to be said for passion though."

"Oh. Right." Realizing what he is speaking about, Daniel flushes and looks down, suddenly uncomfortable. "Right."

"As for your problem with the guilds, few in this hall would find your circumstance a problem. Guilds rarely chase after melee fighters," Litzburn waves his hand around the training hall where his students work hard to hone their abilities. "Still, that is little comfort for you. For myself, I joined the moment I could - though that was after I completed my own Beginner Dungeon. Mary, on the other hand, waited for many years before she did, preferring to adventure on her own."

"Mary has a guild?" Daniel perks up, remembering his earliest friend and the owner of the school he sits in.

"Yes, but hers would not fit you. She joined the White Scales, and they only recruit Expert Adventurers and up," Litzburn answers. "If you decide to join a guild, be sure to understand what they ask for and what is required to leave them. Each guild must register their charter and members with the Adventurer's Guild itself, so it's always best to speak with them directly."

"Thank you," Daniel nods, standing up finally. Well, at least he had learned a little more, but mentioning the Guild reminded Daniel that there was another who he could ask for advice. "I think I'm done for the day."

"Yes, I certainly agree," Litzburn chuckles, clapping the younger Adventurer on the back. "Come back another day. We still need to work on your form."

"Afternoon, Liev." After standing in line, Daniel is finally able to speak with the scruffy, red-headed attendant.

The middle-aged man looks up, rubbing at an ink splotch on his fingers absently. "Daniel. I see you are back. Did you just return?"

"No, we arrived last night. I was hoping to speak with you?" Daniel gestures over to the tables to the side and Liev nods, waving one of the other attendants to take over his spot.

"What is this about?' Liev sits, noting the absence of Asin and wondering if there are issues with the pairing. It was after all not uncommon for adventuring parties to break up.

Once again, Daniel speaks of his invitations to join the guilds, leaving out his issues with Khy'ra. He was still somewhat embarrassed he discussed the matter with Litzburn and was certainly not going to bring it up again, especially with Liev. After he is done, Liev sits silently, staring at the younger man and then sighs, fingers rubbing together again as he scrubs at the ink spot. "I'm sorry, Daniel. I should have informed you about them before you left."

"It's fine," Daniel says immediately.

"No, I should have warned you. I knew local groups would want to work with you, but I had forgotten your generosity with your healing gifts. It was bound to attract attention on your travels," Liev continues before shaking his head. "I should have warned you."

"Warned me?" Eyebrows lowering, Daniel squints at Liev as he considers the words.

"Yes. The guilds that Adventurers make within ours, they are both a great help and a great hindrance," Liev says. "We have had to forcefully disband more than one group, relieving the leaders of their membership and reassigning Adventurers. It is a lot of work because some can't handle the power that such a group can provide. The benefits they speak of are true, but many groups also attempt to control their members quite firmly for these benefits.

"I would have wanted you to avoid their attention for a while longer, but it is done. For now, I recommend you complete your current quest. Whatever your decision, being both more experienced and with better armor will stand you in better favor."

"Should I join one then? Litzburn suggested I do."

"Litzburn did well with his guild before he retired. Others haven't been as lucky," Liev answers immediately. "If I were you, I would not trust my ability to others, no matter how kind they seem."

A wry grin twists his face as Daniel nods. Right. His Gift. He had forgotten again how that could make things more difficult for him. "Thanks, Liev."

"It is a big decision, Daniel. Take your time making it," Liev says, smiling and stands. "Now, if that is all…?"

Daniel nods absently, letting the man leave as he falls back into thought. Neither of these men had helped him make a decision. Well, except perhaps about Khy'ra.

"Daniel," Khy'ra smiles slightly, having spoken only after watching as Daniel finishes wrapping up the cut on the carpenter's arm. The carpenter bobs a head in thanks to both, heading out of the examination room to drop a coin in the donation jar.

"Khy'ra," Daniel answers, shifting slightly. Having nothing more to do and tired of thinking, he had come to the Clinic to work.

"How are you?"

"I'm… well." Daniel rubs at his neck, extending a hand tentatively. Khy'ra crosses over, taking it and he smiles slightly, relaxing.

"I'm... sorry," said Daniel.

"As I said, you have nothing to be sorry to me about. Your apology should be to yourself," she says, leaning forwards and kissing him gently. "I just wanted you to think it over."

Daniel nods, "Yeah. I think I understand what you were saying."

"Good," she smiles slightly, giving him a hug. "I just wanted to say hi. There's still a lot of work to do. But we can speak, tonight?"

"Tonight," Daniel replies, smiling and returning the hug before reluctantly letting her go.

"So, you've been approached by the guilds then. At least, they don't know of your Gift," Khy'ra says, looking up at him from his chest as they lie on her bed.

"Yeah, Liev says it would be worst if they did," Daniel answers. "It's stupid really; it's not as if I could use it during combat or something."

"Mmm…. You are too used to having it, Daniel. Having your party, your entire guild constantly in top shape? Not having to spend gold on potions? It would be a great help. Too many groups find themselves forced to either work partly injured or tired or spending large sums on potions. And on longer delves in more advanced dungeons? Your Gift would be a lifesaver," Khy'ra says. "You have a lot of power here, a lot of leeways."

Daniel slowly nods, absently letting his hand run down her bare back, feeling the smooth skin under his fingers, "So you think I should join a guild?"

"Mmm… I think you shouldn't stop doing that. And that you should remember your earlier lesson."

Daniel pauses, hand hovering for a moment. Earlier lesson? Oh… As he begins to put it together, he finds his thoughts interrupted by soft lips. Right - some other things take precedence.

Chapter 14

"Morning, Asin." Daniel greets his friend, up bright and early and waiting at the Dungeon entrance. She nods in greeting, sniffs once and smiles slightly. Daniel sighs, realizing that his surprise had been given away by her superior senses. He reaches into his backpack, extracting the sandwich for the Catkin who devours the stacked bacon and ham delicacy.

When she is finished, Daniel says, "I think we should focus on the seventh floor for now. Farm it for as much stone as we can. If we ask Liev for the conversion rate for the two B Grade stones for the smaller stones, we can focus on just getting the smaller stones. I think it'll be safer for us rather than risking, well, deeper levels. What do you think?"

Asin nods in agreement. Yesterday's experience a stark reminder that while skill and tactics made a difference, they were both under-equipped and under-leveled. One small mistake could end in tragedy.

Resolved, the pair head down once more to the seventh floor, intent on just farming the Ogres for their stones. No risky attacks, no pushing things. Slow and steady was what they would do.

"Yahooo!" Screaming, the half-naked Adventurer runs ahead of the pair, throwing himself at a pair of Ogres the two had earlier targeted. Running behind him, his friends call out a quick apology as they overtake the two to back up their friend.

"Hey!" Daniel grumbles, lowering his crossbow. Damn it. That was the second time that day that this group had stolen one of their kills.

Asin chuffs out too in anger, her tail lashing sideways as she watches as the five adventurers split the Ogres. The half-naked warrior with the oversized sword takes on a single Ogre by himself while his friends work on the last, crippling and killing it quickly. They work smoothly together, constantly harrying and attacking the Ogre in such a way that the monster is never able to fully focus on any one of member.

The half-naked warrior, on the other hand, is full of vigor with very little skill, quite willing to trade blow for blow with the Ogre. In fact, the Ogre seemed to be worse for wear as the Adventurer just shuddered slightly from each blow, a light red mist beginning to rise from his body as he was injured.

"Go," Asin says after a moment, shaking her head. They might as well move on, hoping to find another group. As annoying as it was, today had still been a decent day. Daniel nods, mentally gauging which direction to go from his minimap before walking forwards. There was a pair of small caves down this way that often held the floor Champion.

The pair treks forward in silence, paying attention to both the ground and their surroundings. Asin still has to stop Daniel from walking into a hidden pit, chuffing in humor. At his excuse, she just wrinkles her nose, and Daniel edges around the trap, grumbling quietly to himself. Behind him, Asin smirks, though she knows that her friend is unable to smell the open earth beneath the layer of grass that covers the trap. Humans and their pitiful noses.

As they near the caves, Asin's ears begin to twitch. She moves forward quickly, overtaking Daniel as she scans the ground ahead of them for further traps now that she knows where to go. Soon enough, they spot the Ogre Champion himself and the chest behind him. Standing over eleven feet tall, the Ogre Champion is clad in leather armor and wears a pair of metal gauntlets that cover its arms. As they near, the Champion lets out a roar in challenge, rushing the pair.

Daniel raises his crossbow, firing immediately and sinking the bolt into the creature's torso. The blow does nothing to slow the monster even as Asin runs to the side, charging a knife with Piercing Shot as she runs. Throwing the knife, she immediately follows up with Fan of Knives as she releases another knife, focusing on buying time for Daniel to load and fire his crossbow again. The Ogre Champion refuses to be distracted though, catching the first knife on its gauntlet and ignoring the pair of knives that strike it subsequently as it bears down on Daniel.

When it is within ten feet, it jumps and swings its fist, attempting to crush Daniel. Rather than blocking the monster, Daniel drops and rolls, abandoning his crossbow as he comes to his feet. Quickly equipping his shield and mace Daniel starts circling the monster, searching for an opening even as Asin continues to pelt the creature with knives.

The Champion snarls, ignoring the annoying Catkin and the knives that sprout from its back as it jumps forward again, swinging a looping right fist and then following up almost immediately with a straight left. Daniel ducks the first and then is forced to put both shield and mace together to block the second, stumbling backward from the sheer strength of the blow. Even as he attempts to regain his footing, the Ogre steps forwards and leads again with a left, smashing Daniel's hasty guard into him and sending him sprawling to the ground. As Daniel spits out blood from a cut in his mouth, he struggles up to his feet, eyes sparking with restrained fear.

As the Ogre steps forward, Asin's bolo hits, wrapping around the creature's legs. It jerks the Champion to a halt, forcing it to stumble as small lightning arcs jump between its legs. Asin immediately follows up with a Piercing Shot, the thrown knife plunging into the creature's supporting limb and forcing the Ogre to the ground.

Rolling quickly, Daniel just barely manages to avoid being crushed, the unwashed scent of the Champion crossing to his prone form. Kneeling, Daniel sees the elbow the Ogre is using to prop itself up, and he stands, triggering Perin's Blow to smash the limb downwards into the ground. The blow cracks the elbow, forcing it to bend as it meets the ground and Daniel immediately attacks the arm again with another pair of Skill-aided strikes.

Arm twitching, the Champion lashes out, catching Daniel in the side. The Adventurer twists his body, rolling with the blow as best he can. Woozy on his feet, Daniel is forced to cast a Minor Healing on himself as he patches himself up from the multiple heavy blows he has received.

Rather than allowing the monster the chance to stand, Asin rushes forward while Daniel recovers and ducks in close to the Ogre, plunging knives into the back of the creature's exposed thighs, attempting to hamstring the opponent. White sparks fly, and the Champion forcibly defecates itself as the electricity robs the Champion of its bodily functions. The unexpected attack forces Asin to flinch, assaulted as she is by the sudden noxious and unexpected onslaught. Distracted for a brief moment, she does not notice the leg barreling into her side until it is too late and she crashes into the ground, her arm breaking with the impact.

The crippled Champion struggles to its knees, roaring in defiance as Daniel, fully recovered, rushes it. He ducks under the right jab that comes at him, jumping into the air and triggering a Shield Bash as he slams his shield right into the bridge of the Ogre's nose. As the Ogre grips its shattered nose, Daniel throws his body into the next attack that lands against the monster's temple to end the fight.

Limping over, Asin lets out a low yowl of pain to attract Daniel's attention. He then moves to set her arm before he heals her. She whimpers, feeling bone grate as he adjusts her injured limb before the cool wash of the spell rolls over her inflamed nerves. Still, through the pain, she watches the cave entrance and the mana stone in the chest in case of thieves in red cloaks. Having done what little he can for the moment, Daniel hurries over to pocket their loot before returning to help the Beastkin again.

"Enough for today?" Daniel asks, his mana all used up.

"Yes," Asin nods, slowly limping forward. Her arm felt fragile as it always did after a healing and the bruise on her hip was not fully fixed as yet.

"Here, let me fix that…" Daniel reaches out to extend his Gift, and Asin hisses at him, realizing what he is up to. While she doesn't know what exactly the Gift costs him, she understands that all Gifts had a cost. "Asin…"

"Small. I fine," Asin insists, forcing herself to walk with less of a limp.

"Asin…" Daniel prods her, and she grumbles, looking at him. "We're partners."

"Mana. Later," Asin insists and then pauses, adding. "Monster Gift."

"Umm…"

"Fight monster. Use Gift," Asin tries again.

"Okay," Daniel sighs, walking a few further steps and then stopping. His crossbow! Hurrying back, he gets it and checks it over for damage as he returns to his friend who is rubbing at her side. While he isn't happy with her decision, at least she compromised. And he could too.

As they walk back, they spot the group of Adventurers from before, though they are missing one of their numbers. As they near, they see that the group is tying together a series of ropes and are standing around the now-exposed pit trap.

"Problem?" Daniel asks as he nears them, curious more than anything else.

"Our friend fell down the pit trap, but he's okay," a hammer wielding Adventurer answers for the group. "He was hurrying to get to the Champion and well…"

Asin's ears twitch as she listens to the familiar voice of the half-dressed Adventurer shout at the party to hurry up. Obviously, the fall had done little harm to the hardy Adventurer. Prodding Daniel, she gestures for them to keep walking and Daniel nods, turning away.

"Hey, did you two just come from the Champion?" a female Adventurer asks, her voice high and melodic as she hands her part of the rope over.

"Yes," Daniel answers.

"Damn, just the two of you? And you're barely hurt!" Admiration fills her voice as she eyes the pair. "You guys must be pretty high level."

Daniel shrugs and Asin says nothing, though her tail curls slightly in amusement.

"Shit. Now we've got to tell Omrak that you guys killed the Champion," groans another Adventurer. At this statement, all his friends look crestfallen. While the group contemplates this dire news, the pair head off.

"We could leave him there…" Asin overhears one last suggestion as the pair limp off.

That evening, Daniel and Asin are seated in the Spinning Top, sharing a meal after a hard day's work. It was a good haul for their level, and the two were celebrating with a good meal and drink. Staring at their now empty plates, they were contemplating the apple pie on offer, wondering if they could fit another piece.

A noise catches the attention of the pair, seated in the corner as they are. The large, half-dressed man in furs cries out in happiness, striding over and grinning widely. "I have found you!"

Daniel frowns, shifting back in his chair and letting a hand drop to his lap. Asin makes no overt move either though her tail starts waving lazily. While it was unusual, it was not unheard of for Adventurers to seek retribution for kills stolen. As the Adventurer nears them, Daniel is surprised to see how young he his - barely more than sixteen at a guess, his face unlined and still growing, hair a pale yellow. The Adventurer moves fluidly, though his encounters earlier in the day show on his shirtless and muscular torso. Still, the bruising seems to be doing little to slow down the exuberant youngster.

"Yes?" Daniel asks, realizing that the Adventurer tops him by nearly a foot. And he might not even be done growing yet!

"I wanted to meet the two mighty Adventurers who beat the Champion by themselves. Such bravery must be toasted! I am Omrak, son of Losin," the youngster speaks, his voice so loud it is almost a shout. He gestures over the nearest waitress. "Come, serve these heroes a drink. I shall take an ale."

"Noisy!" Asin scolds, rubbing at her ears.

"It is very much so, is it not? This a good tavern!" replies Omrak, his volume not changing. "And who are you, heroes?"

"I'm Daniel, and this is Asin," Daniel answers, gesturing to his companion before continuing. "And she was speaking of you."

"Ah." Pausing, Omrak lowers his voice to a stage whisper, "Is this better?"

Asin rolls her eyes as the waitress comes over with three mugs, one filled with Sabu and the other two ale. Eyeing Asin's drink, Omrak says, "What is that purple mixture?"

"Sabu. It's a traditional Beastkin drink," Daniel replies and glances at the mug before he smiles, relaxing slightly. "Thank you for the drink."

"Not at all. Congratulations on killing the Champion. I see my companions were in error - you heroes are entirely uninjured. You must be truly mighty warriors," Omrak says.

"Uhh… no. We healed up," Daniel replies while Asin returns to scraping her plate clean.

"Yes. Of course, you heroes would be able to afford a great many healing potions. They are extremely expensive here, are they not?" Omrak says again, rubbing at his side. "I, myself, have had to purchase a few."

"We did notice your… particular fighting style," Daniel replies, then seizing on the chance adds. "There was a red mist coming from you while you were fighting?"

"The Battle Rage! It is a Skill for our warriors, but it is not as useful against a single opponent," Omrak clarifies, grinning. "You Southerners do not have its like. It gives one extra strength and deadens the pain of the fight."

"That's pretty nice," Daniel nods, realizing where Omrak must come from. Further to the North, past the Gray Mountains was a deep valley that bisected the land where numerous smaller city states existed. Further North of these city states, a small sea separated their lands from Squalak. The mountainous countries that made up that land were well known for calling those who lived further South of them in less harsh and cold climates Southerners.

"Come, let us toast!" Omrak gestures to their drink and Asin sighs, picking up her drink as Daniel does too. "To Great Heroes. May our names be written in the stars!"

Drinking from their cups, they look at Omrak who stands there grinning at them for long moments. As things grow uncomfortable, Daniel coughs and adds, "Would you care to join us?"

"Yes!" Grabbing a nearby seat, Omrak sits down. "Come, heroes; let us speak of our adventures."

Asin rolls her eyes again but stops when Omrak drops coin on the table as he waves the waitress over. "I require dinner and more drinks for my friends!" Well, perhaps Asin could stay if he was paying. Free drinks were free drinks.

A week later, the pair walk into Maxwell's store. It had been a long week, working the seventh level again and again for mana stones but they had finally earned enough to cover the cost of the two B Grade stones they were missing as well as to pay for their living expenses for a few more weeks.

"At last! I thought you two would never be done," Maxwell grumbles, taking the pouch and staring at the stones within. He checks them over carefully, nodding in satisfaction. These stones would be more than enough to power the furnace while he was working on his Masterwork. "Are you getting my venom sacs then?"

"Yes," Daniel answers, smiling slightly. "We're going out in two days."

"Two days!" Maxwell says, his voice rising. "Why are you taking so long?"

"We need maps, equipment, provisions," Daniel says. "We also have our lives to live you know. We've been down in the Dungeon every day since we got back from your trip."

"Still…"

"Two days. If we are lucky, we'll get the sacs easily and be back in a few days. Then it'll finally be done," Daniel says and then continues after a pause. "Can I see the pieces?"

Maxwell shuts his mouth around further protests and sighs, waving Daniel over. Ever since Daniel had arrived back, he had been taking measurements and building out the pieces of armor for Daniel, laying each completed piece at the back. While the pieces were mostly finished, final adjustments would need to be made when Daniel put the pieces on to ensure the armor fit comfortably and allowed a full range of motion. As Daniel's eyes fall on the helmet, he reaches out to gently stroke it before glancing at Max.

"Could I maybe put a deposit on this? I don't really have a helmet…" Daniel asks tentatively. It was outside of their contract after all. Maxwell frowns and then looks at the youngster once more before he shakes his head.

"No." Seeing Daniel's crestfallen face, he holds it up to him. "You can keep it. I trust you. Now, put it on and let me adjust it."

Grinning, Daniel takes the arming cap from Maxwell first and then slides on the helmet. The conical helmet covers most of Daniel's face, leaving only his eyes and his mouth exposed, the lower cheek guards flaring downwards a distance. Asin nods approvingly, lips twitching slightly as Daniel shifts around uncomfortably as Maxwell checks the chin straps and the fit. If Daniel was going to wear a helmet and cut down on his senses, he might as well go all the way.

Pulling the helmet off Daniel's face, Maxwell sets to fixing it immediately. Daniel walks over to his friend, murmuring, "You?"

"No," Asin shakes her head and then taps her ears. "No hear. No smell. No see. Bad. Very bad."

"Mmmm…" Daniel grunts and then shrugs after a moment. It was her choice, though as fighting got fiercer, her ability to dodge all blows would become more and more difficult.

Seeing and smelling his concern, Asin chuckles and taps her temple again, "Enchantment. Protection. Buy soon. Daniel pay me."

Daniel frowns for a moment, piecing together finally that she would buy a protection enchantment instead from the money he owed her. Feeling somewhat more comforted, he absently pats at his wallet. Giving away three-quarters of his earnings constantly and having to earn the mana stones meant that he was living lean these days. Still, a custom suit of armor would be worth it, he could feel it in his bones. As Maxwell calls him over, Daniel hurries to him as Asin, bored, bids them farewell. They had set their meeting time in two days, and she had much to do before then.

"So soon," Khy'ra says dejectedly, slowly rotating her spoon around the bowl of soup in front of her. Seated in the Spinning Top that evening, the Elf digests the information that Daniel is about to leave again.

"It'll only be a short while this time!" Daniel answers her hurriedly, squeezing her hand. "And I've got tomorrow off if you can get it…"

Khy'ra flashes Daniel a small smile, unwilling to explain that it was his leaving Karlak soon that brought down the Elf. The experienced Elf and former Adventurer knew that with his new armor, it would only be a few months after that before Daniel was done with the Dungeon and thus this town. "Tomorrow… I have meetings in the morning, but I can take the rest of the day off," she says firmly. If she was to lose him, she might as well enjoy it while she could. It was after all her way.

"That's great! I have to do some shopping anyway for the trip," Daniel says, reaching out to squeeze her hand and smiling. "I also have something I want to show you in my room." Khy'ra laughs and, realizing what he said, Daniel begins to blush. "No, it's a helmet!"

This just makes Khy'ra giggle more, and Daniel just gives up, hanging his head. Elise, drawn over by the sight of a giggling Elf raises an eyebrow.

"Daniel has a helmet he wants to show me. In his room," giggles Khy'ra.

Elise, obviously not finding the joke as funny as the Elf, sniffs and walks away. This does little to ease Khy'ra's giggles, though she does reach out to grab Daniel's hand again and give it a squeeze. Tomorrow would do and as many tomorrows as she could get.

Chapter 15

The Pearly Forest was situated southwest of Karlak and technically was still part of Brad. However, the presence of the Querk Spiders and other monsters made the ownership of the forest more theoretical than fact. Spread over hundreds of kilometers, it included lands in both Brad and the Borderlands where the Orc tribes roamed, unchecked.

Still, as dangerous as living next to the forest was, the easy supply of lumber and monster parts for alchemical solutions drove the growth of small frontier villages and the farms required for sustenance. Eventually, the forest would be clear-cut to such a point that a new fort and village would spring up, and the old one would become just another border village.

It was to one such village that Asin and Daniel had visited before they journeyed into the forest itself. Rather than trek through the wilderness on a wild search for the Querk Spiders and the venom sacs they required, the pair had decided to pay for the information from local hunters. Querk Spiders were dangerous, and while their venom sacs were prized, there was significantly easier game to be hunted. As such, it was easier for these hunters to avoid known lairs which gave Adventurers like Asin and Daniel a chance to purchase maps like the one they were even now perusing.

Head bent over the document, Asin and Daniel murmur softly as they peruse the scratched together map. Unfortunately, none of the Hunters they had spoken to had a mapping proficiency, and the document they held could only be barely considered a map through a very broad definition of the term. Twice already the pair had gotten lost in the forest in their search for the first lair, though at least Daniel's own Skill was allowing him to quickly develop an understanding of the layout of their surroundings in his mind. In time, they would certainly be able to navigate the forest significantly easier.

Ears twitching, Asin steps away from Daniel swiftly, drawing her knife. Turning slowly, her gaze locks to their left and Daniel quickly follows suit after stuffing the map away. Even as he reaches for his mace, a small gray creature bounds forwards on three legs in an attack only to be caught in mid-air by Asin's blade. It drops bonelessly, but behind it come even more monsters.

"Gray Mus," Daniel mutters unconsciously as he squats to get a better angle to hit the small, fast moving rodent-like creatures. As their name implied, the rodents were gray in color, each about a handspan in size with a pair of extremely sharp front teeth. While not dangerous individually, the Gray Mus were aggressive pests that reproduced quickly and were willing to swarm larger prey. Still, attacking two full grown humanoids was unusual.

As Daniel swings at the first Mus that nears him, he is distracted by the loud cracking of a branch further behind the tide of creatures. The targeted Mus does not even stop, fleeing past Daniel as their natural predator in the forest comes barreling after them.

The Tento Gulo darts outwards, its long brown body hugging the ground as vine-like tentacles topped with stingers lash out, one after the other to carry the unlucky Mus to its long, snouted maw. The brown-black monster with its long-lean body and oversized head crunched down on each Mus that entered its mouth, needle-sharp teeth tearing apart its unlucky prey.

Asin, having sent a last dagger into a Mus watches as the unlucky rodent is speared as well and brought to the Gulo's mouth, her blade still lodged in its body.

The Gulo pauses its pursuit, staring at the two Adventurers, tentacles whipping around itself. Daniel stays crouched down, watching the monster as Asin readies a pair of throwing knives. For a few tense moments, both parties stare at one another before the Gulo slowly backs away, drawing its captured prey to its mouth as it does so.

It is only when the creature is finally gone that both Adventurers relax, chuckling at each other. There was little be gained from fighting the monster - after all, they were not here to gather Gulo parts. Better to keep on task.

As they finally near the location of the first Querk Spider, Asin prods Daniel to let her take the lead. Now that they are close, her better awareness and perception of the surroundings were important, especially as Querk Spiders were well known for ambushing their prey.

Asin leads Daniel in a circuitous route, skimming around the uneven earth and stepping on branches when she is able. Daniel follows her movements precisely, keeping an eye out for additional dangers. It is only after ten minutes of such walking that Asin come to a stop, pointing down to a particular, nondescript spot. This, then, would be the new lair of the Querk Spider.

The Querk Spider lived in burrows in the ground with small doors. Unfortunately, due to their size and deadliness, the Spiders would often move these burrows to new locations as it attempted to 'trick' new prey. They were known to even create false burrows, slowly guiding prey to its real location where it waited, ready to pounce from underneath the ground to bite and inject its venom into its prey. As a precaution, both Adventurers had vials of anti-venom purchased in Karlak from the apothecary, but neither looked forward to using it.

As planned, Daniel slowly edges around the corner of the burrow before setting himself. At his signal, Asin walks forward slowly; her tail curled up underneath her body as she readies herself to jump away. When the Spider attacks, it is so fast that Daniel barely sees it move, the trapdoor pushed upwards as the arachnid rears on its legs to sink its fangs into Asin.

Asin jumps back, the yellow-brown stocky arachnid landing where she was. In size, it is only half of hers, barely three feet long from abdomen to thorax but its strong jaws glisten with venom. Surprise attack failed, the Spider begins to scurry back into the safety of its burrow.

Daniel is moving, however, jumping forwards from the side and lashing out at its abdomen with Perin's Blow. The monster is too fast though, and instead of smashing the creature into the air, he smashes one of six legs. This barely slows the Spider down, and before the Adventurers are able to attack again, it has pulled its trapdoor covering over its burrow. As Daniel reaches over to pull against it, Asin barks out a, "No."

"Ba'al's Vomit," Daniel curses, stepping back and away from the trapdoor. They have no way of knowing if the monster will attack again and the trapdoors were reinforced with the creature's silk. It would be pointless to attempt to shatter it without enchanted weapons. "I'm sorry, Asin. I should have been there faster."

Asin nods jerkily, getting her breathing under control. The Spider was fast. Leading Daniel via a safe route out, the pair move away from the lair. It was unlikely the Spider would come out again today.

Daniel huffs as another Spider slides away safely beneath its trapdoor, making the young Adventurer tremble with rage. Forcing himself to calm down slightly, Daniel walks away disconsolately while Asin picks herself off the forest floor, wiping away mud and leaves from her toned buttocks.

"This isn't working," Daniel says, and Asin can only give a short nod. In a day and a half, they had only found three such Spiders and had failed to kill two of the three. Of the third, Daniel's attacks had been so strong that he had accidentally crushed the venom sac.

Exhausted, the pair stares at where the Spider continues to hide. "Let's take a break for now."

Asin can only nod and lets Daniel lead them to a nearby stream where they set-up for lunch. The pair are quiet as they consider their plans, attempting to see what they can do to change their tactics. At this rate, it would take weeks before they could gather those three venom sacs.

A day later, the pair crouch down in front of a new Spider's lair. Daniel moves to the side once again, crouching down while Asin gently prods their bait. It had taken them the better part of yesterday and this morning to find their bait, though they had been lucky enough to capture three of the split-horned rabbits at once. Now, one of the rabbits had a rope tied around its body and Asin is prodding it, forcing it to head towards the Spider's trapdoor.

There is no warning as the trapdoor is pushed aside and the Spider lunges, fangs spearing the unlucky rabbit. Poison is pumped into the gray, squirming creature and the rabbit's struggles slowdown. As the Spider begins to skitter backward into its burrow, Asin is hauling on the rope that has been looped around a nearby tree, taking up the slack. The Spider jerks to a halt, half in the hole as Asin strains against the monster.

Before the Spider can release the rabbit and escape their trap, Daniel has rushed forwards. Rather than targeting the Spider this time though, he aims his attack at the trapdoor the Spider still holds with two of its legs. Triggering Perin's Blow, he smashes the trapdoor in the side, ripping it free from the Spider's grip and sending it flying into the distance. Without its trapdoor, the Spider spins to attack Daniel, the rabbit dropped and forgotten.

Daniel catches the attack high on his shield, sinking low and letting his knees absorb the shock before he triggers a Shield Bash, slamming the Spider into the air. As it lands, he takes a careful step to the side and crushes a leg, his mace cracking the spindly, hairy appendage.

Asin is scrambling forwards as well, ducking low so that she can slice at both legs on her side with her knives. She scores cuts against both, damaging the legs but as the creature spins again, she finds herself quickly coated with spider silk that the Querk Spider uses to defend itself, spewed forth from its spinnerets. The silk is sticky and tough, restricting her movements and Asin grunts in pain as she attempts to escape.

Seeing his companion in danger, Daniel lays into the Spider, forcing the monster to pay attention to him as he works on the creature's legs. Staying close, he shoves the creature and bashes its jaw when it attempts to push the young Adventurer aside, forcing the monster to give him its legs. Another leg is crippled and then a third soon after, the monster unable to move as fast anymore. As it scrambles aside, attempting to escape now, Daniel darts around to mash the monster's other legs, leaving the creature chittering in anger.

Smiling grimly, Daniel ducks back to look over to his friend. At first, he coughs and then he finally has to giggle a little. To escape, Asin has had to cut off the affected fur, chopping around the silk where it has stuck itself to her body and her clothing. The random patches of uneven fur and gaping holes around her cloak and shirt make Daniel grin, an action that makes Asin hiss at him in anger and dismay.

Freed, Asin stalks right past Daniel, careful to avoid the remaining silk to attack the monster. Drawn back to the task at hand, Daniel works on crushing the abdomen to put an end to the monster, careful to avoid the head where the glands lie.

The monster dead, Asin proceeds immediately to carefully cut up the monster, working to extract the venom sac without damaging it. She chuffs in anger, shaking the blood from the meat and examining the venom sac before discarding it as damaged, working even slower now to extract the second. This is more successful, and Asin purrs happily, her tail waving absently.

Grinning, Daniel holds out the enchanted storage pouch for Asin who carefully stores the gland in it. Even enchanted, the gland would only be good for seven days, but without it, the entire venom would degrade within a day. Still, Daniel cannot help but grin, spotting the bare spot on her tail where Asin had to rip the silk off.

"That's one," Daniel says, and Asin nods. She would need to be more careful on the next Spider. It wasn't as if she carried that many sets of clothing.

"Are you done laughing?" Daniel grimaces, tugging at the silk that binds him down. Two Spiders, one sac and a day later, Daniel is caught in spider silk. His shield is stuck to his body, his legs webbed together and he's lying on the ground, able to roll only a short distance back and forth.

Asin sniggers and shakes her head, wishing for a moment there was a way to mark this moment for all time. Daniel groans and just leans his head back on the ground, exercising his patience.

"Asin!"

"That'll be a silver for each," the shopkeeper smiles, pointing to the set of dissolution potions on the counter.

"A silver!" Daniel chokes. "They only cost 20 coppers in Karlak!"

"True, true."

"So, 20 coppers, right?"

"In Karlak. It's a silver each here." The shopkeeper smiles again. "You taking them or not?"

"Aaarrggghh!" Fishing the six silvers out, Daniel snatches up the potions after paying. They had used their initial two potions, and they were already wasting half-a-day traveling back just to get a restock. They could not afford to waste more time.

"My… face!" Clawing at the silk that has stuck to his face with one hand, Daniel has to remember not to reach with his other hand when he realizes he is unable to move his first. His assailant, having dodged and sprayed Daniel when he first attacked, scrambles away for the nearest tree, dragging the young Adventurer along the ground. Daniel scrambles for his pouch as he bumps over a root, struggling for breath through the corner of his mouth. Hand closing on the potion, he works the stopper free to pour it over the spider silk.

As the Spider reaches the nearest tree, a blurring blue-wreathed dagger pierces its body. Too aerodynamic to pin the creature, it still makes the Spider jerk, slowing its forward momentum long enough for Daniel to pour the potion over the silk. It immediately begins to dissolve as Daniel struggles with the web and breathing.

Asin does not stop, tossing knife after knife at the Spider. Angered, the Spider spins around and attacks Daniel, the long chelicerae in its head shutting on either side of the Adventurer's leg. Only one fang manages to get around the leather armor on Daniel's leg, sliding past the armor and injecting poison into his body. Even as Asin sinks another knife into its body, and Daniel smashes against it, the Spider does not let go, pumping more and more venom into Daniel. As it dies, Daniel is finally able to tear the last of the silk from his face and use both hands to pull its jaws apart.

Asin scrambles over, handing him a potion to combat the paralysis that rushes through Daniel's body. Shivering, Daniel curls up on his side and vomits half the contents of his stomach up. Once Asin has checked with Daniel that he will be fine, she drags the body away, working on the Spider to locate its venom sacs. She grimaces, finding one crushed and the other only half-full. Putting it aside, she mentally does the math. Today was the fourth day since they first managed to get their first sac. Another day and it would rot, so they either had to get one today or risk not having enough. For a time, she watches Daniel who continues to shiver before she hurries over to check on their bait. Only one last rabbit left before they had to find more live bait.

This was going to be tough.

"Last chance." Asin points, holding up both the map and the rabbit. Having gone through the vast majority of the easy to get to lairs, the pair would either have to revisit old lairs or journey deeper if they failed again. Daniel grimaces, nodding, running a hand through his hair and finding it catching on remaining spider silk. Lips twisting, he reaches down to pull out his boot knife to cut the glob of silk out, tossing it aside. Well, at least he did not have to worry about a haircut anytime soon.

"Then we better get this right," Daniel growls, rolling his wrist and mace. Days of tramping through the forest, hunting down Spiders that might or might still be in the locations marked on the map, trapping and dragging live animals and then brief minutes of scrambling, fighting and sometimes, winning, has made the Adventurer short-tempered. So much work for so little gain. No wonder most Adventurers charged such a high rate for these sacs - it wasn't difficult so much as annoying.

Flank, rabbit, charge, and smash. Everything this time works smoothly; the Spider is caught out and its trapdoor is sent spinning away. Asin ducks in close this time and works on the back leg, one after the other while Daniel works on distracting the Spider. He mostly blocks, attacking only once in a while when he has a clear shot, too wary to lash out aggressively.

The monster crippled, Daniel grins and stretches when Asin hisses. He spins around, his eyes widening as he spots the pack of wolves behind him. They let out a little growl, and Daniel slowly edges around the monster towards Asin who has a pair of daggers held out. The wolves snarl again, slowly pacing forwards as they drive the pair away from the Spider.   Neither Adventurer wants to start this fight though - they are outnumbered and tired.

Once they are a distance away, the two look at each other as they slide their backpacks on and begin jogging away. Silence lingers for a time as they put distance between them and the pack before a curse flies out finally.

"Ba'al's vomit!"

Chapter 16

Two and a half weeks later, a pair of tired, dirty Adventurers walk into the city of Karlak. The guards nod in recognition to Daniel as he half-heartedly waves in greeting before paying the entrance fee. The two Adventurers trudge in, Asin's tail hanging low and waving disconsolately as they walk, ears pressed low.

The only time the pair perk up is as they pass by a roadside food vendor, the smell of slowly rotating meat sparking a glimmer of interest. Daniel moves over, purchasing a half-dozen sticks from the lady, before handing the pieces over to Asin who scarfs her food down without a word.

At Maxwell's shop, the armorer is stalking back and forth shouting at his apprentices. When he sees the pair, he opens his mouth to berate them for being so late and then stops, his eyes sweeping over their tired, drawn forms. Asin holds up the bag without a word which Maxwell grabs. She hisses, "One day," before stalking away, a cryptic sentence that takes Maxwell only a moment to puzzle out.

Daniel nods too, waiting for Max to check the contents before he walks off, too tired to explain the delay. The last few weeks had been a hell of bad luck, bad planning, and more bad luck. Having lost the Spider to the wolves, the pair had to discard the first sac. For the next few days, they had struggled to find more Querk Spider lairs. When they had finally collected all three sacs and were hurrying back, Daniel had slipped while crossing a log bridge into the water, spilling both himself and the pouch. By the time they had finally managed to fish the pouch out of the water, all three sacs had been compromised, forcing the pair to begin collecting again.

No surprise then that words had been said, none of which were friendly or nice after the incident. The rest of the quest had been completed in a tense, mostly silent atmosphere. If it had not been for Asin's insistence on carrying the pouch, she would have left immediately upon entering the city. As it was, the pair had agreed to ignore one another's existence for the next three days.

Daniel stumbles into the Spinning Top, waving to Elise. She comes over, grimacing and murmurs to him. He stares at her blankly for a time before he slowly exits, heading to the next inn down the road. Daniel's room had been given up for the week, and because of that, Elise had rented it out. She was now filled up and unable to accommodate him.

Groaning, he flops in his room, staring at the peeling paint and the water-stained ceiling. He exhales, breath flowing out with a huff and then he shuts his eyes, exhaustion finally claiming him. As he falls asleep, a last thought crosses his mind.

"I need a bath."

Dawn comes too early, bright morning sunshine sifting through the cracked shutters and waking Daniel. He groans, rolling on his side and slowly stands, making his way downstairs for breakfast. Breakfast is surprisingly decent, the porridge filling and warm and the sides of bacon and mushroom heaven sent. Resolved to start becoming human again, Daniel heads upstairs to get his towel and a change of clothing from his bag. Today would be an errand day, one filled with taking care of the many small tasks that need completing after a couple of weeks in the forest. He had socks to darn, clothing and his body to wash, weapons to properly care for, broken equipment to repurchase and more errands to run. Tonight… Tonight he would see Khy'ra he promises himself.

A couple of days later, the pair meet up at Maxwell's shop. Asin stands at the corner, offering her friend a slight smile with a cocked head. Words were said, and relations had strained, but he was her friend. Was she his still? The returning smile from Daniel and the cup of offered tea answers her questions, and her tail relaxes, turning back to swinging idly. A slight flicker of disappointment runs through Asin, she had hoped for more of Elise's heavenly cooking rather than tea, but tea would do.

Daniel does not notice, his attention caught by the 'Closed' sign. As they rap on the door, there is silence for minutes. A second knock brings a harried apprentice to open the door, only for it to be shut again with a whispered the only excuse, "Not now!"

As Daniel raises his hand again, the bar is dropped with a finality, leaving the pair to stand in the early morning chill. Daniel grimaces, staring at Asin who returns his look before she shrugs. Well… Not now then.

"This is… nice," Daniel says as he bends down, picking up the mana stone from the Ogre. Asin nods firmly, stretching herself out as they stare around the grassy plains of the seventh floor. It was nice to be back on the seventh floor.

Questing had been necessary, even important. They had learned more of the world, fought in a new dungeon, met new Adventurers and would eventually get Daniel his first full set of custom armor. It had been important, but the Dungeon was much less frustrating. Even the sixth floor and the caverns seemed nostalgic now, difficult but at least they were always progressing. Questing was important, but for now, Daniel was happy to be a real Adventurer, delving into dungeons and facing the monsters that Ba'al would release on the world if it could.

"Next?" Daniel points with his mace before letting it rest on his shoulder, eyes crinkling in humor as Asin finishes stretching and nods. She absently scratches at a bare spot; fur ripped off from the fight. Catching his gaze, she sends him a mild glare before giving up and sticking out her tongue at him before

she scampers ahead. Even the loss of her fur would not make her sad today -
they were back, doing what they should be doing.

It is three days later when the pair finally finds the door to Maxwell's workshop
open. Inside, only a single tired apprentice sits at the counter, barely able to keep
his head from drooping. Spotting the pair, he gestures them deeper into the shop
to the actual smithy portion without getting up from his seat. It was painful being
at the bottom of the ladder the apprentice thought to himself as he forced a smile
for the next customer.

Behind, Daniel is practically bouncing forwards. He stops when he spots
Max who is holding a breastplate to his chest, stroking it gently and buffing the
silver inlaid runes. Even to their untrained eyes, the pair can see the difference
and care in craftsmanship between the work before them and their own gear.
After a time in which Max continues to be oblivious to the pair, Daniel clears his
throat.

"Oh, it's you, boy!" Max says as he looks up, eyes deep set and red rimmed.
He sets the breastplate down reverently, waving Daniel to the side. "Right, let's
get you fitted."

A few minutes later, Daniel is fully outfitted in his armor and forced to do a
series of calisthenics. Max asks questions, checking on fit throughout the process
though occasionally Daniel has to clear his throat to bring the armorer's attention
back to him. After having dressed and undressed a number of times, Max is
finally happy with the fit. "Good… good. That's it."

Daniel nods slowly, rotating his hips and torso and then gently bouncing up
and down. He grins, the armor barely making any noise, so well was it fitted. He
nods firmly to Max, offering his hand. "Thank you!"

"You're welcome," Max shakes his hand and then glances to the side where the enchanted bracers lie. "You know, I could buy those off you and resell them for you. I won't even take a commission."

Daniel opens his mouth and then shuts it, staring at his first ever magical item. He reaches out, letting armored fingers glide across them before he slowly nods. That was the life of an Adventurer, wasn't it? Taking what was useful, discarding what was not. He wanted, no, he needed to progress.

Max calls out without hesitation to his apprentice, making the youngster take the bracers away for cleaning. Obviously, a little work needed to be done before he would dare show that work in his store!

Turning to Asin, he grins at her. "I have a little something for you too." Reaching behind, he pulls out a small, thin metal gorget with a separate plate piece that hangs down the front which he hands to her. It is not wide at all and curves slightly down in the front and back to allow greater movement. As Asin takes it, her eyes widen at how light the piece is. Seeing her reaction, Max smirks. "I had some extra steel."

Asin takes the piece, quickly buckling it on and adjusting the leather straps to ensure it sits properly. Max looks it over and nods after a moment, more than pleased with the fit. As Asin fingers the collar, wondering at the cost of getting such a piece enchanted by Tharuk, she can only add, "Thank you."

"You're welcome." He smiles again, his hand unconsciously resting on the breastplate next to him. "Now, get out!"

The pair quickly exits, understanding how mercurial Max could get, especially after spending the last few days with little rest. A shared glance is all the pair need before they begin to trot quickly to the Dungeon. Time to try out their new toys!

"Let's go, big boy!" Grinning, Daniel hefts his shield and mace as he runs forward. They had been extremely lucky, having literally stumbled upon the Ogre Champion a bare two hours after making their way down to the seventh level. Chest and Champion in their sight, the pair immediately charge the creature before them.

Daniel skids to a stop just outside of the Ogre Champion's range, dodging the blow that swings down in front of him and digs a divot into the ground. Behind, Asin throws a series of knives that multiply, cutting into the Champion and distracting it. Daniel darts in immediately to the left, swinging his mace into the creature's side and feeling a bone crack as Perin's Blow catches it. However, even as the monster is lifted off the ground, it backhands Daniel, the club smashing into the Adventurer's side.

The club cracks into his body hard, throwing him off his feet and forcing Daniel to work to recover his balance. He grins, elation running through him as he realizes that he is barely hurt - that blow itself should have seriously bruised, if not broken his ribs. More confident than ever now, Daniel darts back in as Asin throws another knife filled with blue energy, the Piercing Shot drilling into the Ogre's eye.

As the creature rears back in pain, clutching at its ruined orb, Daniel crashes into the monster with his shield, triggering a Shield Bash into its short ribs. The monster leans over, allowing Daniel to lash out with a pair of Skill enhanced blows even as Asin closes and hamstrings the Champion. Crashing to the ground, crippled and in pain, the monster is quickly dispatched.

Asin and Daniel stare at the blue lights as they slowly dissipate, shaking their heads in amusement. It seemed strange that such a simple change would make such a difference, but with less concern about getting hurt, Daniel found himself being more aggressive. This took the pressure off Asin who was then able to focus on dealing damage and distracting the Champion. It was a knock-on effect that made it possible for what was a difficult fight before to become so much simpler.

On retrieving her knives, Asin moves to pick up the mana stones before getting a confirming nod from Daniel. Time to head for the eighth floor then.

Three hours later, Daniel pants as he stands above the pair of fallen Ogre corpses. The eighth floor had much the same geography as the seventh - wide open lands with glowing blue cavern walls. However, the Ogres came in pairs at least and sometimes as many as four at a time. Fights were more difficult as the Ogres often grouped up, attacking Daniel in a desperate attempt to overwhelm him. Often, Daniel would be forced to stay on the defensive, pulling the monsters with him while Asin finished one, relieving the pressure sufficiently for Daniel to fight back.

Rotating his shoulder, he forces his breathing to slow down, trying to calm down his heart. This last group had managed to take his feet off him, and he had spent a good few minutes curled up, being beaten on by the enormous monsters. His new armor and careful positioning had allowed him to survive, though he ached all across his body. Rubbing at a bruise on his face, he focuses on casting a Minor Heal, his body stitching itself together, as Asin finishes collecting the stones. Healed, he finally pays attention to his new notification.

Level Up!

Adventurer Level 7

You have gained 5 attribute points

Finally! He had managed to get past the level he had lost and was finally climbing again. He might not reach Level 10 before the end of the Dungeon, but at the least, he was on the way. There was a lot of work left, and he certainly felt that they needed to spend more time working this level, but soon, soon, they'd be done!

Name: Daniel Chai

Class: Level 7 Adventurer (0%)

Sub-classes: Level 7 (Miner) (14%)

Human (Male)

Statistics

Life: 243

Stamina: 243

Mana: 177

Attributes

Strength: 23

Agility: 21

Constitution: 29

Intelligence: 18

Willpower: 18

Luck: 14

Skills

Unarmed Combat: Level 3 (38/100)

Clubs: Level 9 (74/100)

Archery: Level 2 (48/100_

Shield: Level 8 (24/100)

Dodge: Level 6 (09/100)

Combat Sense: Level 6 (17/100)

Perception: Level 6 (27/100)

Mining: Level 7 (78/100)

Healing: Level 8 (98/100)

Herb Lore: Level 3 (31/100)

Stealth: Level 2 (14/100)

Cooking: Level 3 (29/100)

Singing: Level 2 (14/100)

Skill Proficiencies

Double Strike

Shield Bash

Perin's Blow

Mapping (II)

Spells

Minor Healing (I)

Gifts

Martyr's Touch - The caster may heal oneself or others by touch and concentration, sacrificing a portion of his life to do so. Cost varies depending on the extent of the injuries healed.

Chapter 17

Learning magic was strange, especially when one's previous experience with learning magic was through a Skill Up mused Daniel. Seated across Khy'ra's dining table this evening, the black-haired Adventurer watches as she weaves the spell slowly again, eyes squinted to catch each change in formula and mana flow. As she finishes the spell, she lets the magic disperse and slumps backward, rubbing her temples.

There were three portions to learning any magical spell. First, came the knowledge of the subject matter - a requirement to understand how the magic interacted with the substance or individual it affected. It was why more Advanced Spells were locked till one gained a greater level of the underlying skill. Second, came the spell formula which was a combination of alchemical formula, a way of thinking and a method of mana weaving all combined. Lastly, came personal flair - the way a student learned to apply the first and second portions of knowledge in their own understanding of mana. Of course, as every teacher had their personal flair, the process of studying a spell required a student not only learn the spell but learn how their master cast it and how to strip out the portions that did not work with their particular understanding and ability with mana.

A common saying was that magic users spent as many years searching for a teacher as they did learning magic itself and why teachers were particularly picky about students. A bad match between teacher and student could result in months if not years of wasted effort by both parties.

Unfortunately, Daniel neither had the time nor money to find a suitable instructor. He only had one particularly generous, beautiful elf that was willing to spend date night at home, casting and recasting a spell again and again so that he could attempt to learn it. Focusing, Daniel tried again, slowly pushing the mana out as he recalled the arcane formula.

"Yes… no, too much, just a little…" Khy'ra whispers encouragement along as they work together.

An hour later, Daniel is done as his mana is drained. Khy'ra smiles, pushing him back in his seat and plopping onto his lap. "Good! Very good."

"Ughh… I barely got past the first sequence," Daniel mutters as he wraps his arms around her body, squeezing it gently and nuzzling her neck.

"It was our first lesson," the Elf points out and then leans down, letting his breath tickle her ear. "You'll do better the next time. Just keep practicing."

Daniel nods, already distracted by the squishy, pleasant presence on his lap. He takes her ear into his mouth, nibbling on the lobe as Khy'ra catches her breath, squirming slightly. There were certain advantages to this kind of lessons for sure.

"Asin," Khy'ra calls out in horror, rushing forward to grab the young Catkin's arms. "What happened?"

Asin begins to growl and purr, answering Khy'ra in Catkin while Daniel stands stupefied, wondering what the fuss is about. As Khy'ra strokes one of Asin's arms and the patch of bare fur before pointing to another, realization slowly arrives. The pair continues to converse in Catkin, growling and purring at each other as they start walking off, leaving Daniel to follow after. His attempts at learning Catkin had been abject failures, his ear unable to locate the differences in words well enough for him to even begin learning thus far.

Resolving to follow along without complaining, Daniel perks up slightly halfway through their walk, the group having left the city a while ago. Khy'ra's not-so-covert glance and quick grin is enough to let him know that he is the object of conversation, though neither lady seems inclined to enlighten him further. Left alone, Daniel can only brood about what they might be discussing about him for the rest of their walk.

"Tharuk!" Khy'ra calls out to her friend, waiting for the Dwarf to exit his workshop before waving to him. Hours of walking has the group finally arriving at the lonesome building that makes up the Dwarf's workshop and home. "I brought visitors."

Tharuk laughs out loud and waves to the Elf, nodding in greeting to both Asin and Daniel. Asin bows slightly while Daniel waves, both sniffing the air as they smell lunch on the stove.

"Aye, lass. I remember. Lunch is nearly ready," Tharuk replies and waves them in, returning to his kitchen while the group takes seats around his cluttered kitchen cum workshop table. Asin's nose twitches, mentally cataloging the spices that are being used – Bloor, cinnamon, cardamom, Hunik salt, duck fat.

Seated together, Daniel whispers to Khy'ra, "What were you talking about?"

"Girl stuff," Khy'ra says.

"You were laughing!"

"We were," Khy'ra replies and refuses to say more.

"Right, lunch! Grab your plates, you lazy lot!" Tharuk cries out from the kitchen, drawing the attention of the group. Lunch is a pleasant, tasty and filling stew that is rapidly consumed with the freshly baked bread Tharuk pulls from the oven. It is only as they near the end does Tharuk bring the conversation back to the reason they came. "So, I hear one of you has a commission for me?"

Asin nods, holding up the steel gorget for Tharuk. "Shield."

Tharuk raises an eyebrow, picking up the gorget and looking it over. He hums and haws as he tests the piece, squinting and brushing fingers across it before slowly nodding. "Good work. Master-level crafting and materials. I can work with this for sure. A Shield Enchantment is costly though, more than most."

Asin nods. "Have coin."

Tharuk raises a slight eyebrow before he gently places the gorget down and begins to stroke his beard, staring at Asin, "Well, since you're a friend of Khy'ra, I can do it for fifteen Gold."

Daniel coughs, his eyes wide and Khy'ra sighs, grabbing his hand and standing up. "We'll just leave you two then."

Asin just nods, continuing to stare at Tharuk as she hisses, "Four."

"Four! I'd have to sell my house at Four! Eleven," Tharuk says and then in the silence as Asin stares at him, gestures to the side. "Pie?"

As Daniel is dragged out by Khy'ra, Daniel plaintively cries, "I wanted some pie too."

"The Dungeon is closed!" a voice shouts into the Top where Daniel has finally managed to get a room again. Seated in the dining room with Asin and Khy'ra for dinner later that evening, the shout catches everyone's attention.

"What?"

"No…"

"That's not possible!"

"What did he say?"

"QUIET!" shouts Elise as she strides over to the street youth who has brought the news. She prods him in the chest, getting him to repeat his message. When he is done, he is already running to the next inn after getting a tip from Elise. She turns to everyone who is waiting. "The Dungeon doors are closed. Adventurers can exit, but no one can enter. There is a lot of noise coming from the Dungeon too, grinding and screeching."

A hush falls over the inn, many Adventurers looking at one another in search for an answer. Eventually, all eyes fall on Khy'ra, waiting for the wise and long-lived Elf to speak. She smiles at everyone, waving slightly before she speaks, her mild voice carrying. "It's changing its configuration. It sometimes happens with Dungeons, though it's rare. It'll re-open."

The Adventurers, guards, and other patrons relax slightly.

Ken calls back with a question. "How long?"

"I don't know. It's variable. Maybe a day, maybe a week, maybe a few months." Khy'ra shrugs before adding, "It depends on how much is changing. The longer it's closed, the more it will have changed."

This statement makes a few Adventurers shift uncomfortably. Many made their daily living working the second sector of the floor, breaking down crawler walls and collecting crawler sacs for a living. It was good money that held little risk for these experienced Adventurers and a change in the Dungeon could mean a loss of their livelihood.

Daniel and Asin exchange worried glances. Their journeys and the needs of the quest had driven them to rely on their savings more than they had liked. It was only in the last few weeks that they had begun to replace their spent coin. A long break could be difficult for both of them. Without a word, they both stand and head for the door, Daniel snatching a quick kiss with Khy'ra first as she gets crowded by other Adventurers.

Best see what quests were available before they were all snatched up.

"Omrak?" Daniel frowns, walking over to the big warrior who is standing disconsolately by the Quest board in the Adventurer's Guild. A week after the closing of the Dungeon, the board was now bare as Adventurers scrambled to get what little jobs there were to fill their coin purse. Sadly, few Adventurers had much in savings - their lifestyles rarely predicated long-term plans.

At his name, the young Adventurer turns, flashing a strained smile at Daniel and Asin, "Morning, heroes!"

"Where's your party?" Daniel asks as he looks around and Omrak's face falls again.

"Gone," he mutters and then straightens his broad shoulders. "They have left for Peel."

"Split?" Asin clarifies and Omrak nods slightly, his face tired.

At Daniel's frown, Omrak adds, "My party, they felt I was fighting too recklessly. Using too many health potions."

A memory of the laughing warrior, standing and trading blows with Ogres flash through both Adventurer's minds. "Why don't you wear armor?"

"I have no coin," Omrak grimaces, his gaze lingering longingly on Daniel's leather armor that he wears today. "It is impossible. I fight as hard as I can, and no matter what level I go to, I can never earn enough!"

Daniel opens his mouth and then shuts it, unsure of what to say. Asin offers a slight, toothy smile before she waves goodbye. As there are no jobs again this morning, she has other duties to attend to. Daniel nods goodbye to his friend as Omrak continues to stare at the board. "Well, I guess I should get to work."

"Work?" Omrak says.

"I'm at the Clinic for now," Daniel replies and then eyeing Omrak he adds. "You know, I heard that Levi near the docks is always working for strong dock workers to help unload the barges."

"Thank you! I will speak with this Levi. It is not the work of heroes, but even heroes must eat." Without waiting further Omrak dashes out, a wide grin on his face. Daniel just looks at the disappearing form of the large Northerner, somewhat bemused. Well, he had best get to work too.

The distant cry of a newborn baby and the creaking of old wood are the only noises that break the silence of the night. Seated at Khy'ra's kitchen table, Daniel nurses a cup of tea in the dark, staring unseeing into her kitchen. Sleep has eluded him again tonight, his thoughts unwilling to still even as he lay in bed with his girlfriend.

He had been putting off the decision for weeks now, the pressing question of whether to join a guild. At first, he had delayed it till he had completed his quest. Then, he had delayed it to 'test' his new armor. Then, he had made excuses that he was learning a new spell for free with Khy'ra. During the day, when he worked at the Clinic, these excuses made perfect sense. However, late at night, with no Dungeon in the city nor work to keep his mind busy, his excuses felt like what they were, excuses.

He was delaying making a decision, procrastinating, because he did not want to make one. He knew, truly knew, that he had no desire to be a Questor, solely living on the returns of quests like others. Nor did he wish to be a Lifer, working a section of Dungeon over and over again like a, like a Farmer. Both those decisions were easy.

Joining a guild though, becoming part of something larger, that was more difficult. He could not casually dismiss that opportunity. Guilds would allow him to grow, to become stronger faster. He would not need to rely on his girlfriend, would not have to scramble and scrabble for coin to develop his arms and armor. He would have more party members, more training, more opportunities.

And yet… And yet.

"Daniel?" Khy'ra walks into the room, pulling her robe closed as she turns to his moonlight-silhouetted form. Seeing her, an involuntary smile crosses Daniel's face, his face lightening. He holds a hand out, and she takes it, sliding onto his legs with ease as he hugs her to him. She bends down, trading a kiss before she murmurs, "Problems?"

"Just… thinking," Daniel answers and hugs her again, resting his head on her shoulder. Khy'ra nods slightly, staying quiet till Daniel breaks the silence himself. "I was thinking about the guilds again."

"Oh," her reply is soft as Khy'ra struggles to keep her tone neutral. She knew this day had to come, but still…

"I just, it makes sense you know?" he says plaintively. "There's so much to gain from it. I'm doing okay right now, doing good, but… it makes sense!"

"Mmmhmmm," Khy'ra replies, biting her lip in the dark to not add anything.

"I just…" He hugs her again, staring into the dark. "I wanted to be an Adventurer ever since I was a kid you know. I heard all the stories, remembered all the names. Going into the deepest Dungeons, fighting the hardest monsters, being the best and keeping everyone safe. It was what heroes did.

"And I can do that. I have to do that with a guild. No hero ever grows without a guild, a strong party beside him. I know that. But…" Daniel shakes his head, whispering the last. "I don't want to go."

"Because you're scared?" Khy'ra turns, meeting Daniel's eyes at last. "Or because you're comfortable?"

"I'm… happy," Daniel answers her after some thought, his lips twisting crookedly. "I'm happy, learning with you and Asin. Fighting my way through slowly. I hate questing, but even then, when we are done, it's so satisfying."

"Then that's your answer," Khy'ra says.

"But…"

"Daniel. A word of advice from an old… Adventurer," Khy'ra says, smiling slightly. "When you look back at your life, it's not the stories that you remember. Or the Dungeons you visit or the monsters you vanquish. It's your friends and your struggles. You have time. Time to join a guild. Time to get better. I know it doesn't seem like that, but you do have time. Enjoy it while you can."

Slowly nodding, Daniel leans against her. A small part of him still wonders if this is the right choice, but… he was happy. Was that not what everyone truly wanted? Even if he had to leave, perhaps he could be happy here for a little longer.

Bursting through his clinic door, the messenger pant as he catches his breath before he announces his news, "It's open!"

Daniel opens his mouth and then shuts it, his eyes lighting up with excitement. He glances at his latest patient and then casts Minor Healing, the open cut on her hand stitching close as Daniel grins, grabbing his cloak from the coat hanger. As he hurries out, he looks to the receptionist who laughs, waving Daniel away. She understands she cannot stop him. After all, everyone here was a volunteer.

As he runs along, Daniel finds himself joining a stream of other interested parties. He notices other Adventurers, of course, on-sight, but there are numerous other citizens who hurry along. Nearly three weeks of having the town's biggest income earner being shut down has hurt the livelihood of many, and so, the interest is not unexpected.

As Daniel finally reaches the town square, he finds it already crowded. He growls slightly, unable to press forward or see anything. After a while, hushing noises are made, and the crowd slowly falls silent as the Guard Captain stands, shouting.

"The Dungeon is open. No one has been allowed in as yet. All Adventuring parties are to visit the Adventurer's Guild to receive their entry number. Entry will be gated from tomorrow onwards. Now go home!"

As the word gets passed down, other guards start taking up the call, directing the crowd out of the town square. Questions are rebuffed, and slowly Daniel manages to make his way to the Guild Hall. As he nears, he spots a familiar figure crouched on top of a statue, licking the fur on her hand.

"Asin!"

The Catkin stares and then waves, dropping down to meet him. Her grin widens as she meets Daniel's excited gaze. The Dungeon was open!

###

Book 3

A Dungeon's Soul

Chapter 1

Dawn light filtered through the wooden shutters of Daniel Chai's room in the Spinning Top. He shivered, pulling his blankets closer to his body for a moment as the late autumn morning chill made itself known to him. Long years of discipline forced him to sit up now that he was awake. He ran a hand through his hair, smiling slightly at the uneven cut that Khy'ra, his girlfriend, had given him. She was a dangerous Adventurer, a beautiful Elf, and a kindly Healer, but the one thing she was not was a decent barber.

After stretching slowly to his full five foot eight inches, Daniel walked to the windows after wiping himself down, sliding a shirt back on. He threw the shutters open and looked out at the sprawling city of wood and stone before him, then leaned outwards slightly as he stared at the center of town to spot the Dungeon entrance and the Adventurers' Guild. Early as it was, he could see streams of Adventurers entering and exiting the Dungeon, traversing the pathway between Guild and Dungeon to sell their loot before resting.

The Karlak Dungeon had reopened in the last few days after being closed for weeks as the Dungeon reconfigured itself. The wave of relief that had risen through the city when it was made clear that it was still a Beginner Dungeon had been palatable. As every Adventurer had to start again from the first Level, the Adventurers' Guild had instituted a lottery system to stagger entry. Eventually, the more experienced Adventurers would trickle down to the lower levels and entry would no longer need to be staggered, as the Adventurers would all be spread out across its many levels. Eventually.

Daniel sighed again, pulled his head back in, and finished dressing. Unfortunately, their party had drawn a slot for tomorrow, leaving them to wait another day. Weeks without their most important income source meant that he needed to work whatever jobs he could find on the quest board if he wanted to eat tomorrow. Staying in bed was not an option.

Walking down the stairs, he waved to Elise, the Spinning Top's owner, who was delivering food to the floor. The matronly blonde smiled at Daniel, nodding to a free table while she delivered watered-down beer, wine, and a mix of eggs, bacon, and leafy greens to the table. Daniel idly noted that the plates were nearly overflowing with greens as the very last harvest had been pulled from the ground. Soon, only canned vegetables and a small variety of magically preserved vegetables would be available.

"Morning, Elise," Daniel greeted the innkeeper as she arrived with his breakfast. Elise just flashed him a smile, too busy to chat while he dug into the meal with gusto. As he finished up, Elise dropped off a pair of wrapped lunches at his table.

Outside, having retrieved his leather armor, shield, and mace, Daniel quickly joined the flow of humanity as he headed to the Guild. Daniel casually eyed the crowds who were mostly made up of human townsfolk with the occasional glimpse of a Beastkin. Early as it was, most Adventurers were either already in the Dungeon or still asleep. Once he arrived at the Adventurers' Guild, he found his partner, Asin, waiting for him.

"Morning, Asin," he greeted his friend and fellow party member. The smaller Catkin was crouched on the stairs that led up to the building, licking at her paw while her tail lazily waved in the air behind her. Jade eyes glinted in amusement as Daniel handed her the packet of food, which she quickly slipped into her bag, ensuring it was strapped in and out of the way of her additional throwing knives.

"Daniel," Asin purred. The Catkin as always kept her speaking to the minimum, being one of the unlucky few who found it painful to speak in the human tongue of Brad. Unfortunately, as hard as Daniel worked at it, he found it difficult to shape his throat and tongue to speak the common Beastkin language.

"Checked out the quest board yet?" Daniel asked as he walked up the stairs. Asin stood smoothly, her movements all feline grace. At the shake of Asin's head, Daniel nodded contentedly. Inside, the Adventurers' Guild buzzed as Adventuring parties cashed out Mana Stones, hung out regaling each other with tales of the new floors, and generally made a mess. Asin's ears perked up as she swiveled her head from side to side, listening in on the conversation. Being the third day of the Dungeon opening, talk mostly centered around the first floor and as such, Asin learnt nothing new.

The quest board was literally a pair of rolling wooden boards upon which the attendants at the Guild posted new requests. The board itself was separated into three portions depicting the most common quest types—Delivery, Collection, and Miscellaneous. Unlike the previous few weeks, the board was not stripped bare of all quests as more and more Adventurers went back to the Dungeon to earn coin.

Lips pursed, Daniel slowly read through the posted offers. Unlike many of his peers, the former Miner had been taught to read, so he ignored the symbols posted on the bottom right for the illiterate, instead studying the board for a suitable option.

"Ah, brave heroes! The morning's fire greets you all!" The roared greeting makes Asin wince. Everyone in the Guild briefly turned to view the youthful barbarian who was the cause of the ruckus. Standing nearly a foot taller than Daniel, the blond-haired, tunic-clad muscular Northerner towered over the Adventurers within, a friendly smile on his face as he walked in. Carrying only a single, large sword, the barbarian strode over to the quest board, his grin widening as he spotted Asin and Daniel.

"Morning, Omrak," Daniel greeted the youngster, shuffling over slightly to give the barbarian space.

"This? Is this quest worthy of a hero?" A brief few seconds later, Omrak was pointing out a quest with a meaty finger.

"Uhhh …" Daniel read the quest notice, lips twitching. "That's a request for beaters for the upcoming Fall Hunt. It's a few days away and you'd need to make your way there. Not bad pay though."

"Ah …" Omrak rumbled, staring at the quest. Daniel raised an eyebrow and Omrak shrugged as he answered the unspoken question. "I have no party. I must wait a few more days before entering the Dungeon. This quest work, it is less than heroic but better than the docks."

"No luck with finding a party so far?" Daniel asked.

"No. I fear I must wait for a new group or grow strong myself," Omrak said, clapping a hand to his chest.

"Well, we're going in tomorrow …" Daniel began to say before he was elbowed in the side by Asin. She snarled at him, making him blink.

"Hero Asin …?"

"Later," Asin growled as she dragged Daniel to a nearby booth. She lowered her voice then, snarling at him. "No offer."

"But why?" asked Daniel. "It won't be for long and he needs some help."

"First floor. Lousy stones. Split three way," Asin said, her tail lashing out behind her.

"Uhh …" Daniel quickly parsed the sentences together before he blinked. "You don't want to help Omrak because we won't earn enough?"

Asin nodded firmly, making Daniel grimace.

"He's not earning a lot right now. It won't hurt for him to join us and we could use his help at lower levels. He's roughly on the same level as we are so he wouldn't be holding us back," Daniel said quickly, lining up his arguments.

"Expensive," Asin repeated.

"Yeah, but he can carry more than we can."

Asin paused, clearly taken by that thought. Pressing his advantage, Daniel continued, "You know you can't carry much and neither can I. With more help, we could potentially clear the second floor in a single day."

Asin frowned before she finally answered, "Third."

"That's …"

"Third."

"Fine!" Daniel grimaced, knowing that pushing to do three floors in a single run was going to be difficult. However, the Guild had agreed that any party that managed to make it to the third floor would be eligible to enter the Dungeon at any time. Having won her way, Asin stalked back to the big barbarian who had been watching the argument with interest.

"Join. Carry. Go fast," Asin hissed at the big man, holding her fingers up as she spoke. "Equal share."

Omrak grinned, clapping the diminutive Catkin on the shoulder and staggering her. "Thank you, hero! You shall not find fault in our progress. I shall be your shield, your sword, and your back!"

"Loud!" Asin complained to Daniel as she grabbed a quest off the board and stalked off to join the line awaiting an attendant.

"Omrak, quieter, please," Daniel said, grinning slightly at his Catkin friend, who was rubbing her shoulder discretely.

"Of course, hero!" Omrak said in a stage whisper.

"Tomorrow, at the entrance. Dawn."

"I shall be there. But for now, I must meet with the Master of Docks. I shall avail myself to the boats one last day."

"Yeah, you do that. See you, Omrak." Having said his goodbyes, Daniel strode over to his waiting friend, who held the quest notice out for Daniel to read. He winced as he read it over, grumbling. "Really?"

"Good coin."

"I know …" Daniel sighed again and slipped the quest notice into his pouch. Well, he was asking her to help.

Hours later, Daniel stifled a slight groan as he hauled the next basket of fish up the steep hill. As Omrak would have said—this was not a hero's work. However, it was decent-paying work for both of them—at least, so long as the fish were swimming. It was the last week of the run and the Fishermen's Guild had finally opened up fishing on the river, ensuring that the nets and fishing traps were running full-bore. Even if Adventurers were not the preferred day laborers, this week any extra pair of hands was gratefully taken.

Daniel just wished that he was not stuck doing the heavy labor. Unfortunately, like most of the hired Adventurers, he had no Skills or background in crafting, so fixing the nets or the traps was out. His only saving grace here was his strength and endurance, and so he found himself trudging up the hill with baskets filled with fish. In the river, Asin—with her natural grace and her superb aim—was having the time of her life with the nets. Even without a Skill related to fishing, she was pulling a significant number of fish out.

As he came back down the hill, Daniel watched Asin tromp out of the freezing water to warm up against the nearby braziers. Enchanted galoshes kept her feet and thighs warm but did nothing for her torso. Daniel had to hide a smile when she finally exited and shook herself hard, sending droplets of cold water cascading from her fur. A choked snort from behind him told Daniel that he was not the only one to find the wet Catkin amusing.

If he had to spend a day outside of the Dungeon, this was not a bad way to do so. Still, as Daniel stretched and looked up into the sky, he could not help but look forward to the next day.

"Daniel," Khy'ra greeted him as she entered her house. "I got your message at the Clinic."

"Khy'ra." He bent forwards, planting a quick kiss on her lips before he turned back to frying the fish. One good thing about working the river today—dinner was easily served. "Everything good at the Clinic?"

"The usual." Khy'ra shrugged. "Nothing that needs your Gift, though if you could spare a few minutes later, we have a few patients that could use a Healing."

Daniel nodded, relieved that he would not be required to use his Gift. A small number, maybe one in a thousand, were Gifted with an ability upon birth. The usefulness and strength of the ability varied but what never did was that the use of a Gift had a cost. For Daniel, that cost of using his Gift was the loss of a portion of his memories, his experience, his Skills. However, his Gift also provided him an uncanny understanding of the body which allowed him to learn and progress in the use of more traditional Healing magic.

"After dinner," Daniel said.

"Of course. Worked the river today?" Khy'ra asked as she walked up beside him, breathing in the aroma of the fried fish. She could smell crushed pepper, the pork fat that she had saved, dried thyme, red peppers, and something else. Brows furrowed, the Elf stared at the tantalizing dish.

"Asin's recipe," Daniel answered, prodding the fish once again before taking it out of the frying pan.

"Should I get the milk then?" Khy'ra teased as she walked to set the table.

"I fixed it," Daniel said proudly. Once again, he was grateful that the Catkin was as dedicated to good food as he was—his journeys in the last few months had taught him that this was not the case with most other Adventuring parties. On the other hand, the Beastkin had a tendency to eat intensely spicy foods—something that puzzled Daniel, considering their expanded senses.

"Oh good," Khy'ra said, and Daniel laughed. As much as Khy'ra complained, he could still recall her stuffing her face without complaint the last time Asin was here cooking for them all.

"You're headed into the Dungeon tomorrow?" Khy'ra asked as she finished setting the table, watching as Daniel fished out the bread from the oven. There were many reasons she cared for this young Adventurer, but the way he fed her certainly helped. A touch of sorrow flickered across her face as she recalled that he would be leaving soon. Like most humans, they stepped into and out of her life.

"Yes. Do you recall the Northerner? Omrak?"

"I've seen him around. Big man."

"Uhh …" Daniel paused, noting the admiring tone in her voice before he shook away the flash of jealousy. "Yes. He'll be joining us. At least for a few levels."

"Mmmm … that's good," Khy'ra said around a mouthful of fish.

Daniel blinked, uncertain of whether she was referring to his cooking or Omrak. Seeing his confusion, Khy'ra's eyes crinkled in humor and Daniel realized she had done it on purpose. Seeing him growl playfully at her, the Elf finally relented.

"It's good that you've gotten more help. There are a lot of Dungeons that can't be completed without more members," Khy'ra clarified. Daniel nodded, knowing what she said was true. However, both he and Asin were workaholics, and finding others who were willing to keep up with them would have been difficult. Daniel, however, had a very good feeling about Omrak.

Biting into the fish himself, Daniel turned the conversation to Khy'ra's day, pushing aside thoughts of the Dungeon and Adventuring. They would have more than enough to discuss tomorrow.

Chapter 2

"Morning, Liev," Daniel greeted the red-haired, scrawny Guild attendant. Leaning against the wooden counter, Daniel proffered their chit in exchange for the entrance seal.

"Daniel, Asin. And Omrak?" Liev stared at the blond giant, lines on his face deepening as he raised an eyebrow in inquiry to the pair. After receiving a confirming nod, Liev just shrugged and added Omrak's name to the seal. "Have you been keeping up with the news?"

"Yes, but best to go over it again," Daniel answered for the group. Asin pursed her lips slightly, eager to leave, but said nothing. Behind, Omrak looped his thumbs in his belt, pushing his giant sword that hung by a shoulder sheath down his chest to the side.

"Right, first floor has Kobolds. No change there," Liev said. "Second floor, we've got Elemental Turtles. Slow but tough. You either need to flip them or shatter their shells. As you know, breaking the shells in combat will decrease the chance that they'll drop when the Dungeon dismisses the body and the Guild is buying the shells. We're paying two copper per shell currently. No traps reported.

"No group has managed to make it to the third floor as yet. The first floor is relatively small—about three-quarters the size of the old first floor. The second floor makes up for it, being about thrice the size. It's a mixture of water pools and caves, so you'll need to be careful about walking around. There are no natural lights and the Guild has not installed any thus far, so you'll need to bring your own for the second floor. An extra pair of clothing is also recommended, and rope."

Having finished his rundown, Liev waited patiently for any questions. Seeing none, he finished.

"That's about it for the Dungeon so far. We did get a letter indicating that we should expect at least a few interested Advanced parties soon."

Daniel grunted at the news, not entirely surprised. The bonus for completing a new Dungeon added to the allure of the unknown was bound to draw some more experienced Adventurers. Even so, Asin hissed slightly, while Omrak was either oblivious to the implications or uncaring, having shown no reaction to the news.

"Thanks, Liev. We'll see you tonight?" Daniel asked.

Liev nodded in agreement, watching the trio leave with a slight smile on his face before he turned to the next group.

"Do we have everything we need?" Daniel asked the group on the short walk to the Dungeon entrance. Unlike other cities, which made a big showing of the Dungeon, Karlak's entrance was a simple stone building with large double doors flanking it. Daniel's lips twisted wryly at the sight of the doors—he had never seen them closed other than for the reconstruction.

"About time you got in. Been lazing around?" Ken, the chubby middle-aged town guard, called out to Daniel and Asin when they arrived. He gave a cursory glance at the seal they offered, dropping it into the pouch that waited beside him. "Well, I won't keep you. I expect stories and drinks tonight at the Top, though."

Daniel smiled at the noisy guard, offering a quick nod to Curtzman on the opposite side before he led his party inside. Neither of the other Adventurers had offered much more than a nod to the pair of guards—Asin because the guards generally treated her kind with a significant degree of distrust, and Omrak because his run-ins with the Karlak guard had mostly occurred late at night, and ended up with him in the cells waiting to sober up.

Inside, the stone building led immediately to a familiar grey entranceway. As they reached the entrance, both Daniel and Omrak stepped forwards to lead the way. Daniel twitched, staring at the Northerner who was in the process of unsheathing his greatsword.

"I shall lead the way, Hero Daniel. It shall be my honor to be your shield," Omrak declared.

For a moment, Daniel felt a sense of vertigo as he adjusted his thinking. Omrak was right—being both a bigger, stronger, and more skilled melee fighter, Omrak was the better choice to lead the way. Especially as the first couple of floors had been reported as trapless. Daniel looked over the Northerner again, noting that outside a leather groin cup, Omrak still had not managed to save up for a suit of armor. In fact, aside from his greatsword and a knife that was so big it could be considered a short sword itself, the barbarian was the most lightly equipped of the group.

Daniel, was dressed in the breastplate and pauldrons of his old leather armor. While he would have preferred to use his newly acquired suit of iron armor, the dangers of the watery second level kept him dressed minimally. If he did fall in, he could discard his shield and mace and swim to the surface with what he currently wore.

Asin, was equipped with a light surcoat of untreated leather, a pair of crossed bandoleers holding throwing knives across her chest, and more strapped to her legs. On her hips, she carried a pair of larger fighting knives that she used when she needed to get close. Hanging from a series of straps behind her, were the bolos she had purchased in Peel. To top it all, he spotted the enchanted lightning bracers and the enchanted Shield gorget that she wore instead of more powerful armor.

All three Adventurers of course carried their other gear, packs filled with rope, lamps, food packets, trap balls, and other essential delving gear. Asin, catching his serious study of their equipment, snorted lightly and Daniel gave a wry smile. Okay, it was only the first few floors of a Beginner Dungeon.

The first floor was a total sense of déjà vu for the entire group. The low ceilings and narrow passageways meant that Omrak spent a significant portion of the time bent over, carrying his sword in one hand. The smooth, Mana-imbued stones that made up the passageways, glowed with a soft blue light that offered the group enough illumination to see easily, though they all knew that after a few hours they would feel the subtle strain.

What was different was the sheer number of Adventurers. Early as they were, staggered entry or not, the number of Adventurers walking through the first floor was unusual. It was no busy city street, but for a Dungeon, it could be considered uncomfortably busy. Many of the Adventurers held maps in their hands, sketching in new corridors and marking intersections, while others rushed down the passages as they attempted to either locate more monsters to kill or complete mapping the floor for the experience bonus.

In either case, after a long hour of not locating a single monster, both Asin and Omrak were growing impatient.

"Bad luck," Asin grumbled, jerking her head to the Northerner.

"Asin …" Daniel began. It was not as if the crowding was Omrak's fault.

"My blade hungers for blood too, Hero Asin," Omrak said. "Though perhaps we can seek blood in less cramped quarters."

The loud reverberations of Omrak's declaration made Asin wince, her sensitive ears twitching. She growled softly, about to chastise him again, when she heard something. Having glanced back to look at his friend, Daniel saw her ears twitch and her tail straighten.

"What is it?" Daniel asked softly.

"Kobold," she answered, and pointed down the hallway. The word had not fully left her mouth before Omrak let out a yell of excitement, charging the monster. As he took the corner, he barreled into the wiry, long-limbed Kobold who was rushing to check out the noise as well.

Bowled over, the short monster was only beginning to struggle to his feet before a massive fist, swung in a tight, left hook, connected with its face. It lifted the Kobold entirely off its feet and slammed the top of its head into the wall, cracking it open. It was not a fact that Omrak noticed as his foot swung forwards to end the fight.

Slain, the Kobold's brownish-gray body glittered and broke apart, the corruption by Ba'al dispersed. In return, the Kobold left an unused, rusty shiv and a tiny Mana Stone. The Mana Stone was the core of the monster, the way that Erlis was able to manifest Ba'al's corruption in a Dungeon and the entire reason for the Dungeon's existence. Omrak bent down, picking up the stone, and then turned to offer it to Asin at her yowl. She took it quickly, sliding it into a secure pocket inside her leather vest before the party moved on.

As they traversed more and more of the first floor, Daniel started offering more concrete directions as he guided the group through the floor. Each turn, each new cavern and passageway, was added to his mental map of the underground, a gift of his Mapping proficiency. In a few hours and a few more Kobolds, the trio found the stairs down. Without a word, the party trooped down. The first floor held no challenges and, even worse, no coin to be earned.

The second floor was, as Liev warned, a significant contrast. Gone were stone hallways and narrow passages to be replaced by large wet grottos. Water dripped, ran, and pooled everywhere with only wet walkways treading through the cave. The group[took a brief moment to register themselves on the portal stone before they carefully made their way forwards.

Bearing a lantern each, Omrak and Daniel slowly walked forwards, taking care with each step. Behind them, Asin rolled her eyes and let out a lazy yawn, her pupils wide as they drank in the meager light sources. Unlike the first floor, the party met their first attacker within minutes.

The Elemental Turtle surged out of the water and clamped its stone-infused jaws around Omrak's boot, taking them all by surprise. Omrak snarled, jumping away reflexively and shaking his foot in a futile attempt to detach the creature. Howling, he put his foot down and readied his sword to cut the monster but is beaten to the act by Daniel, who'd anticipated Omrak's failure. Crouched low, Daniel swung his mace down hard, smashing the turtle on the shell hard enough to shatter it. Injured, the turtle opened its mouth to die a moment later as Daniel repeated his attack.

Pushing by Daniel, Asin huffed in anger as she picked up the only drop, a small Mana Stone. She looked at Omrak and then Daniel before she said, "No smash!"

Daniel offered a shrug in apology while Omrak inspected his foot, prodding at the bruised ankle. After he'd taken a tentative step, Omrak nodded to himself and stalked forwards as he paid closer attention to the water. Daniel's eyes narrowed as he gauged the damage from the slight hint of a limp that Omrak showed.

"Omrak, one second," he called out to the Northerner. Stepping forwards, he placed a hand on him and cast a quick Minor Healing. The spell wiped away a portion of the Barbarian's fatigue, his accumulated bruises, and the injured ankle.

"Ah!" Omrak drew a deep breath, the sudden absence of pain euphoric. "Your Healing is welcome if unnecessary. It was a minor injury."

"I doubt we'll get anything but minor injuries," Daniel said, glancing around. The turtles were annoying but, at their level, not dangerous. Not unless the group decided to have a nap at least.

"Very true, these are not ballad-worthy enemies," Omrak said, and Asin rolled her eyes. She turned her head, tracking the ripples in the water a distance away, her lips pulled apart to show glittering carnivorous teeth.

"Too far …" Daniel said, and Asin nodded. Still, she kept an eye on it as Omrak took off again.

"Let's map the place. Remember, our goal is the third floor," Daniel said, and the giant ahead of him rumbled agreement.

Fire turtles. Water turtles. Lightning turtles. Stone turtles. Air turtles, which were just strange with their tiny wings and their tendency to drop onto the party as an attack. Hours later, as they approached evening, Daniel was growing truly sick of turtles. The party had quickly developed a method of dealing with the monsters, but it did not make the repetition and annoyance any less.

Omrak had switched out his greatsword for his knife, using the pommel to smash apart turtles, or stabbing them in the guts after he flipped them over with his arms. Daniel's trusty mace was aptly suited for killing these monsters, and it was only Asin who lacked the brute strength or proper weaponry who found herself mostly ineffective. If not for her enchanted bracer that added small arcs of electricity to her attacks, she would have been rendered utterly ineffective. As it stood, Asin spent most of the level spotting for the two melee fighters.

On Omrak's back, his bag had begun to bulge with the Dungeon-created shells. Outside of a single, swirling, fire-patterned shell, all the others had been added to the pile. Asin kept that shell herself, intending to add it to her collection of rocks at home.

"Break?" Asin huffed as her stomach rumbled.

Looking around the cleared cavern, Daniel nodded and unslung his backpack, taking a seat near a rock a short distance from the water. The trio quickly took seats facing each other, allowing them to keep track of the cavern while they ate.

"You don't eat much, do you?" Daniel said, glancing at the wrapped sandwich that was dwarfed in Omrak's massive hands.

"Ah …" Omrak said as he visibly hesitated.

Asin let out a huff before she picked up a small stone and tossed it at Daniel's head. Daniel flinched, and glared at his friend while she snorted and pulled apart part of her own sandwich, offering it to Omrak wordlessly.

"I could not …"

"Eat," Asin growled, prodding him. "You fight."

Omrak stared at Asin, confused.

"She means you've been doing most of the fighting," Daniel clarified for Asin, who gave an appreciative nod.

"Ah …" Omrak glanced at the offered sandwich again before he took it in his hand. "My thanks, Hero Asin."

When Omrak took a bite of the sandwich, his eyes widened, and he began puffing, his mouth wide open. Daniel choked off a laugh, realizing what had happened even as Omrak hastily drank from his waterskin.

"You are a true hero to eat that," Omrak said, eyes filled with admiration as he watched Asin continue to chew on her sandwich and spiced meat. Offering the half-eaten portion back to Asin, Omrak said, "I fear this challenge is beyond me."

"It is an acquired taste," Daniel said, eyes crinkling in humor. Asin just sniffed, though Daniel noted the lazily swinging tail that indicated her own amusement. Pulling apart his own sandwich, he traded with Omrak for the remains of the portion offered to him. "Tasty though when you've gotten used to it."

Omrak's eyes widened even further as he watched Daniel take a bite of the sandwich, the stocky Adventurer's only visible reaction a slight increase in mouth-breathing.

"Truly, I am in the company of great heroes."

"Floor guardian?" Omrak rumbled in question as they peered into the large cavern. Inside, a single Elemental Turtle sat, surveying its surroundings. Its shell swirled in a pattern of red, gray, and their first white, indicating an attunement to fire, earth, and another element. The monster was twice the size of their previous opponents, just over four feet in length and a foot-and-a-half tall.

Elemental Turtle Champion (Level 4)
HP: 280/280

"Probably. See the stairs?" Daniel said, nodding past the Guardian to where a set of stairs led down.

"Yes. This should be a good fight," Omrak said as he sheathed his knife and pulled out his greatsword. Asin winced as he did so, Omrak having forgotten to keep his voice low as he had grown excited at the prospect of battle.

Turning its gaze to where the three hid, the Turtle let out a low roar accompanied by a surge of fire. The trio scurried backwards, hiding behind an outcropping till the flames died; Asin growling softly in displeasure at having lost the element of surprise.

The moment the fire died, Omrak charged from cover, screaming his own challenge. The Turtle counter-charged, at the last moment pulling its head back into its shell as it noted Omrak swinging at it. The sudden change in the monster's momentum made Omrak's attack fall short, the blow only landing at the edge of the blade and making a minor chip on the turtle's shell. The turtle's initial momentum unchecked, it knocked the barbarian off his feet, forcing the Northerner to flip over the shorter monster.

Behind Omrak, Daniel followed more carefully. Hunkered low, he engaged Double Strike, his own Skill Proficiency that made his mace blur as it smashed into the Turtle's shell. Each attack chipped away at the shell but left no other visible damage.

Hissing, the Turtle pulled itself out of its shell, snapping at Daniel. Daniel caught the attack low on his shield, stumbling slightly as he attempted to regain his balance from the low-angle of the attack. As the Turtle readied itself to bite again, a fan of throwing knives arrived, lightning sparking as they embedded themselves in the exposed body.

In pain, the Turtle snapped itself back into its shell and in doing so, knocking the knives free. Omrak's own swing, cutting horizontally, missed the legs and knocked the shell sideways, sending it spinning. For a moment, the Adventurers wondered if their eyes were playing tricks on them as the shell glowed with an inner white light.

Moving forwards cautiously, Daniel readied himself to continue the attack on the monster. When it popped its head out, Asin sent a knife at it, which was blocked by the monster charging forwards. Asin snarled slightly, readying another knife even as the Turtle opened its mouth to breathe fire again. Staring at the glowing mouth, Daniel ran sideways towards the water's edge and ducked low, covering his body with the shield even as the flames roared out.

Omrak, behind Daniel, took a more direct route, jumping over the attack. The barbarian swung his blade down, the greatsword cracking the shell with a loud clang of metal. To the side, Asin threw a Piercing Strike that drilled through the monster's leg, laming the Floor Champion.

The turtle roared in pain, glowing white as it struggled to heal the wounds. Water spilling from his body, Daniel ran from the shallows to lash out at the Turtle, who dodged by retracting into its body. Frustrated, Omrak tossed his sword aside and grabbed hold of the edge of the monster, flipping it over with a surge of strength.

Its soft under-belly exposed, both Asin and Daniel pummeled the monster with attacks, its healing factor unable to keep up. Omrak, having retrieved his sword, dealt the final blow by plunging his blade into the monster's exposed underbelly. Motes of blue light burst forth, dancing across the group before leaving the Champion's giant shell and a Mana Crystal.

The group panted in exhaustion, adrenaline slowly draining away. Daniel straightened before casting his Minor Healing on both Omrak and himself, fixing the accumulated injuries in the party. Omrak grinned, battle lust still riding high in his eyes, while Asin just shook her head. Being their only ranged attacker had its advantages.

After some searching, the group finally found the floor chest that the Champion was guarding. Within was the floor's Mana Crystal reward, a much larger and higher-grade crystal. As always, Asin pocketed the crystal for the group, her tail waving in happiness.

"Down?" Asin asked.

"Just to register ourselves," Daniel cautioned, and Asin nodded agreement. It was too late to start another floor.

Outside, after having registered themselves on the third-floor portal stone and transporting themselves back, the trio stretched. Daniel shared a friendly greeting with the new guards before the group walked towards the Guild Hall in good spirits. They had finished both floors in a single day!

"Omrak, are you going to need to fix your sword?" Daniel asked, recalling the massive blow that the Northerner had landed.

"No. Lund's Blessing is on my weapons," Omrak answered. At the raised eyebrow he received, Omrak explained. "It is a Skill Proficiency that increases the durability and strength of my weapons. My sword will not require fixing."

"Huh," Daniel said. As he considered Omrak's fighting style, Daniel could see how such a Skill Proficiency could be useful. He ran a finger along the edges of his mace, noting the deformed metal. Soon, he would have to look into either getting a new weapon or fixing this one. Luckily for Daniel, maces required significantly less care than swords. A blunt mace was still dangerous, after all.

Inside the Guild Hall, the group approached Liev when it was their turn. Asin quickly handed over their Mana Stones while Omrak proffered the bag of shells. Liev waved the group over to a nearby wider table so that he could properly assess their earnings. As Liev sorted and counted their earnings, muttering the totals of each item, both Asin and Omrak watched over the proceedings with rapt attention.

"Nine silver and four copper," announced Liev as he finished. Asin and Omrak both nodded immediately and then shared a long, considering look at each other. Daniel, on the other hand, had been watching the other Adventurers stream in, content to trust in his friends.

"That's a lot," he said. His first foray into the Karlak Dungeon had only netted him four silver from what he recalled.

"Yes. The Champion's shell is good quality and rare, and the Mana Stone you brought back is of slightly higher quality than previously," Liev said. Good as the haul was for the level, for a group of their size, the nine silver worked out to only three each. A decent but not special haul.

"We also made it to the third floor," Daniel added, curious to see if they needed a seal for that too.

"Really? Congratulations. I will inform the guards," Liev said. Normally he would have asked for some form of proof, but these two he trusted. After Liev had paid out the group, Asin sorted out the change before the group confirmed plans to test the third floor tomorrow.

Chapter 3

"This is a weird floor," Daniel muttered, pushing against the walls. The group stood just outside the portal room of the third level, poking and prodding at the walls and floor in confusion. The entire floor was built of a strange, flexible substance that reformed when pushed. In fact, the greater the force used to push against the walls, the faster the wall reformed. An experiment by Omrak had thrown him off his feet after he had punched the wall.

"Very strange," Asin hissed, her nose twitching. The entire floor smelled strange to her, a slightly acrid, sour smell that she had not encountered before. It made her fur stand up slightly and slowed the lazy, unconscious swinging of her tail.

"Asin, can you take the lead?" Daniel asked. Like his friend, he sensed something strange in this floor and wanted the Beastkin's better senses in front.

As Asin loped forwards, Daniel nodded for Omrak to follow along while he brought up the rear. What kind of monster took to living in a place like this?

The answer to that was as strange as the floor itself. Their first warning was the echoing squeaks of expelled air mixed with the sound of continuous collisions against the walls. The group tightened their formation, Daniel hefting his shield while Asin crouched low and to the side.

The noise culprit bounced around the corner at speed. A reflexive thrust by Omrak and a thrown knife by Asin both missed as the fast-moving monster pinged off one wall to the next. It slammed into Asin's shoulder, throwing the Catkin off balance, before bouncing to hit the flat of Omrak's blade to ricochet off the ceiling towards Daniel. Unable to dodge fully, Daniel bent his head low, letting the monster impact against his helmet. Most of the force was absorbed by the helmet, but it still made Daniel's neck ache.

As quickly as it had attacked, the monster was gone, bounding past the group. They straightened, staring at one another in confusion. None of them had managed to get a good look at the monster before it had left, leaving them even more puzzled.

A few minutes later, the trio were alerted to more incoming monsters. Asin crouched low again, her ears swiveling as she tracked the attackers, while the others got ready to fight. This time they were approached by a pair of the creatures, bouncing down the long hallway. Asin, tracking their movements, waited until the lead monster had bounced hard before she threw her knife. The Catkin snarled in anger, misjudging the speed, and tried again. This time, she managed to nick the monster, which let out an angry squeal.

Omrak waited till the nearest monster was within range before he swung, his greatsword whistling through the air and missing both monsters. The lead attacker caromed off a wall, slamming into Omrak's thigh and then his abdomen in short order before it hit the ceiling and rebounded back to attack Omrak again. The second monster ricocheted off the ground and slammed into Asin's stomach, bowling her over before it bounced to the ceiling and then Omrak's head, its new trajectory aimed directly at Daniel. Lightning danced when it hit Asin, but it seemed to do little to slow the creature.

Daniel, offered more time to set himself, launched a Shield Bash at the monster. The shield smashed into the monster, compressing the creature and sending it backwards towards Asin at speed. Asin flinched reflexively, raising the knife she held in her hand and accidentally impaled the fast-moving monster. Under the combined momentum, she collapsed backwards, staring at the dead monster held fast on her knife.

Omrak, finally fed up, reached out and grabbed the monster as it bounced on the barbarian's shoulder again. He snarled as the monster clamped teeth around his hand before he continued to crush the creature. Even with his Skill Proficiency of Lesser Strength Enhancement, the monster refused to die. In fact, the harder he squeezed, the harder it seemed to push back. With a yell, Omrak clamped a second hand around his own and exerted even more force, finally finding the hard core that made up the creature's internal body and crushing it.

Asin meanwhile stared at the impaled monster, a roughly spherical creature whose body felt very similar to the material of the walls around them. It had a series of small, tiny legs all around its body which it used to propel itself around, and as Omrak had found out, an inner, solid core.

Twinkin Sphere

HP: 0/27

The creatures finally broke up into motes of light, leaving behind Mana cores and a sliver of their stretchy skin.

"So … that happened," Daniel finally said into the silence.

"Head's up!" Daniel shouted, swinging his mace with full force at the bouncing monster hours later. Struck, the monster compressed and flew backwards towards Omrak, who shifted the angle of his blade slightly, letting the monster split itself apart on the edge of his sword.

To Daniel's left, Asin threw a Piercing Shot that drilled and pinned another Sphere to the wall. It struggled for a moment before finally expiring, breaking up completely. The third monster bounced off Daniel's shoulder, bruising him before getting away.

Chuckling to himself, Daniel rubbed at his shoulder through his armor while the others regrouped. After hours of wandering the third floor, the group had learnt three things. Firstly, there were no traps in this Dungeon. Second, it was rare for the Twinkin Spheres to hang out after its initial attack. Lastly, while attacks came regularly, the monsters did not seem to be able to do much damage with each attack.

"Shall we go?" Daniel asked, and at Asin's nod, they continued to move deeper into the Dungeon. A short few minutes and a pair of attacks later, the group found themselves overlooking their first true cavern on the floor. They gaped at the numerous columns that dotted the floor and snaked upwards while a small, steep path led down to the cavern floor. In a corner, they could see another staircase, leading down to the fourth floor. Flickering in the low light of the Mana-imbued walls, the group noticed scores of the Twinkin Spheres bouncing around, smashing into columns and each other with wild abandon. Dotted throughout the cavern were more exits, leading to different locations. Occasionally, Spheres would bounce into or exit those entrances.

"We have to get down," muttered Daniel.

"Dangerous," Asin said.

"Aye, a single hit is nothing for Heroes like us. But on that trail and with that many …" Omrak rumbled. Daniel blinked, looking at the barbarian. Well, it seemed he did have a cautious bone in his body. "Still, a hero can only go forward. I shall lead the way."

Or not.

"Uhhh …" Daniel said, cudgeling his brain for a better plan.

"Rope," Asin said, already unslinging her backpack. Daniel nodded quickly in agreement. It only took them a few moments before the trio had roped themselves together. As an additional precaution, they tied another rope to a nearby column and looped the ropes they tied on themselves to it. A last knot at the end of the rope gave them some additional safety before they tossed the ropes down the entrance.

"Come, we shall reap a whirlwind of …" Omrak paused, staring outwards. "Spheres."

"Go." Asin prodded the giant who shifted away from the sharp claw.

Exiting the cavern, the trio slowly edged their way down to the cavern floor, eyes alert. The Twinkin Spheres at first seemed oblivious to their descent but soon the trio saw a change in their movements. More and more monsters began angling towards them. Curling up slightly behind his shield, Daniel growled as he readied for the fight. Ahead, Omrak had switched weapons to his large knife, wielding it in his left hand while the right gripped the rope. Asin pulled her melee knives as well, ready to defend herself as the monsters closed in.

Daniel took the first few attacks on his shield, letting each monster bounce off it into the darkness. His mace was pretty much useless as a weapon against these monsters, and so, he could only guard himself as they edged down. Asin twisted and ducked, slashing at passing monsters and occasionally taking a blow to her body. Omrak, the largest of the trio, was beaten black and blue by the bouncing creatures even as he swung his knife in mostly futile swipes.

"Keep moving!" Daniel shouted through the storm of noise as the Spheres assaulted them. Under the deluge of monsters that started arriving in greater and greater numbers, Omrak missed Daniel's shout and began to focus on defense and attack, coming to a complete stop.

Asin, smaller and lighter than both, curled up closer to the wall. Knives held in her hands, the Catkin swung at any movement she spotted even as arcs of electricity danced all around her as the monsters struck her and her enchanted aura. Growling as she grew increasingly bruised, Asin slapped the gorget and the rune on it, activating the Shield spell. It flared into light, her aura strengthened such that the monsters bounced off it before impacting her. Given a brief respite from the attacks, Asin stood and started throwing knives, engaging her Skill Proficiency, Fan of Knives to give Omrak a brief moment of relief too.

Omrak, having realized the futility of standing and fighting had already begun edging his way down. In the gap created by Asin's knives, the Northerner rushed down. Keeping a hand up to protect his face, he hurried down the pathway, almost tripping on his feet in his haste. Each blow seemed to draw a deeper red glow from his body that spread outwards, his movements growing more sure. On the ground, the barbarian drew his sword, the weapon dancing as it sliced apart Twinkin Spheres, a wide grin appearing on Omrak's face.

Behind, Asin quickly slipped pass Daniel to make her way to the bottom of the cavern to take station slightly behind Omrak. In the safety of his larger form, Asin cut at the monsters that Omrak missed before they could bounce away again. Daniel was the last to arrive, hunkered down behind his shield as he was. Once on the floor, he took station to Omrak's left, providing his meager support by blocking attacks from one side. Of the three, his greater degree of armor and shielding ensured that he was the least hurt.

"How many are there?" Daniel gasped.

"One. Two. Many!" Asin snarled, pinning another Sphere.

"COME. FACE ME. I AM OMRAK, SON OF LOSIN," shouted Omrak as he whirled his sword around him. Out of the corner of his eyes, Omrak saw something larger flying through the air, a sphere the size of Daniel's shield. Before Omrak could attack it, the humongous Twinkin Sphere slammed the barbarian off his feet.

"Champion," Asin snapped, and Daniel nodded, bending down to cover Omrak as he laid a hand on the Northerner. Cracked ribs, bruised muscles, and a bit lip was what Daniel sensed with his Gift almost immediately. He grunted as he pulled his Gift back, even as the memory of his latest bread recipe slipped from his mind as payment. A Minor Healing would fix up Omrak.

Before Daniel was able to cast the spell, Omrak surged to his feet with a roar. His eyes bloodshot, red light leaking from his body, the Northerner scanned for the monster, idly slicing apart an attacking Sphere. Already, the combined efforts of the trio had reduced the monster numbers significantly, such that attacks came only occasionally.

"There!" Daniel said as he spotted the bouncing Champion.

Omrak shifted, his sword ready as the Champion lined itself up for an attack. Disregarding Omrak, it bounced towards Asin, only to be intercepted by Daniel, who Shield Bashed the monster backwards to Omrak. The momentum was so great that Daniel felt the muscles and tendons of his shoulder tear slightly. It was not for naught as Omrak speared the Champion on his greatsword, ending its life. Soon after that the group cleared the cavern and retrieved all the stones, before they hurried down to the next level.

In the safety of the foyer of the fourth floor, the group rested. Daniel groaned, casting Healer's Mark on all three of them before casting Minor Healing again on Omrak, who was the most gravely wounded. His work as the group's healer complete, Daniel sighed, resting against the wall as he waited for the healing spells to take effect. Already, he noted how large a drop he had experienced in his Mana from these simple spells.

While the group waited, Daniel glanced at the notification on his screen and his full Status Screen.

Skill Level Up

Club Skill has increased to Novice level. +5% damage for all club-based weapons.

Name: Daniel Chai

Class: Level 7 Adventurer (31%)

Sub-classes: Level 7 (Miner) (14%)

Human (Male)

Statistics

Life: 243

Stamina: 243

Mana: 177

Attributes

Strength: 23

Agility: 21

Constitution: 29

Intelligence: 18

Willpower: 18

Luck: 14

Skills

Unarmed Combat: Level 3 (38/100)

Clubs (Novice): Level 1 (04/100)

Archery: Level 2 (48/100)

Shield: Level 9 (44/100)

Dodge: Level 6 (19/100)

Combat Sense: Level 7 (03/100)

Perception: Level 6 (77/100)

Mining: Level 7 (78/100)

Healing: Level 9 (44/100)

Herb Lore: Level 3 (31/100)

Stealth: Level 2 (14/100)

Cooking: Level 3 (89/100)

Singing: Level 2 (14/100)

Skill Proficiencies

Double Strike

Shield Bash

Perin's Blow

Mapping (II)

Spells

Minor Healing (I)

Healer's Mark (I)

Gifts

Martyr's Touch—The caster may heal oneself or others by touch and concentration, sacrificing a portion of his life to do so. Cost varies depending on the extent of the injuries healed.

Not as good as a Level Up but he would take it, thought Daniel. Beside him, as their wounds healed, his party members also regarded their own notifications.

"More?" Asin asked, after the group finally looked away from their notifications.

"I am willing," Omrak said, stretching.

"No, let's go back," Daniel said. "We've got a bunch of stones and it's getting late. I'm also nearly out of Mana so if there's something out there …"

"Level Four!" Asin pointed out.

"Yeah … and that was a Level Three. We didn't have the right equipment. We're doing great, Asin," Daniel argued back, while Omrak watched quietly.

Asin stared grumpily at Daniel before she turned to Omrak. "Vote!"

"Let us continue. I yearn to see what comes next," Omrak rumbled, and Asin flashed a grin at Daniel. The stocky Adventurer just sighed and waved them towards the entrance. Well, it certainly looked like they would be checking out the next Level.

"Crossbow?" Asin asked, staring upwards as they stood under the Dungeon sky. And sky it was, for there were even clouds that floated above along with birds. It was the birds that Asin watched, their long and sharp talons glinting. Standing in the exit, she drew a deep breath, tasting the scents in the air. Even now, underground, it smelled of fresh air and grass, trees and flowers. Even a wind ruffled her fur.

"Didn't bring it," Daniel said, and Omrak shook his head in turn.

"Net. Bow," Asin muttered to herself, and Omrak had to nod in agreement. It seemed that a net to catch the fast-moving monsters or a bow to kill them at a distance would soon be added to the list of things a Karlak Adventurer required. It certainly would be a boon for the city's merchants.

"I fear we must turn back. We are not equipped for this," Omrak rumbled, and Asin reluctantly nodded. As much as she wanted to check out the floor in more detail, she was now outvoted.

"Well, at least we made it this far," Daniel consoled the group as they retreated back to the foyer and exited the Dungeon. Reaching the fourth floor in only two days was quite good, especially considering the fact that the Dungeon itself only had ten floors maximum as a Beginner Dungeon. As they exited, Asin shot one last, longing look over her shoulder.

Chapter 4

"Daniel. Asin. Omrak," greeted Liev as the trio walked to his counter. He raised an eyebrow as Omrak turned, dropping his backpack on the table. Like the Dungeon, the Adventurers' Guild had seen a minor transformation as well. Gone were the chest-high counters that the attendants had worked from. Instead, tables had replaced the counters with sufficient space for Adventurers to deposit their loot. Unlike the old Karlak Dungeon, the new Dungeon seemed to excel at providing additional drops.

"Is it worth anything?" Daniel asked as Liev examined the Twinkin Sphere skin.

"Mmmm … we can offer you a copper per five skins," Liev said at last, putting the skin back on the counter. Asin hissed at that, her eyes narrowing in distrust. "This is a new loot drop. Until we learn more about what potential uses it might have, the purchase is purely speculative."

Asin growled again while Omrak just shrugged phlegmatically.

"Asin, do you want to keep this? Maybe once they know what it is …?" Daniel asked.

The Catkin snarled at Daniel before catching herself, staring at the pieces before she nodded in reluctant acceptance. Omrak scooped up the pieces and stuffed them back into his bag, clearing the table for Asin to deposit the Mana Stones. When Liev reached the large Mana Stones from the Champion and the floor chest, he stopped and raised a bushy red eyebrow.

"Did you find the stairway down?" Liev said.

"Yes, we're registered for the fourth floor," Daniel said proudly.

"Very good! I do believe that makes you the first group to get that far," Liev said, smiling slightly. "Well done."

"Your thanks are appreciated, Attendant Halliope," Omrak said. Daniel blinked, trying to recall where he had heard that name before. After a moment, he dismissed it. He had probably heard someone else call Liev by his family name at some point. It might even be a fragment left behind by his Gift. It was uncommon, but occasionally his Gift took fragments of a memory rather than complete sections.

"You should look at the quest board then. We just posted it today," Liev said, smiling at the group as he finished counting their earnings. The pile of coin he pushed forwards was significantly smaller than yesterday's, which made Asin grimace as she divvied up the amount.

"Thanks, Liev, we will," Daniel said, waving goodbye to the redhead attendant as he walked over to the board. He did not need to ask which quest Liev had directed him to, for the posting dominated the board.

Dungeon Completion

The Adventurers' Guild of Karlak has authorized a one-time payment of 50 Gold for the completion of the newly reorganized Karlak Beginner Dungeon. This is an open request available to all parties. quest completion will be ascertained via the delivery of the Dungeon Boss's Mana Stone.

Daniel read the notice before Omrak's insistent elbow made him read it out loud. Omrak sucked in a breath on hearing the quest reward.

"I could buy a farm …" Omrak muttered to himself.

"Farm?" Asin and Daniel's harmonious cry of incredulity made Omrak look at them puzzled.

"Yes. The farm next to my father's would be suitable," said Omrak. Thinking back, he continued, "It lies on good earth and is fed by the same river as my father's. The family needs more land. I believe we shall dedicate a third of it to cattle. The market for good beef is always strong."

Daniel just continued to stare at the teenaged giant next to him, trying to imagine the muscular, shirtless barbarian pulling up weeds. Asin worked her jaw for a moment before she finally shook her head, prodding Daniel to make him shut his mouth. Omrak was oblivious to their reactions as he continued to detail his ideal farm.

"… and Greel can collect the shit!" roared Omrak with laughter at a joke that only he could understand.

"Oy! Shut it," called another Adventurer, to whom Omrak bobbed his head in acknowledgement.

"Safe to say we're going to try for it?" Daniel said, filling in the silence. He knew he had no need to ask Asin. It was more likely for her to turn down a meal than a chance to earn more coin. Especially as the quest coincided with something they were already doing.

"Yes!" Omrak nodded again, Asin inclining her head in agreement as her tail lashed out behind her in excitement.

As Daniel opened his mouth to continue, a commotion in the Guild entrance drew their attention. A party of four Adventurers strode in. The first wore full plate armor, his face covered by a helmet. Dirt and dust from the road caked the armor, dulling its shine, but Daniel could tell it was of high quality almost immediately by the lack of noise as the fighter moved. Behind him, a scarred older man walked, his shoulders broader than Omrak's but a few inches shorter than the youngster. The older man carried the largest pack of all, his body bowed slightly under the weight. Following the pair, a bookish younger man walked, looking around with a studied air while a last, shorter, and quieter fighter brought up the rear.

"Mage," Asin growled softly.

"How …?" said Daniel.

"Pouches." Asin gestured to the belt and Daniel looked, finally spotting the indicated items.

"I don't …"

"Mages must carry their spell components with them. The numerous pouches are often a giveaway," rumbled Omrak.

"Oh …" Daniel shook his head, still uncertain about the reasons for this.

"Mana less. Crushed crystal expensive," Asin explained.

Daniel blinked, nodding. Healing magic never needed a catalyst—the bodies they worked with were the catalyst that was used. When cast, the Spell took a small portion of the healthy body as the template and developed from there. It was why illnesses that degraded the whole body or old age were nearly impossible to cure—the Healer had no template to work from and had to substitute their own Mana. While a good Healer might slow the aging process using just Mana, it was to such a low degree that most did not bother.

Mages who were attempting to alter the very fabric of nature would need to carry a catalyst of some form to start the process. A crushed Mana Stone, which was basically pure Mana, could be substituted, but of course, was expensive. What Daniel had not known was that other reagents could be used. After all, Daniel had never met a Mage in-person before.

Lost in thought, Daniel missed the rest of the entrance of the group. When the stocky Adventurer started paying attention again, he was surprised to note that the plate-mail-clad fighter was a brunette female who had stowed her helmet under one arm.

"We just came from Silverstone. What do you mean you can't let us in till tomorrow!" the woman demanded, her voice cultured and smooth. Around her, the Guild had fallen silent as everyone listened in.

"I'm sorry, but Guild rules are clear. Every group must take their turn on entry. As tomorrow is the last day of the group entrances, I can fit you in then. But not a moment earlier," Liev said, entirely calm.

"This is ridiculous. We will finish your Dungeon in a week!" she snapped, her hands pressing down on the table. "Let us in and get this done and we'll be gone."

The warrior woman either ignored or was oblivious to the indrawn breath and hisses her bold statement caused among the other Adventurers. The shorter party member at the rear, though, was not, hunching lower as he squirmed in embarrassment.

"Amrah, this is sufficient," the scrawny Mage said. "I would prefer to rest anyway."

The brunette warrior turned, glaring at the Mage, but then deflated. "Fine. Get us a token for tomorrow then, attendant. Make it out to the Crimson Elms."

When the group finally left, the Guild Hall broke into excited babbling.

"Advanced party?" Daniel asked Asin and Omrak, knowing in his heart that they were.

"Yes."

"It is clear."

"Damn …" Daniel sighed, looking towards the quest reward. Their chances of winning it was now gone. They stood no chance against an Advanced team. Asin followed his gaze before she shrugged, tapping her coin pouch as she eyed the deepening sun.

"Dungeon tomorrow?" Asin asked to confirm plans.

"I fear I might not be able to acquire such equipment as necessary by tomorrow," Omrak rumbled. "It is late."

"We can skip the nets for now," said Daniel, staring into the distance. "You don't use a bow or crossbow, do you?"

"No. It is not traditional for my people. I am well versed in the throwing axe, though I lack one," Omrak said.

"Not a problem; I know someone who probably stocks some." Daniel grinned and said to Asin. "We'll get going then."

Asin nodded, before she waved goodbye to the pair, who immediately headed out of the doorway.

A short while later, the pair of Adventurers were banging on the door of Max's shop.

"He's a very good armorer. Also carries some weapons, though he doesn't specialize in it. We did a quest for him not so long ago so he kind of likes us," explained Daniel to Omrak.

"Some of us like to sleep," the armorer and weaponsmith grumbled as he dragged open the bar across his door. "If it weren't for you, Daniel …"

"I know. I know. I've got news for you though," Daniel said as he stepped in, while Max wandered around the shop lighting the lanterns. Omrak walked in, his eyes drinking in the displays of armor and weapons he could never have afforded.

"Well, out with it!" grumbled Max.

"We managed to make it to Level Four! Now, on Level Three there's these weird monsters called Twinkin Spheres …" Daniel immediately launched into an explanation of the monsters. Max nodded, listening as he stroked his beard in thought. Behind them, Omrak perused the store, searching for a suitable weapon.

"… so we were thinking it'd be nice to have a net. For all three levels. They'd catch the turtles and fish them out, grab the Spheres and we could even use them against the birds," finished Daniel.

"And they'll need to be weighted," muttered Max, and nodded. "We can make that. Simple work, in fact."

Omrak cried out, pulling forth a pair of throwing axes in their sheaths from a weapon rack near the back of the shop. Grinning, the large Barbarian held up the pair to Max.

"How much for this, Master Tradesman?"

"That'd be two silver for you," Max said. "And before you ask, that's as low as I'll go."

Omrak nodded, pulling the sheath off the head of one and looking at the edge. He frowned slightly, turning it side to side before checking the next one. "This is not your work."

"No. Apprentice work. Good enough to sell, though."

"Aye, but not as fine as your other equipment." Omrak hefted the axes one last time before he slid them into their sheaths. Hefting his pouch, Omrak turned to Max, "Two silver is fair."

"Good. You going to change out that mace of yours anytime soon, Daniel?" Max asked, glancing at the battered weapon by the stocky Adventurer's side. "Seen better days."

"Mmm … not yet."

"Well, let me know when you're ready. Now shoo! Some of us have lives."

Chuckling, the pair quickly exited the shop soon after, parting ways as they left.

In the Clinic, Daniel stretched. After a hard day's dungeon delving, most others would be taking a break. For Daniel, as he had a little Mana left and a girlfriend who worked at the Clinic, he found himself finishing up his day in the small examination room and office.

"You need to eat more than potatoes," Daniel sighed, waving a finger at the muscular man before him. "Meat. Fruit. Have a stew once in a while."

"But I don't like anything else," the large man whined.

"Then you'll continue to be tired. Can't do anything for you," Daniel said, pointing to the door. "Your body isn't getting what it needs. Eat properly."

Daniel watched the man leave glumly and shook his head. It bothered him that he could feel the deficiency in the man's body with his Gift, but he had no idea what it was. Last winter, he had seen quite a few of these cases, which led him to believe it had to do with the reduced food types available to his patients.

Even with the combined knowledge offered by the Elves and Dwarves, there was much that they still did not understand. He often felt like he was blindly subscribing cures because they worked, without understanding the why.

As the door opened, Daniel shook his head and focused on his new patient. Another patient who had waited too long before visiting, ensuring that a simple cut was now infected. Grunting, Daniel reached for the basin of water to clean the wound. Having wiped away dirt, pus and blood to see the cut properly, Daniel cast Healer's Mark on the man.

"Wait outside; don't touch the wound. It'll heal in an hour. When it's healed, you can leave," Daniel said, a slight headache reminding him that he was close to running out of Mana.

"I have to …"

"Don't. Leave," Daniel snapped, fixing the man with a glare. The laborer looked at the large, stocky Healer before him and remembered that as nice as he was, he was also an Adventurer. Dealing with a stubborn laborer would not be a problem for him.

"Yes sir!"

Daniel rubbed his forehead and washed his hands as the man left. Maybe he should have just washed it down with Dwarven Whisky. It normally worked. However, the stubborn idiot probably would never come back if it did not. Even before his breath had caught, the door opened again with another patient.

"You look like you could use a night's sleep." Khy'ra's voice floated to Daniel's ears as he sat quietly, eyes closed. As he opened his eyes, Daniel realized that he had actually been sleeping for a bit.

"Sorry. Long day," Daniel said. "The patients …?"

"Are gone. Sent them home for today." Khy'ra walked over, grabbing his arm and then wrinkling her nose. "What is that smell?"

"Twinkin Spheres. Level Three monster. Very strange …"

"Huh. Bath house first then," Khy'ra said, pulling Daniel up with one hand. "Come on, you can tell me all about it there."

Later, in a private room in the bath house, Daniel stared at the delivered plate of food. He poked at it, glancing over to his girlfriend before he asked, "I didn't realize they let you eat in here."

"It helps if the owner owes you one," Khy'ra said, arching her back slightly as she dug fingers into her lower back. "Ugh …"

"Here, let me do that," Daniel said, pulling her over to help and copping a quick feel. Khy'ra snorted, shaking her head, but relaxed into his strong fingers.

"Can you afford this, though? A private room is expensive," Daniel said, glancing around.

"It's fine."

Daniel fell silent, working the knots out of her lower back. This display alongside the continued existence of the Clinic once again made him wonder exactly how successful an Adventurer Khy'ra had been before she retired. While he knew that she received funds from the City and other donors, he doubted it was sufficient. And if Khy'ra lived a mostly austere life, her occasional indulgences seemed to be particularly spectacular.

"Thinking again," Khy'ra said, interrupting Daniel's musing. "You should be eating before it gets cold."

"Yeah, sorry." Rather than admit his actual thoughts, Daniel said, "We had an Advanced team arrive today. They'll probably take the Dungeon clear quest."

"Why?"

"Probably for the quest."

"Why do you think they'll win?"

"They're an Advanced team," Daniel said, frowning. It was obvious, was it not?

"And …?"

"They've got more experience than we do! Better equipment, better Skills," Daniel said, exasperated.

"Not necessarily. And it's not all important."

"I don't understand."

"Think about it, Daniel. Would a high-level Advanced group travel all the way to just complete a Beginner Dungeon? How much did that Advanced Group you worked with make in one day on the first floor?"

Daniel opened his mouth and then shut it, thinking back to his visit to Silvestone. She was right, Nico and his party had only completed Peel because it was on their way. They would not have traveled to Karlak just to complete the Dungeon. The experience bonus and the earnings, even with the quest, would not have been worth the travel time.

"They're still an Advanced Group …"

"That just means they've completed a Beginner Dungeon," Khy'ra said. "The difference between a Beginner Adventurer and a new Advanced Adventurer isn't that great. Not like it is for the gap between Advanced and Expert. And don't forget, a party is more than their levels. It's the Skills and the teamwork that matter."

"You think we can complete the quest?"

"I don't know. And neither do you."

"Oh …" Daniel blinked. Khy'ra as always was right. It was annoying sometimes dating a couple-of-hundred-years-old Elf who had seen it all before.

"Daniel …" The Elf frowned, staring at the young man before she shook her head.

"What?"

"Never mind."

"What?"

"Why are you an Adventurer?" Khy'ra finally asked.

Caught off guard by the question, Daniel paused in silence as he tried to find the answer to that. 'Because I wanted to be' was not really a good answer. Neither was 'I didn't want to be a Healer or Miner'. Neither really spoke to why he wanted to be an Adventurer in particular. Brow furrowed, he tried to work out a proper answer for Khy'ra, who nibbled on the dishes while she waited.

"Well … I guess I wanted to see the world," Daniel finally said.

"Mmm … so why not be a questor?" Khy'ra asked. Questors were Adventurers who specialized in fulfilling quests. They rarely, if ever, entered Dungeons.

"I don't like quests. They are boring," Daniel said. "It's the same thing, all the time. There's no… thrill, no danger."

Khy'ra laughed, shaking her head. "And that makes you a true Adventurer. But what do you want from it?"

"Well … I …" Daniel paused as he attempted to find a reply.

"Perhaps something to think about for later. Now, let's eat before the tub gets too cold!" Khy'ra said, pushing a plate towards Daniel. She knew better than to push him, not now.

Chapter 5

"Good balance," Asin said as she watched the borrowed throwing axe embed itself in the tree. Inside the Dungeon on the fourth floor, the group had taken a short stop to allow Omrak a chance to refresh his throwing Skills. Nearby, Daniel sat with his crossbow knocked, clad only in the helmet, breastplate, shoulder pauldrons, and bracers of his plate armor, watching the skies for potential trouble. Thus far, none of the birds had come close.

Unlike other floors, this one seemed to stretch forever, a single trail leading forwards through the plains. Daniel knew that much of this was illusion—that there was a definite wall in the distance and all around them, but the illusion was so convincing, he struggled not to accept it. As the wind rustled the grass, he stared at the scrawny tree that the pair had taken to punishing.

"We done yet?" Daniel asked impatiently.

"I believe I have regained most of my former skill. Let us seek glory!" Omrak replied, his voice a roar. Asin, next to him, winced, edging away.

"Don't go too far, Asin, we'll need to cover each other," Daniel said as they started to walk forwards. Asin just left in a huff, though she slowed down to let the pair close in. Hefting the extra quiver of crossbow bolts over his shoulder, Daniel followed along.

"You wear only part of your armor today, Hero Daniel," Omrak mentioned as he walked alongside.

"Figured it'd be easier to move without the leg armor," said Daniel.

"Truth. I find great freedom in not having armor," said Omrak.

"I thought you couldn't afford it."

"That too," Omrak replied cheerfully.

A few minutes later, as the group followed the path, Daniel spotted the first sign of trouble. A trio of the birds had started winging their way towards them. He hefted his crossbow, waiting. He knew he was a poor shot, so he had no intention of firing early.

Ahead of him, Asin had stopped and drawn a single throwing knife. She sniffed, tasting the air as she waited for Daniel to shoot first. Omrak absently flipped his own throwing axe in his hand, being relegated to the last attacker. After all, he only had two hatchets, so losing or breaking them was a serious concern.

The trio watched the birds wing their way to them, getting closer and closer. Wide wingspans, a long-hooked beak, and sharp talons that glinted kept the three watching. Just as Daniel raised his crossbow to aim at them, they turned and flew away, circling the group as they climbed high above the trio.

"Weird," muttered Daniel. He could not think of a monster that actually refused to attack.

"Go?" Asin asked after they watched the birds circle for a few minutes with no sign of coming down.

"I guess," Daniel said. He could possibly hit one of them, but he really did not trust his aim. He could still remember missing stationary tree trunks a short few months ago. For that matter, he'd never tried to shoot directly into the sky before.

The group started walking again, occasionally looking upwards at the circling birds. Not long later, a pair of birds winged over as well. Again, the group set themselves, and again, the birds winged away before the trio could attack them. Joining the initial three, the new pair continued to circle the Adventurers.

For another uneventful hour, the party continued to trudge the Dungeon level, unmolested. Twice more, birds winged towards them before finally joining the group above, circling the trio. In time, the group found themselves craning their neck upwards constantly, trying to discern what was happening and wary of attack by the large number above them.

"Horses," rumbled Omark.

"Uhh …" Daniel frowned, tilting his head to the side. He heard nothing in the wind.

"I feel the trembling in the earth. Many horses," Omrak said.

"Not horses," Asin said, exhaling with a huff. "Something ground."

"Ground …" Eyes wide, Daniel squatted and placed a hand on the ground. He hissed, looking around desperately. "That's a Tremqua Worm!"

"I know not this monster," Omrak said, staring at the ground intently as if, by sheer force of will alone, he could see through it. "How do we fight it?"

"You don't," snapped Daniel. Nothing, no rocky outcroppings, no solid earth. He cast his mind back, eyeing his minimap and then snapped, "This way!"

Daniel took off at a run, leading the group to his new destination. His friends rushed along behind him, Asin quickly catching up and loping alongside. Instead of speaking, she kept her breath for the sprint. As they ran, the trembling grew in strength such that even Daniel could feel it through his reinforced, solid boots.

The group burst into the clearing of gravel that Daniel recalled seeing, only stopping when they were a good ten feet in. Breath heaving, Daniel eyed the ground as he spoke between breaths, hands still flexing around his crossbow. "The Worms travel deep underground until they are ready to attack. Then they surface. That's when they are most dangerous. If we survive that, they'll travel just below the surface until we kill them."

"Why are we here?" Omrak asked, staring warily at his feet as the rumbling increased.

Asin's ears perked up, her hand to the ground as she attempted to sense where the monster would erupt from. Daniel swayed lightly on the balls of his feet as he answered, "They're so large that it takes a while for what they eat to expel. If they eat the rock, it slows them down. A bit."

Daniel was sweating, his breathing slightly faster than normal. Asin, having seen the unusual distress her friend was in, called out, "How know?"

"What?"

"Worm. Know?"

"I fought them as a Miner," Daniel said. "My … we …" Memories of his father, of waiting and waiting for a man who never came back. And the story that came out later of a Tremqua Worm attack. It had been the worse attack the Mine had experienced in ages, one that killed a half-dozen Miners.

Daniel shivered, his mind wandering as he was caught up in old memories. He did not notice the change in vibrational speed that indicated the monster was close. Asin realized her error with a start and dashed over, tackling Daniel a moment before the monster burst from the ground. The Tremqua Worm looked much like a normal earthworm, segmented body and a wide mouth that swallowed the earth as it lunged upwards. Unlike an earthworm, though, its body was as thick around as Omrak's waist.

The smaller Catkin was unable to move Daniel aside in sufficient time completely, the Tremqua Worm gripping and ripping part of his leg off. Daniel screamed in pain even as the monster twisted in the air, arching its body to fall towards the pair of tangled Adventurers. It slammed into Asin's back, only a last-minute activation of her Shield rune stopping the monster from ripping a hole through her back. The Catkin whimpered as the force of the blow compressed her chest even under the protection of the rune. Unable to pierce her defense, the Worm began to dig along the ground to escape.

Omrak roared, charging towards the pair and swinging his sword at the exposed segment. It took the giant of a man a single swing, muscles flexing as the blade parted the monster's body in half. Omrak howled in glee, using the momentum of his blade to slice again at the portion of body left behind as it still squirmed. The top half fled into the ground, squirming away before Asin could twist around to attack it.

Daniel was curled up on the ground, hands clamped down on his injured calf to slow the flow of blood as he cast Minor Healing. The first spell scabbed the wound over, after which he cast Healer's Mark before he pushed himself to his feet. The crossbow banged on his thigh as he stood up, ignored by Daniel in favor of his mace.

"Where is it?" he snarled, realizing he had not even taken off his shield. Now, he had not the time to do so.

"There." Asin pointed with one hand, holding the other above her head ready to throw her knife. Omrak continued to slice and kick the half of the Worm that still squirmed, intent on killing it.

Daniel watched as the monster twisted, coming around to where he stood. Struck by a sudden thought, he waited patiently till the monster was nearly on him before he jumped and swung his mace into the ground while activating his Skill Proficiency Perin's Blow.

The attack doubled the strength of his strike, passing through the earth to the monster. It injured the Worm, making the monster swirl away. Daniel snarled, taking a step forwards and triggering another Perin's Blow immediately, but only managing to catch the end of the monster, making it change direction again.

Daniel was distracted from his obsession with the Worm by a pained yowl. Asin had a deep cut along one shoulder, her other hand waving a knife against the birds that were dive-bombing her. Before Daniel could take this in fully, he realized that a bird was coming at him. He threw himself to the side too late, claws screeching against his breastplate from the failed attack. Omrak fared the best of all as he ignored the attacks, preferring to return hurt for hurt. When bird met blade, bird lost spectacularly.

Asin rolled and came up with a pair of blades in her hands before she threw them at the birds, engaging Fan of Blades. Each blade exploded into multiples, spinning through the air. Most missed, unaimed as they were, but some hit and offered Asin more time to continue her attacks.

Daniel, relieved that his armor was sufficient to ward him for the moment, refocused on locating the Worm.

"Omrak. Move!" Daniel roared as he charged forwards, desperate to save his friend. Omrak danced aside, moving his feet as he swung his sword above him. Already, red mist filled the air around Omrak as he took more and more damage. With another roar, Omrak buried his sword in the ground a moment too soon to decapitate the Worm. Unable to stop, the Worm smashed into the buried metal and squirmed to get around it.

Daniel, finally caught up, swung his mace again, triggering Perin's Blow one last time. The attack left a deep depression in the ground as the monster was crushed, earth churning as it died. Crouched low, Daniel looked up to see that Omrak was guarding him from further attacks from the birds as he swung his blade around to his own detriment. Blood flowed from open wounds, deep cuts along his torso including a few inches of flesh that hung loose from his shoulder.

Eyes narrowed, Daniel reached out and cast Healer's Mark on Omrak. Already, Daniel could see the blood flow slowing. Turning his head to the side, he spotted Asin continuing to attack the quintuplet of birds that targeted her, her movements as graceful as always as she danced away from them. Still, the Catkin was bleeding from a dozen minor wounds including a scrape along one cheek.

No longer distracted, the group focused on dealing with the attacking birds. Daniel even found time to recock his crossbow and fire it. Once. And miss. Both Omrak and Asin dealt with the flying monsters quickly, injuring wings and sending the birds crashing to the ground.

Panting, Asin gripped her shoulder where she had wrenched it accidentally. Behind the Catkin, her tail swung lazily, belying her ragged state. "Bad shot."

"Keep laughing and I won't heal you," Daniel threatened as he walked over, his own wound finally healed.

Asin stuck her tongue out as Daniel placed his hand on her shoulder, casting Healer's Mark. Turning around, Daniel spotted Omrak, who was busy digging into the earth for the Mana Stone.

"Tough," Asin said, her moment of humor gone.

"The monsters? Alone … maybe not. But together …" Daniel shook his head. He definitely felt he had made a mistake not wearing his full suit of armor.

"A glorious fight," Omrak said, grinning. "Blood and feathers. All around."

Asin snorted before she pointed to the way they came and tilted her head to the side. Daniel blinked, glancing backwards and then at Omrak. Either choice they made, it was unlikely they would finish the level this day.

Chapter 6

"Temqua Worms and Grish Raptors," Liev said as he wrote down the information the group provided. "Working together too. Very interesting."

After their first fight, the trio decided to retreat the entrance before wandering in an elaborate circle to draw additional Temqua Worms. Interestingly enough, unlike other levels, the fourth level had few attacks and the group only had a chance to test their Skills out twice more before they called it a day.

"Good-sized stones, though," Liev said, tapping the trio of large Mana Stones that he had set apart. "C-grade eights and nines are very good for the level. Of course, the Raptors are only D-grade tens, so it balances out."

"No drops," Asin added, shaking her head.

"True. The second level seems to be the best level for the Farmers for now," Liev mused before he let his eyes wander over the stones again. "Anything else?"

"No, that's about it," Daniel said.

"Well, you're still in the lead," Liev reassured the group as he finished totaling up their earnings. "I'm sure you'll work out a plan to get through the floor soon."

"I think, well, it shouldn't be a problem tomorrow," Daniel replied, glancing to his friends, who offered nods in exchange. It seemed strange to be progressing through floors so quickly, but really, the first few floors had mostly been a matter of searching for the exits at their levels.

"Well, I guess we'll see you tomorrow," Daniel said, waving goodbye.

"Yes, tomorrow," Liev said as he worked to hide his yawn.

Outside, the group glanced at one another before Daniel spoke up, "Drinks at the Top?"

Quick nods of confirmation lead to the group taking a stroll down to the nearby inn. The Spinning Top was not the only inn in town, but it had three things that made it a popular watering hole. Firstly, the cooking was above average to superb. Secondly, Elise kept a clean and well-mannered location. And thirdly, and perhaps most importantly, it was close to the town center. For weary Adventurers, finding a place to sit and eat after a long day's delve ensured that the Top was constantly busy when the Dungeon was open.

Inside, Daniel quickly spotted and snagged the very last open table. It was in the far corner of the inn, a decent distance from the fireplace but also the farthest away from the Top's most recent star attraction—the Crimson Elms. Seated on their chairs, the group regaled the rapt audience with tales of an Advanced Dungeon.

Any other day, any other group, Daniel would have been right there with the rest of the Adventurers, drinking in the stories like the lifeblood they were. Stories, no matter how exaggerated, often held hints for Beginner Adventurers of what to expect in future Dungeons. A survivor, no matter the reason why, had something to teach. And in a profession where so many died, any crumb of knowledge was important.

"They cleared the third floor today," Elise said as she deposited the tankards of ale and a cup of sabu for Asin. The Catkin immediately grabbed her drink, sticking her nose in the rim and inhaling the sweet smell of fermented fruits.

"Oh?" Daniel tried to feign unconcern, which made Elise smile.

"Yes. They were telling that story earlier," Elise said. "Three of today's special?"

"Four!" roared Omrak as he lowered the tankard of ale and wiped at his mouth. "And another drink!"

"Right away." Elise smiled, heading back to the bar to pass on the order.

"I had to kill the Griffon Champion all alone while Rickard and Will were holding the rest off. Harald was out of Mana after calling his Gravity Well spell and grounding the Griffons. Now, I ..."

"Ouch!" Daniel snapped as he pulled his arm back and rubbed at the spot where Asin's claw had drawn blood. He turned away from listening to the Crimson Elm's leader to focus on his own party.

"Talking," Asin said. "Tomorrow, we run?"

Daniel blinked and nodded, rubbing his chin. It was the continuation of the discussion while they waited.

"I say not. They are small monsters. Unworthy of running from," rumbled Omrak. "We should walk forward with confidence. We know how to defeat those Worms now."

"You know," Daniel grumbled. Unlike the rest of them, Omrak had the ability to stab his sword straight down into the ground due to his combined Skill Proficiencies. He could spear the monster as it rose, injuring and driving it away. It made him entirely safe from the attacks. "The rest of us are working it out."

"Bah. Your Skill injures them," Omrak said.

"If I hit at the right time. Too early and it does nothing."

"Is same for me," Omrak shrugged. "All fights are a risk."

"Run," Asin said. "Down. More monsters. Coin."

Daniel nodded to that. It was a definite point. The level seemed to be straightforward—all they had to do was run in a straight line along the path to find the exit. If they did that, they should find it. They might skip the Champion this round, but if they could complete the level, they might earn more on the next level. Pride or not, their goal was to earn coin after all. Today's earnings were even lower than yesterday's. In the end, it was his shrinking coin purse that made up Daniel's mind. "We'll run."

Omrak hmphed and crossed his arms. His sulk lasted until the plates of sliced lamb appeared, at which point it disappeared as quickly as the food into his mouth. Asin inhaled the strong scent of lamb mixed with herbs, doused in a gravy of fermented bean and meat juice. She grinned, slicing apart the potatoes first and dragging the tuber along the gravy before popping the meal into her mouth. She sighed slightly, the mixture of rich thick gravy and steamed potatoes settling her hunger.

Plans made, the group fell silent. Tomorrow would be interesting.

Jogging in full plate sucked, Daniel decided. It was hot, it was heavy, and it was exhausting. Ahead of him, he could see Asin crouched with a hand to the ground, feeling for the tremors that indicated a Worm. Daniel had left his crossbow behind, having decided against the extra weight today, so it would be up to Asin and Omrak to protect them against the birds. Not that Daniel himself had been of any real use before anyway.

Omrak, beside him, jogged along easily, chuckling at Daniel. Without armor, the giant barbarian had a much easier time of it. "There are more birds now than ever."

"Yes," Daniel panted.

"I believe they come because we have not stopped," Omrak rumbled, gesturing above. "I fear we run into danger."

Daniel nodded, waving to Asin to stay where she was. She frowned, raising an eyebrow in enquiry when they closed.

"We must fight soon. Or if we are forced to later, we will be at a disadvantage," said Omrak.

Asin growled and then looked up before curling her claws on the ground. "One closing. Maybe outrun. If Daniel faster."

"Not happening," Daniel gasped as he sucked in lungfuls of air. He forced himself not to bend over, to stay standing. He did, however, pull his helmet off to cool down and allow himself to drink from his waterskin easier.

"Fight."

"Good," rumbled Omrak as he stepped aside and unsheathed his sword before burying it in the ground and stripping off his shirt. Undressed, Omrak lifted his sword again and began to tap it on the ground, just lightly as he waited in an attempt to draw the monster to him. Daniel moved aside quickly to give Omrak space as he scanned the horizon.

"Is that the Elms?" Daniel said as he squinted back the way he came. In the distance he could see figures moving and the Elms were the only others on the fourth floor thus far. A moment later, he saw the birds that had collected above the other group suddenly collapse as if a giant hand had crushed them. The Elms broke apart and alternately stomped, kicked, stabbed, and smashed the ground. Or more likely, the monsters that were on the ground. It took the group barely a half-minute before they started walking again. "I guess that's what Gravity Well does …"

"Focus," Asin hissed at Daniel, and he found himself grimacing again. Right, they had their own monsters coming in soon. He fell silent, head bent as he focused on the trembling in the earth as the monster coasted inside the ground. Daniel was once again grateful that whatever made it possible for the Tremqua Worms to move at such speed underground also made it possible to detect them so easily.

Asin yowled slightly, arching her back in anticipation of jumping, before she looked to where Omrak continued to bang on the ground. Omrak stopped his tapping after a moment and then roared as he plunged the blade into the earth, leaping backwards immediately after.

Cued to attack, Daniel dashed towards the sunken blade. The Tremqua Worm burst forth from the ground, injured by the strike with its mouth torn open on one side. Even as it raised itself off the ground and twisted to hide again, Daniel reached it. The stocky Adventurer roared as he loosed Perin's Blow, smashing the monster higher into the air. The Worm's body elongated under the attack and pulped under the mace, splattering Daniel with warm blood.

Above, the birds dived and were met by Asin's Fan of Knives. The survivors flocked closer, the lead bird struck by Omrak's thrown axe and falling to the ground in a bloody fan of feathers and meat. Daniel paid no attention to what was going on above him as he pounded on the Tremqua Worm with his Skill. Even the bird that attempted to pierce his armor with its razor sharp beak and peck at his body from its perch on the ground failed to draw his attention.

Asin almost chuckled as she watched Daniel, one hand swinging and cutting any attacker while the other tossed knives underhand. The Catkin would have to spend a few minutes finding all of them later on, but it was why she marked each knife with her scent each morning. It was a tactic that only worked for a Beastkin and one she had not shared with her party members, nor did she intend to. Asin idly hopped to the side, scooping up another pair of knives she had left in the ground for easy access while they waited and continued her attack.

One last blow and Daniel rose fully, idly catching a swooping bird against his shield. The raptor smashed directly into it, its claws and wings compressing briefly before it found itself on the ground, stunned by the sudden stop. Daniel stepped forwards quickly, stomping down on an exposed wing as he surveyed the battlefield.

Omrak, bare-chested and bleeding again, was swinging his sword around and batting birds to the ground around him. Occasionally the Northerner would take a step aside as injured raptors attempted to hop their way to him. Injured and bleeding though he might be, Daniel could tell that Omrak was not being hindered by his injuries. Knowing that, Daniel took the time to attack the monsters that had been grounded. Omrak's fighting methods were strong, powerful, and dangerous—but they were not designed to allow a Healer to approach and lay hands on him for healing. It was a definite concern and one that had Daniel considering learning the ranged variations of his healing spells.

Minutes later, the group found themselves free of monsters. During the cleanup, a second Tremqua Worm had surfaced and attempted to attack Asin.

The agile Catkin had proceeded to jump straight into the air and throw a Piercing Shot directly down its throat, immediately killing the monster, much to Daniel's chagrin. In truth, locating and picking up the various Mana Stones was more difficult than the initial fight.

"Better?" Daniel asked as he glanced at Omrak, who stood stretching, his wounds scabbed over and slowly healing under Daniel's spell.

"Yes. My thanks again, Hero Daniel. It is a marvelous thing to have a Healer in your party."

Asin chuffed her agreement before looking around the ground once more. Satisfied they had collected both knives and stones, she pointed down the road. Time to go. The Crimson Elms were on their way.

"I need a break," Daniel said, his breathing heaving hours later. The only reason it had taken so long before he called it quits again was his Healing magic, and even that was limited by the amount of Mana he dared use. "How big is this level?"

"Big," Asin said.

"It does seem extensive," Omrak added, shaking his head as he surveyed the land around him. Twice more already the group had needed to pause to deal with the building numbers. Behind them, the Crimson Elms continued to trudge onwards, more than content to let the Tremqua Worms attack as they walked. "It reminds me of stories of the Lowna Plains."

"It reminds me of the road from Peel," muttered Daniel wryly. Flat, boring and endless that road had been. "You know, this level might end up being an easy one for most groups."

"Hmmm?" Asin growled as she chewed on a strip of jerky.

"The monster attacks are few and far between. Once you know what to expect, it isn't difficult to deal with. It's also a single flat plain, so if there are a lot of parties, you might not even be attacked," Daniel explained. "In other levels, you don't want to cluster up. Too narrow corridors, too small caverns. Here, there's no reason not to."

Omrak nodded slightly, rubbing his chin. "Yes. And the features are the same as before. Unlike the second floor, where the water levels alter the paths."

"Exactly. No surprises, no changes. This will be an easy level," Daniel said, his breathing slowly coming under control. Pulling some jerky from his own pouch, he began to chew on it as he waved for the group to start walking. They would eat and move.

"Why?" Asin asked and waved her hand around the Dungeon at their puzzled glances.

Daniel shrugged and Omrak stayed silent. It was generally believed that Panqua, Erlis's, son was the one who managed the actual Dungeons. Apocryphal stories even had Adventurers running into the god in Dungeons, gifting reward and punishment for those who succeeded and failed spectacularly in equal measure. Still, stories from the church or not, no one actually understood why or how he did what he did or when. Because of that, most Adventurers ignored what little was known, focusing on the rather more important day-to-day aspects of surviving the Dungeons.

It was late afternoon by the time the Elms finally caught up with the group. As the day lengthened, Daniel found himself slowing down even further, such that the group had taken to just walking for the last few hours. That had increased the number of Worms who latched onto the group, which forced them to slow down further and wait for each attack.

"Not running anymore?" their leader said the moment they had caught up. Daniel pressed his lips together, refusing to rise to the bait, while Asin just growled.

"No," Omrak replied cheerily. "We see no end to this level as yet."

"Well, you did well. For a Beginner group," she continued. "If you follow close enough, we'll keep the monsters off your back too."

"It would be our honor to join in glorious battle with such great Heroes," Omrak said.

"That's not—"

"Ah, you would prefer not to fight such paltry monsters? We will be honored to ensure your weapons are not demeaned by their blood."

"No—"

"No need for thanks, great Hero," Omrak continued, waving his hands around. "We will do our best to fight under the eyes of ones so great. Perhaps some pointers would be helpful."

"Look, you—"

"Leave it, Amrah. We'll move faster if we aren't having to deal with the monsters," said the Mage.

Amrah looks dissatisfied at that, growling softly beneath her breath. Still, she said nothing further as she stomped onwards. The large warrior on their side followed quietly, though the slightest smile could be seen on his lips.

"Thank you, great Heroes!" Omrak called.

In answer, the Mage raised his hand and called forth his spell, the birds that had gathered falling to the earth. The Crimson Elms continued their walk while the trio found themselves dealing with the injured monsters. When they were done, the Elms had already moved on, leaving them to collect the Mana Stones.

"Did you do that on purpose?" Daniel said.

"Do what?" Omrak replied, a wide smile still on his face. Daniel squinted at the large barbarian suspiciously while Asin just snorted, continuing to pick up the Mana Stones.

"Hurry. Catch up," Asin said, pointing to the group a distance ahead.

"Right, right." This was going to be a long day.

Chapter 7

"A day and a half journey, eh?" Liev said, rubbing his chin. He stared at the tired, dusty trio that stood before him. "That explains the lack of monster attacks."

"Uhhh …" Daniel said.

"Levels require Mana to create. The larger the level, the more Mana. Beginner Dungeons are Beginner Dungeons partly because there is only so much Mana that they have access to. It's why they are limited to ten levels," Liev continued. "More Mana spent on a level to make it larger means less monsters."

"Interesting," Asin said approvingly.

"You did not fight the Champion?" Liev asked, glancing at the stones before him.

"No, the Elms did."

"Did you see it?"

"Yes. It was enormous—thrice as large as a normal Worm. No birds, though—not any more than normal," said Daniel. "Tough and you have to be much more careful than before. You really can get injured."

"Did you reach the fifth level?" Liev asked as he finished totting up their earnings.

"Yes. We didn't explore, though," Daniel said. "It was just a room with a door. Didn't want to test the door out."

"A door?" Liev said, running a hand through his red hair. "Well, might be many things. Going in tomorrow then?"

"Definitely," Daniel said. His earlier misgivings were still there, but after meeting the group, he knew he would not give up. If they lost, they lost—but he was not about to let the arrogant Crimson Elms saunter in without any challenge.

Asin beside him just nodded, already splitting the coins. The pile was significantly higher than their previous trip. Playing clean-up for the Elms had at least been highly profitable, if demeaning. She quietly handed the coins over to each group member before flashing the group a grin and offering a wave before she left.

Omrak picked up the coins, sliding them into his pouch. The barbarian stretched before he spoke. "I shall see you tomorrow. Hero Daniel. Attendant Halliope."

Daniel nodded goodbye, pocketing his own coin as he headed out.

In the inn, Daniel sighed, stripping a shirt off to wipe himself down. As frustrating as the day was, he did have one small thing to smile about.

Name: Daniel Chai

Class: Level 8 Adventurer (02%)

Sub-classes: Level 7 (Miner) (31%)

Human (Male)

Statistics

Life: 257

Stamina: 257

Mana: 186

Attributes

Strength: 25

Agility: 22

Constitution: 29

Intelligence: 19

Willpower: 19

Luck: 14

Skills

Unarmed Combat: Level 3 (43/100)

Clubs (Novice): Level 1 (14/100)

Archery: Level 2 (48/100)

Shield: Level 9 (74/100)

Dodge: Level 6 (23/100)

Combat Sense: Level 7 (18/100)

Perception: Level 7 (04/100)

Mining: Level 7 (78/100)

Healing: Level 9 (64/100)

Herb Lore: Level 3 (31/100)

Stealth: Level 2 (24/100)

Cooking: Level 3 (99/100)

Singing: Level 2 (14/100)

Skill Proficiencies

Double Strike

Shield Bash

Perin's Blow

Mapping (II)

Spells

Minor Healing (I)

Healer's Mark (I)

Gifts

> Martyr's Touch—The caster may heal oneself or others by touch and concentration, sacrificing a portion of his life to do so. Cost varies depending on the extent of the injuries healed.

The increase to his attributes was as always, extremely helpful and been quickly allocated. Daniel also had a Skill Proficiency point to allocate this Level. He had a few options, including taking some of the Skills he had ignored or upgrading an existing Skill, but there was also new options to consider.

The first was from achieving a Novice level in Club Proficiency. He had two options at this point. He could either purchase **Mighty Blow,** which was a more powerful version of **Power Strike,** or he could purchase **Elemental Blow**. It imbued his own attacks with an additional elemental force, much like the elemental bracers that he once wore and that Asin still did.

In addition, with a higher Skill level in Combat Sense, he now had the option of purchasing a new Combat Sense-related Skill called **Find Weakness**. It was a Skill Proficiency that innately made him understand where he could attack to increase the amount of damage. This was particularly important when fighting new monsters, since their weak spots were not always apparent immediately.

As always, he could also dedicate his Skill Proficiency to increasing one of his existing Skills, but those, while useful were not particularly interesting. One day perhaps, he might acquire **Triple Strike**, but for now, it's beginner variation worked well enough. Nor did he desire to spend his point on upgrading his Healing spells. At the very least, he wanted to wait till he could acquire a ranged variation.

Both new options were powerful for different reasons, but in the end, he found himself selecting **Find Weakness**. The reason was simple. **Elemental Blow** required him to use Mana, something that he needed for Healing. **Find**

Weakness, on the other hand, was a passive Skill Proficiency and thus was more powerful overall.

Having made his decision, he selected it and looked over the information silently.

Find Weakness

Increased understanding of opponents and ability to detect weaknesses.

Skill: Passive

Cost: N/A

Effect: User has a 20% + 5% chance per level of Combat Sense to find weakness

Satisfied with his choice, Daniel sighed and closed his eyes. Even if it was in the middle of the day, the Adventurer had been awake and moving for a day and a half as it stood. He was exhausted and tired and really just needed some rest.

Later that evening, Khy'ra pushed open the door to his room. She laughed, seeing the sprawled-out form of the Adventurer as he lay there, shirtless with a touch of drool slipping out of the corner of his mouth. The Elf moved into the room, pushing against Daniel's discarded clothing on his desk to clear some room for the food she had been acquired downstairs.

"Daniel," Khy'ra said as she gently pushed against his shoulder.

"Mmmrrpphfff."

"Daniel, dinner," Khy'ra said again, prodding his shoulder harder. He rolled over and the Elf grinned impishly, sneaking a finger between his armpits to tickle it.

"Aaargh!" Daniel said, sitting up and glaring at her.

"Evening," Khy'ra said, leaning over and kissing him on the lips. "I brought dinner. You need to eat."

"Mmm … I guess." Daniel rubbed at his face to clear the sleep from his eyes before he swiped at his mouth just before his stomach growled. "What would I do without you?"

Khy'ra fell silent at those words, turning away to pick up the plates and return with them to the bed. She handed Daniel's plate to him while she began to poke at the crust of her pie to mix it in.

"Did I say something?" Daniel asked, frowning at the sudden change of atmosphere.

"No, you didn't. Not really. It's just, well, you are going to be gone soon," Khy'ra said. "It's just coming up so fast."

"Oh …" Daniel blinked, shaking his head, and then he reached out and hugged her. "I'm sorry."

"It's fine," Khy'ra said, her voice soft and slightly tired. "It's fine. It's not as if I didn't know to expect this."

Daniel nodded into her hair, just hugging her harder. That too was true.

"Eat," Khy'ra said again, elbowing him slightly to make him let her go. "I keep telling you that recently don't I?"

Daniel laughed slightly, and then turned to his pie. She was right. Still … he would miss her. They ate in silence for a time, both of them lost in their own thoughts, before Khy'ra shook her head, visibly pushing the morose thoughts aside.

"Come. Summer is not ended," she said.

"It's autumn."

Khy'ra smiled, kissing him on the lips. "Now, tell me about your delve."

"Well, we tried running the floor. That was a mistake. If I didn't have my Gift …" Daniel said, Khy'ra leaning in with interest.

Chapter 8

Standing on the fifth floor after the first doorway, the group stared at the small tile-set arrayed before them and the locked door. Even Omrak's great strength had been unable to budge the handle and striking the door had not worked either. It was obvious that they were meant to solve the puzzle of the tiles.

"What do we do?" Daniel said, staring at the set of multi-colored tiles. It was a large set, thirty pieces wide and thirty pieces long with a series of five colors. All the spaces but one were filled.

"Move?" Asin growled, pointing at the tile space that was open.

"I guess," Daniel said, and glanced at Omrak, who shrugged.

"Right, move it is," Daniel said, and gently pushed one tile to the next. The moment he did, three of the red tiles that were now in a same line shimmered and disappeared. "Huh."

Omrak glanced down at the tile set, noting the disappearance before he returned his gaze back to the room, his sword held at the ready. Asin's lips peeled backwards in a predatory grin before she prodded another tile in the open space to make a set of four. These tiles shimmered and disappeared, other tiles above clanking together as if pulled by a force. This created another set of colored tiles which disappeared too before the experience repeated once more.

Without being asked or asking, Asin began to move the pieces. Daniel watched her for a few moments more, before he finally turned away to stare around the room. A few minutes later, Asin let out a frustrated yowl. The Catkin had seven pieces left and three colors, none of which could be shifted. Unable to continue, the board shimmered.

At the same time, a portion of the wall lowered, and a trio of elemental turtles waddled out. Immediately, Omrak jumped forwards and started attacking the creatures, his giant sword cutting and smashing the monsters. Daniel jerked himself to a stop, waiting for a monster to make its way pass Omrak before he could attack. Asin just waited, the room too small for her thrown weapons to come into play safely.

After the monsters were killed, Asin looked back to the board, which had reset itself with a different configuration of tiles. Lips pursed, she nodded to herself and started to move tiles around.

"Asin, can one of us have a try?" Daniel asked as he watched Omrak pick up the ex-Kobold's Mana Stone.

"No," Asin snarled, glaring at the board.

"Okay." Daniel backed off. After over a dozen rotations, Asin seemed to have gotten better, with only a few final tiles left. "The better you do, the easier the monsters that come out when you fail."

"I would almost ask you to fail more, Hero Asin," Omrak said, glancing around the walls. "The monsters we have fought have been less than challenging."

"No. Pass," Asin said as she prodded at the board. Daniel sighed, and he went back to leaning against the door. So far it seemed that every wall could open, so the doors themselves were the only stable portion of the room.

"JAKA!" Asin shouted, jumping to her feet and laughing.

"Finished?" Daniel asked as he pushed himself off the door. Asin nodded, proud, as Omrak walked to the door, his sword held ready. Asin jumped over to the door, grabbing at the handle and yanking it open. Inside, there was just another room.

"Oh hell," Daniel muttered as they all walked in. "This is a puzzle floor, isn't it?"

Asin nodded and the trio looked around the room, taking it in. There was a single mauve-colored door in the room with a small cylindrical tube that was attached to the door where a handle would be. In the center of the room were three containers filled with red-, blue-, and yellow-colored liquids and a separate, empty container.

"We must match the liquid colors to the door," Omrak said.

"You know of this?" Daniel said.

"It is a common puzzle," Omrak said as he walked forwards. "May I?"

"Sure …" Daniel said.

Asin blinked as the large Northerner began to pour the colored waters into the empty container without hesitation. It took barely a few seconds before Omrak was done, holding the container up to the light.

"Good?" Asin asked, peering at the container and its contents. An unfortunate aspect of being a Catkin was her reduced ability to judge colors, at least as the humans saw it.

"A touch more red," Omrak said, and walked back, fixing the liquid quickly before he poured the entire concoction into the handle. The door shuddered for a moment and Daniel hefted his mace, wary of additional monsters. He only relaxed when the door popped open and another empty room was showcased.

"Good." Asin loped forwards, clapping Omrak on the shoulder. Omrak just shrugged, accepting the compliment.

"Did we just get transported back to the start?" Daniel asked, staring around. The last puzzle they had faced was a riddle. A single wrong answer and they were back in the tile room. Daniel exhaled roughly as he stared at the tile set Asin had taken charge of once more.

"It does appear so, Hero," Omrak said.

"Daniel. It's Daniel," Daniel muttered irritably as he rested against the door again.

"Of course, Hero Daniel."

"No. Just Daniel."

"Yes, Hero Just Daniel."

"You're joking, right?"

Omrak just smiled while he glanced back to Asin and the tile set to see how far she had gotten.

After a second failed attempt by Asin, Daniel turned to Omrak. "What made you come to Karlak? There must have been closer Beginner Dungeons."

"Four," Omrak said. "None were suitable for melee fighters alone. I had planned to complete Karlak by myself."

"What changed?"

"Coin," Omrak answered with a self-deprecating laugh. "I could not progress as fast as I earned. A group aided that."

"Huh," Daniel said. The grinding of a wall rising made the stout Adventurer turn, glaring at the Kobold that came out. Idly, he caught the attack high on his shield and twirled his mace around, slamming it into the space between the Kobold's third and fourth ribs, pulping its heart and killing it immediately.

"Asin, how are we doing?"

"Close. Easier now," she muttered, staring at the option she had now. Daniel just bent down to collect the Mana Stone before resting against the wall again. This was going to be another long day.

"Late day," Liev murmured, staring at the small portion of coins the trio offered.

"Puzzle floor," Daniel grumbled. At Liev's raised eyebrow, he detailed the floor for Liev who nodded.

"Ah, those were always enjoyable," Liev said, smiling at his own memories.

"Huh. For you maybe," muttered Daniel. Four times more the three had managed to get past the first room. They had even finished the third room once, but each failed attempt after the first room sent them back to the first room to start again. It did not help that the questions in the third room, like all the other puzzles, changed constantly, such that a correct answer once was no guarantee of a correct answer the next time.

Each new room was a different puzzle, the fourth a series of levers and ropes which controlled weights that had to be perfectly aligned. This puzzle Daniel had taken a shot at, and failed. Omrak continued to be the star performer of the group, never once failing to match the door's color.

"Are the Elms out yet?" Daniel asked.

"No," Liev said, shaking his head. He paused, staring at the trio before he continued slowly, "They might decide to spend a little time on this floor on purpose."

"Why?"

"They have a Mage with them," Liev said, as if that explained everything. The confused looks he gets from the others makes him continue. "Mages gain experience from knowledge and puzzle-solving. A puzzle floor like this could progress a novice Mage by a few levels."

"Oh …" Daniel said. Well, that made sense. Healers, real Healers with the Class and all, gained experience from Healing. It made sense that Mages would gain experience from puzzles and gathering knowledge.

"Best not to rush," Liev cautioned. "We lost Ilona's group today. Pierson's group found their corpses on the third floor next to the Champion."

"But … they were—" Daniel said, stuttering a little.

"Stronger than that? Not if you push too hard. A mistake and you're dead. You know that," Liev said, shaking his head. "Just because it's the lower level, it doesn't mean you can push it too hard."

Daniel grimaced as he accepted the coins from Asin. Liev was right, even if Daniel hated that fact. Caution, no matter what rewards were available, was important. They needed to slowdown and take it more cautiously, even if the fifth floor did not pay well. Even if they were not gaining much in terms of experience.

"Take care, Liev," Daniel said, waving goodbye to the red-haired attendant. Already, the others in his party had broken off, heading home after taking their share of the day's earnings. They had an early start tomorrow.

Chapter 9

"We should be exploring level seven, not playing stupid puzzles," snapped Amrah, as she stared at the Mage over dinner a week later in the Top. Daniel and Asin were quietly eating their meal not far from them that evening, enjoying the warmth from the fireplace close to them. The trio of Adventurers were still stuck on the fifth level, though at least they now knew that there were eight rooms in total. The last room held no puzzle, just the Floor Champion. If they could puzzle-out and beat the seventh room by tomorrow, they might finally be able to move on.

"We agreed to split our time," Harald the Mage said calmly. "Is this a formal request to change our agreement?"

Amrah growled but sat down with a thump, refusing to meet the Mage's eyes. A slight smile crossed Harald's face before he turned back to his drink. It had been over a week since their arrival and by now, the lure of an Advanced party had died down. There were still those who asked for and listened to the stories Amrah was more than willing to tell, but for the most part, the Adventurers had their own stories to tell.

The town buzzed with commerce now, and even Elise was talking of expanding her inn. The new levels had sparked the imagination of many wannabe-Adventurers who were arriving in a constant flow and taking up all the rooms in the inns throughout towns. Even experienced Beginners were willing to test out the new Dungeon, especially as the wider range of floors provided a more diverse training experience. Karlak was fast becoming a city that catered to a wide variety of Adventurers. It was said that Vinnie, the only bowyer in town, was now so busy that he had tripled his prices.

Daniel glanced at Asin, curious to see if she had noted the conversation. The Catkin offered a simple nod while she sipped on her Sabu, ears twitching a moment before she turned to the door with a smile. Khy'ra entered a moment later dragging along a protesting red-haired attendant. Spotting the two, she bee-lined towards them immediately.

"Daniel, Asin," Khy'ra greeted them before bending down to place a kiss on Daniel's lips. "Keep an eye on this one. And you. Sit."

Liev, grumbling, sat next to the bemused pair.

"I'm here under protest."

"Healer's orders," Khy'ra said as she plunked down a pair of foaming beer mugs. "Scoot. You're not dating Daniel."

Liev grunted, shifting seats and letting the Elf sit next to the stout Adventurer.

"Where's Omrak?"

"Dock," Asin said.

"He's still working down there?" Daniel asked, blinking. That he did not know. For that matter, how did Asin?

"Coin."

Khy'ra smiled slightly, listening to the pair, while Liev sucked down his beer.

"Not seen you out in a while, Liev." Daniel turned to the redhead. Liev coughed, clearing his throat as he finished up his beer.

"Yes. Well, a new Dungeon requires a significant amount of work. A very large amount of work," Liev said, and sighed. "I really should be back there. There are reports to file, maps to be commissioned, complaints to deal with …

"Owww!"

"No. You need a night out. And some decent food," Khy'ra said, pulling her hand back.

"You didn't have to hit me," Liev muttered, rubbing the top of his head.

"No, but it was fun," Khy'ra mocked the old attendant before she shook her head. "Gods, this reminds me of the last time I had to drag you for a break."

"In Corabia?" Liev said.

"Yes," Khy'ra said, smiling slightly. "We had to pull you from the library by force just to get you to eat after three weeks."

"They had dozens of books I never did see anywhere else. I had to copy them down," Liev said.

"That's what you always said." Khy'ra rolled her eyes.

"You two adventured together?" Daniel asked, glancing at the pair.

"Yes. It's good to get out once in a while and keep the hand in," Khy'ra said, smiling. "Not that we do it much these days, but …"

"But bills must be paid," Liev finished for her. "And we've all got expensive habits."

"The Clinic isn't a habit." Khy'ra pouted and Daniel nodded, giving her a quick squeeze around her waist. The waitress walked by, dropping off their plates.

"Of course not," Liev replied, smiling quietly as he scooped up some mashed potatoes on his fork. He paused, holding the fork in hand, and added musingly, "We never did make it to the Rysy Spires."

"No. Maybe another time," Khy'ra replied.

"Isn't that the Master Dungeon?" Daniel said. "One of a dozen in the world?"

"Yes. One of the two that lie within the borders of Brad," Liev said. It was actually part of the reason why the Kingdom had as much sway as it did. As Adventurers made up a significant portion of the Kingdom's armed forces, their ability to conveniently progress within the confines of the Kingdom ensured that they could contribute significantly to any conflict. It also meant that they often would act as ambassadors when they visited nearby kingdoms to clear those Dungeons.

"Dechen Cave?" Asin said, pointing between the two.

"Not me," Liev answered, shaking his head. "Nothing interesting there for a Mage. No spell books or tomes or anything else."

"Just a couple of times," Khy'ra answered.

"Couple?" Asin's eyes widened, staring at the Elf.

"I was led through it the first few times," Khy'ra reassured Asin, waving a hand down. "It's not as difficult as most think."

Liev snorted at her mock humility. Daniel just sat there, staring at his girlfriend. There obviously were a few things that he did not know about the beautiful Elf. Or, considering how old she was—probably more than a few things.

Still, he leaned over and murmured into her ear, "Is that how you keep the Clinic funded?"

"Mostly. I get donations of course and they help," she replied in a whisper, glancing over at Liev. "I hope you don't mind. He just needs some time away, but he won't take it."

"No," Daniel chuckled and then suddenly grinned. "Liev, so you've delved with Khy'ra before. I'm sure you've got a few stories …"

Khy'ra let out a little gasp and proceeded to glare at Daniel. He chuckled at his girlfriend's reaction until she elbowed him in the ribs, whereupon he gave her a quick kiss before looking back to his new prey. The red-haired attendant watched the byplay between the two before he smiled, saying, "Well … there are a few. There was this time in Sopot …"

Daniel settled in with Asin to listen to Liev talk of Khy'ra and their old adventures. Yet, in the corner of his mind, he turned over the idea of the two Master Dungeons, one of which even his accomplished girlfriend had not completed.

Chapter 10

"Is it just me or is this Dungeon a lot weirder than it used to be?" Daniel asked the next day, his eyes wide. It only took them a single try to make it all the way through the other rooms and now they stared at their last obstacle—the Floor Champion. The Champion's room itself was bare bones, illuminated by a series of torches with flames of varying colors.

"Weirder," Asin confirmed.

"What do we attack?" Omrak said, his voice puzzled.

"Ummm …" Daniel squinted at the monster, which was made of colored squares that constantly shifted. The monster had no head or true body, the entirety of its form morphing and twisting. Stranger, the colors in each block shifted as well. Daniel's new Skill Proficiency did not seem to be giving him any hints as yet as the monster lacked any eyes, ears or other clear weaknesses. "Hit them all and see what happens?"

"Fan?" Asin asked, pulling a series of knives from her hand.

"That works. Omrak and I will follow up if we see anything. Omrak, go high and I'll go low," Daniel decided firmly as he leaned back around the doorway and cranked his crossbow to insert a bolt.

"Ready," Daniel said.

Asin flicked a glance to Omrak who gave a single nod before she spun around the corner and dashed into the room, throwing her knives and triggering her Skill Proficiency. Her knives bloomed, multiplying and striking the monster across its cubed bodies. Most deflected off the creature's armor, only a pair sinking into a blue cube.

Immediately, Daniel sighted and fired his arrow at a blue cube that was holding the creature off the ground. Omrak cast his throwing axe as well, but both attacks bounced off. Daniel hesitated, confused for a moment at this unexpected development. A moment and then he released his crossbow, allowing it to drop to the ground as he charged the monster.

Omrak was ahead of him, swinging his sword at each cube while dodging the sudden changes in direction as best he could. Asin scampered to the side as well, flinging her knives at random cubes as they attempted to figure out what the puzzle solution in this case was.

"Green!" Ormak roared as his blade sank into the colored cube. He tore the blade out even as Daniel, a moment later managed to land his own successful blow. Asin's thrown knife a few seconds later clattered off a similarly colored cube at the creature's top.

Omrak, his attacks no longer working, had switched to randomly striking again. A sudden shift in the cubic body resulted in the Northerner being smashed without warning, throwing him back. Daniel, nearby, could almost swear he heard the bones break. He had no time to pay attention to his friend as the monster now turned its attention to him. Forced to defend himself, Daniel worked his shield and mace together to block and parry attacks that came in sudden surges of colored blocks.

Omrak returned to the battle in a violent explosion, his sword bashing the monster away from Daniel. Daniel exhaled with relief, spending a moment to catch his breath. There had to be a pattern to how you could win, but so far, they had not figured it out. The vulnerable cubes did not change after each attack, nor did they rotate in any specific order or location. They were timed in some way but that in itself was not sufficient. Daniel drew another deep breath, readying himself to step forwards, when the light flickered again. Drawn to the torches, he frowned. One torch, the one that was colored green, seemed stronger than the others right now.

Acting on instinct, he called out the color. Asin did not break step as she avoided an attack and sank a knife into an exposed green cube. Omrak was too busy to attack as he defended himself and by the time Daniel ducked and twisted out of the way from the monster's attacks, the flame had flickered. However, Daniel could see Asin's blade embedded in the green cube.

"Yellow," Daniel called out as he slammed his mace into the appropriately colored cube. "The torches. Follow the torches!"

Once they had figured out the monster's vulnerability, the battle became easier. Each attack that injured the monster slowed it down further, made the shifting in blocks jerkier. Attacks that had bruised and injured before were made simple to avoid or block, and when the monster finally stopped rotating and twisting, the trio collapsed, tired. Daniel groaned slightly as he forced himself up, walking over to Omrak to cast Healer's Mark on him and then moving to Asin, who was rubbing at her ankle. He smiled slightly at her nod before he pulled open the Floor Chest to pocket the Mana Stone. Well, that was not so bad. Certainly, the information would be something that Liev would be grateful for.

As the group entered the sixth floor, they were forcefully reminded of the previous second sector of the Dungeon, where the Draxillan Crawler used to live. Unlike the previous caves, the passages here were all on one level. but they were very much caves with dirt floors, dripping waters, and passages that they had to walk through.

"Crawlers?" Daniel muttered, looking around. This seemed similar, but the fact that it was all on one level seemed to indicate another type of monster was here. Perhaps the Dungeon just decided to repeat the similar layout because it was easier. Or was it the god, Panqua? Was he influenced by what had been present before? Did Dungeons or Panqua care?

"No." Omrak walked forwards and pointed to the ground. "These tracks are different."

Asin walked over, squatting down and running clawed fingers along the tracks. She held her palm out to them, measuring size and later, depth with furrowed brows. Humanoid tracks, in a way. "Thin."

"Yes, definitely," Omrak said. "Skeletons?"

Asin hissed at the mention before she stood and pulled out her melee knife. Daniel hefted his own mace as he stepped forwards to take the lead on instinct. Omrak growled softly as he stared at the corridors before he sheathed his own sword and pulled out a throwing axe to wield.

"Well, let's try this out," Daniel muttered, walking forwards into the dark, lit only by the torch that Omrak helpfully held for them. After all, they had time since they had completed the previous floor so quickly. At the least, they could learn what monsters they were to face.

A part of Daniel sighed, wondering if he would ever get to use his crossbow. It certainly felt like he kept getting relegated to being the melee fighter—even Omrak was better and faster with his throwing axes than he was. Then again, perhaps if he spent more time on the range, it would help as well.

Daniel's musings about his shortcomings came to an abrupt end as the clinking, grating sound of bone knocking on bone travelled through the air. He frowned as he raised his shield higher before entering the cavern. Inside he quickly spotted a dozen skeletons, held together by eldritch means. Bones floated above one another or scraped together when a movement came too fast like when the creatures turned to the new intruder, mouths opened wide. To Daniel's surprise, the group let loose an unnerving, otherworldly howl that froze the Adventurers in their tracks while the Skeletons charged.

As the first Skeleton reached him, swinging its boney hands at Daniel's face, Daniel jerked back, brought to his senses by the attack. His helmet saved his eyes and face, but the monster still left a long, bleeding scratch against his exposed chin. The pain shocked Daniel into action, his mace swinging sideways to beat a hand aside even as he hunkered down beneath his shield.

Behind, Asin was shocked awake by the underworld stench. Dry earth, musty bones, and something else, something unnatural, assaulted her sensitive nostrils. She snarled in a low rumble as she darted past the still-frozen Omrak, elbowing him in the side as she moved to guard Daniel's left.

Omrak grunted in shock, the pain bringing him back to the unfolding battle. Roaring in rage, Omrak stepped forwards to Daniel's side before he chopped down with his axe at an exposed bone. The shorter axe swung down, barely missing the stalactites that hung from the ceiling, before cracking into the collarbone of the skeleton. Again and again Omrak attacked, rage taking over his senses at the unnatural fear the monsters engendered within him. By sheer strength, Omrak was able to smash the bones apart, but it took multiple strikes.

Daniel with his mace was the most suited to this, the metal edges crushing and pulping bones with each strike. Occasionally, Daniel would take a step forwards and lash out against another monster to help the monsters focus on him as the spearhead of their tight triangle. Without weapons, the monsters were unable to injure the well-protected Adventurer, allowing him to wade into the group.

As Daniel pulled back from crushing the ribcage of one Skeleton, he found his mace arm grabbed. The Adventurer jerked backwards as he attempted to pull away but was unable to loosen the monster's grip. He struggled for a moment as the Skeleton threw its body on top of his arm, forcing Daniel to lift the entire monster. Another Skeleton grabbed at his shield as he was distracted, pulling it down as a third monster launched itself at the Adventurer directly. Only a last-minute lowering of his helmeted head allowed Daniel to protect his face as the monster tried to bite at the exposed flesh. Even still, the monster managed to sink its teeth into his cheekbone, ripping the flesh free.

Asin hissed, seeing Daniel trapped and fighting the monsters, but was unable to move to help. Each cut with her knife sent arcs of lightning along the opponents' yellowish-white bones, but the attacks seemed to do little. She could only buy time, distracting the monster as she attacked it, keeping it from piling on her friend.

Help came in the form of strong fingers as Omrak reached between the ribcage of the Skeleton holding Daniel's mace down, gripping the spine and lifting the monster upwards before tossing it at Omrak's former opponent. The action freed Daniel's arm at the cost of his mace. Able to move again, Daniel spun and smashed his gauntleted fist into the skull of the Skeleton that had latched itself on to his body in its attempt to eat his face. Daniel snarled and punched the monster again and again by instinct, fear, and anger mixed in equal measure as he pummeled his attacker.

When the Skeleton's head finally shattered apart, the bloody jawbone and skull falling to pieces, the creature dropped from Daniel's body. Panic subsiding slightly, Daniel stared at the Skeleton that still clutched at his shield, and triggered Shield Bash, slamming the shield a few inches forwards and throwing the Skeleton away.

"Here!" Omrak growled, tossing Daniel back his mace.

His weapon returned, Daniel stalked forwards to finish his own opponent. It took a brief few seconds for Daniel to smash apart his single enemy before he returned to give aid to Asin, whose opponent was chipped but still standing.

"Looks like they die if you smash the skull open," Daniel said after he cast Healer's Mark on himself to begin the healing process.

"Yes. But it must be smashed fully," Omrak said, glaring around at the fading bones. Asin pulled her knife to her, testing the edge and grimacing.

"Knife no work," Asin complained, her tail wagging side to side.

"Aye, it is only my Skill that allowed me to use my axe," Omrak agreed. "And I am unable to use my sword in these caves."

"Back?" Asin asked, frowning as her tail lashed out behind her.

"I'm doing okay," Daniel pointed out. "Mostly."

"Do you believe we can complete the level with you leading the way?"

"Probably?" Daniel said, surveying the damaged skeletons that lined the floor. "This is only Level Six."

Omrak glanced at Asin, who just nodded resignedly. For a moment more, Omrak hesitated before he finally agreed. "Very well, Hero Daniel. We shall be in your hands."

"Then let's go. At the least, we can map out some of this level." Hefting his weapon, Daniel strode forwards.

It barely took them another twenty minutes before they found another group of Skeletons. Daniel approached quickly, rushing forwards and to the right as he bashed one monster into the other seven, leaving one untouched. The attacked Skeleton flew backwards, its lighter body no match for the greater strength and Skill. It slammed into the other monsters behind it, tangling the group up and causing a few to fall. Roaring in approval, Omrak dropped his axe to sweep his sword out of its sheath. This cavern was taller and wider, large enough that he could wield his weapon with ease. As the undead monsters struggled to their bony feet, Omrak laid into them with a vengeance. Asin in the meantime backed up Daniel, ready to step in to help him if he needed it.

Not that he did at this point. The single standing Skeleton reached outwards, attacking Daniel, but was blocked with a hard parry that cracked its arm bones. On the return, Daniel crushed its temple, sending the monster staggering backwards. Out of the corner of his eye, he saw that Omrak was about to be swarmed.

"Yours," Daniel shouted as he bull-rushed a Skeleton on the edges. This monster had lost its arm but showed no sign of slowing down as it attacked the Northerner. So intent was it on its objective, the Skeleton never saw Daniel's tackle that sent it flying into a nearby wall. Spinning on his feet, Daniel used the edge of his shield to crack the spine of another Skeleton before crushing its head with his mace.

Omrak, bleeding and beleaguered, was forced back further towards their entrance. The Skeletons continued their single-minded pursuit, leaving Daniel their exposed backs to attack. Seizing the opportunity presented to him, Daniel attacked with wide, powerful swings and quickly ended the fight. By the time he was done, Asin had finished chipping away at her own opponent.

"Easier," Asin growled.

"No scream," Daniel replied, and blinked. Ugh, he sometimes fell into Asin's talking pattern without thinking.

"Yes. Did we surprise them?" Omrak asked.

"Perhaps," Asin sniffed, and shrugged as she spent the time looking around for Mana Stones. Daniel bent down to help her, his eyes roaming over the two entrances. Left, or right? Truly, it did not matter right now—they just needed to map the Dungeon till they found the staircase down.

"This is going to take a while," Daniel said, shaking his head as he stared at the map only he could see. The minimap showed the sprawling complex they had walked in the last hours, multiple passageways that led from each cavern that had to be explored individually. Worse, they often found small passages which had to be carefully squeezed through and verified, as some of those passages would open into wider or larger caverns. It meant that they had moved slowly, checking side passages and small openings as they walked along. Eyeballing the map, Daniel sighed. They had barely covered a quarter of the ground that a 'normal' level would have, and it was time to head back.

So busy was he that Daniel missed the small opening by his feet, his steps carrying him past before he could see the Skeleton that pushed itself free. Asin, who was directly behind Daniel and checking for traps ahead of them saw the monster too late. A boney hand grabbed her ankle, pulling her to her knees even as the Skeleton continued to crawl out of the hole, levering itself up along her body. Nails clawed into the Catkin, digging into fur and the flesh beneath, opening long wounds along her frame. Close enough now, the Skeleton bit down on an exposed thigh, teeth rending flesh.

As the Skeleton raised its head from the injury, blood running down its teeth, Omrak reached forwards and gripped the monster by its neck. Eschewing his axe, Omrak smashes the monster directly into the cave walls again and again. Skin and fur tore from Asin as the creature was ripped away, freeing the Catkin to send a Piercing Shot down the hole to crack the skull of the next Skeleton that pulled itself forwards.

Having heard the commotion behind him, Daniel turned around and quickly moved to take station before the hole.

"Sorry!"

Asin just yowled in frustration and pain as she backed away to let the warriors deal with this next threat as she scrambled for bandages. Forced to crawl out one by one, it was a simple matter for Daniel to end them all. Monsters torn apart, Daniel moved to place a hand on Asin, healing her as he muttered an apology again. This Dungeon wore one down, never letting you spend a single moment to yourself. Always, always there was a danger.

Asin, fur and skin slowly regrowing, bent down to pick up the Mana Stones and yowled unhappily, her tail lashing out behind her. So many were in her pouch now, but each Mana Stone dropped was tiny and dark, lacking none of the luster a good stone might have.

"Sorry again," Daniel said, looking around at last. "I missed it. Should have paid more attention. It was just so small."

"Small," Asin agreed.

"Har! You say so," Omrak grumbled, rubbing at his head where he accidentally knocked it again on a stalactite. The cavern in this portion of the Dungeon was so low that Omrak had knocked his head more than once. Already, Daniel had been forced to deal with one nasty bleeding scalp wound and an incipient concussion. "I fear this cave will end me before our opponents.".

"Good time to stop anyway. About time to go back," Daniel said, pointing back the way they came. "We won't finish this level today. Maybe not for a few days."

Asin nodded, scratching at an ear. "Map?"

"I'm making it," Daniel said.

"Buy," Asin said, shaking her head. "Elm sell?"

"Oh …" Daniel frowned but finally nodded. The Catkin was right, if there was a faster option here, they should go with it. Though he doubted the Elms were that confident that they would sell the location and route to the next stairway down.

He pondered that thought while he led the way back, their return uneventful but for a few further attacks, which the group dealt with simply enough. Still, by the time the party finally made their way into the Adventurers' Guild, the group was dragging their feet. It had been a long, cramped, and tiring day.

"Sixth floor?" Liev said, glancing at the crystals arrayed before him as he did the calculations. There were a lot certainly. "I hear it's infested with Skeletons."

"Infested. That works," Daniel said. "The Elms didn't sell a map, did they?"

Liev shook his head, swinging his pad around for Asin and Omrak to confirm before he drew forth the requisite cash.

"Didn't think so." Daniel sighed. This was definitely going to take a while.

Chapter 11

"How's it going?" Khy'ra asked Daniel as she lay in bed, watching the young man working at his desk. Daniel blinked and looked up from the parchment upon which he was drawing the map for the sixth floor. The party had spent four days on that level and it seemed that while it was not significantly larger than a 'normal' floor, the numerous connected and dead-end passages meant that more space was compacted into the same area. At least it did not seem like the level's layout changed.

"Slow. We might have to do an overnighter tomorrow if we want to finish it," Daniel said. "We keep running out of time."

Khy'ra smiled slightly, watching Daniel, before she stood up and walked over to look at his map. Blonde hair cascaded down her back as she did so, and Daniel took a moment to enjoy the view. The Elf smiled slightly when she noted that, leaning over to tap him on the nose while she glanced at the map. After a moment, her finger dropped to a blank spot on it.

"There. Your staircase will likely be around there."

"How do you know?"

"Experience," Khy'ra said before she held up a finger. She walked quickly over to her chest, bending low to wave a hand at it before she pulled forth a rolled-up map. Returning, she waved her hand over the map and murmured a word. Suddenly, lines began to trace over the map, quicker and quicker till before them was a detailed drawing of a Dungeon.

"Look familiar?" Khy'ra asked, and Daniel nodded. That was the third floor of the old Karlak Dungeon. The moment he did, Khy'ra said another word in Elvish and the map changed again.

"Peel, sixth floor."

"Porthos, seventh floor."

"Alytus, fifth floor."

"See the pattern?" Khy'ra asked after flipping through numerous Dungeon maps on her magical map.

"No …" Daniel said, shaking his head. If there was one, it was more subtle than he could see.

"Well, when you can, you'll start to understand how the Dungeon is laid out. Might save you some time in the future," Khy'ra said, and then glanced at his original map as she rolled up her own. "Of course, it won't help much with your problem."

"No, too many passages," Daniel confirmed, sighing.

"Come on, let's go to bed," Khy'ra said, tugging on his hand and laying an inviting kiss on his lips. "The Dungeon will still be there tomorrow."

Drawn by Khy'ra's hand, Daniel discarded the map behind him.

The next morning, Daniel was yawning as Asin walked up to the Dungeon entrance. She raised an eyebrow, surprised at seeing Daniel there before her.

"Early."

"Yes." Daniel yawned again, then smiled slightly. He reached down and picked up some brown packages wrapped in parchment paper and twine. "Don't have much of a lunch today. I did pick up some pack meals from the Guild for today and tomorrow."

Asin sniffed, obviously displeased, but took the packages to slip into her bag. As the wind shifted, she caught Daniel's scent and Khy'ra intermingled with their night's strenuous activities. Nose wrinkling, she stepped away to crouch beside the entrance.

"How are things going?" Daniel asked after a while to fill the silence.

"Good."

"Really? You've been pretty stressed about our earnings recently."

"Low," Asin agreed.

"Never seen you that worried before."

Asin just shrugged, not meeting his gaze.

"Asin, we're friends. You know you can talk to me about things, right?" Daniel probed again.

Again, the Catkin just nodded, and Daniel gave up, lips compressed in a tight line. Perhaps he would ask Khy'ra later when he had a moment. The two had certainly developed a curious relationship. Daniel's thoughts were interrupted as Omrak neared them. Daniel absently noted that Omrak was wearing a simple, visorless helm today, his first real piece of armor. Time to get to work.

"Ouch," Omrak growled, rotating his shoulder. A trio of Skeletons had managed to get hold of his hands, hampering his movements while a fourth had pounded on him. The group had found a cavern filled with Skeletons, their presence hidden by a convenient wall, and found themselves swarmed before they could pull back. Every single one of the party now bore wounds from the battle, Asin barely escaping with her life by scampering up a wall and staying out of reach of the Skeletons.

"Sorry. Nearly done," Daniel said. His plates of iron armor had protected him from most direct attacks, but between the gaps and along the edges where armor met cloth, he was scratched and bruised.

"No like," Asin said as she collected another stone and dropped it into her pouch. "Can't hurt."

Not exactly true, Daniel thought as he spotted a throwing knife and handed it back to his friend. Her Piercing Shot could drill through skulls, killing the monster immediately. Unfortunately, each use of her Skill drained her Stamina, ensuring that she could only activate it occasionally. Otherwise, her attacks were minimally effective.

"Well, we've begun the unexplored region of this side of the map. Hopefully we'll find the way down soon," Daniel said placatingly. Not much else he could say. "When everyone's ready, that is."

"A minute," Omrak said, testing his shoulder again. It still pulled sharply when he rotated his shoulder, drawing a wince from the large blond man. "Perhaps I could use a Healer's Mark."

Hours of walking, squeezing, crawling, and occasionally climbing later, the party had mapped out another section of the Dungeon. Unfortunately, their last section had led to a dead-end, and so the group found themselves backtracking to their last unexplored location.

"That's … new," Daniel muttered as he poked his head around the corner. Asin's warning had pulled the group to a halt before they entered, and now the trio watched the group of Skeletons and Skeleton Champion standing eerily still in a previously empty cave. The Skeleton Champion looked no different from its brethren except for a deeper, darker discoloration of its bones, and the pair of short swords it wielded.

"Champion," Asin growled softly, testing the edge of her throwing knife.

"See if we can kill it beforehand?" Daniel suggested.

"I can try," Omrak offered, hefting his throwing axe.

"Both."

On a silent count of three, the pair surged forth from their hiding spot and threw their respective weapons. The knife and throwing axe whipped through the air before they were deflected in quick succession by the Champion's swords.

Omrak stood there, stupefied, while Asin scrambled to pull her bolas from her belt. At least those worked, especially in such a large crowd. Daniel, seeing that the attack was finished, stepped forwards to take the charge.

The normal Skeletons rushed forwards, bones clicking together as they came on with their hands outstretched. The Champion stood still, however, instead issuing its paralyzing scream. The group winced as one, feeling the supernatural fear course through their limbs to slow them down. At least now, they had gained sufficient experience to resist the initial freezing effects of the scream. Even so, Asin found herself fumbling the grip of her bolas, dropping it on the earthen floor.

The first Skeleton was on Daniel before he could activate his Shield Bash, slowed down by the scream as he was. He could only hunker beneath the shield, taking the attack and stepping backwards to absorb the charge as even more Skeletons piled on. Seeing an opening, he roared and sent his Skill Perin's Blow directly into the ribcage of one monster, shattering the bones and sending them flying backwards in a hail of shards. Gravely injured, the monster collapsed at his feet, while Daniel stepped to the side to avoid a grasping arm.

Behind him, Omrak brought the pommel of his axe down on the crown of a Skeleton, compressing the monster and knocking it off its feet. With a backhand strike, he cleaved open the ribcage of another that was attempting to circle the group. This attack was minimally effective at deterring the creature as it regained its feet and continued its approach.

Finally on her feet again, Asin skipped backwards and to the left before tossing the bolas underhanded at a Skeleton in the back. It wrapped around the targeted monsters and another's legs, tangling both up and buying time for Daniel.

Using the brief moment afforded him, Daniel focused and let loose a Shield Bash against his current opponent, sending the monster stumbling backwards. In the opening, he engaged his Double Strike to crack a hip and then the skull of another Skeleton. Before he could reset his guard, a sword darted forwards, skipping along his chestplate and missing his face by inches. Not giving Daniel time to rest, the Skeleton Champion lashed out again with its other sword, a blow that was barely blocked by Daniel's shield.

The pair dueled for a moment, Daniel blocking attacks with his shield and mace, and the Champion cutting and stabbing with speed and precision. Daniel grunted as he stepped backwards again as he attempted to regain control of the fight. Unable to assist or hold the attention of the other monsters, the Skeletons began to circle around the Champion and Daniel to attack his friends.

Asin yowled as she scrambled backwards, throwing another bolo to entangle the feet of a Skeleton that chased her. It was a delaying tactic, but at least it meant she only had two to deal with. Beside her, Omrak roared as a Skeleton gripped his thigh, its mouth clamped around his leg. The Northerner was unable to deal with it as he held a second clawing Skeleton aloft by its ribcage and struck at a third even as another pair attempted to close in on him.

Daniel grunted as another strike slipped past his guard and bounced off his upper arm armor. The Skeleton Champion was significantly more skilled than he was, Daniel was quickly realizing. A muted cry of pain from behind him reminded him that Asin was in trouble and he made a quick decision, raising his shield slightly higher.

The Champion was quick to take advantage of the situation, its sword lashing out. Trusting in his armor, Daniel surged forwards at the same time, twisting his shield so that he could slam its edge into the Champion's neck even as he engaged Perin's Blow. The Champion ducked low but failed to clear the shield completely. The top of its head was caught by the improvised weapon and the Skill-driven blow rocked the monster backwards.

Panting with exertion, Daniel stepped forwards and kicked the monster directly in its chest to send the Champion sprawling backwards. Daniel then spun to the side to look over his companions. To his surprise, it was Omrak who most desperately needed his help, swarmed as the Northerner was by the Skeletons. Daniel rushed the monsters and triggered Double Strike again, each attack targeted at ripping a monster off the giant. He grimaced as an abrupt shift by the giant made one of his strikes glance off Omrak's arm, even as it ripped the skeleton off.

Freed at last, Omrak struggled to his knees. Enraged and glowing red, the Northerner pinned a Skeleton under one knee and pulled another down by gripping its pubic bone. On the ground, the monster was smashed repeatedly in its face by Omrak, cracking the orbital bone and finally shattering the skull in its entirety.

Daniel, his initial charge spent, proceeded to bend lower and push his shield into the midsection of a nearby Skeleton, pushing it away from Omrak and into the Champion. Crouched beneath his shield, Daniel proceeded to lash out at any opening he saw beneath his shield, crushing ankles and tibias as he spotted them. A sword flicked past the shield, coming at an angle and cutting deep into Daniel's side near his arm where his body was left unarmored. The attack forced his arm to collapse, the Skeleton he had been holding aloft crashing down on him.

Daniel tottered for a moment on his knees before he shrugged his shoulder and tossed the sprawled over monster behind him. The Champion stepped into the opening, a sword raised to plunge at Daniel's exposed throat. It was only a thrown knife that sliced through the air to crack into the monster's temple that threw the blow off to clatter uselessly off Daniel's armor.

Forcing what little strength he had into his knees, Daniel triggered Perin's Blow again, catching the Champion in the spine as he stood. The explosion of force threw the Champion backwards and left its spine broken. Daniel had no time to stop to gloat as he turned back to help his friends mop up the last of the monsters.

With the Champion broken and unable to continue fighting, the other monsters were quick to fall. Now that Omrak and Daniel were able to handle them, Asin scampered back with the remaining pair of Skeletons she had been distracting. Afterwards, the group sat in place, breathing deeply as they waited for the magical healing to slowly patch them together. Daniel grimaced, glancing at his remaining Mana pool, and walked over to Omrak, casting Minor Healing to help patch the open wound in his thigh. He would need to cast Healer's Mark at least a couple more times to heal the big man full which would significantly reduce his existing pool significantly. As it stood, he had used his Gift on the most serious of his own wounds to conserve Mana.

"Swords." Asin pointed at the pair of bone swords that lay on the ground.

"Omrak, can you carry them?" Daniel asked, gesturing to the weapons. The Northerner grimaced but walked over, picking up the pair and testing them.

"Good balance," Omrak stated. Touching a finger to the edges, he pulled his finger away with a whistle. "Still sharp."

"Could be good money," Daniel said, rubbing his chin.

Omrak nodded as he began to tie one sword to his own, electing to hold the second in hand. Asin, having recovered her breath, had pulled open the chest to reveal the floor stone. She held it aloft for everyone to see, a grin on her face. This was a stone she could be happy about.

"Better?" Daniel chuckled slightly and then winced, his ribs bruised from the repeated pounding. Better to get moving before they stopped for the day. Pulling himself to his feet, Daniel led the group to the next passageway, keeping his eye out for more skeletons. A short half-hour later, Daniel's eyes widened slightly as he received a notification as constant use of his healing skills finally resulted in an upgrade to its abilities. It did not take him much time to make the decision.

Minor Healing (I) upgraded to Minor Healing (II)

Heals minor wounds.
Effect: Heals Intelligence + Healing Skill level of wounds
Cost: 20 Mana

It was still an expensive spell, but it now healed a third more. It was comparable in terms of the amount healed now with Healer's Mark, but unlike Healer's Mark, which healed over a period of time, this was close to instantaneous. That was the reason Daniel decided to choose to upgrade this spell rather than Healer's Mark. One could keep them going on long delves, the other could save a life.

"Daniel," Omrak growled, bringing the Healer's attention back to the present. Daniel stared forwards, his attention drawn to the Skeletons stumbling forwards towards the party. They were in a small space here which meant there was no way for the monsters to flank them, but it also meant their continual screams would jar his nerves. Good thing they couldn't get past his armor. Settling into his stance, Daniel hefted his mace. No need to waste Stamina on special attacks here.

Seated in a larger cavern, the party rested their feet after a long day of searching. They had covered miles of underground passages, their only source of light the Mana lantern carried by Omrak. Miles of mapped passages behind them, the trio sat eating their meal together.

"How much more?" Omrak asked as he bit into his sandwich.

"No idea," Daniel said, looking up at the minimap. "Still, I think we're close. Maybe a few more hours if we are willing to continue pushing it."

"Tired," Asin growled, rubbing at her calves.

"There is danger in continuing without rest," Omrak said around a mouthful. "We risk running into further ambushes."

"True," Daniel said, frowning as he assessed his own body. He had less than a fifth of his Mana left and that needed to be held in reserve for combat. Fatigue ran through his muscles, his eyes bloodshot and aching from constant squinting. They could attempt to rest here, but the way the Skeletons roamed, it was unlikely to be a restful night. That left them one last option. He focused internally, pulling on his Gift and sending it coursing through his body. He felt his memory, his experience, slip from him as he washed the fatigue away.

Refreshed, Daniel walked over and placed a hand on Omrak's shoulder. A quick assessment made him blink—he had not even noticed the broken rib. That the Northerner had managed to walk and fight so long without complaint was amazing. Focusing, Daniel patched the rib and then cleared the chemical fatigue from Omrak's body, before doing the same for Asin.

"We good?" Daniel asked, stretching slowly. The physical exhaustion was wiped away, though the mental tiredness was still there, if lessened. A few more hours. He could do that, Daniel told himself.

"Aye. Thank you again, Hero Daniel," Omrak rumbled, and Asin nodded in agreement. Together, the trio stood and walked forwards into the darkness, a single light illuminating their way. In the clatter of their footsteps, Daniel wondered what new memory he had lost.

Chapter 12

"A Labyrinth." Daniel exhaled, staring at the maze that sprawled in front of them. As he had thought, it had only taken them another few hours to find the way down. However, as they poked their heads out of the entranceway of the staircase, all they could see was the start of the maze, its stone passageways spread out before them.

"This is what has held the Crimson Elms behind then," Omrak stated.

"Maze." Asin walked forwards, sniffing and eyeing the innocuous stone walls. Her fur ruffled slightly, and she paused before she took the next step, crouching and holding her hand above the gap between the two stone slabs on the ground.

"Trap," Daniel said before she could. He reached into a pouch and pulled a weighted ball, showing it to the Catkin. Asin quickly stepped back, nodding to Daniel. With an underhand toss, Daniel landed the ball on the stone slab, which flipped itself around, exposing a pit for a brief second.

"Seesaw trap," Omrak said, walking forwards and prodding the trap again to set it spinning.

"Yes," Asin said as she slowly moved along the edges of the trap to test the next stone piece. This one did not move. "More?"

Daniel frowned, mentally weighing his exhaustion. "No. We should go back."

"Test more," Asin said, moving forwards slowly as she prodded. "Extent."

"Not a good idea," Daniel said. "We're tired."

"Faster. Learn now."

"Daniel is right, Hero Asin, we are all exhausted," Omrak said.

"Asin …" Daniel started.

"No." Asin turned and glared at the duo. "More coin."

"Why, damn it?" Daniel stepped forwards and found himself stopping at the last second when he remembered the trap.

"Need," Asin said.

"So does Omrak. He doesn't even have armor and takes more damage than any of us," Daniel growled. "And he's saying we should go back."

"Show. Later," Asin finally huffed. "Test now."

Daniel gritted his teeth and then finally nodded. Fine. They would test the area for a bit, learn a little more about the labyrinth. But he wanted an answer.

"Tripwire. Darts."

"Deadfall. Spikes."

"Minotaur. Yours."

"Pitfall."

"Pressure. Fire."

A good hour and a half later, Daniel raised his hands as he called out, "Enough, Asin."

Asin paused, staring at Daniel, before she touched the pouch by her side. The Minotaurs were not particularly numerous, but it seemed the longer they stayed in the Labyrinth, the faster they came, tracking the group. Still, they were definitely more profitable with properly sized and lustrous Mana Stones. As for the traps, they had not found a new one recently.

"Okay," Asin relented, her tail no longer waving, her fur wilted.

"Finally," Omrak muttered, shaking his head as Daniel led the group back. Asin's ears twitched for a brief moment but stilled, the Catkin prowling behind the group as the trio edged around the marked traps.

"We coming back tonight?" Daniel asked. Inside the Dungeon, it was hard to tell the time, but it had to be early morning. By the time they had slept and woken up again, it would be late afternoon at best. Thankfully, the Dungeon made no difference if it was morning or evening.

"Yes." Asin nodded. "Need gear."

"We'll take some of today's earnings for the trap finders and more rope," Daniel said.

"Omrak. Buy?" Asin tilted her head to the side, looking up at the large Adventurer.

"I can do so. I believe I know what is necessary." Omrak nodded agreeably.

"Good."

Daniel blinked, having thought that he would be the one to do it. After all, that was what he normally did. He frowned slightly, wondering what it was all about, but then shrugged as he hopped over the trip wire. It did not matter, not really.

Still, he wondered.

"Daniel."

The knocking on the door woke Daniel from his sleep, making him groan. It felt like he had just gotten to sleep before he was woken. He stretched slowly, moving over to the water basin to splash his face, when another insistent knock disturbed his thoughts.

"Coming," Daniel called out around his washcloth. Grabbing his shirt, he shook his head to clear the cobwebs from his mind. Physically, there was just a residue of the exhaustion from yesterday. Mentally, though, he felt he could have spent another day in bed.

Pulling the door open, he saw Asin with her fist raised to knock again.

"Asin?" Daniel said, puzzled.

"Show," Asin said, before gesturing for Daniel to come. At his confusion, her tail twitched as she added, "Coin."

"This couldn't wait?" Daniel grumbled as he tucked his shirt in.

"No."

Daniel clamped his teeth around the words that threatened to spill out and walked back into his room to grab his mace and coin pouch from the bedstand before he walked with Asin down the stairs. He knew better than to push the Catkin to explain things before she was ready.

As they walked, Daniel glanced over at his friend, noting how her fur was still slightly wilted and not as well kept as usual. She moved with her usual grace but with a slight hitch in her steps that only someone who had spent as much time with the Catkin as he had would have noticed. Being both friend and her healer gave Daniel a unique insight into his party members he was becoming to realize. As Daniel walked, he idly noted their route, realizing that he probably knew where they were going.

"Are we headed to the butcher?" Daniel asked, frowning.

"Yes," Asin answered before falling silent. She refused to answer any further questions, not even after she burdened Daniel down with the carcass of a pair of pigs, carrying a large bag herself too. After that, she threaded her way through the streets towards the Beastkin quarter.

"Am I just here to carry things for you?" Daniel grumped as he lurched behind the Catkin, carrying the meat.

"Wait."

The encumbered pair finally came up to a sprawling two-story building in the Beastkin quarter. Asin skipped past the main door immediately, leading him to a side door, which she proceeded to kick. When it opened, she handed her bag over to the large Bullkin inside, who gripped it and held a hand out to Daniel. Daniel frowned before handing his own burdens over, the glimpse of the inside detailing a large kitchen. The Bullkin snorted and growled afterwards to Asin, who yowled back, the pair holding a brief and noisy discussion before the door closed suddenly in their faces.

Finished, Asin turned away and gestured for Daniel to follow.

"Is that it?" Daniel asked, shaking his head. "That's your explanation? Meat to some building?"

"Yes." Asin stopped and pointed backwards. "School."

"You're feeding a school?" Daniel said slowly, frowning at her nod. "I'm going to need more than that."

"City no pay. No food. Children hungry. I buy," Asin said slowly, and exaggeratedly. "Expensive."

"How many children are in there?" Daniel asked as he reached for his pouch, his own generous nature tugging on him.

Asin hissed at him, stalking off.

"What?"

"Beastkin," Asin growled, and pointed around and then added, "Human. No help."

"Then why did you show this to me?" Daniel said.

"Insisted," Asin said as she turned back to her friend. "My problem. I deal. Tired now. Evening."

"Asin …" Daniel started and then fell silent, watching her walking away. Damn it, Asin.

Chapter 13

Labyrinths were a traditional level in most Dungeons, and depending on the level of the Dungeon, could sprawl over a few kilometers or tens of kilometers. However, no matter which level of Dungeon it was, the monster that inhabited it was the same—the Minotaur. Bipedal, seven-foot-plus monsters with muscles that rivalled Omrak's and a bull's face, they were equipped, or not, dependent on the Dungeon level. For a Beginner Dungeon like Karlak, the Minotaurs were unarmored and wielded copper swords and axes, which disappeared after their defeat.

Spinning around, Omrak swung his sword in a diagonal from his lower left to his right shoulder in a cut that battered aside the Minotaur's copper sword, tearing open its chest. Beside Omrak, Daniel fought much more guardedly, taking the Minotaur's strike on his shield and sliding it off to his left while he crushed the arm as the monster tried to retreat. Forced to drop the sword, the Minotaur backed away, swinging a hook that Daniel ducked beneath to continue his attack. Behind, Asin watched the pair fight as she ran her finger along the edge of a throwing knife, waiting.

"Thanks for the help," Daniel grumbled as he watched the Minotaur corpse disappear.

"Dangerous. Move bad," Asin explained, and then shrugged. "No need help."

"Aye, we required no help," Omrak said, picking up the Mana Stone and tossing it over to Asin to pocket. "Next trap?"

"Darts. Pressure and tripwire," Asin said, pointing down the hallway.

"Right," Omrak said, pulling out a ball to roll along the ground. Afterwards, he walked forwards slowly with the sword pushing ahead of him to trigger the tripwires.

Daniel followed along slowly as he stared at the map inside his head. The labyrinth was huge, and while they were following the time-honored tradition of staying to the left, it did mean they constantly found dead-ends. Interestingly enough, he had a nagging feeling that something was not right about this maze yet. It was a feeling that had yet to crystalize, which was why he kept silent, for now at least. Either way, there was a lot of ground to cover this evening.

A few hours later, the Catkin paused as she was about to take a step forwards. She pulled her leg back, crouching down as her ears twitched. In a moment, both Omrak and Daniel could hear it. A grinding noise that slowly increased in volume that seemed to surround them all.

"What is this?" Omrak growled, hands tense on his sword.

"The walls are moving," Daniel said, looking around himself. "The labyrinth is reshaping itself."

"Midnight," Asin guessed.

"Yes, probably. So that's why the Elms have been stuck," Daniel said, sighing. Between the traps and the shifting maze, each party had only a single day to attempt this.

"Problem. Out," Asin said, pointing back the way they came.

Daniel frowned, before he realized what she was saying. If the way back had changed, they were now lost in the middle of the maze without a way out. Or through. While the group obviously carried enough food for a few days, the possibility of getting stuck in the maze for all that time made Daniel shudder. It was a Miner's worst nightmare.

Both Asin and Omrak were silent as well as they considered the fact that now, they had no choice but to find a way out.

As the grinding and rumbling slowly came to an end, Daniel hitched up his bag, glanced at his friends, and said, "Let's go."

Nodding, Asin stepped forwards and started checking over the ground in front of them for traps. Omrak followed behind, watching for traps as well and monsters.

An hour later with no attacks, the trio glanced at each other. It was possible that the monsters had pulled back during the transformation and were only now filtering into the rest of the Dungeon. The other, more disturbing possibility was that they were actually cut off, their particular location within the Dungeon a completely enclosed route. It was a thought that none of the trio cared to share with their friends since there was nothing they could do about it. Still, the fear at the potential of being trapped, even for a day, made the trio move slightly faster than they should have.

Asin stepped forwards, placing her leg against the stone slab, and then found herself tipping forwards as the slab slipped open beneath her weight. Pitched forwards, she threw her hands backwards in a futile attempt to stop her plunge. Only a desperate grab by Omrak on her cloak halted her fall before he yanked her to safety.

Yowling in distress, Asin rubbed at her throat where the rough handling had bruised it. Still, she nodded her thanks to Omrak. The giant Northerner did not notice this, having edged over to stare at the slab of stone while he wedged it open with his sword. Surprisingly, instead of a simple deadfall, the edges of the trap were filled with spikes that were certain to injure any unlucky Adventurer. Thankfully, it was not a large fall, just under six feet. Not lethal, but painful.

"You okay?" Daniel asked.

Asin nodded slightly as she tried to control her breathing and slow her heart. Eventually, she stood up and walked around the edge of the trap, ready to test for the next section. Unfortunately, the Dungeon had no easily discernable ratio of traps to corridor, which meant each section had to be checked carefully.

"We can take a break if you want?" Daniel called out after her as he brought up the back.

Rather than answer him directly, Asin just continued to move forwards slowly.

It was a relief when they eventually ran into a group of Minotaurs. The Minotaur group had just turned the corner and, on spotting the trio, roared before they charged. The lead Minotaur stumbled slightly as it hoof caught a tripwire, righting itself soon after and continuing the charge. Daniel growled at the unfairness of it all as the trap refused to trigger. Asin in the front stood up swiftly, drawing and throwing her knife and activating her ability Fan of Knives at the same time. Knives split again and again, plunging into the monster's body.

Injured, the Minotaur next ran into Omrak and his sword. Raised above his head, Omrak suddenly stepped forwards and swung the sword down, splitting its skull open between its horn. Daniel finally managed to get his crossbow loaded, the newly released bolt catching a Minotaur right above its hip and spinning it about with the force of impact. His crossbow empty, Daniel dropped the weapon and ran forwards to meet the remaining half dozen with mace and shield.

Asin continued to harass the monsters with her knives, dancing to the side with each attack. A thrown knife spun through the air, sparks of electricity dancing as it lodged in a Minotaur's bicep, forcing its attack on Omrak askew. Daniel Shield Bashed an incoming attack, the powered block ripping the sword from a monster's hand before Daniel began his series of attacks.

A few minutes later, the trio were left panting amongst the shiny blue sparkles of light as the corpses dispersed. Recovered, Daniel walked over to Omrak to cast Healer's Mark and bandage his ribs where a cut had opened up. No point in stitching it; the spell would fix the damage soon enough. Or, as Daniel eyed his friend, perhaps the second use of the spell.

Asin limped over and prodded Daniel, pointing to the cuts on her thigh and upper arm in order. At the end, she had been forced to jump into melee combat to ensure an injured Minotaur did not flank the pair. Unfortunately, the huge height and strength difference had left the Catkin at a serious disadvantage.

Still, for all their injuries, the fight had lifted the mood of the group. Fighting for their lives was a danger that the trio were used to. Slowly starving to death, trapped underground was not for Asin and Omrak. As for Daniel, it was a danger that he had thought he had left behind. Grinning slightly at each other, the trio collected the Mana Stones and moved on.

The good news, thought Daniel, was that they were definitely not trapped in a portion of the labyrinth by the shifting of the walls. At least, if they were trapped, the portion they were trapped in was huge. The bad news was that, even after four hours, the party still had not found a way out. Since each corridor was the same, there really was no way to tell if the exit was around the next corner or a hundred corners from now.

By now, the thrill of the initial fight had gone away, and even subsequent fights had not brought any of the excitement back. Now, it was just the slow grind of checking for traps, walking along blue-tinted corridors and the occasional, hectic fights.

A sullen silence had fallen among the group as they concentrated on their respective tasks. Daniel scanned for trouble ahead and behind them, while Asin checked for traps, and Omrak watched her and marked the traps they found. Occasional grunts and whispered words of warning were the only sounds that emanated from the group, as they plodded through the labyrinth.

Eventually, it was Omrak who broke the silence. "Is this the same passage? Again?"

"Yes," Daniel said, pointing down to the third of four passages that split from here.

"Did we just walk in a circle," Omrak growled, hands tightening on his sword.

"Yes," Daniel answered again while Asin crept forwards, prodding at a suspicious stone. A hiss and a dart flew out from the side, striking the stone on the opposite wall. The Catkin did not even blink, just edged to the left to test the next stone.

"Are you sure about your map?" Omrak asked, leaning forwards.

"Yes," Daniel replied again.

"Stop it. You can speak in full sentences," Omrak snapped, stomping his foot.

"Why?" Daniel paused and then added, "There's nothing else to say. We just need to keep walking."

"For how long? We've been down here for hours now. We can't even tell how long," Omrak said, waving a hand at the enclosed corridors. "It'd be at least seven, eight hours."

"Yes," Daniel said, stretching. "Do you want to take a break? We probably have the rest of the day."

"A break. I just want out!" Omrak snarled. "I want to stop walking around in a circle. I want to know we're actually getting somewhere."

Asin scurried to the side, a hand touching the top of a throwing knife as her eyes narrowed at the raging giant. Daniel stared at Omrak, opened his mouth and then shut it before he finally tried again. "I can't guarantee we can get out. But we are getting somewhere. Slowly."

"We only have your map to tell us," Omrak said, gritting his teeth. "What if you die. What if you get hurt or separated? What happens to us then?"

Daniel started to answer and then paused, actually considering Omrak's words. Finally, he said, "You're correct. We'll take a break and I'll draw a map for us."

Omrak, mollified, finally nodded and flopped to the floor before he reached for his pack to find something to eat. Asin took a seat as well, pulling her waterskin to sip at it. Better to drink slowly—relieving oneself in a Dungeon was never enjoyable. Daniel rubbed his temple as he dug out some parchment and some charcoal to sketch the map that he saw in his head. A part of him, a deep part of him, resented having to do this. However, Daniel squashed the emotions as he worked on the paper. Omrak was right. They definitely did not want to get lost—even if they were following the old wall-following rule, it was no guarantee that they would find the exit that way.

Better to sketch the map, know where they were going, and if they finally found themselves where they started again, they would at least have a map to start from. As it stood, they had already investigated two different islands on the chance that the stairways down were in them.

Daniel was fast beginning to understand why multi-week trips into Dungeon levels were a thing. It had been hard to grasp the complexity of exploring Dungeons before, but being trapped inside the Labyrinth—even if it was for only a few hours—was a definite learning experience. Twenty-five minutes later, Daniel finished the parchment and handed it to Omrak.

"Keep it. Mark it as we go along," Daniel added, and Omrak nodded grimly. The big Northerner opened his mouth to say something else and then shut it, shaking his head.

The echoing roar made the trio shift in their steps again before they glanced at one another. Asin snarled slightly but moved forwards again to the next set of paving stones. That roar, louder and more challenging than ever, had been echoing through the corridors for the last half-hour, getting slowly closer and closer. Slowly was the pertinent word, though.

"Closer. A lot closer," Omrak muttered, sliding the map back into his pouch.

Daniel nodded, putting his mace back into its loop in his belt before he picked up his crossbow. He cranked the crossbow back and slid a bolt in now that he knew they were likely to meet the screamer soon. Then perhaps they would find out who it was, though Daniel had his suspicions.

Asin nearly had the entire passageway cleared before she paused, sniffing the air. She waved the group back even as she drew more knives. It did not take long before the other two heard what Asin had smelled already—company was coming.

Three Minotaurs and a Minotaur Champion walked around the corner, weapons held in their hands. As a group, the Minotaurs rushed forwards while the Champion, standing half a foot taller and nearly the same again wide, rushed forwards while letting loose an all too familiar scream. Daniel hissed, his crossbow raised and firing even as the throwing axe and throwing knives took their attackers in the chest. Daniel's jaw dropped as he watched the Champion pull one of its compatriots into the path of his bolt before he let it go, letting the injured Minotaur stagger back to its feet, clutching its arm.

Omrak surged ahead as he picked up his sword from the passage, holding it diagonally as he charged. As he neared, he swung it, a glowing yellow light filling the blade. A hasty block by his target did nothing to slow the unstoppable cut, the Minotaur's blade shattering as it connected with Omrak's glowing weapon. A moment later, the Minotaur's body was bisected as well.

Asin cursed as a second Piercing Shot was dodged by the Minotaur Champion as it bore down on her. He was stopped only by Daniel, who lunged forwards, triggering a Shield Bash. The Champion twisted at the last second, taking the strike in his shoulder and staggering backwards. Given a bit of space,

Daniel stepped quickly to the right and struck with Perin's Blow at another Minotaur, sending it crashing into the wall.

Omrak grunted his thanks even as he sidestepped quickly, dodging a strike from his opponent while he cut at its leg. The Minotaur snarled as its muscles gave way while Omrak doubled down on his attack. Behind, Asin threw her knives at the Minotaur Daniel had hurt, keeping it from rejoining the fight.

Daniel turned back around to meet the Champion, catching a downwards strike on his shield. He found himself driven to his knee by the attack, the blow hard enough that his entire arm collapsed backwards to hit him on his head. Even before he could stand, the Minotaur Champion was slamming its sword down again, forcing Daniel to stay on his knees and reinforce his shield arm with his other hand.

Asin spotted the difficulty that Daniel was in and whipped a Fan of Knives at the Champion, the knives sinking into its body. The attack provided Daniel a moment to scramble backwards. As he stood, Daniel attempted to raise his shield arm and failed, the constant blows having dislocated it and his attempts at moving send fresh pain shooting through his body. The Champion, having recovered from Asin's attack, lowered its head and charged Daniel, closing in on him quickly. Daniel ducked sideways, dodging the charge mostly and hitting the monster as it passed.

Turning around quickly, the Champion shifted, putting Daniel in the way of Asin's knife, which clattered off his backplate as he stepped to keep himself in front of the monster. Daniel blinked, startled by the noise and impact, a moment's distraction that let the Champion roar and swing its sword forwards, its blow catching on Daniel's left pauldron. He groaned, the impact bruising his body again.

Asin, snarling, backed up to give herself more space to throw her knives. She sent them overhand, the knives arcing over the top of Daniel's head to target the Champion, who bobbed and weaved. Seeing the monster distracted, Daniel lunged low and triggered Perin's Blow against the monster's knee, feeling it crack as the knee gave way. Standing swiftly, Daniel then triggered a pair of strikes to finish the monster off while Asin sank a couple of electrified knives into its body. Crippled, the Champion did its best to fend off the joint attacks but finally collapsed, leaving Daniel panting from deep exhaustion.

Omrak, having finished his own opponents, stared down at the monsters and the bruised Daniel, shaking his head.

"A great opponent," Omrak rumbled.

"Urgh." Daniel groaned, leaning against a wall as he healed himself.

"Well, at least I'm not the one injured this time," Omrak said, grinning. He frowned suddenly, twisting to the side as lights began to play along the ground. "What's that?"

The pair just shook their heads, staring at the lights and gripping their weapons. They only relaxed when the lights stopped glowing to reveal a familiar treasure chest. Asin grinned, skipping over to open it, while Daniel sank back down, feeling the dislocated shoulder slowly grinding back into place.

Even after he healed, they still had to find a way out.

Chapter 14

It was probably, by Daniel's estimation, an hour past noon. It was hard to tell of course without the sun, but having been a Miner before, Daniel had gained some skill at guessing such things. The group had finally decided that it was best to rest for a few hours after Asin had been speared in the leg from a trap she had missed. After healing her, Daniel was completely out of Mana, and further attempts at exploration from the exhausted party had been left for later.

In an attempt to ensure their safety, the party had backtracked to a single, relatively trap-free corridor and set up camp in its center. After a hurried discussion, both Asin and Omrak bedded down while Daniel refreshed himself with his Gift. He would, in a few hours, take a nap himself to refresh his mind, but his Gift left him able to withstand the rigors of the Dungeon better. Now, if only he could remember what it was that had left him when he had activated his Gift. Somehow, Daniel knew that the memory was important.

Shaking his head, Daniel chewed on the beef jerky as he watched both sides. His crossbow lay next to him, fully loaded and ready for use. Alone with his thoughts and the insistent snoring of the Catkin, Daniel could only sit on watch, attempting to keep himself from falling asleep.

This was their first true test as a party with Omrak in it and, thus far, Daniel felt things were going well. Sort of. Everyone was short-tempered, and the once talkative Northerner had slowly grown more and more sullen. That actually helped, since Daniel knew that Asin found the constant chatter annoying, so Omrak growing silent helped her not lose her temper. The only downside was that Omrak's temper was somewhat more volatile, but it could be worse.

Eyes half-closed, Daniel blinked as he heard the clink and scrape of movement. He reached for his crossbow, waiting for the noise to resolve itself.

Eventually, the noise faded, and Daniel leaned back, resting once more. It was going to be a long few hours.

"Mmmmpphfff…" Daniel groaned, rolling to his feet. He'd only had a half-hour of rest as it stood, and his head felt worse than before, filled with wool and grit. Still, they could not waste any more time. They needed to complete this level before it reset.

"Coffee?" Omrak offered Daniel the mug as he stood up.

"Thank you." Daniel sipped on the mug and then blinked, staring at the warm mug. He frowned, looking around and not seeing the fire. "How …?"

"Northerner secret," Omrak said, grinning hugely. "Drink up. We should begin."

Daniel glared at how chipper Omrak was but fell silent, deciding to just drink up and enjoy the unexpected luxury. In a few moments the group was packed and on their way back to where they last left off, searching for the way down or the exit.

An hour later, Asin's ears twitched. She held a hand up, calling the group to a stop as she listened to the voices. Frowning, she tapped her ears and then waited for the pitiful humans to finally hear what she did.

Seeing that the Catkin did not seem perturbed, the pair waited patiently. Soon enough, they picked out the voices in conversation before the Crimson Elms came walking out from a side corridor. Leading the group was the short, quiet man from before and, directly behind him, staff held aloft, was the Mage. His staff was glowing red and where the light fell, traps that were hidden glowed.

"Cheating," Asin muttered, and Daniel could only nod. Still, the pair were quick to note where the traps on this corridor were. No reason to not make use of the unexpected bonus.

"Well, look who it is. We heard you might be down here," Amrah said, her eyes dancing over the trio scornfully.

"Heroes," Omrak greeted them with a smile, absently tucking away their map. "Did you just enter?"

"Of course not," Amrah said, snorting, and then raked her eyes over the disheveled group. "Get caught in the change?"

"Yes," Daniel said, stepping forwards as he eyed the other group. "Are you charting your way in?"

"Of course." Amrah smirked. The larger fighter said nothing, just watching the group while the Mage tapped his staff on the ground impatiently.

"Amrah, we should be moving along," Harald said. Amrah glanced at the staff again and nodded, moving to walk pass the group.

Daniel, however, stepped sideways slightly, blocking their way as he cleared his throat. "We were actually hoping you could share your map. It'd help us get out."

Amrah frowned and then glanced to Harald, who shook his head. Daniel grimaced and stepped aside without being asked to. The Crimson Elms moved right past the group, stepping between the Adventurers and, in the shorter fighter's case, brushing against Omrak as he walked past. The party stayed silent, watching them leave, before the group headed down the corridor, skipping past the traps that had been highlighted.

"That's the way out …" Daniel said, pointing to the way the Elms had come from.

"Eventually," Omrak said, rubbing his chin. "Probably."

"Definitely. Though, it'd take a while to get there," Daniel added.

"No, go on," Asin said, pointing down the corridor.

"We've been in here for a while," Daniel said as he surveyed the tired group.

"No. Go on," Asin said, shaking her head. When Daniel started to look mulish, she pointed down the way they came and which the Elms had continued on.

"Bad. Probably." Since they had started from within the Dungeon, there was no guarantee that the way they had not gone was not the way out.

"Bad." She pointed again to where the Elms had come from.

"Good." Asin pointed.

"Hero Asin is correct," Omrak said. "It would be wrong for us to give up now. The Elms have actually reduced the area we must search."

"We are assuming they did their job properly," Daniel muttered. Asin nodded and then pointed again down the corridor.

"Voted."

"Fine," Daniel grumped, shaking his head. It seemed they were going to do or die then. Well, preferably not die.

It was a short five minutes before they reached the next turn. Omrak reached into his pouch and then stopped, groping the leather pouch. He frowned, searching again, and then he pulled it from his belt to turn it inside out.

"Something wrong?" Daniel asked, even as Asin worked on the next corridor on the right.

"The map. It is gone," Omrak said.

"Did you drop it?"

"No. I put it in my pouch," Omrak said slowly. "I drew in the corridor on the right. Just before the Elms arrived."

"The Elms ..." Daniel frowned, his eyes widening. That shorter fighter, he had brushed up against Omrak. "He didn't, did he?"

"I believe the Elms are less than heroic," Omrak said, growling softly. "I do not believe I dropped it."

"Should we …?" Daniel muttered, staring backwards. If they had the map, they would be able to skip to the end where the group had started exploring. Daniel stared up at the map in his head, mentally judging distances. After a few minutes, he swore softly. Assuming they did not have to face any Minotaurs, the Elms could reach the end of the map in two or three hours of straight walking. If they decided to, they would only have to check out the opposite direction that the team had chosen not to explore.

"Damn it," Daniel swore softly. This would give them a huge lead. Of course, the question would be if the staircase was down that way. Or the Elms could wait and backtrack and follow behind Daniel and his team, searching down this part of the maze using the same assumption that Daniel and his team were using to skip the Elm's route.

"Trap," Asin called out.

"Asin, did you hear …?" Daniel said.

"Yes. Trap," Asin reiterated, and pointed downwards before stepping over the trap to check on the next stone.

Omrak stared at the Catkin and then opened his mouth before he shut it. His lips twisted as he stared back to where the Elms had left, before he turned to Daniel, opening his mouth. Daniel on the other hand shook his head, cutting Omrak off. The Northerner growled, but subsided as he realized he was outvoted.

Damn it. But Asin was right—confronting the group would do nothing. Better to focus on what they needed to do.

Blood running down his arm, Omrak roared as he tackled the Minotaur that had cut him. Falling down together, he scrambled up the monster's body, holding its arm down as he began to land punch after punch into its face, knuckles tearing skin and fur. Behind, Asin ducked beneath a strike and lashed out again with her knives, cutting the tendons in the Minotaur's elbow before she lunged forwards, opening the wound wider. Daniel, hunkered beneath his shield, fought his own opponent more carefully, trading strikes.

A short few minutes later, the trio stood victorious staring at the staircase down. They had found it, finally. Not without running into this last batch of monsters.

"Ready?" Daniel asked. Omrak nodded but Asin just stared into space, growling softly to herself as her tail waved lazily.

"Asin?"

"Busy," Asin hissed before continuing to stare into space.

"I believe she has Leveled Up," Omrak offered, and Daniel nodded in belated agreement. Well, they could wait. The pair moved aside to sit down while they waited for Asin to be done. Idly, Omrak took his sword out and began to clean it and, after a moment, Daniel followed his example to care for his own gear.

"I noticed you have a new ability," Daniel said to fill the silence.

"Yes, I gained it last Level," Omrak said. "The Fangs of Zemur."

"You don't use it often."

"It requires significant amounts of Stamina. My father always said to use such abilities sparingly."

"Ah …" Daniel fell silent. "Your father was an Adventurer?"

"No. A farmer."

"Oh …"

"In the North, all are taught to fight. We are not numerous and so all must enter the Dungeons to quell the monsters. My father ventured into many before he gained his name and inherited the land from his father."

"I never really knew mine," Daniel said, feeling a familiar ache in his chest at that thought.

"My condolences."

"It's fine," Daniel said before he fell silent. Omrak, sensing the mood that Daniel was in, focused on caring for his blade. After a time, Asin finally nodded to herself. The pair stood up, walking to her.

"What did you get?" Daniel asked curiously.

"Serpent's Tooth," Asin said. "Poison."

"Oh …" Daniel frowned. He was not entirely sure he liked that answer. Poison could be helpful, but if one of them got injured by it, it could make things more difficult. He certainly had no spell to cure poison. Still, it did shore up one of Asin's major weaknesses, which was her inability to inflict significant amount of damage. At least, he thought so.

"Well, we good to go?" Daniel asked, and after receiving the confirming nods, the trio trooped down the stairs. Finally, they would be able to exit this level and the Dungeon. Best of all—this left them in the lead again.

Chapter 15

"Three more floors at most," Khy'ra said, smiling softly at her boyfriend. He lay lounging on the bed, holding her hand as she sat next to him.

"That's right," Daniel said.

"Do you know what you're going to do when you're done? There's a lot more Advanced Dungeons and a few Beginner ones close by too."

"Mmmm … I was thinking that Peel might be good to finish. It shouldn't be too hard, and we know about it already," Daniel said. "I haven't spoken to Asin or Omrak about their plans."

"Always good to ask your party members," Khy'ra chuckled.

"I don't know if Asin would come with us, though," Daniel said, grimacing. Omrak, Daniel was pretty certain would be happy to come.

"The school?"

"You know?" Daniel asked, surprised. After a brief moment's consideration, Daniel realized that of course the Elf would know. Khy'ra was an important part of the city and spoke with a wide range of citizens everyday. "It's important to her. And if she left …"

"There wouldn't be anyone helping out," Khy'ra finished for him.

"She wasn't doing this before, was she?" Daniel said, and Khy'ra shook her head.

"The Council cut the budget when the Dungeon was closed. Said they couldn't afford it anymore."

"But the Dungeon's open again."

"Oh Daniel." Khy'ra smiled softly at her boyfriend. "It's never that easy. They've been wanting to cut it for ages. This was just an excuse."

"Is there … is there anything I can do?"

To this, Daniel received a quick kiss on the head. "If I think of anything …"

"Tell me," Daniel said. He knew Asin had told him not to get involved, but this seemed so unfair. However, he could think of nothing that he could do—he did not even know where to start to help. A city budget was not something you could hit or delve. And contributing to the school, well, it was a short-term solution.

A day later, the group found themselves on level eight, staring at a familiar vista. The trio glanced at one a nother before laughing, walking forwards into the large caverns. As Daniel stared at the map in his head, he laughed softly. This was literally the same level eight as before the Dungeon had changed its configuration.

Feeling more relaxed, Daniel directed the group down to where they last left off and the staircase to the ninth level, glad to finally be on familiar ground once again.

With a grace that belied his stature, Omrak ducked beneath the Ogre's club and swung his sword in a short horizontal strike that ended in the monster's knee. Twisting his blade, the Northerner ripped it upwards, opening a wider wound on the creature's thigh. Using the impetus of standing, Omrak kicked forwards and sent the injured Ogre sprawling backwards before he reset himself for his next opponent.

"Should we help him?" Daniel asked, having dispatched his own Ogre.

Asin shook her head, squatting on the corpse of the Ogre she had stabbed in the eyes. The giant Northerner had rushed forwards to meet the first group of six ogres on his lonesome, wielding his sword and screaming with battlelust. Omrak had dispatched the first Ogre with his new Skill before he was bogged down fighting the others. It was only the arrival of the pair that stopped him from being flanked. Omrak, however, did not seem intent on sharing the last three monsters at all, wide strikes and frenzied darting ensuring neither Adventurer could close in and aid him safely.

Not that he needed it. Daniel winced as Omrak lopped off a hand and then, on the return cut, opened up the Ogre's stomach. The Northerner seemed to revel in the open space and monstrous opponents, wielding his sword with wild abandon. The incidental wounds he picked up just added to the strength of his attacks. In truth, this was a horrible match for the Dungeon. Not only did the wide-open caverns that made up the Ogre floor allow Daniel to use his plate armor and crossbow to full effect, the numerous monsters allowed Omrak to unleash the full range of his fighting style. Even Asin, with her new Skill, could contribute to the fight. The group was tearing through the floor like Asin's chili and Omrak's guts.

That evening, when the trio emerged, they did so with smiles on their faces. Not only had the party cleared the Ogres without a problem, the Mana Stones each of the Ogres dropped was of good value and as frequent as the attacks. They had even inadvertently managed to stumble upon the Ogre Champion and the floor chest, a battle that had ended with Daniel spending nearly half his Mana patching up the stubborn Northerner, who had traded blows with the Champion till one fell. It was quite apparent to Daniel that the group had grown stronger during their time through the new Dungeon. The fact that they knew what traps, what terrain, and what tactics to expect had made the floor so much simpler than their previous experience on this floor. In addition, Daniel could not help but smile at the fact that he had now reached Level 9.

In a good mood, the party tramped into the Adventurers' Guild to drop their day's earnings off with Liev.

"Good day?" Liev asked, noticing the smiling group. Quick nods from all three made him return the smile before he sobered up. He hated to tell them this, but it had to be done.

"The Crimson Elms were just in. They've cleared the eighth floor too."

The trio stared at Liev, their good mood suddenly deflated.

"How?" Daniel said.

"It's not a hard floor," Liev said, lips twisting slightly. "No puzzles, no difficult traps, no mazes. And they bought the map to it since the layout didn't change at all."

"Oh …" Daniel groaned and rubbed his temples. There were only two floors left that were possible and the last floor might just be a Boss Monster.

Asin growled, tugging on Daniel's arm. She pointed back the way they came to the Dungeon entrance. Daniel shook his head automatically, already mentally assessing his Mana stores and the weariness in his body.

"No, Asin," Daniel said. "I just used most of my Mana healing us before we came up. There's daring and then there's reckless. This is reckless."

Omrak watched the pair argue, his hand absently stroking the hilt of his pommel.

"Quest," Asin said, her tail lashing out behind her.

"It's a whole floor. Maybe two. We've never fought a Dungeon Boss either, Asin," Daniel growled, shaking his head. "No. It's too dangerous."

"Try," Asin said again, pointing.

"No," Daniel said.

Omrak, watching the two, cleared his throat. "Perhaps, Heroes, I might offer a suggestion."

Daniel and Asin both shot a glare at the youngster before they paused, remembering that he was a part of the party. Daniel nodded jerkily and Omrak smiled at the two.

"Let us rest for a few hours. Tomorrow at dawn, we can begin and not leave till we complete the quest. It will give Hero Daniel time to recover his Mana and us to gather what supplies we need," Omrak said.

"That's …" Daniel began and then stopped, shrugging. "That's reasonable."

Asin growled, looking unhappy, but she finally nodded.

"Liev, can we use our earnings to purchase some of the Healing potions the Guild stocks?" Daniel asked.

"Of course," the redheaded attendant said, smiling slightly at the group as he busied himself with sorting the last of the stones.

"Also, there's something strange about the ninth floor," Daniel said, lowering his floor. "Tell me what you think about this …"

The ninth-floor annex looked like every other annex they had seen thus far, a simple carved stone room illuminated by Mana-imbued stone. Daniel hefted his mace, rolling his shoulders as he banished his doubts concerning their plan. If they pushed through on this floor, perhaps they had a chance to win the quest rewards. Waking up early in the morning, packing for a multiple-day delve, this was the last roll of the die for them.

When the group stepped out, familiar underground cave corridors awaited them. The corridors and caverns were a mix of natural and sentient carved surfaces that sprawled outwards, passages and exits leading not only from ground level but ten or twenty feet up, all illuminated by the lightest of Mana-imbuing. Some of the exits were blocked by familiar grey- and brown-colored walls, while the slightly acrid smell of Ixillian Crawlers' chemically altered saliva permeated the air.

"Remember, they're likely to be just the harassers," Daniel muttered, staring at the walls. It was the only explanation that Liev could come up with, that the

Crawlers were being reused to provide cover for something more dangerous. Daniel sighed, shifting slightly in his leather armor as he committed the room to memory. Knowing what they were walking into, he had downgraded to his lighter and less bulky armor for the most part. Sadly, his enchanted bracers had been sold, leaving him wearing his iron bracers. Still, at least this way he was less likely to get stuck.

"Let us begin," Omrak growled, shifting his backpack to settle more comfortably behind him.

With a nod, Asin led the way, choosing one of the initially larger passages. Past experience had told them to be wary of traps on these levels, so leaving the Catkin to lead was the smart choice. Past experience had also indicated that what started out as a large passageway might easily become something a lot smaller.

It was a bare five minutes before they encountered their first monster. It oozed from a cavern ceiling as they walked, landing with a splash on top of Daniel. Immediately, the slime's acidic body began to eat into Daniel's armor, its body flowing around his protection to burn his skin. Daniel's shout of surprise was enough to warn the other two, which allowed Asin's quick reactions to dodge another falling monster. Omrak was not as lucky, the creature having missed the Northerner's torso but still managing to wrap a flailing appendage around his thigh. Unlike Daniel's, Omrak's began to let loose a series of light shocks, making the big Adventurer's thigh muscles clench and release.

Daniel swiped at the slime on his shoulder, his gloved hand brushing through the monster and doing no damage. He frantically tried again as the creature burned through his flesh, setting his nerves alight. Omrak, knife in hand, swiped at the main body of the creature attacking him with as little success. It was only Asin who managed to hurt her opponent. A thrown blade passed through a slime body, sending sparks of electricity shooting through it. Left behind by the blade were traces of poison that began to discolor the purple gelatinous monster, tendrils of green creeping deeper and deeper through the gelatinous body. The purple monster shook and shuddered at the attack, lurching forwards in its attempt to attack the Catkin.

Daniel saw none of that, his focus on the monster on his shoulder. As he swiped again at the creature, something caught his eye. A small, floating blue stone within the creature. Inspiration struck and on his next attack, he reached out and grabbed the stone that attempted to float aside. Too close and too spread out on his body to get away, the stone was easily grasped and pulled from the slime. In a moment, the entire slime's body broke apart without its core, falling away from Daniel's body.

"The stones. Destroy the stones!" Daniel shouted in relief.

Heeding Daniel's advice, Omrak attacked the slime's glowing core. Unlike Daniel's, though, this monster had only laid a few tendrils on the Northerner and, as such, was better able to dodge and shift its stone. Eventually, Omrak landed a blow that shattered the stone and ended the monster.

"Bad. Destroy stone," Asin muttered, pointing at Omrak's. Her own slime had expired from the poison and repeated shocks shortly before Omrak's.

"It was killing me," hissed Omrak.

"Yes. Not dead, good," Asin said, and pointed to the stones. "Less coin, bad."

Daniel ignored the pair arguing, his hand on his own shoulder as he cast his Healer's Mark on himself. Silently, he assessed the damage with his Gift and hissed at the results. In the short battle, the acid slime had eaten not only through his skin but into some of the underlying muscle and nerves itself. Daniel gritted his teeth and focused, healing nerves and muscles before stopping. Better to let the spell finish the job.

"Slimes," Daniel said finally, rejoining the conversation that had finally stalled between the other two Adventurers. "Is there another way to kill them?"

"Poison. Electricity," Asin said.

"Neither of which Omrak or I have," Daniel pointed out.

"Fire?" Omrak said, touching his backpack. "I have torches."

"Wet." Asin pointed to where the slime had been, the body having dispersed.

"True, but we might as well try it," Daniel said, nodding to Omrak, who was already pulling out a torch from his backpack. At least with his mace, he had a better chance of hitting the stone than Omrak with his knife or sword. When Omrak had the torch lit, Daniel jerked his head to Asin and the group started off. Now that they knew what to expect, the imposing ninth floor seemed less threatening. Dangerous, lethal, but less threatening.

Fire worked. Sort of. It was not a strong weapon—a torch thrust at a slime could burn it, hurt it, but you also risked the torch being extinguished. Omrak soon learnt that it was actually better for him to almost hit a slime, to keep the torch close to the body and let the heat that emanated from the torch do its job, rather than stabbing it in like a sword. It was not perfect; it was in fact nearly as ineffective as using his bladed weapons. Nearly.

At least they were not fighting a fire slime. Exploration over the last few hours had made it clear that there were a multitude of different forms of slime present on the ninth level. Each carried its own danger—fire slimes spat out flaming portions of its body that refused to die off and exploded upon death. Earth slimes carried numerous rocks within their body, giving the slime the potential to strike and defend itself from Daniel's mace. Air slimes no longer crawled, spread, or glooped their way, but floated through the air in an attempt to enclose and suffocate.

And of course, the Crawlers made their presence known, sometimes at the most inopportune times. Armored carapaces that crawled through the Dungeons, walling off sections and attacking with little care for their lives. They were not deadly if taken on alone, but when combined with the slimes which were resistant to most normal attacks, had proven a dangerous combination.

Daniel shook his head as he surveyed the surroundings while Asin explored the cavern they had exited into. The Catkin as always was checking for new traps, though thus far, there were none but the usual pitfalls, which were easy enough to avoid. Behind, Daniel could hear pained grunts as Omrak pulled himself along the final narrow passageway. For some reason, the Crawlers never finished sealing the passages, leaving the Adventurers a small but tight exit. Tight enough that the large Northerner was finding it difficult to squirm his way out.

"Do you need help?" Daniel said for the third time.

"I shall manage, Hero," Omrak grunted out, his voice strained.

"Okay then." Daniel fell silent again, letting his gaze roam over the surroundings, wary of another attack. The slimes did not wait around like other monsters, roaming from cavern to cavern and seeming to prefer ambushes rather than straight fights. With their gelatinous bodies, they could squirm through the smallest cracks and appear without warning.

"Aaaarrrgghhh …" Omrak roared as he shoved his arm and shoulder through the gap and grasped a convenient stalagmite. Gripping it tight, he pulled his body again, wide shoulders stuck on the edges. His shirt, abused once too often, tore, and the Northerner found himself swearing.

Daniel, his attention drawn to the partially exited giant, never saw the swarm of Air Slimes float down from a passageway high up in the ceiling. They made no sound as they controlled the winds around them, the group of five slimes splitting off with one going after Omrak and two others for the free pair.

It was only the shift in air currents that gave Daniel a fraction of a moment's warning. He shifted to the side, shield rising and bashing the slime away. He jumped back quickly as the second slime swooped in on him and then raised his shield up to Bash it. He surged forwards and his shield smashed the slime backwards, sending the gelatinous blob to smack into a cavern wall. That dealt with, Daniel spun around, only to have to throw himself backwards in an ungraceful sprawl as the monster attempted to land on his face again.

Asin, on the other hand, took a more direct route, sprinting around the cavern and throwing her knives at the monsters. Each attack sent dancing sparks of electricity and purple streaks of poison, injuring the monsters that attempted to catch the elusive Catkin. As she darted right past Daniel, she swiped a clawed hand at the monster that attacked him and then sprinted to where Omrak, unable to protect himself, was struggling against his own slime. Caught unawares, the slime had engulfed his face and pushed a part of itself down his mouth before he could stop it.

Daniel snarled, ducking under another swoop by the slime that attacked him before he spun and lashed out with his mace. It caught and ripped a glob off it, missing the all-important core however. Dancing to the side again, Daniel was forced to bob and weave as he attempted to hit the core again and again.

The fast-moving, darting monsters were hard to hit as they attempted to land on the Adventurers. Forced to duck and swipe, it was Asin's slimes that finally expired first from repeated exposures to lightning and poison. The Catkin paused, scanning the surroundings, and snarled, seeing that Omrak was no longer struggling. She darted over, claws appearing in her hands as she scrabbled around the slime, before finally succeeding at pulling the core out. Almost immediately, the slime dissolved, but Omrak did not move.

Asin snarled and slapped the big Adventurer in the face. Omrak did not react at all and the Catkin spun, already calling for Daniel. Daniel Bashed his last slime with his shield, this time managing to force its core from its body, killing it. Freed, Daniel looked to Asin and then Omrak, his eyes widening.

The healer darted forwards, a hand outstretched to touch the large Adventurer's still body. The moment contact was made, he sent his Gift into Omrak's body. Lips tense, he noted that the large Northerner was no longer breathing, though his heart still beat. Only a single surge of power was needed before Omrak gasped out loud, his body forced to breathe again.

Asin let out a held breath, her tail waving again as Omrak hacked and coughed. Daniel reached forwards and, gripping Omrak's upper body, ripped him from the opening. The large Northerner screamed as the ragged edges of the passageway tore his clothing and skin apart. Daniel unapologetically bent down, laying a Healer's Mark on the large Northerner before he turned back to scan for more trouble. The big Adventurer just curled up, hacking and coughing as he regained control of his body.

As Omrak slowly recovered, Daniel shifted his gaze to the Northerner every once in a while. That was too damn close.

Chapter 16

Hours of crawling, walking and climbing had left the group no closer to finding the exit. The ninth floor sprawled, with each cavern having multiple exits at any one time. Each of those exits, no matter how small, had to be verified and checked. And through all this, the party had to be wary of the slimes that could appear at any time, or the Crawlers that traversed the caverns.

One concern that Daniel held close to his chest was the potential that the Crawlers had blocked the staircase down, ensuring that the group would be unable to find the exit. It was a minor concern since they would eventually map the entire location and, if necessary, they could backtrack. The greater concern was that eventually the Elms would be here too, searching.

"Hold," Omrak said as he scrambled around in his pack to find another torch. Whenever they could, the group had used bigger passageways, if for no other reason than to not waste time as Omrak relit his torch. In the end, they had begun sending Asin ahead on smaller passageways to allow her to scout them out. It saved them time, especially as many of these passageways were found to be connected to another, previously explored location, or one that could be accessed more easily.

"Sure," Daniel said, settling in to watch for slimes. Asin ignored the command as she looked for additional passages. It was, after all, her role in the group.

"I disliked this section before," Omrak said, looking around the dimly lit location. The torch did little to increase the illumination in the caverns, instead layering slightly brighter spots over less illuminated areas. "It has not improved."

"These slimes are tough," Daniel said, shaking his head. "I regret giving up my bracers."

"Enchanted weaponry would be useful. My brother has an enchanted knife, one that burns with a flameless heat," Omrak said. "It would be useful here."

"Or a shovel," Daniel said. "Something to scoop the stones out."

"A shovel …" Omrak rubbed his chin and then laughed. "That would work. Pity I did not bring one."

"Looks like she's ready." Daniel nodded up to Asin, who was waving them to her. "Time to get going."

"Yes." Omrak stepped forwards and then paused, clapping Daniel on the shoulder. "Thank you."

Daniel just nodded, embarrassed by the thanks. Chuckling, the Northerner walked forwards and ducked low as he got ready to squeeze into another too-tight passage.

Late that evening, the group had finally called it a day. They had covered a lot of ground but still had not found the exit. After careful scouting, Asin had determined that there were only a couple of entrances in the cavern they squatted in, giving them their best chance of a peaceful night's rest.

Not that they expected a good rest. It was clear that this floor was extremely busy with the slimes and Crawlers, ensuring that the group constantly had to be on watch. They would definitely have to rest in rotating watches.

"Should we go back?" Omrak asked, chewing on his dinner of dried beef jerky and bread.

"Why?" Asin asked.

"Both Daniel and I struggle with the slimes. It is only your Skills that have given us an edge. With appropriate equipment, we could travel faster," Omrak answered. Daniel stayed silent, content to let the two argue.

"How much? Map," Asin asked, turning to Daniel.

"Maybe half?" Daniel said. It was hard to tell, what with the sprawling passages that could cut off without warning.

"No," Asin said, shaking her head.

"Why?" Omrak growled. "Each fight is a risk for Daniel and me. It would be better for us to fight at full strength."

"One day. Half. Back. Half-day. No. Race," Asin explained, tail lashing out behind her angrily. After she was done, she rubbed at her throat. Talking so much always hurt.

Omrak just stared at Asin, confusion on his face, before looking to Daniel. He sighed and explained, "It's a half-day to get back. Then we're a half-day back in to where we are and maybe, we'd be faster. Probably. But it takes us only a day to finish half, so we only need a day to finish. That about right Asin?"

She nodded and then added one last word: "Race."

"Right, and we're in a race," Daniel said.

"You agree with her?" Omrak said, looking to the shorter Adventurer.

"I think … yes. I think we should push ahead. That was the plan," Daniel replied.

"Very well," Omrak conceded, looking somewhat annoyed but accepting. "I shall take first watch."

Daniel just nodded. He would take mid-watch. His Gift let him last longer than the other two after all. Even a few hours' sleep would help them all, fitful and split as it might be.

Sleep that evening had been less than restful. The group had stumbled awake twice, fighting off the intrusion of a Crawler and then a group of slimes. Even then, the catnaps they had managed to catch had refreshed the group sufficiently enough that they were able to start exploring in the early hours of the morning. Now, in the midafternoon, the group were crouched, staring down at the enormous cavern laid out before them.

"What is that?" hissed Daniel as he stared at the green gelatinous cube that dominated the cavern before them. Unlike the other slimes, which were often only a foot or so across, this one was nearly six feet wide. It would be a simple matter for a creature that big to swallow an Adventurer whole.

"Big slime," Asin said, running a finger along a knife. Eyes narrowed, she searched for signs of the Mana Stone within its body. If they could destroy it, that would end the fight no matter how big the slime was.

"It must be the floor Champion," Omrak rumbled quietly.

"Definitely," Daniel confirmed, shaking his head as he considered his attack options. Shield Bash would do nothing to the monster, other than perhaps displacing some of its body. Neither Perin's Blow nor Double Strike would injure it, and his latest Skill Proficiency was not an active weapon. He could see where the Mana Stones were, but it did little good when the stones were embedded so deeply in the monster's body.

"I fear I would be of little use here," Omrak said, having done his own assessment as well. It would take a lot of torches to injure it and they just did not have the time.

"Around?" Asin pointed backwards and the group grimaced. One thing they had noticed with the new Dungeon layout was that often the staircase was situated very close to the Champions. It was a change from previous layouts and could potentially be just a matter of the lack of Adventurers sending the Champions to spawn again. In either case, the chances were that the staircase was near here—potentially just past the Floor Champion.

"Probably for the best," Daniel muttered at last. Omrak nodded and the group quietly creeped backwards. No sense in attempting a fight where two thirds of the group could do little to it. Still, Daniel pondered what they could do with what they had. Surely there was a way to win that fight.

Hours later, the group found themselves collected once more near the entrance to the Champion's chamber. Thus far, they had not seen sight nor sound of the Crimson Elms. Considering the size of the cavern, that meant very little. Still, the party held a little hope that they were still ahead of the Elms. Having explored the gaps in the maps in Daniel's mind, they now found themselves back where they started hours ago.

"Any ideas?" Daniel asked, staring at the chamber.

"I fight. Poison. Run," Asin said.

"That seems foolhardy," Omrak pointed out. "I would not agree to that."

"I have to agree. Your Skills might be the most effective, but it still takes a while for the slimes to die. Something that big …" Daniel said, shaking his head. "Going in alone is a bad idea."

Asin growled but just nodded, her tail lashing out behind her. She turned to stare at the pair, waiting to see if they had any other ideas.

"I was thinking …" Daniel started, and then stopped. A part of him seriously did not like the idea he was about to suggest. Old training, old habits, said it was a bad idea. Still, it was the only one that he could think of. At his friend's encouraging nods, he finally gives voice to his thoughts. "We could use oil. Douse it in the oil flasks we have left, set it on fire."

Omrak hummed, rubbing his chin in thought. "It is big enough. Though, such a large monster on fire …"

Daniel could see it in his mind's eye. A flaming cube that rolled around the cavern, setting everything it touched on fire. Worse, he knew that too much fire could potentially be dangerous for them—creating bad air that could hurt, maybe even kill the group. It was always a concern in real mines—though how it worked in a Dungeon, Daniel did not know. His little experience with the Dungeons indicated that they did not act the same way mines did, that concerns like bad air and buildup of dangerous gasses did not occur. Still…

"Idea?" Asin said, prodding Omrak, who shook his head. At that, Asin pointed to Daniel and finished the conversation. "Oil."

Saying it and doing it were two different things. The party quickly laid out their plans, divvying up the bottles and the last of the torches between Daniel and Omrak. They would be in charge of throwing and lighting the monster on fire. Asin would creep into the room first and begin the attack, using her blades to damage and poison the monster immediately. Once the monster was focused on her, the pair would throw their oil flasks and hopefully set it on fire before retreating as Asin attacked it again.

At first, the entire plan went well. Asin's attacks left streaks of purple poison that slowly spread through the slime, injuring it. Interestingly enough, her knives never left the body of the creature, instead held and caught in the viscous liquid that was its body. The oil flasks, thrown at the monster, shattered, spreading its contents on the creature. Or in one case, was swallowed entirely. When the pair managed to stab the slime with their torches, it lit the flames and sent shudders through the Jell-O body.

What they did not expect was the way the monster then proceeded to swallow the majority of the flames into its body, extinguishing them within its core. So surprised were they that the pair nearly did not move away in time when the monster charged them, flames still licking along its surface. Scrambling backwards, the pair split up as they rounded a particularly wide stalagmite.

Behind, Asin hissed in anger as her poisoned and aura-enchanted blades continued to fly true and were ignored. She targeted all across the slime's body, determined to spread the poison faster as the monster kept its core away from her. Yet, nothing she did seemed to draw the monster's attention as it darted towards Daniel.

Daniel scurried away, trying to circle around the cavern, and give time for Asin and Omrak to continue their attacks. Omrak pulled his last flask from a pouch, throwing it at the monster. The oil relit on the dying flames on the surface of the slime's body, sending the slime shuddering as it started to twist its body inside out. Bereft of oil, Omrak pulled out his sword and targeted the edges of the creature, lopping off pieces. The shorter Adventurer darted in, using the edges of his shield to scoop out parts from the body as well. If they could not kill it with fire, they would have to do it the hard way.

Focused on attacking the monster, Daniel did not notice that the slime was no longer shuddering but rearing a portion of its body straight up. With a sploosh, the entire stretched cube fell on Daniel, engulfing him in the viscous fluid. Almost immediately, Daniel could feel the acidic properties of the slime start acting on his skin, attempting to eat away at his body.

Pain immediately filled his existence. The slime attacked his bare skin and slowly penetrated between his armor and clothing, burning layers of skin. Worse, it attacked his eyes, ears, and nose as it attempted to invade his body. Mouth closed, Daniel reached out to clamp a hand over his nose and squeeze it shut. As his body burned, Daniel attempted to focus to cast a spell, but pain robbed him of his concentration. Trapped in his body, Daniel could only squirm and thrash as the monster ate away at his body.

Omrak snarled in surprise, his sword flashing again and again as he carved bits of the monster. Asin dashed forwards as well, pulling her larger melee knives from her sheaths before she began slicing into the monster, dodging side to side after each strike. Each attack left streaks of purple in its body and sparks of electricity that fried and stilled the portions contacted. Yet, each of their attacks still did little to reduce the large slime that continued to strip the skin from Daniel's body.

Screaming in muted pain, his mouth clamped shut, Daniel reached inwards. He found his Gift, waiting as always for him. With a thought, Daniel released the

Gift through his body and focused it on his senses, which were slowly being eaten away, patching his eyes and ears together even as he felt his memories disappear. His free hand continued to thrash about, trying to grip something, anything.

Seeing that his attacks were doing little, Omrak dodged to the side again and thrust his sword forwards. The blade plunged into the monster, piercing through gelatinous flesh all the way into Daniel's own body. In the beginning, the pain from being impaled was hidden beneath the cascade of other pain signals, but as Daniel's body thrashed around again, he finally noticed the shard of steel in his body. His free hand reached out and gripped the blade reflexively and then Omrak pulled the blade backwards. Daniel, his mind clouded, felt himself drawn forwards and gambled as he reached to grip the giant sword with both hands. Seeing that Daniel had a better grip now, Omrak tugged harder, drawing the Adventurer out of the body.

At first the slime did not notice their motions, focused as it was on the danger that Asin posed. However, as Daniel began to move through its body more quickly, the slime shifted, pulling its body to recover the beleaguered Adventurer. In doing so, the slime shifted its Mana core closer to the Catkin.

Asin snarled and lunged forwards, plunging her hand into the body up to her shoulder. The slime shuddered, its body trembling as the arcs of electricity that surrounded Asin's aura interacted with its body, injuring it. The slime stunned for a second, Asin was able to grasp the stone and yank backwards, extracting it finally from the slime.

Daniel, partially pulled outwards, fell to the ground as the monster exploded, its body no longer held together by the Mana Stone. Almost immediately, the slime's body began to disperse, leaving the stripped, partially digested body of the Adventurer on the floor. His Gift, running on automatic, patched his body together, replacing skin and muscle, repairing his eyes and ears. After a few minutes, Daniel was able to grasp hold of his senses and stop his Gift, using his Mana to cast a Healer's Mark on his own body.

Only when Daniel sat up did Asin come over, her own arm burnt and damaged from her attack. Daniel placed a healing on it too before he looked to Omrak, his eyes still blurry. For a moment, Daniel attempted to find the Northerner, and it was only Asin's guidance that he saw the blond Adventurer in the corner, throwing up.

Daniel tried to speak and coughed, his voice raw. He swallowed a few more times, casting a Minor Healing on himself before he could do so. "Is he okay?"

"Bad. No skin," Asin said, pointing to Daniel.

"Oh …" Daniel said. He began to think back to what had happened and flinched mentally as his mind refused to return to those dire minutes.

"Okay?" Asin asked softly, placing a hand on his shoulder.

"I … I will be," Daniel said finally as he sat up. As he raised a hand to brush his hair back, Daniel stared at the uncontrolled shaking in it. Perhaps he was more injured than he thought.

Finding the staircase down after Daniel had recovered only took them a few more hours. Before they had left, they had a spirited discussion on whether to go on. In the end, it was Daniel's insistence that they finish this—or at least, learn what the last floor was like—that drove them on. Injured, tired, and mentally scarred or not, they were nearly done.

As always, the annex for the tenth floor was a plain, bare room. The trio slowly stared around them, eyeing the simple wooden door that blocked the way in.

"Ready?" Daniel asked, a tightness in his chest as he stared at what might wait for them. This was it. One last floor, one last Boss. And then they would be done.

Asin just yowled while Omrak nodded. It was time to check out the last floor.

Chapter 17

The room that the three of them walked into was circular in design, reminiscent of an ancient colosseum. Clean brown sand, a wide-open sky and walls that were over ten feet high that led to a stand. The trio clumped together as they walked in, eyeing the empty stretch of sand.

"What is this?" Daniel muttered.

Asin shook her head, her tail lashing out behind her as she stalked forwards with an eye on the ground. The creaking of wooden winch made all three look up, staring as the gate ahead of them slowly opened. Out from the gate came a trundling boar that was over twenty feet tall, hairy bristles and long tusks snorting. Immediately on spotting the party, it rushed them, picking up speed as the three scattered, Asin to the far right and Omrak to Daniel's left.

"Why me?" Daniel cried out as he realized that the monster was charging him. It wasn't particularly surprising, since he was in the middle but Daniel could not help but feel somewhat prosecuted. Having realized he couldn't get away, Daniel hunkered down beneath his shield and reinforced the shield with his other hand, breathing slowly as he timed his counterattack.

With a roar, Daniel countercharged the monster and engaged his Shield Bash. The boar smashed him backwards, not even pausing as Daniel's attack connected and cracked his shield and a tusk at the same time. The Adventurer was thrown backwards, flying through the air to impact the wall and crash to the ground. The boar swerved away, ignoring the fallen Adventurer.

Omrak, having seen that he was not targeted, had charged back to the monster and, as it began its turn, swung his sword. Skin parted as the muscle was torn apart by the blade, ripping a deep gash on the boar's flank. As the boar finished its turn and charged towards Asin, Omrak dashed forwards to the slowly moving Daniel.

Asin snarled, running backwards as she threw another series of knives at the monster. Each of her attacks barely pricked the boar, its tough hide stronger than armor. Only a Piercing Shot had thus far managed to penetrate its body. Still, the Catkin did not give up as she sprinted to the wall as the monster bore down on her.

It was only a few seconds before it hit her that Asin jumped, claws extended as she sprawled against the wall and held on to it. The boar, unwilling to smash directly into the wall, was forced to swerve at the last second, only its tail brushing against Asin. Even that was enough to rip her away from the wall and leave a quickly blossoming bruise.

Spluttering, Daniel pushed himself upwards as Omrak put the waterskin away. Already the Northerner was moving away from Daniel, sword raised as the boar targeted him. He crouched low, sword held near his knee as he waited for the monster to arrive. Snorting and growling, the boar picked up speed as it closed in on Omrak.

Daniel pushed to his feet just as the boar collided with Omrak. Sword held low and pommel dug into the ground, the large Adventurer had used his large sword as an improvised spear and impaled the Boss monster on it. Thrown backwards from the impact, Omrak hit the wall and bounced off it before being trod upon by the boar's back foot.

Dashing over, Daniel placed a hand on Omrak's shoulder even as the big Adventurer struggled to his feet. Concentrating, Daniel laid Healer's Mark on his friend and then Minor Healing, before he turned to search for the Boss. Asin, having run back, threw her bolas at the creature's leg in a vain attempt to trip the monster. The bolas caught but were so stretched out, they ripped apart without slowing the monster down. Thankfully, instead of directing itself at any single

Adventurer, the board dashed to the other side of the arena as it built up speed again.

"You okay, Asin?" Daniel called out as she neared, placing Healer's Mark on her the moment she was within reach. It would help a little bit but for the most part, Daniel looked to conserve the remainder of his Mana for when it was going to be really needed.

Asin pulled another pair of throwing knives into her hand from her backpack, staring at the boar that had just turned around. Growling softly, the Catkin took off at an angled run, already throwing her knives at it, using Piercing Shot to help cover the distance.

"Crossbow," Omrak suggested as he stood up, searching for his sword. He spotted it a moment later, still embedded in the monster's body. The Northerner reached for his knife, taking off running, while Daniel sheathed his sword and reached for his slung crossbow.

A brief inspection showed that it was still working, if worse for wear. Quickly, Daniel cranked the crossbow back and pulled a bolt out before he tossed it away and reached for an unbroken one. The crossbow might have survived Daniel being thrown around, but it seemed that some of his bolts had not. Finally loaded, Daniel swung the crossbow back up to target the charging boar. At least, Daniel thought, even he could not miss a monster the size of a barn.

The boar had turned again and somehow, between the time that Daniel was loading his weapon and the last time he saw her, Asin had managed to mount the creature. Crouched above the monster, lightning arcs shooting as the monster contacted her body, the Catkin stabbed and cut with her weapons as she attempted to flay the monster alive.

Beneath her, the boar charged the Northerner, who stood, crouched and waiting. At the last moment, Omrak threw himself forwards, grabbing his sword and rolling to the side at the same time. The sword slid sideways as the opposing forces of the roll and charge tore open the wound, forcing a cascade of blood to pour out.

Daniel exhaled, firing his crossbow, and then reloaded immediately even as the creature turned, attempting to come around and attack the beleaguered, blond Adventurer. Omrak, clipped by a hoof, struggled to his feet, his sword behind him as the boar finally slowed down and turned to attack, only to receive another crossbow bolt in its face. It snorted and squealed but stayed on task as it moved to gore Omrak.

Omrak in turn swung and cut at the creature's nose, forcing the monster to be wary of his attacks. No longer charging, the monster did not have the impetus of its momentum to bowl over the large Northerner and so they feinted with sword and tusk. All the while, Daniel and Asin continued to attack it.

"It's slowing down!" Daniel said as he dropped in another bolt. The successive attacks and blood loss was taking its toll along with the continued presence of the enchanted Catkin above and her poisoned weapons. Strong and powerful as the boar was, it could only take so much damage.

Ducking a swipe with one tusk, Omrak stood and lunged forwards, blade sinking into a cheek before he attempted to tear the blade free. However, unbeknownst to Omrak, his sword was stuck between some teeth which caused his motion to grind to a stop. In that brief moment, the boar twisted its head again to lash out with its remaining tusk. Omrak was thrown to the side, his back torn wide open.

Daniel shouted out loud in the vain hope of attracting the monster's attention as he ran forwards, holding the crossbow up to his body as he closed the distance to his fallen friend. Closer now, he raised the weapon and, working on intuition, pulled the trigger and sent the bolt flying to embed in the boar's eye. The monster snorted and jerked reflexively as it was blinded, having missed Omrak's prone form by inches as it slammed into the wall.

Asin was thrown to the side by the impact, unseated from the top of the monster but the Catkin hung on grimly as she plunged her knife once again into the monster's body. Even now, she could see the slow spreading of the poison. All they needed to do was wait and her Skill would kill it.

Bent over Omrak, Daniel swiftly cast his Minor Healing spell once and then again before he surged to his feet. Hefting his remaining weapon, Daniel got ready to do battle with the Boss. Crouched low, he grimaced as a sharp pain in his lower back shot up his spine. He shook his head, focusing on the monster, and decided to try Perin's Blow as the monster lunged forwards. Tusk smashed backwards, the boar growled and flicked its head, its mane flowing out behind it. While the monster was dazed, Daniel lashed out with his mace, beating on the monster's snout and pulping it, sending the monster into a rage.

As Daniel attracted the monster's attention in front, Omrak staggered to the side, his body leaking red light. He roared as he reared back, sword held in hand, then he swung downwards, shearing through the boar's front right leg. As the boar collapsed, Asin threw herself off, rolling and rolling before struggling to her feet and spitting to clear her mouth of sand.

The trio quickly backed off from the crippled Boss. Daniel sagged to the ground as the injuries to his body finally caught up to him. Beside him, Omrak roared as the red light continued to glow from his body, while Asin hastened the monster's death by tossing the last few of her knives.

Enraged and stubborn, the boar pulled itself along the ground, inching towards Omrak, who stood, waiting. When it was finally in range, the large Northerner stabbed his sword into its eye, driving the blade all the way into the brain. A last, shuddering jerk sent Omrak flying one last time before the monster died.

"Daniel?" Asin said, walking over to her friend. The short Adventurer waved her away, slanted eyes tightening in pain as he waited for the Healer's Mark he had placed on himself to do its job. It would not heal him fully, but it was all that he could do.

Omrak, curled up on his side, was unconscious when Asin managed to make her way to him. She prodded him a few times before she gave up, sitting down to watch over her friends as they recovered.

Chapter 18

A half-hour later, Daniel finally sat back up and walked over to Asin. Omrak continued to snore, his body drained from the fights. Daniel frowned, touching him for a brief moment to ascertain that he would survive, before he walked over to the large chest that Asin has been staring at.

"That our winnings?" Daniel asked, pointing.

Asin nodded, fished in her pockets, and pulled out the largest and clearest Mana Stone Daniel had ever seen.

"What is that? A B class four?" Daniel said.

Asin, for once, just shrugged. It was not as if she had seen a stone like this before. It was certainly an improvement over the B Class 12 that the previous Karlak Boss had given out.

"Did you open it??" Daniel asked, pointing to the chest, and Asin shook her head. She sighed, going back to staring at the chest. After a moment, Daniel walked over to Omrak and prodded him with his foot in an attempt to wake him. It took the careful use of his Gift to prod the Northerner awake.

Omrak rose from the ground, sword clutched in his hand, to stare at the empty field of battle. He groaned slightly, head still hurting from repeated hits, before he spotted the chest and relaxed.

The group, gathered together, stood and stared at the chest, wondering what was within.

"Asin?" Daniel finally said, pushing the patiently waiting Catkin.

No sooner had the words left his mouth than was the Catkin pounced forwards, pulling the chest open. Within, there were two pieces of equipment. A simple hammer with an engraving on it, and a thin, black leather breastplate. The three Adventurers looked at the equipment, frowning, before the Catkin picked them up and handed them around.

Daniel clutched the hammer, staring at the spike that protruded from one end, and looked at the group, who just gave him a slight nod. Omrak took the breastplate, his hands running over the leather.

"This is magical," Omrak said.

"Should be," Daniel answered, sliding the hammer into his pack. It was obvious that the hammer with its etched runes was definitely enchanted in some form. Better not to use it yet. "We can ask around to get them identified. When we're back."

"Asin, you are bereft of a prize," Omrak said.

"Stone. Mine," Asin said, patting her hip.

Daniel just nodded happily in agreement while Omrak glanced at Asin's pouch and then the armor in his hand. Finally, he nodded. Daniel understood what he probably was thinking, that they had no way to tell how powerful or even if the item itself was not cursed. But that was part of the gamble of being an Adventurer.

The three Adventurers slowly limped out of the Dungeon, their movements slowed down from exhaustion and injuries. Yet all three could not help but trade grins with one another and the guards as they exited.

"Did you finish it?" Ken asked, the large guard holding back a smile.

"Yes," Daniel said, and Ken raised a hand to clap his friend on the back and then decided against it. Daniel was not healed enough for that kind of boisterous congratulations.

"Tough fight?" Ken's question was more a statement. Daniel offered a slight nod before he gestured to his friends who had not stopped walking. "Go."

Daniel quickly hurried to catch up with his friends as they entered the Adventurers' Guild, managing to do so before they entered the hall. As they walked in, the Guild slowly fell silent as Adventurers and attendants spotted the trio. An Adventurer who was working with Liev quickly stepped aside as he waved the three of them forwards. Something showed on his face, something that Daniel could not place, but which twisted his stomach.

"Liev," Daniel said as he pulled the hammer from his belt. Asin had already reached for her pouches, placing the pair down and pulling down the edges of one to reveal the Boss Mana Stone. Omrak was slower as he struggled to pull the leather armor from his pack, but he eventually did. Through all this, the silence resounded through the room, stretching tight.

"Daniel. Asin. Omrak," Liev said calmly. He reached out and touched the Boss Mana Stone and slowly turned it about. When he next spoke, the redhead tried to keep his voice professional. "Congratulations."

"Did we do it?" Daniel said, somehow knowing the answer.

"No," Liev replied, shaking his head. "The Elms were in half a day ago. I'm sorry."

The three groaned in unison, their faces fallen as they traded looks between one another. Half a day. They were short by just a little. If they had explored a little more the day before, if they had skipped sleeping. If they had the right weapons. Around them, now that the bad news had been imparted, the Guild came back to life.

"You'll want to speak with Tharuk about the hammer," Liev continued, fingers lightly brushing the steel weapon. "I'm sure he'll be able to verify its details. As for this." Liev reached out to run a finger along the edges of the armor. "May I?"

After Omrak's agreement, Liev hefted the armor, running his fingers along the seams and down the bare front of the armor. He turned it inside out, staring at the clear back before he brushed a sharp fingernail along the front once more. Finally, he placed it back down on the counter. "This is unenchanted, as you probably guessed. No runes, no markings. Remarkably resilient, though. I would say it's from a Black Rhinoceros."

"Unenchanted?" Omrak repeated, his face crestfallen.

"Yes. It's very difficult to enchant Black Rhinoceros hide. Even untreated, it's stronger than most iron," Liev said. "Save enough, get a good Enchanter, and you'd have an amazing piece of armor."

Omrak's face lit up again as he took back the armor, stuffing the supple but tough piece into his pack. Asin, who had been quietly watching, prodded the stone, her ears tilted down. Liev smiled slightly, pulling the stone closer for inspection.

Daniel turned away while Liev spoke with Asin, rubbing at his eyes where tears threatened to spill. Damn it. They had been so close. Exhaustion combined with the comedown from the fights and delve threatened to break his control. He could not help but think that this was expected.. They were an Advanced Team after all. They never stood a chance.

"Daniel?" Liev called again, and the short Adventurer blinked, turning back to the counter. On the counter was a crystal ball, one that he had not seen in ages. "If you'll extend your hand?"

Daniel slowly complied and, guided by Liev, placed his hand on the crystal ball. It flared to life for a moment, Liev murmuring arcane words as he adjusted Daniel's status.

"Done."

Daniel smiled slightly, pulling his hand back from the crystal. Like his friends, he decided to take a look at his newly updated Status.

Name: Daniel Chai (Advanced Rank Adventurer)

Class: Level 9 Adventurer (63%)

Sub-classes: Level 7 (Miner) (04%)

Human (Male)

Statistics

Life: 281

Stamina: 281

Mana: 206

Attributes

Strength: 27

Agility: 24

Constitution: 30

Intelligence: 21

Willpower: 20

Luck: 15

Skills

Unarmed Combat: Level 3 (93/100)

Clubs (Novice): Level 2 (17/100)

Archery: Level 2 (68/100)

Shield (Novice): Level 1 (24/100)

Dodge: Level 7 (83/100)

Combat Sense: Level 7 (78/100)

Perception: Level 7 (56/100)

Mining: Level 7 (78/100)

Healing (Novice): Level 1 (41/100)

Herb Lore: Level 3 (31/100)

Stealth: Level 2 (24/100)

Cooking: Level 4 (03/100)

Singing: Level 2 (14/100)

Skill Proficiencies

Double Strike

Shield Bash

Perin's Blow

Find Weakness

Mapping (II)

Spells

Minor Healing (II)

Healer's Mark (I)

Gifts

Martyr's Touch—The caster may heal oneself or others by touch and concentration, sacrificing a portion of his life to do so. Cost varies depending on the extent of the injuries healed.

Later that day, the three Adventurers found themselves seated in the Spinning Top, nursing their injuries and sorrows. Their initial elation over completing the Dungeon had disappeared long ago and now the three sat, nursing their food in silence. They had failed at the quest, failed to beat the Elms.

Khy'ra walked into the inn and leaned against the doorway for a second, staring at her boyfriend before she sighed, noting how the glum trio had infected the entire Inn with their sorrow. Taking a seat next to her boyfriend, the Elf tilted her head as Daniel looked up at her.

"Is this how a team that just completed their first Dungeon looks like now?" Khy'ra asked, shaking her head. "I might be old, but surely the time traditions haven't changed that much."

"We lost," Daniel said, running a finger around some spilled beer. "By half a day."

"And?" Khy'ra said, shaking her head. "Did it mean you didn't get your Dungeon completion equipment? Did you miss out on the Stone itself?"

"No ..." Daniel said, noting the tone she held. He knew what was coming.

"Then celebrate," Khy'ra said, rapping her knuckles on the table to get the attention of the other two. Not that they were not listening in already. "Last lesson. There's always something wrong, always something depressing about this job. A bad delve, a lost friend, a missed quest. This job, this career, it's all about regrets. Always, always celebrate your successes. Otherwise, put your hammer down now. If you cannot celebrate when it is called for, you are in the wrong profession. It only gets harder from now on."

Daniel cast his head down, his hand caressing the hammer he had just won. He looked at Khy'ra and she flashed him a smile, and he found himself reaching for her hand, squeezing it. This success, this win, was a bittersweet one for her too. And yet, she was smiling.

Celebrate when you can …

"Elise! A round for everyone," Daniel said, calling to the innkeeper and forcing a smile on his face. Omrak roared his approval, pounding his drink on the table and splashing Asin who growled at the large, loud Adventurer.

"Noisy!"

A week later, the trio found themselves meeting up in the Top in the early morning. Daniel rushed down the stairs, shirt still untucked as he hauled his packed bag with him. Below, Asin and Omrak rolled their eyes as the Adventurer arrived late once again.

"Sorry, sorry!" Daniel apologized as he sighted his friends.

"Khy'ra?" Asin asked, looking up the staircase.

"Coming," Khy'ra said, following behind Daniel at a more sedate pace and giving the Catkin a quick hug. "I wouldn't miss seeing you off."

"School?" Asin said once she was released.

"Don't worry. The Stone will keep them fed for a while and we wrangled a slight return of the funds. Being a local hero gave your dad some leverage with the

Council," Khy'ra assured the Beastkin. "And I promise, your dad and I will make sure the funds you send back get put to good use."

"Goodbye," Asin said, her face falling slightly before she stepped away.

"This is for lunch," Elise said, walking out with a series of wrapped packages that she quickly distributed. "Don't forget, Mary's still waiting for you. And I'll expect a letter once in a while."

Daniel nodded, hand gripping Khy'ra's. The Catkin and Northerner shared a look before they walked out, leaving the two lovebirds alone.

"Khy'ra …" Daniel started, before he was hushed by a finger on his lips.

"No. We said it all. Did it all," Khy'ra said, eyes twinkling slightly at the last. "It's enough. You have a life to live. And so do I. Come back, when you can. Write, when you can. But live your life."

Daniel smiled slightly, kissing her fingers, and nodded. He turned, walking away, and rubbed at his eyes as he left to join the pair who dutifully ignored him as they left the city. On the road, outside, the trio looked at one another.

"Is this the right road to Peel?" Daniel finally said as they trudged along.

"No," Asin stated, glaring at him.

Daniel blinked, mouthed *oops* as they turned around. The trio laughed, shaking their heads as they made their way to the next Dungeon.

###

Author's Note

If you enjoyed reading the book, please do leave a review and rating. Not only is it a big ego boost, it also helps sales and convinces me to write more in the series!

If you enjoyed this, check out my other series:
- Life in the North (An Apocalyptic LitRPG)

    and

- A Gamer's Wish (An Urban Fantasy LitRPG)s

For more great information about LitRPG series, check out the Facebook groups:

- Gamelit Society

About the Author

Tao Wong is an avid fantasy and sci-fi reader who spends his time working and writing in the North of Canada. He's spent way too many years doing martial arts of many forms and having broken himself too often, now spends his time writing about fantasy worlds.

For updates on the series and my other books (and special one-shot stories), please visit my website: http://www.mylifemytao.com

Or sign up for my mailing list: http://eepurl.com/c35JS1

Or my Facebook Page: https://www.facebook.com/taowongauthor/